Floella's Favourite
Folk Tales

Floella's Favourite Folk Tales

FLOELLA BENJAMIN

Illustrated by Jennifer Northway

Beaver Books

A Beaver Book
Published by Arrow Books Limited
62–65 Chandos Place, London WC2N 4NW

An imprint of Century Hutchinson Ltd

London Melbourne Sydney Auckland
Johannesburg and agencies throughout the world

First published by Hutchinson Children's Books 1984
Beaver edition 1986

Text © Floella Benjamin 1984
Illustrations © Jennifer Northway 1984

Printed and bound in Great Britain by
Cox & Wyman Ltd, Reading

ISBN 0 09 947660 6

Contents

Introduction	7
Why the Agouti Has No Tail	9
Akim the Mermaid	13
How Anansi Got His Stories	18
Why Thunder and Lightning Live in the Sky	24
Fee Fee Foo	28
The Mouse Who Wanted to Be King	32
Dry Bones' Party	37
The Crow and the Sparrow	41
Why Anansi the Spiderman Makes Webs	46
The Mean Pear Seller	51
The Fish Prince	54
Sun and Moon's Party	59
The Tree House	62
Kisander and Her Pomsitae Tree	73
Tiger Son	76
Valiant Victor	82
The Metal Man	89

Introduction

When I first tried to recall the stories I was told as a child in the West Indies, I really had to rack my brains to remember exactly how they went. I remembered all the characters, like Anansi the Spiderman, Dry Bones and the Agouti, but I had to ask my mum, who has a marvellous memory, to tell me the stories again. That's the beauty of traditional stories; they are handed down from generation to generation, with each family having its own slightly different version. So collecting the West Indian stories for the book was quite easy for me after all.

Gathering the stories from Africa, India and China was a bit more difficult – until I hit on a great idea: every time I saw a Chinese, African or Indian person in a bus queue, on a train, in the local shop, or in a restaurant, I would ask them to tell me the favourite story from their childhood. I must have listened to dozens of lovely stories from many people who were more than delighted to recall the traditional tales of their homeland. And I would like to thank them – especially the passengers of the Victoria line tube train where, one day, I had the whole carriage giving their versions of stories.

In this book I have tried to include the ones I liked best; some are well known, others less so. I had a lot of fun collecting and writing them, and I will be passing them down to my own son, Aston. I hope you enjoy them, too. Oh, and don't forget to pass them on. On and on!

Floella Benjamin

Why the Agouti Has
No Tail

An agouti is a small animal that lives in the West Indies. It looks something like a squirrel, only it doesn't have a tail. A long time ago, however, the agouti did have a fine tail and this is the story of how it lost it.

Once upon a time the dog and the agouti were very good friends and lived together happily. One day Agouti and Dog were lazing in the garden, enjoying the afternoon sun when along came Goat, who was looking very pleased with himself.

'What are you so happy about?' asked Dog.

'I've been invited to a party,' replied Goat with satisfaction.

Now, both Dog and Agouti loved parties and when they heard this their ears pricked up.

'What party is this?' said Agouti. 'We want to come as well.'

'Oh, *you* can't come,' said Goat haughtily. 'This party is only for animals which have horns.' Then he trotted off with his head in the air.

Dog and Agouti looked at each other. Neither of them had horns and that meant that they would definitely not be going to the party.

'Oh, dear,' said Dog. 'I do love parties; there is always lots of food to eat.'

'This has spoilt my whole day,' said Agouti, and he went indoors to sulk.

The next day Dog and Agouti went into town. The news of the party had spread and everyone was talking about it, especially the animals with horns. Apparently, the party was to be held on a small island some distance away. There was to be a barbecue and lots of rum-punch to drink. All the horned animals were to leave for the island, by boat, the next morning and return in the evening after the party.

'It's not fair,' said Dog. 'I must find a way to go to the party.'

'But you don't have horns,' said Agouti. 'You would soon be spotted and then there would be trouble.'

'Don't worry, I will find a way,' said Dog, and he disappeared into the forest, leaving his friend Agouti behind.

Dog walked along a narrow path which led through the trees. He just had to think of a way to get invited to the party, but however hard he thought, he couldn't come up with any ideas.

Suddenly, as he rounded a corner, he saw a pile of old bones in front of him on the path. They were the remains of a cow that had died many years ago.

What luck, thought Dog, as he spotted a lovely pair of horns amongst the pile of bones. He picked them up and tied them to his head with a strong piece of vine. Then he rushed home to show his friend Agouti.

But Agouti was not very pleased when he saw Dog with the horns. 'It's all right for you. You are large enough to pass as a horned animal. But what about me? I would soon be spotted. There are no horned animals as small as I am. I still can't go to the party.' Agouti was more miserable than ever and he sat in a corner and sulked.

The next morning Dog was up bright and early. He tied the horns to his head as tightly as he could. 'Come down to the jetty with me, Agouti,' he pleaded, 'and see if my disguise works.'

Reluctantly, Agouti agreed. He was interested to see if Dog could get away with the deception.

The jetty was bustling with horned animals, all waiting for the boat to arrive and take them across to the island. So none of them noticed as Dog, wearing his horns, slipped quietly amongst them.

Agouti watched as Dog climbed aboard the boat and sat down next to Goat. His heart beat faster, as he realized that his best friend was going to get away with the trick and go to the party without him. He was so jealous that, before he could stop himself, he cried out, 'Stop! Stop! There is an imposter aboard.'

At this, all the horned animals looked at Dog and saw that he had tricked them. They picked him up angrily and threw him into the water.

When Agouti realized what his jealous betrayal had done, he turned and ran as fast as he could, with Dog close on his heels. He ran and ran as fast as his short legs could carry him, but Dog was angry and humiliated and soon caught up with Agouti, who scurried into a nearby hole. But Agouti wasn't quite fast enough and Dog snapped off his tail as he disappeared down the hole.

Well, needless to say, Dog and Agouti were no longer friends, and if you are ever in the West Indies and you see a dog scratching and barking at a hole, it is probably because there is an agouti down there. That is how the agouti lost its tail.

Akim the Mermaid

Once upon a time, in Africa, there lived a girl called Akim. She was very beautiful and kind, and many young men asked for her hand in marriage. But her parents wanted to make sure that the man she married was the right one for her.

Eventually, they decided on a young man who lived several villages away. He was brave and strong and came from a wealthy family. Although Akim had never met the young man, she felt sure he would be a good husband and she accepted her parents' decision without question. So, the marriage was arranged and a date set for the ceremony.

'It is the custom for the bride to go to her future husband alone,' said Akim's father. 'But, as you are going so far away, your younger sister will accompany you, so that you will have a friend to talk to when your husband is out hunting. You will also take a woman servant with you, to help with the cooking and cleaning in your new home.'

When the time came for Akim to leave, all the people of the village turned out to wave goodbye and wish her luck. Akim was sad to leave her home, but at least she had her sister and the servant woman to keep her company.

They walked all day, carrying their heavy bundles of belongings. Eventually, they came to a lake where they stopped to rest. 'The village is on the other side of this lake, mistress,' said the servant woman. 'Why don't you bathe and prepare yourself to meet your future husband?'

Akim thought this was a good idea, so she undressed and stepped into the cool, refreshing water.

Suddenly, the servant pushed Akim with all her might until she disappeared under the water, into the deepest part of the lake. Akim's little sister cried out and ran to the water's edge, but there was no sign of her sister. 'Why did you push her?' cried the little girl.

'Shut up, and listen to me! From now on, you will call me Akim. I will marry the man who was chosen by your parents. If you dare to tell anyone, I will push you into the lake as well!' said the wicked woman. 'You will be my servant now, and you will do exactly as I say or you will be sorry.'

The little girl was very frightened, so she did as she was told. Then the wicked servant put on Akim's clothes and together they went into the village, where the young man was anxiously waiting.

When he saw his bride he was a bit disappointed. He had been told that Akim was very gentle and kind. But when he looked at her, he thought she looked bad-tempered and disagreeable. However, the marriage had been agreed and he was a man of honour, so he married the wicked woman the next day.

He had built a fine house for his new wife to live in and the wicked woman lived there, waited on hand and foot by Akim's poor little sister, who was too frightened to tell anyone what had happened. The little sister worked hard from morning till night, cleaning and cooking, while the woman did nothing except shout orders at her.

'Go to the lake and fetch some water,' she shouted one day, 'and hurry back, or I will beat you!'

The young girl took the large water jar to the lake. When she reached the water's edge, she bent down to fill up the jar. Then, to her astonishment, she saw her sister Akim rising up from the depths to meet her. 'I thought you were drowned!' cried the little girl.

'I nearly was, but the kind Spirit of the Lake saw what that evil servant did and wouldn't let me die. Instead, I was turned into a mermaid. Look!' At this, she wriggled out of the water on to the bank.

Her sister was amazed at the long fish tail Akim had grown, but was overjoyed to see her dear sister alive. She told of the cruel servant woman and how she had masqueraded as Akim and had married the young man in her place. She also told of how she was forced to work every day as a servant.

When Akim heard this she was very angry, but there was little she could do as a mermaid. 'I will ask the Spirit of the Lake for help,' said Akim. 'Perhaps there is a way we can expose that servant's treachery. But, for the moment, you must say nothing of our meeting to anyone. Just go back to the village and carry on as before. Come here each morning so that we can be together.'

All this time, the husband had been feeling very miserable. The lovely woman he had hoped to marry had turned out to be cruel and selfish. She beat her young servant and never did any work herself. All she did was sit around all day and complain.

One day, when he was out hunting, he was feeling particularly downhearted. So he sat down by the side of the lake and gazed sadly into the water. 'Oh, I am so unhappy,' he sighed.

Suddenly, the surface of the lake rippled, and the man heard a voice. 'I am the Spirit of the Lake,' it said. 'You are the victim of a wicked trick. Your wife is not the girl you were supposed to marry.'

At this, the man jumped to his feet in astonishment. 'Then tell me, how I can find my true bride, O Spirit of the Lake!' he cried.

'Tomorrow morning, go to the side of the lake where

your wife's servant collects water, and hide in the bushes. Then you will discover the truth.'

The next morning he did as the Spirit had said. It wasn't long before Akim's sister arrived. He watched as she knelt by the water and cried out, 'Akim! Akim!'

After a short while, the most beautiful mermaid came up out of the water and slid on to the bank. He listened as the two girls talked of the wicked servant and how the Spirit of the Lake had promised to help them.

When he had heard enough, he jumped out of the bushes, knelt down beside the mermaid, took her hand and said, 'So you are the real Akim. You are as lovely as I was told. That evil woman will be punished for her crime, and you will be my true bride.'

When the Spirit of the Lake heard this, the spell was broken and Akim's tail disappeared.

'Oh, Akim,' cried her sister. 'How wonderful – you're back to normal again!' And they hugged and kissed each other with joy.

Then they went back to the village and told the story to the chief, who was very angry. 'Bring the wicked servant here!' he commanded.

The woman was dragged from her house and brought before the chief. When she saw Akim and her sister standing next to the man she had so cruelly tricked, she fell down and begged forgiveness.

'How do you want me to punish this woman?' the chief asked Akim. 'Should I have her thrown into the lake and drowned?'

But Akim was not a vengeful person. She asked only that the wicked woman should be driven from the village for ever, so that she could marry and take her rightful place beside her husband and live happily with him as his true bride.

How Anansi Got His Stories

Anansi the Spiderman came to the Caribbean from West Africa many years ago. But his adventures are still talked about in Africa. He is very clever and cunning, and he has a special gift that has made him famous: at the first sign of trouble or danger he can turn himself into a spider.

Anansi stories have not always been called Anansi stories: they were first known as Tiger stories. You see, Tiger was the most powerful of all animals and everyone in the forest respected him.

However, Anansi wanted the stories to be named after him. So, one evening, Anansi went to see Tiger, who was lying in the shade of a tree. Anansi gossiped for a while with Tiger until eventually he felt the time was right to ask his favour. Being very cunning, Anansi thought he would start by flattering Tiger.

'O magnificent Tiger, you are not only brave and strong but also wise and clever. Your fame has spread throughout the land, and everyone knows of you and respects you. But as for me, I am weak and insignificant. If only I had something to make people respect me and remember my name.'

Tiger enjoyed being flattered by Anansi and wanted to prove to all the animals what a clever ruler he was. So he turned regally to Anansi and said, 'Perhaps there is some way I can help make others remember your name.'

'Well, there is one favour I would like to ask of you,' said Anansi.

'What is it?' said Tiger. 'Speak out!'

'O brave, wise Tiger,' said Anansi, 'the stories we all know are named after you; but how wonderful it would be if they were named after me! Then everyone would remember my name.'

Tiger opened his eyes in surprise. He hadn't expected Anansi to ask such a big favour of him. He loved the stories and didn't want to lose them, but he felt he could not say no in front of all the animals which had gathered around. After all, he had offered to help Anansi.

Then he had an idea. 'Yes, Anansi, the stories will be yours, on one condition,' said Tiger. 'You must capture Snake, who lives down by the river, and bring him to me alive. If you complete this task, then the stories will be named after you.'

As Anansi wandered off to attempt his task, Tiger and the other animals laughed at the thought of Anansi the Spiderman capturing Snake, who was both strong and clever.

That night Anansi lay awake trying to think of a way to capture Snake. At last, he had a very clever idea and could hardly wait to try it out.

When the morning came, Anansi rushed down to the path that Snake usually took every day up from the river. He started to dig a deep hole and then placed an egg at the bottom of it. Anansi felt sure that when Snake passed by and saw the egg in the hole he would climb in to get it, for Snake loved eggs. Once inside, he would not be able to get out because of the steep sides Anansi had built.

Anansi hid in the bushes and waited for Snake to pass by. It wasn't long before Snake came slithering up the path and saw the hole with the egg in it. But Snake was no fool, and he did not climb into the hole; he simply coiled his long tail around an overhanging branch and slid his long body down into the hole to reach the egg, which he swallowed in one!

Oh, dear, thought Anansi, Snake is much cleverer than I thought. I will have to try another plan to catch him.

This time Anansi built a cage from bamboo sticks and placed a ripe, juicy calabash mango inside. Then he left the door of the cage open and waited, ready to slam it shut once Snake was inside. But Anansi had not made the cage big enough, and Snake put just his head inside the cage and ate up the juicy mango.

Once again Anansi had failed. It looked as if he would never have the stories named after him. He sat miserably by the river, thinking what to do next. Then he noticed Monkey fishing and it gave him an idea . . . .

He ran home, found a piece of rope, and made a noose at one end. He put the noose on the ground, covered it with leaves, and on top he placed a piece of goat meat which his wife had cooked for dinner that night. Then he sat on the branch of a tree nearby, holding the other end of the rope, and waited patiently for Snake to come past.

At last along came Snake, who spotted the meat and, sure enough, began to eat it. Quietly above, Anansi waited for the right moment to pull the noose tight around Snake's head. Then suddenly he tugged on the rope as hard as he could; but Snake was much heavier than he had expected and the next thing he knew he had landed in a heap beside him.

'So, Anansi,' said Snake, 'it's you who has been trying to trap me all week. You'd better have a good reason for it, or I will swallow you up.'

'Oh, please don't, I beg of you,' pleaded the bruised Anansi. 'I do have a good reason, but now I'm sure to lose my bet.'

'What bet is this?' asked Snake curiously.

'I have a bet with Tiger,' said Anansi, 'that you are the longest creature in the forest. Even longer than the tallest bamboo tree over there.'

'You are quite right,' said Snake. 'I am the longest creature in the forest. You win your bet.'

'But how can I prove it to Tiger?' said Anansi.

'That's easy,' said Snake. 'Cut down the bamboo and put it beside me and you will see.'

This was just what Anansi wanted Snake to say. He hurried off to the nearby bamboo grove, cut down the longest bamboo shoot he could find, and rushed back to where Snake was waiting. Snake immediately stretched out beside the bamboo.

'There you are,' said Snake proudly. 'Am I not longer than the bamboo?'

'Mmmm, not quite,' said Anansi, 'but if you stretch as hard as you can you will be longer and then I will win my bet.'

'How's that?' asked Snake, stretching as hard as he could.

'Well,' said Anansi, 'you are so long I cannot watch your head and tail at the same time.'

'Then tie my head to the bamboo,' said Snake, 'and then go to the other end of the stick and watch my tail.'

'OK,' said Anansi, as he excitedly tied Snake's head to the stick and rushed down to the other end. 'Come on! Stretch! Stretch!' he shouted. 'You are nearly there – just a bit more.'

Snake gave one last push and at that moment Anansi seized the opportunity to tie Snake's tail to the stick as well.

'Well, I never, Anansi's done it! He's captured Snake alive,' shouted all the animals in amazement, as Anansi passed them by, carrying Snake to Tiger.

Tiger was surprised, too, that Anansi had captured Snake alive, and he had to keep his word.

'Well done, Anansi,' said Tiger, 'you are clever and cunning and deserve to have the stories named after you.'

And that's how the stories of Anansi the Spiderman came to be.

Why Thunder
and Lightning Live
in the Sky

Many, many years ago Thunder and Lightning lived on earth like everyone else. Lightning was young and quick-tempered and caused his mother Thunder much distress.

No one liked either of them very much because of their noisy, troublesome ways. If Lightning didn't like some-one he would fly into a violent temper, striking out in every direction and destroying everything in sight. When-ever Thunder saw what her son was doing she would call out loudly to him to cease. But her voice was so loud that it shook the earth and frightened the villagers.

Everyone became very tired of Lightning's violent out-bursts, which were always followed by his mother's deafening shouting. So they decided to complain to the king, who decreed that Thunder and Lightning must leave and live on the outskirts of the village where they would annoy no one.

This worked for a short while, but soon Lightning was back to his old ways, burning, killing and generally caus-ing trouble, always closely followed by his mother rebuking him in her loud, thundering voice.

Once more the villagers went to the king, who decided that Thunder and Lightning should move even further away to the distant mountains, and he ordered them never to return to the village again. Thunder and Light-ning didn't like being exiled; they rumbled and flashed

angrily as they left and they could be heard complaining for weeks afterwards.

It was not long, however, before Lightning returned. He had been plotting his revenge and he showed no mercy as he set fire to the dry crops, causing bush fires to rage and farm houses to burn to the ground. Of course his mother chased after him, bellowing at him to stop, but he took no notice of her and continued to wreak his revenge.

But this time Lightning had gone too far. The villagers felt they could no longer endure his spiteful and wicked ways, and they demanded that he and his mother be banished from the face of the earth. So the king ordered that they be sent to live in the sky where they could do no more harm.

When Thunder and Lightning heard what their punishment was to be, they begged and pleaded for forgiveness, promising never to disturb anyone again. But the people no longer trusted them, for they had broken their promises before. So the king asked all the birds – the parakeets and cockatoos from the forest, the flamingos from the lakes, the eagles from the mountains and the vultures from the deserts – to come and pick up Thunder and Lightning and fly them high up into the sky, which was to be their new home. The birds were only too pleased to help, for they too were fed up with the noisy, inconsiderate pair.

So hundreds of birds flocked around Thunder and Lightning and picked them up with their claws and beaks. They flew them up and up into the sky until they were high above the clouds, and there they left them.

Everyone thought the birds had finally taken Thunder and Lightning to a place so far away that they would never disturb anyone again.

But this was not quite the case, because even now we

still get visits from them, with Lightning losing his temper and sending bolts of fire down to the earth, and the deafening voice of his mother, Thunder, never very far behind.

Listen out for them next time there is a storm.

Fee Fee Foo

There was once a king who had three beautiful daughters. They were so precious to him that he never allowed them to leave the palace grounds to play with the other children. The girls were so well guarded that no one outside the palace even knew their names.

The king thought himself very clever to have kept the names of his daughters so secret, and he decided to hold a grand competition to see if anyone could guess what they were. He offered a prize of as much gold as the winner could carry away from the palace, and this attracted people from all over the kingdom; but no one managed to guess even one of the names, never mind all three.

When Anansi heard about the competition he decided that he would try to win the prize, but being Anansi he thought of a crafty way to find out the girls' names.

That afternoon, while the girls were out playing in the palace grounds, Anansi slipped into the palace, carrying three lovely bunches of flowers. He crept past the guards and up the stairs to the three sisters' bedroom and he placed a bunch of flowers on each of their beds. Then he hid in the cupboard and waited. When the girls returned that evening and saw the pretty flowers, the youngest said, 'Oh, look, Fee Fee Foo and Sugar Blossom, look at these beautiful flowers. Who could have left them?'

'Who indeed, Tinky Tangle?' said the other two. 'Let's go and ask our father if it was him.' And they picked up the flowers and went to show the king.

When he heard them go, Anansi came out of the cupboard, climbed out of the window and over the palace wall, and ran home as fast as he could.

The next morning he called on Rat, Goat, Donkey, Hare and Dog and told them to collect their steel drums and meet him at his house as quickly as they could. When they were all assembled Anansi led them towards the king's palace.

'Why are we going to the palace with our steel drums?' asked Goat. 'We have already tried to guess the names of the king's daughters and failed.'

'Ah,' said Anansi, '*I* have not yet failed, and if you do as I say we will all soon be rich!'

When they reached the palace gates, Anansi told his friends to play a calypso rhythm on their steel drums and he began to sing:

> 'Tinky Tangle, Sugar Blossom
> And Fee Fee Foo,
> Where are you?
> Where are you?'

'Now join in!' shouted Anansi to his friends, and they all marched into the courtyard singing the calypso:

> 'Tinky Tangle, Sugar Blossom
> And Fee Fee Foo,
> Where are you?
> Where are you?'

When the king heard the sweet music, he came out into the courtyard to listen, for he loved a good calypso. But when he heard the words, he realized that someone had guessed the names of his daughters.

Then he spotted Anansi. 'I might have known it would be you, Anansi!' he cried. 'I don't know how you did it,

but you and your friends are the winners; take as much gold as you can each carry.'

Rat, Goat, Donkey, Hare and Dog all looked at Anansi with joy and amazement. Now they realized why he had asked them to bring their steel drums! They ran through the palace filling them to the brims with gold, then they happily struggled home under the weight of their newly won treasure.

From that day on, the king allowed his three daughters to play with other children, who would come to the gate and sing:

> 'Tinky Tangle, Sugar Blossom
> And Fee Fee Foo,
> Where are you?
> Where are you?'

And Tinky Tangle, Sugar Blossom and Fee Fee Foo would answer:

> 'Here we are, here we are,
> Happy to play with you.
> Tinky Tangle, Sugar Blossom
> And Fee Fee Foo.'

They were happy now, for they had lots of new friends to play with, thanks to Anansi.

The Mouse Who Wanted to Be King

A long time ago, in India, there lived a little mouse – just an ordinary mouse with brown fur and long whiskers. He lived under the floorboards of a house in the poorest part of the city and he had to search hard for scraps of food to eat.

One day the mouse was sitting underneath the verandah of the house, where it was cool and shaded from the hot midday sun, when he heard a commotion going on in the street. He peeped his head out to see what was happening and saw a great procession of magnificent elephants passing by. Riding in a gilded basket on the back of the most splendid elephant was the king.

The king was dressed in beautiful robes of red silk, embroidered with gold. On his head he wore a turban into which were sewn rubies and pearls, and on his feet he wore sandals of the finest leather.

When the little mouse saw the king and all his finery, he said, 'If only I were king, I could wear silken robes and jewels instead of dull brown fur. I could live in a palace and eat the finest food instead of living under the floorboards where I have to scratch for crumbs.'

All that night the little mouse lay awake thinking about what he had seen. Then, just as the sun was coming up, he had a wonderful idea. He marched round to the cloth merchant and demanded to see the owner.

'I am the Mouse King,' he said. 'Give me some of your

finest red silk cloth or I will tell my subjects, the rats and mice of the city, to come to your shop and gnaw holes in all your cloth!'

The cloth merchant was so afraid of rats and mice invading his shop that he did as the mouse asked and gave him some of the material.

The mouse took the piece of cloth to the tailor, who was busy making a coat with the help of his children. When they saw the little mouse they all stopped work.

'I am the Mouse King,' said the little mouse. 'Make me a fine robe from this cloth or I will command my subjects, the rats and mice of the city, to invade your shop and gnaw holes in all your suits and coats.'

This so frightened the tailor and his children that they started work on the tiny robes immediately, while the mouse waited impatiently.

Soon the garment was finished and the mouse put his fine robes on. He stood in front of the mirror and admired himself; he walked up and down trying to be as king-like as he could. He made such a funny sight that the tailor's children could hardly stop themselves giggling.

The mouse took a long piece of the cloth and wound it around his head like a turban, then he strode off towards the cobbler, who was sitting cross-legged in his shop hammering a pair of shoes. When he saw the strange little mouse in his silk robes and turban, he stopped work and said, 'What can I do for you, little mouse?'

'I am the Mouse King and I command you to make for me a fine pair of sandals from the softest leather you have,' said the mouse grandly. 'If you refuse, I will tell all my subjects, the rats and mice of the city, to invade your shop and gnaw at all your leather.'

The cobbler thought the mouse looked very funny in his robes and could hardly stop himself from bursting out with laughter. But he decided that he had better do as the mouse asked, for he did not want hundreds of rats and mice to gnaw at his leather.

Very soon the mouse had a lovely pair of sandals made from the softest leather the cobbler could find. The mouse put on his new sandals and strutted up and down the street in them. Now I look like a king, he said to himself. He did not see the people in the street laughing at the funny little mouse in his fine clothes.

The next day the mouse put on his new clothes and set off for the king's palace. He walked up to the gates, which were guarded by two soldiers. 'Stand aside,' he ordered. 'I am the Mouse King and I am here to see your ruler!'

The soldiers looked at the little mouse in his fine robes and could hardly believe their eyes. 'Of course, Your Highness,' said one of them, trying not to laugh, 'follow me.'

The soldier led the mouse to the throne room where the king sat on a great golden throne. The soldier marched up to the steps which led up to the throne and bowed. 'Your Majesty,' he said in a loud voice so that everyone in the huge room could hear, 'you have a royal visitor. May I present His Royal Highness, King Mouse!'

There was a stunned silence as the little mouse walked boldly up to the throne. 'Greetings, O King,' he said. 'I have come with a proposition for you.'

The mouse took his time, stroking his whiskers once or twice before he spoke. 'If you do not give me half your kingdom at once, I will command all my subjects, the rats and mice of the city, to invade your palace and destroy it!'

At this, the king stopped smiling and a look of anger came over his face. 'How dare you come here and threaten me,' he bellowed. 'I have a good mind to order my palace cat to chase you away.'

As he spoke, a huge white cat appeared from behind

the throne and leapt towards the poor little mouse, who squeaked in terror and scampered up on to a nearby table, shaking with fright as the cat fiercely swished its tail from side to side.

Just then the king's little daughter, who had been sitting on her father's knee, said, 'Oh, father, he is such a funny little mouse with his silk robes and sandals, let me keep him as a pet.'

Now, the king loved his little girl more than anything in the whole world and it gave him great joy to see her happy, so he snapped his fingers and the fierce cat went back to its basket behind the throne. A cage was brought and the little mouse was put inside.

'Oh, thank you, father,' said the princess. 'I shall look after the little Mouse King and feed him on scraps from the royal kitchens every day, and I shall make him a bed of soft straw to sleep on.'

So, you see, the mouse *did* get to live in a palace after all and he never had to scratch around for food again.

Dry Bones' Party

Dry Bones lived by himself on top of a mountain, where none of the animals ever went. It was a very dry and barren place, not suitable for anything except Dry Bones. He would spend his days alone, cackling and rattling around the mountainside, discouraging anyone from coming near.

Then one day, to the animals' surprise, word spread that Dry Bones had invited them all to a party where, he promised, there would be plenty to eat and drink.

Now, the animals did not like Dry Bones, but they loved a good party, especially if there was plenty of food. So when the day of the party arrived, all the animals turned up. They couldn't believe their eyes when they saw the table laden with delicious food.

Soon the party was in full swing and everyone was enjoying themselves – except Monkey. He knew Dry Bones hated all the animals and liked being alone, and he was curious as to why he was suddenly being so kind to them.

While all the other animals were eating and having a good time, Monkey noticed Dry Bones quietly slip out of the room. So he followed him round to the back of the house to see what he was up to. At the back of the house Dry Bones had built a fire, and on the fire was the biggest cooking pot Monkey had ever seen.

Monkey climbed on to the roof of the house and

looked into the pot to see what Dry Bones was cooking. But when he looked down, he saw that there was nothing in the pot but boiling water. As Dry Bones stirred the pot, he started to cackle in his croaky voice:

> 'More bones for Dry Bones,
> More bones for Dry Bones.
> Fat bones, juicy bones,
> More bones for Dry Bones
> Tonight . . . Ha! Ha! Ha!'

Then, to his horror, Monkey realized that he and all his friends were in great danger. Dry Bones *did* have a reason for inviting them all to the party. They were to end up in the pot!

Monkey knew he had to warn his friends, who were all having a great time inside. He rushed back into the party, screeching and chattering at the top of his voice: 'Run! Run! Run for your lives!'

At first everyone was too busy enjoying themselves to take any notice of Monkey, and anyway he was always screaming and chattering about something or other.

When Monkey saw that no one was paying attention to him, he jumped on the table, sending cups and plates and food flying, which made everyone stop and look at him in amazement. 'Run! Run for your lives, everyone!' screamed Monkey. 'The party is a trap. Dry Bones has plans for a feast of his own. And that feast is us! Run! Run now!'

At this, all the animals scattered in every direction. Through the doors and windows they jumped and scurried, then down the mountainside they ran as fast as they could, with Dry Bones rattling behind them. Finally, when all the animals had reached the safety of the forest and had disappeared into their hiding places, they chanted back up the mountain:

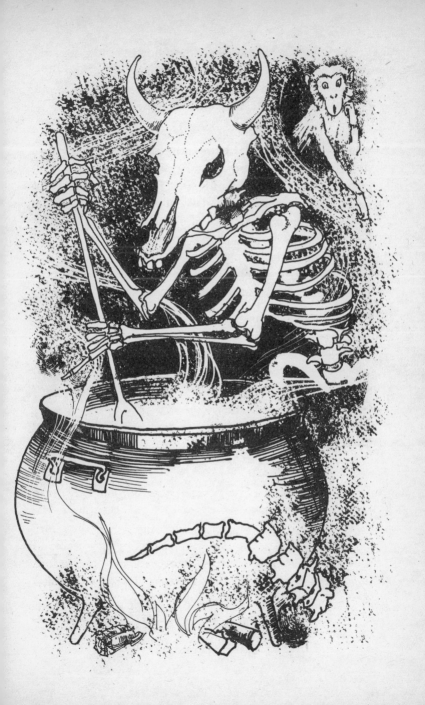

>'No bones for Dry Bones,
>No bones for Dry Bones.
>No fat or juicy bones,
>No bones for Dry Bones
>Tonight.'

When Dry Bones heard the animals taunting him with their chant, he covered his ears and stamped his feet in anger, for he knew he had lost them and had nothing to show for his night's work. Dry Bones was so angry that you could hear the echo of his bones rattling as he returned to his mountaintop empty-handed and swearing never, ever to have a party again.

'I will have to think of another way to get their bones,' he cackled, and he started to mutter:

>'More bones for Dry Bones,
>More bones for Dry Bones.
>Fat bones, juicy bones,
>More bones for Dry Bones,
>But not tonight!'

The Crow and the
Sparrow

One day the crow and the sparrow decided to have a curry dinner together. The sparrow provided the rice and the crow brought the meat for the dish.

The sparrow was a really good cook, and while she prepared the meal, Crow waited anxiously for his share. Sparrow laid the food out beautifully on the table, which she had decorated with flowers.

When they were about to sit down to eat, Sparrow looked at Crow and exclaimed, 'Goodness me, you are not going to sit down to dinner without washing, are you? Your beak and claws are so dirty. Go and wash them at once.'

Crow was really hungry and did not think he was that dirty, but he thought it was best not to argue with Sparrow, for even though she was small, she was very bossy. So off he hurriedly flew to the nearest stream and said:

> 'Your name is Stream,
> My name is Crow.
> Please give me some water,
>   For if you do so,
> I can wash beak and feet
> And the nice curry eat;
> Though I really don't know
>   What the sparrow can mean,

> For I'm sure, as crows go,
>   I'm really quite clean!'

'Of course you may have some,' said the stream, 'but first you must go to the deer, borrow one of his antlers and use it to dig a small hole, into which the water can flow.'

So off Crow hurriedly flew to find a deer, to whom he said:

> 'Your name is Deer,
> My name is Crow.
> Lend me an antler,
>   For if you do so,
> I can dig a small hole
>   For the water to flow;
> Then I'll wash beak and feet
> And the nice curry eat;
> Though I really don't know
>   What the sparrow can mean,
> For I'm sure, as crows go,
>   I'm really quite clean!'

'Of course I will,' said the deer, 'but first go to the cow and ask for some milk for me to drink. Then, by all means, you may borrow my antler.'

So off flew Crow to find a cow, to whom he said:

> 'Your name is Cow,
> My name is Crow.
> Please give me some milk,
>   For if you do so,
> The antler is mine,
>   To dig a small hole
>   To be my wash bowl;
> Then I'll wash beak and feet
> And the nice curry eat;
> Though I really don't know

What the sparrow can mean,
For I'm sure, as crows go,
   I'm really quite clean!'

'Of course I will,' said the cow, 'but first I need some grass to eat, so that I can make you some milk. Fetch me some, please and milk is yours.'

So off flew Crow to a field and said:

'Your name is Field,
My name is Crow.
Please give me some grass,
   For if you do so,
   Madam Cow will give milk
And the Deer, sleek as silk,
   Will lend me his antler
   To dig a small hole
   To be my wash bowl;
Then I'll wash beak and feet
And the nice curry eat;
Though I really don't know
   What the sparrow can mean,
For I'm sure, as crows go,
   I'm really quite clean!'

The field replied, 'Of course you may have some grass, but you will need a scythe to cut it down. Go to the black-smith and ask him to make one.'

So off flew Crow to the blacksmith and said:

'Your name is Smith,
My name is Crow.
Please make me a scythe,
   For if you do so,
The grass I can mow
As food for the cow,
Who will give me some milk

For the deer, sleek as silk,
   Who will lend me his antler
   To dig a small hole
   To be my wash bowl;
Then I'll wash beak and feet
And the nice curry eat;
Though I really don't know
   What the sparrow can mean,
For I'm sure, as crows go,
   I'm really quite clean!'

'Of course I will,' said the blacksmith, 'but I will need your help to fan the flames of my forge, with your wings.'

So Crow began to flap his wings, and the coals in the forge grew red hot and the blacksmith made him a scythe.

Crow thanked the blacksmith and flew back to the field and cut some grass, which he gave to the cow, who gave him some milk, which he gave to the deer, in return for his antler, which he took to the stream and used to dig a small hole, into which the water flowed. Then he flew back to Sparrow.

But when he got there, he found that Sparrow had not only eaten her share, but also his share of the lovely curry.

'You took so long,' said Sparrow, 'that I thought you weren't coming back. So I ate all the curry. I'm sorry.'

Crow was so angry and hungry that he vowed never to have a wash again.

That is why crows are black all over, even today.

Why Anansi the Spiderman Makes Webs

One day Anansi got together with his friends Hare and Rat, and planted a field of sweet potatoes. They dug the ground, planted the sweet potatoes in neat lines, and waited for them to grow. Every day they would go to the field and pull out any weeds that tried to choke the tender young shoots. Of course, Anansi always made some excuse as to why he couldn't work, and usually spent the day lazing on the grass watching Hare and Rat working in the hot sun.

Eventually, the time approached when the crop could be harvested, and Hare and Rat arranged to meet Anansi the next morning at the field. That night, though, Anansi crept down to the field and dug up some of the sweet potatoes, put them in a sack, and hid it near his home.

In the morning when the three met, Hare and Rat noticed that part of the field had been freshly dug, but Anansi pretended not to notice. As usual, Anansi made an excuse, saying he had a sore back and couldn't work, and sat down to rest in the shade. While they worked, Hare and Rat decided that they would watch the field that night to see if the thief returned

When half the field had been harvested, Hare and Rat decided to call it a day. They waved goodbye to Anansi and said that they hoped his back would be better in the morning so that he could help with the work. As soon as he was out of sight, Hare and Rat ran back to the field and

hid themselves in a bush. After a few hours they began to think that they were wasting their time.

'No thief is foolish enough to return to the scene of his crime so soon,' said Hare. 'Let's go home, I'm tired.'

'Maybe you're right,' said Rat. 'Let's forget it.'

But just as they were about to leave they spotted a shadowy figure approaching. 'Quick, hide,' said Hare. 'We'll catch him in the act.'

So they ducked down behind the bush again and watched as the figure started to dig up the sweet potatoes. Then they crept quietly towards him. When they were right behind him, Rat shouted, 'Caught you, you miserable thief!' At this, the robber spun round in surprise.

'ANANSI!' cried Hare. 'You are the thief!'

Hare and Rat were both so surprised that Anansi had time to make a run for it, but they soon recovered themselves and gave chase.

Before long Hare and Rat started to gain on Anansi, who wasn't a very fast runner. He looked over his shoulder and saw Hare and Rat close behind, and he knew that if they caught him he would be in serious trouble. But just then he saw a large tree ahead and he leapt up into the branches and clambered up to the top, where he sat, trembling with fear. Hare and Rat couldn't climb trees so they stood at the bottom looking up angrily at him. 'You wait, Anansi,' said Rat. 'When you come down, we'll give you what for.'

But Anansi had no intention of coming down; he just changed himself into a spider, as he always did when he was in trouble or danger.

'You will have to come down eventually,' shouted Rat. 'You can't stay up there forever without food.'

When morning came, Rat went home for a rest, leaving Hare to guard the tree. Later he returned to allow Hare to go home for a while.

From his branch Anansi watched these comings and goings with dismay. His stomach began to rumble and he looked around for something to eat; but the tree was bare. Oh, why didn't I choose a mango tree to climb, instead of this old stump, he thought.

As the hours passed Anansi grew more and more worried. He even considered giving himself up, but Hare and Rat were still very angry with him and he soon thought better of it. There must be something I can eat, Anansi said to himself. Then he spotted a few flies buzzing around nearby, and to the starving Anansi even they began to look delicious. So he thought up a way to catch them by spinning a web, and that is why spiders still weave webs to this day.

Eventually, Hare and Rat got fed up with waiting at the bottom of the tree and told Anansi they would forgive him as long as he promised never to steal from them again.

The Mean Pear Seller

Once upon a time, in China, it was customary for traders to set up their stalls outside the gates of large cities where they would sell their wares to passing travellers.

One such trader was a pear seller. He was a very mean man and would charge the hungry travellers high prices for his juicy pears. At the end of the day, as the city gates were about to close, a crowd of poor people would gather around the stalls and the traders would give them any fruit or vegetables that had not been sold; but the pear seller never gave anything away.

One day, as the pear seller sat by his stall, he noticed an old man standing looking at him. The old man was dressed in rags and was obviously very poor.

'Please give me a pear,' said the old beggar.

'Go away, you filthy old man. If you want a pear, then you must pay for it like anyone else,' said the pear seller.

'But I have no money; all I ask for is one pear. I have not eaten all day,' replied the beggar.

At this, the pear seller became very angry because the old man was beginning to attract a crowd. 'Go away, I tell you!' he shouted. 'If I gave every beggar a pear I would soon be poor myself.'

Now, standing in the crowd was a young man, who, although poor himself, felt sorry for the old man. 'Here you are, old friend,' he said, tossing him a coin. 'I'll pay for your pear.'

The old man picked up a pear and ate it. When he had finished, he said to the young man, 'Thank you for your kindness, young sir. Now please allow me to show my gratitude.'

At this, he took a pip from the core of the pear and threw it to the ground. The crowd watched as he covered it with earth and spoke a few words under his breath.

Almost at once a small green shoot appeared. It grew rapidly, and within a few minutes it had become a small pear tree laden with ripe, juicy fruit. The crowd of onlookers clapped and cheered with admiration at the old beggar's magical tree and were even more delighted when he told them to help themselves to the fruit. When all the pears were picked, the tree disappeared back into the ground as quickly as it had arrived.

Now, all this time the mean pear seller had been watching the display of magic, and he thought of a way he might be able to profit from it. As the crowd of people dispersed, shaking their heads in amazement and carrying armfuls of pears home, he went over to the old man, who was sitting by the roadside, smiling to himself.

'Oh, wise old wizard,' said the crafty trader, 'you have taught us all a lesson here today. You proved that it is best to be kind and charitable, for anyone who is will be rewarded tenfold.'

'That is correct,' said the old man. 'You have learnt the lesson well.'

The cunning pear seller looked humbly at the ground and said, 'Then perhaps you could show me the trick, so that I may teach others the same lesson.'

At this, the old beggar laughed out loud. 'Take a look at your stall, pear seller! It looks as though you do not need tricks to show people the meaning of kindness.'

When the mean pear seller looked at his stall, he saw that there was not a single pear left on it. You see, the old man's magic had only made the crowd *think* they had seen a pear tree grow from a pip – the pears were really from the mean pear seller's stall.

The rest was just an illusion . . . .

The Fish Prince

Once upon a time there was a powerful rajah, who lived in a splendid palace with his wife, the ranee. The rajah and ranee were loved by the people, for they were good and generous, and it was a cause of great sorrow to everyone that their beloved rulers had no children. Everyone prayed to the Gods to bless the couple with a child, but sadly the prayers were not answered.

One day some fish were delivered to the royal kitchen to be cooked for the rajah's dinner. Amongst them was one little fish that was not dead. One of the kitchen-maids took pity on the little fish and put him in a bowl of water. Shortly afterwards, the ranee saw him and decided to keep the pretty fish as a pet. And because she had no children, she lavished all her affection on the fish and loved him as a son. When the word spread that the ranee kept a fish and loved him like a son, the people named the fish 'Muchie Rajah' (the Fish Prince).

Soon Muchie Rajah grew too big to live in the small bowl, so the ranee instructed one of her craftsmen to make an ornate tub for him to live in. In time, however, Muchie Rajah grew too big for even the tub to hold him. So, sparing no expense, the rajah ordered a great pool to be constructed in the palace grounds. When it was finished, it had steep sides, forty feet high, from which there projected a balcony, where the ranee would sit and toss tasty morsels of food to Muchie Rajah. Sometimes she would sit there all day, watching the great fish swimming round and round in the pool.

'How lonely you look, my son,' she said one day. 'I will find you a wife.'

So the ranee sent her messengers out to find a bride for the Fish Prince. They went all over the kingdom, asking everyone if they would allow one of their children to marry Muchie Rajah; but they all answered; 'We cannot give one of our dear little daughters to be married to that great fish – even though he is Muchie Rajah.'

When she heard this, the ranee became even more determined to find a wife for her son, no matter what the cost. So she offered a bag of gold to anyone who would allow their daughter to become the Muchie Ranee (the Fish Princess). But not even the poorest people were tempted to sell their children.

At last the news reached the ears of a woman who lived on the very edge of the kingdom. Now, this woman had married for a second time, her first husband having died. She had a daughter by her first marriage and her new husband also had a daughter by a previous marriage. The woman hated her step-daughter and tried, by every means in her power, to make life unpleasant for the girl. She gave her the hardest work to do and the least food to eat.

When the woman heard that there was a large reward being offered for a girl to marry the Fish Prince, she called for the ranee's messengers. 'Give me the gold and you can take my step-daughter to marry the Muchie Rajah,' she said to them.

Then, turning to the girl, she said, 'Go down to the river and wash your saree, so that you will look clean and presentable for the Muchie Rajah.'

The girl did as she was told and went to the river, where she cried bitterly at the thought of being married to the Fish Prince.

As she cried, her sobs were heard by an old cobra who lived in the river bank. When he saw the girl crying, the cobra said to her, 'Young girl, why are you crying?'

'Oh, Cobra,' she answered, 'my cruel step-mother has sold me to be the wife of the Muchie Rajah, that great fish.'

'Do not be afraid,' said the cobra, who was very wise. 'Pick up three stones from the river bank and tie them up in the corner of your saree. The Muchie Rajah whose wife you are to be, is not really a fish, but a real prince who was turned into a fish by a wicked sorcerer. Be prepared, and as soon as you see him, throw the first stone at him; he will then sink to the bottom of his pool. The second time he comes, throw the second stone and he will sink to the bottom of the pool again. When he rises for the third time, throw the third stone and he will resume his human form.'

So the girl carefully tied three stones up in the corner of her saree, waved goodbye to the cobra, and went back to where the ranee's messengers were waiting to take her to the palace.

When they arrived there, the ranee was waiting impatiently, but when she saw the girl, she was most pleased. 'You are very pretty, my dear,' she said. 'You will make my son, Muchie Rajah, a fine wife. You will meet him immediately.'

The girl was taken to the great pool and lowered down the side to a ledge which was level with the surface of the water, and there she was left alone for the night.

She looked at the dark, deep water that lay at her feet, and waited. After a few moments, the surface of the pool was disturbed and she could see the great fish swimming towards her at great speed. As he grew closer, he lifted his head clear of the water and opened his huge mouth. The girl, although terrified, took hold of the first stone and

hurled it at the fish with all her might. No sooner had she done so than Muchie Rajah sank to the bottom of the pool and everything fell silent. The girl waited, breathlessly, her heart pounding against her chest.

Then suddenly the great fish rose again, almost beside where she stood. She hardly had time to throw the second stone, but somehow she did, and the fish sank once again. The girl held the last stone in her hand.

So far everything had happened just as the cobra had said it would. She knew that the fish would approach her again and that she must not fail with the last throw.

Then, without warning, there he was, his great body almost out of the water. As he towered above her, she threw the last stone with all her strength. There was a blinding flash, and there, standing before her on the ledge, was a handsome prince.

The poor girl was so exhausted by her frightening ordeal that she fell to her knees, crying. But the handsome prince knelt down beside her and said, 'Do not cry; you have broken the spell and I am free. Will you marry me and be my princess?'

The next morning the ranee came to her balcony to see how the Muchie Rajah liked his new wife, and she was very surprised to see the handsome young prince standing by the pool with the girl. She ordered that they be raised from the ledge immediately and when she heard their story she was overjoyed.

The news spread throughout the land and the people rejoiced, because they now had a prince and princess. Even though the prince was no longer a fish, the people still called him Muchie Rajah (the Fish Prince), and his wife, the Muchie Ranee (the Fish Princess).

Sun and Moon's Party

Long, long ago Sun, Moon and Water all lived happily on earth together and were all great friends. Sun and Moon loved to visit Water's house, where all three of them would gossip and tell amusing stories to each other.

One day, when Sun and Moon were on one of their regular visits to Water's house, they said to him: 'You have never been to our house. We would love you and your family to visit us, so that we can return the hospitality you have shown us. Surely that's what friends are for.'

'We would love to come and visit you,' said Water, 'but we are afraid that if we came it would mean that you would have to leave your home.'

'But why?' said Sun and Moon.

'Well,' said Water, 'I do not know how to tell you this . . . but your house is too small to hold us all.'

'Oh!' said Sun. 'But it just so happens that we are building a much larger house. When it's finished, will you then come?'

'If it's large enough, of course we will come,' said Water, 'but do keep in mind that my family takes up a lot of room and we would hate to come to your house and damage anything.'

Sun and Moon were overjoyed to hear that Water had finally agreed to visit their home. They worked hard, night and day, to finish their spacious new house. Then they sent an invitation to Water, which read:

Sun and Moon
have pleasure in inviting
Water and all his family
to visit their new home
for tea.

(Please come)

Water felt sure that the house, no matter how big it was, could not hold all of them, but he did not have the heart to refuse his good friends' invitation. So he accepted and began to flow in with his family and the friends who lived with him: in came thousands of fish, hundreds of whales and dolphins and even turtles.

When just a few of them had arrived, Water said, 'Are you sure you still want all of us to come in? We are bound to fill your house to the brim.'

'Of course you are all welcome. There's plenty of room for everyone,' said Sun and Moon.

'Very well,' said Water, and in he and his family poured. Soon Water had risen so high that Sun and Moon had to move to the highest part of their house to avoid getting wet.

'There are lots more of us to arrive yet,' shouted Water. 'Do you still think your house is big enough for us all?'

'We can't go back on our word now,' whispered Sun and Moon to each other. 'We will just have to move up to the sky to make room for Water and all his family and friends.'

So that's what they did, and the party is still going on today, with Sun and Moon high up in the sky looking down at their friend Water.

The Tree House

Once upon a time, in Africa, there were three boys who lived with their father. Sadly their mother had died, so their father had to look after them on his own, which wasn't very easy because he had to go out every day to work on his farm.

While he worked, the father worried about his three little boys, for there were many dangerous wild animals that prowled the nearby forest, not to mention the evil people who would like to steal the three boys away and make them work like servants.

One day the father had an idea. He went into the forest to look for a tall tree, and after searching for a while he found one that was perfect. His plan was to build a house high up in its branches where his boys would be safe from the animals and the wicked people.

First of all, he found some strong vines; he carefully knotted these into a long rope ladder which he rolled up and slung over his shoulder. Then, with his sharp axe tucked into his belt, he slowly climbed the tree. As he went, he chopped off each branch until he was at the top of the tree and the trunk was smooth and free from footholds. Now no one would be able to climb the tree, and the only way up or down was by the rope ladder which he tied securely to a strong branch and lowered down to the ground.

Having done this, he climbed down again and began

collecting logs with which to build the tree house. He tied them into bundles and pulled them up with a long vine, and in this way he carefully built a lovely little house high up in the wide branches of the tree. When he had finished, he climbed down the ladder and looked up into the branches. It was perfect; he could hardly tell there was a house up there, so well was it hidden in the thick foilage.

The man was very pleased with his work and went to fetch his three children at once. When they saw their new home, the boys were delighted and they quickly settled themselves in for their first night in the tree house. They pulled up the ladder and felt safe and secure amongst the branches which swayed gently in the breeze.

The next morning their father got ready to go to work, but before he left he told them what they must do: 'When I have climbed down the ladder, you must pull it up at once. Do not let it down for anyone except me when I return tonight.'

'How will we know you have returned, father?' asked one of the boys. 'We cannot see the ground below, for the leaves are too thick.'

This was a problem the man had not thought of and for a moment he was puzzled. Then he had an idea. 'I've got it!' he said. 'I will say a little rhyme, and when you hear it you will know it is safe to lower the ladder.'

'What is the rhyme?' cried the boys excitedly.

'Now let me think,' said their father. 'I know! I will call my three boys who love to play, *tree* boys! So, sons, listen. This will be the rhyme:

> Three boys, tree boys,
> Your playing now stop,
> Your father is home, so
> The ladder please drop.'

At this, the boys' father set off for work. He climbed down the ladder and as soon as he reached the ground the boys pulled it back up again. 'Remember,' called their father once more, 'do not lower the ladder for anyone but me,' and he disappeared into the bush.

Every morning their father would go off to work and every evening he would return and say the little rhyme and the ladder would be lowered. While he was away the boys were happy in the tree house; they played amongst the wide branches, and the birds which lived in the tree soon grew accustomed to them and would fly into the house and sing prettily as the boys fed them crumbs from the table.

As time passed the boys grew bigger, and one day their father said to them, 'Soon you will be big enough to come to the farm and help me.' The boys were excited at the prospect of going to work with their father and eagerly awaited the day when they would be allowed to do so. 'Maybe next month,' said their father. 'But until then things will remain as they are.' So he climbed down the ladder and watched as they pulled it back up, before setting off to work.

What he didn't see was a pair of sinister eyes watching from the bushes. The eyes belonged to an old crone who lived all alone in the forest – some people said she was a witch and stayed well away from her. She had noticed the goings-on up in the tree and could catch the occasional glimpse of the three strong young boys as they played amongst the branches. How nice it would be if I could catch those three lads and make them work in my field, she thought. I would soon have crops to sell and I would grow rich. But the old hag could see no way of getting up the tree except by the rope ladder which the boys had pulled up.

Then she had an idea. I know, she cackled to herself, I

will pretend to have a message from the boys' father and get them to lower the ladder so that I can climb up and capture them. She went to the foot of the tree and called out: 'Yoohoo, yoohoo, I have a message from your father; lower the ladder so that I may climb up and give it to you.'

When they heard the woman calling, the boys stopped playing and listened. 'That is not our father,' said one. 'We must not lower the ladder to anyone but him.' So they just called down, 'What is the message? We can hear you, so there is no need for you to come up.'

The old woman knew her trick had failed and without answering she ran off into the bushes.

That evening, when the boys' father returned, he called out as usual:

> 'Three boys, tree boys,
> Your playing now stop,
> Your father is home, so
> The ladder please drop.'

He didn't see the old woman hiding in the bushes listening to the rhyme.

Ah, she hissed to herself, so that is the secret of how to get those boys to lower the ladder. I will be back tomorrow and then we shall see what we shall see. Hee! Hee! Hee!

When the boys told their father about the old woman, he said, 'You did well, my boys. Now you understand why we have to be so careful. The woman was lying about the message and would no doubt have captured you if you had lowered the ladder.'

The next morning the old crone waited until their father had left for work, and watched as the boys pulled the ladder up. Then she went to the bottom of the tree and said:

> 'Three boys, tree boys,
> Your playing now stop,
> Your father is home, so
> The ladder please drop.'

When the boys heard this, they stopped playing. 'That's odd,' said one. 'Our father has returned from work very soon and he sounds so strange. Perhaps there is something wrong. Let's lower the ladder and let him come up.'

But the eldest boy was not sure, and he called down: 'We cannot hear you; please say the rhyme again, father.'

So the woman called out as loud as she could:

> 'Three boys, tree boys,
> Your playing now stop,
> Your father is home, so
> The ladder please drop.'

'That is not our father,' said the eldest boy. 'It is that wicked old woman who tried to trick us yesterday. Go away!' he shouted. 'We are not that easily fooled; that is not the voice of our father.'

When the old woman heard this she was furious and shook her fist at the boys as she stormed off into the forest. 'I'll be back,' she shouted as she went.

When she returned to her house, she sat down in front of her cooking pot to think. 'There is only one way I can get those boys to let that ladder down,' she muttered. 'I must make my voice sound like their father's.' So she set about mixing a magic potion that would make her voice as deep as a man's. She put everything she needed into the cooking pot and stirred the mixture round and round as it bubbled over the fire. The ingredients were the most horrible things like frogs' eyes and lizards' tongues, but

the old woman was so determined to catch the boys that she didn't care.

When the potion was ready, she closed her eyes and drank the horrid liquid down with one gulp; it tasted so nasty that she almost fainted. But as soon as she recovered she tried out her voice to see if the potion had worked and, sure enough, when she opened her mouth to speak, out came a gruff, deep voice just like the boys' father's. Straight away she rushed back to the place where the tree house was, stood at the bottom of the tree and said:

'Three boys, tree boys,
Your playing now stop,
Your father is home, so
The ladder please drop.'

The three boys listened carefully to the voice saying the rhyme, then the middle boy said, 'That is our father home from work – let the ladder down.' So the three boys lowered the ladder – and the old crone climbed up it.

When she reached the tree house, she grabbed the poor boys before they had a chance to recover from the shock of seeing the horrible old crone instead of their father. 'Got you!' she said in her deep voice. 'Your days of playing are over; now you will come and work for me.' Then she tied the boys up and carried them down one by one to the ground below, before marching them off into the forest to her house.

When the boys' father arrived soon afterwards, he knew straightaway that there was something wrong: the ladder was still hanging down from the tree and there was no sign of his three boys. He searched in the nearby bush, but they were nowhere to be seen. Then he remembered what the boys had told him about the old woman who had pretended to have a message from him for them. It must be her, said the boys' father to himself. People say she is a witch. She must have used a spell to trick my boys.

He ran as fast as he could to the nearby village and went straight to the chief's hut. The chief was very troubled by what he heard and sent a messenger to fetch the wise old man who lived on the edge of the village. When the wise man heard what had happened, he shook his head.

'I know this woman,' he said. 'She is a wicked witch and it will not be easy to rescue your sons, for she knows some pretty powerful spells. But there is a way that her magic power can be broken.'

'Tell me what it is,' said the boys' father. 'I will do anything to save my sons.'

'Well,' said the old man, 'if you can manage to get hold of the wooden stick she always carries with her, and break it in two, her powers will be broken as well. But I warn you – if she finds out what you are up to she will put a terrible spell on you, so you had better be careful.'

The man thanked the chief and the wise old man and set off to find the witch.

By now it was growing dark and the forest was full of strange sounds as he made his way to where the old crone was said to live.

Presently, he came to a clearing with a small hut in the middle of it. Inside there was a fire burning and he could see the shadow of someone inside moving about. He crept closer and managed to crawl to the open doorway without being seen. Cautiously he peered inside, and there, sitting with their feet and hands tightly bound, were his three sons. The old witch was sitting at the table eating her supper, and leaning against the arm of the chair was her long magic stick. But as the man looked at the stick he realized that he would not be able to grab hold of it quickly enough to prevent the witch putting a spell on him. He would have to think of a clever plan to get closer to it.

He crept silently away into the bushes and ran back to the tree house, where he thought for a while. Then an idea came to him. He took some ashes from the fireplace and rubbed them into his hair to make it look grey. Then he found an old blanket and wrapped it around himself. Next, he took his most valuable possession from its secret hiding place. It was a small golden drum which his father had given to him and which had been in his family for generations. He tied it around his neck with a leather cord so that it hung on his chest. Finally he climbed back down the ladder and broke off a dry branch from another tree to use as a walking stick. He was now ready to put his plan into action and set off back to the witch's house.

As he got close to the clearing where the witch lived, he began to lean heavily on the walking stick like an old man, and with his other hand he held the blanket tightly around him.

The three boys were all asleep in the corner of the hut and the witch was sitting in her favourite chair, smoking a pipe and thinking of work for them to do the next day, when there was a knock on the door. 'Who is that knocking at my door at this time of the night?' she screeched. 'Whoever it is will be sorry!'

She picked up her magic stick and went to the door to see who was foolish enough to disturb her. Standing in the doorway was a grey-haired old man with his eyes closed, leaning on a walking stick.

'What do you want?' hissed the witch.

'Have you a bowl of soup for a blind old man? I have walked many miles today and I am half starved.'

'You can starve to death for all I care,' said the witch. 'Now be gone before I put a spell on you.'

'Oh, please help me,' said the old man. He held out his hand and let the old blanket he had wrapped around him fall open. There around his neck hung the golden drum.

When she saw the gold shining in the moonlight, the old woman's eyes lit up. More gold for my collection, she thought to herself, and it will be easy to steal from this blind old fool.

'Come in, old man, of course I've a bowl of soup for you. Come in and sit yourself down.'

The old man felt his way into the hut and sat down at the table while the witch busied herself at the stove. She thought the old man was blind, of course, and that he couldn't therefore see her sprinkle a powerful magic sleeping potion into the bowl of soup.

'Here you are. I hope you enjoy it,' said the witch with a sly smile, as she handed the old man a bowl of soup. One spoonful of that, she thought to herself, and you will fall into a deep sleep and the gold will be mine.

'Thank you kindly,' said the blind man, and he took a spoonful of the soup. But as the woman looked away for a second he quickly threw it under the table. 'Mmm, this soup is delicious,' he said, 'but I feel very tired all of a sudden. May I lie down in front of the fire and sleep?'

The wicked witch thought her evil plot had worked. She looked at the golden drum eagerly and could hardly wait to get her greedy hands on it.

'Of course you may,' she said, as she helped the old man over to the warm hearth. As soon as he lay down, the old man pretended to fall into a deep sleep and made loud snoring noises.

After a few moments, when the witch felt sure he was soundly asleep, she stealthily knelt down beside him and reached out to untie the cord which was around his neck. Then, all of a sudden, to the witch's surprise, the old man sprang to his feet and grabbed her magic stick. The witch was so shocked that she couldn't even think of a spell to cast. She just sat on the floor with her mouth wide open, and before she had time to gather her wits, the man broke the stick in two across his knee.

There was a flash of light and a noise like the rushing of the wind, which woke up the three sleeping boys in the corner of the room. To their astonishment they saw the old witch slowly crumble into a pile of dust on the floor of the hut, and they couldn't believe their eyes when they saw their father take off the old blanket and shake the grey ash from his hair.

'Oh, father!' they cried. 'We knew you would come and rescue us from the wicked witch.'

'Yes, my sons,' he said, 'you're safe now and she can never harm anyone ever again.'

Their father untied the three boys and they all made their way back to the tree house, where they all lived happily together for a very long time.

Kisander and Her Pomsitae Tree

Kisander the cat had a lovely Pomsitae tree in her garden, with dozens of ripe, juicy pomsitaes hanging in its branches.

Every day, as he passed Kisander's house, Anansi would look over the garden fence at the delicious fruit and wish he could get his hands on it. But Anansi was afraid of Kisander. She was clever and had sharp claws; she could move silently through the forest and could see in the dark. How could he get those pomsitaes, while she was guarding her tree?

As the days passed, Anansi grew more and more desperate to eat the pomsitaes. Finally, he decided to try to steal some, no matter what the danger.

That evening Anansi watched Kisander as she swung in her hammock under the pomsitae tree. Eventually, she went inside and Anansi waited until he thought she was asleep. Then, stealthily, he scaled the fence and crept over to the tree. He climbed up into the branches and quietly started to pick the pomsitaes, which he put into the sack he was carrying. There were so many ripe, juicy pomsitaes that Anansi soon forgot himself and got quite carried away with greed. He began crashing about in the branches noisily. Mmm ... here's a nice one, and another, said Anansi to himself.

It wasn't long before Kisander, who had been sleeping soundly, was rudely awakened by the rustling and mutter-

ing outside her window, and she threw open the door and hissed, 'Who is in my tree, stealing my pomsitaes?'

Anansi was so startled by this that he dropped the sack, which fell down and landed with a thump at the foot of the tree.

'Aha,' cried Kisander. 'There goes the thief,' and she pounced at the sack.

When she saw it was a sack full of pomsitaes, she looked up into the branches above and called out, 'Come down at once, thief!' But as she looked up, with her bright, piercing eyes, she could not see Anansi, because he had changed into a spider, as he always did when he was in danger.

'The thief must have escaped,' said Kisander. 'But at least he has saved me the trouble of picking my pomsitaes.' She picked up the sack and went indoors. But she could not get back to sleep and she paced to and fro restlessly, glancing occasionally out of the window at her garden.

Anansi sat uncomfortably on a branch, trembling with fright. Sometimes he could see Kisander's eyes flashing through the window as she looked up at the tree, but luckily she did not spot him. Then, to make matters worse, it began to rain and Anansi huddled on his branch shivering miserably. There was not even a single pomsitae left on the tree for him to eat, for they were all in the sack he had dropped, so his stomach rumbled with hunger.

Finally, Kisander went back to bed, but it was dawn before Anansi plucked up the courage to come down from the tree and run home as fast as his legs would carry him.

From that day on, Anansi couldn't even look at a pomsitae without remembering his ordeal in Kisander's tree.

Tiger Son

Once upon a time there was a woman who lived with her only son in a small town in China. One day the son was on a journey through the mountains when he was attacked and eaten by a tiger. When his mother heard the sad news, she was beside herself with grief. Her only son was dead and now she was alone with no one to look after her.

Soon her grief turned to anger and she decided that the tiger that had committed this crime should be caught and punished. So she went to the magistrate and asked him to make out a warrant for the tiger's arrest.

When the magistrate heard the woman's request, however, he fell about laughing. 'We can't arrest a tiger,' he said, 'and even if we could, how would we know which tiger to arrest? There are dozens of them in the mountains around here.'

But the woman was so upset that no amount of reasoning could calm her down. 'You are the magistrate,' she cried, 'and a murder has been committed; it is your duty to see that justice is done.'

The people who had gathered around nodded in agreement. 'She's got a point there,' one of them shouted, and everyone laughed. The magistrate shifted uncomfortably in his seat. He could see no other way out of this awkward situation but to issue a warrant for the tiger's arrest, so he took out his pen and wrote out the document. At this, the woman and the crowd were satisfied and went about their business.

Now, every morning the warrants that had been issued by the magistrate the day before landed on the desk of the chief of police and he would assign one of his constables to each case. When he saw the warrant for the tiger's arrest he thought someone was playing a joke on him. 'Arrest a tiger, indeed!' he snorted. But then he had an idea; he would carry the joke one step further. There was a new constable starting work that day called Li-Neng and the police chief summoned him to his office.

'Li-Neng,' said the police chief, 'I have a very important job for you on your first day as a constable. Here is a warrant for the arrest of a dangerous criminal. Be off with you and do not return until you have captured him.'

When poor Li-Neng saw the tiger's name on the warrant, he shook with fright, but he was determined to make a good impression as a policeman and so he set off towards the mountains at once.

He had no idea how he was going to catch the tiger and he spent many days just wandering around without even seeing a trace of one. He began to feel very downhearted, but he was determined not to return empty-handed, so he pressed on. Further and further into the mountains he went until he came to a small lake into which a waterfall cascaded. It was such a pleasant spot that he decided to sit there for a while and rest. He lay back on the soft grass and listened to the sound of the rushing waterfall as it tumbled into the lake. It was so soothing that he soon fell into a deep sleep.

Suddenly, he was awakened by the feeling that he was being watched. He sat up and was so shocked by what he saw that he almost jumped out of his skin. Only a few feet away from him was a huge, fully grown tiger. He was just sitting there staring at him, blinking occasionally. Li-Neng

was terrified. He looked around for a means of escape, but all around were the steep walls of rock. So he decided to put a brave front and demanded, 'Are you the tiger who ate the young traveller who came this way last month?'

The tiger simply blinked and lay down. Li-Neng took this to mean yes, so he said, 'Then I arrest you in the name of the law. Will you come quietly?'

The tiger blinked again and rolled over on his back like a playful kitten, so Li-Neng plucked up all his courage, took a rope from his bag and tied it around the tiger's neck. 'Come along,' he said, 'Back to the town with you.'

The tiger did not resist his pull on the rope, but just walked alongside Li-Neng like an obedient dog. Li-Neng could hardly believe his luck and couldn't wait to see the look on the face of his chief when he arrived back with the tiger.

As he approached the town, everyone who saw him and the tiger ran away screaming with terror. The word spread rapidly ahead of him until it reached the ears of the police chief, who was in a meeting with the magistrate.

'What nonsense is this?' they both asked. In fact, they had both completely forgotten about the warrant for the tiger's arrest.

Suddenly, there was a commotion outside and they both went to see what it was all about. When they stepped on to the front porch of the police station, standing there before them was Li-Neng, with a huge tiger sitting next to him. All around the square the townsfolk were watching from upstairs windows or from the branches of trees where they had fled in terror when they saw Li-Neng coming into town with the tiger.

As soon as he saw the police chief, Li-Neng stood smartly to attention and saluted. 'I have arrested the tiger as you ordered, sir!' He held out the warrant, but the two men were transfixed with terror.

'W-well done, Li-Neng,' the police chief eventually stammered. 'How did you do it?'

Li-Neng was enjoying himself a great deal, but he tried to act as casually as possible. 'Oh, it wasn't very difficult,' he said nonchalantly. 'The tiger has confessed to the crime and has come quietly to face trial.'

'Trial!' blurted the magistrate, who had climbed on to the table by the doorway and was shaking like a leaf. 'Yes. . . . Yes, of course . . . bring the prisoner to the courthouse.'

A short while later the whole town watched as Li-Neng and the tiger sat in the dock and the magistrate, in his robes of office, said in a solemn voice, 'Tiger, you are charged with the murder of this woman's only son.' The magistrate pointed to the woman whose son had been killed. 'Do you confess to the crime?'

The tiger nodded his head slowly and blinked.

'Then I must sentence you,' said the magistrate. 'If you were a human, the sentence would almost certainly be death, but I must say that this case is most unusual. There is no record of a similar case in all my books of law. Therefore, I must think of a suitable punishment. As you are a tiger and obviously do not know much about the laws of man, and considering that you gave yourself up and came quietly, my sentence is as follows: you will go to the woman and try to make up to her for the loss of her son!'

At this, there was uproar in the courtroom. The woman was furious and demanded a retrial, but the magistrate said that his decision was final and that was the end of the matter.

Li-Neng took the tiger to the woman's house and untied the rope from around his neck. The tiger lay down in front of the house, and although the woman shouted abuse at him he just blinked at her, so eventually she gave up and went inside. That evening the tiger stood up and padded softly away into the darkness.

'Ah, I knew it!' said the woman. 'As if a tiger would do as the magistrate ordered! He has gone back to the mountains, no doubt to kill more innocent travellers.'

The next morning, however, when the woman opened her window and looked out, to her surprise there was the tiger. Lying in front of him was the body of a deer which he had obviously killed and carried there. The woman eyed the tiger and the deer suspiciously. 'Is that for me?' she asked. The tiger nodded and blinked.

Now, the woman had not eaten meat since the loss of her son as she could not afford to buy it, so she was soon tucking into a delicious venison stew which she shared with the tiger. Each day, from then on, the tiger returned with something to eat, sometimes it was a wild pig or a pheasant or another deer. He slept on the verandah outside the woman's door and kept her safe from thieves and robbers.

Soon the woman became fond of the great beast and he would place his head on her lap and purr loudly as she scratched his ears. He was like a son to her and, just as the magistrate had ordered he made up for the loss of her real son. Many years later the old woman died and the townsfolk gathered round her grave to pay their last respects. As they were doing so, the tiger appeared and the crowd parted as he trotted to the graveside. The tiger lifted his great head and roared once as if to say goodbye. Then he returned to the mountains and was never seen again.

Valiant Victor

Once upon a time, in India, there lived a weaver whose name was Victor. He was very small and skinny, and everyone laughed at him and teased him about his size. This upset poor Victor a great deal and he would get very angry. 'I may be small and skinny, but I have the courage of a tiger, and one day you will all see how brave and valiant I am,' he would say.

This just made everyone laugh at him even more and they started to call him Valiant Victor. But instead of being ashamed of his nickname, little Victor enjoyed it when people called out to him in the street, 'Hey, there goes Valiant Victor,' and soon he was known far and wide, although he had never done a brave act in his life.

One day Victor was sitting at his loom when a fly buzzed around his head. It was so annoying that Victor threw the shuttle he was using to weave the cloth at the irritating fly. To his surprise it hit the fly fair and square and killed it.

'There, you see,' cried Victor, 'that is how I handle creatures which annoy me, for I am the great Valiant Victor.'

The little man went all over the town telling everyone how he had killed the fly with a shuttle. Of course, everyone laughed at him, but he hardly noticed them, for he was far too busy boasting about his valiant deed. In fact, the more often he repeated the story the more he became convinced that he was the bravest man in the whole town, and finally he decided that it was high time he left and went to seek his fortune elsewhere. So the little weaver packed his bag and set off to find somewhere where his bravery would be appreciated.

Valiant Victor travelled for many days through many towns and villages until he came to a place where the local farmers were being plagued by a rogue elephant. The great beast was trampling their crops and terrifying their livestock. He had even attacked the farmers themselves when they tried to drive him off.

'Don't worry,' said Valiant Victor, 'I will sort out this elephant for you – I am the great Valiant Victor. Maybe you've heard of me?'

The farmers shook their heads; they hadn't heard of him and he didn't look as if he was capable of fighting a fully grown elephant, but they were willing to try anything to get rid of the beast. 'Hurrah for Valiant Victor,' they cheered, as the little man set off without even a weapon to fight with.

'That's the last we'll see of him,' they said, as he disappeared out of sight.

Soon Valiant Victor was alone in the part of the forest where the elephant had last been seen, and he began to stamp around loudly, shouting, 'Come on out, Elephant! Let me see you so that I can catch you.'

After a while there was a great noise of trees snapping and undergrowth being trampled, and at last the enormous elephant appeared. As soon as he saw the great beast, Valiant Victor stopped shouting. His courage deserted him and he turned and ran as fast as he could, with the angry elephant close behind. Suddenly the idea of being a great hero didn't seem so attractive to poor Victor as he looked over his shoulder at the charging elephant. The enraged beast was almost on top of him when Victor ran between two massive trees. The elephant followed at full speed, but then to Victor's relief he got jammed between the two tree trunks. Struggle as he might, the elephant was wedged tight and could not move.

After a while, the farmers cautiously ventured out to see if the little man had been trampled under foot, but to their amazement, there was Valiant Victor sitting a few feet away from the wedged elephant, who by now was so exhausted by his struggling that he was quite subdued. When the farmers asked Valiant Victor how he had managed to catch the elephant, he just shrugged. 'Oh, it was nothing,' he said casually.

It turned out that the elephant had had a nasty thorn embedded in his trunk and the pain had caused him to run amok. When the thorn was removed the elephant soon became his normal self and was released by the farmers to go back into the hills where the rest of the herd lived.

Well, the news spread about Valiant Victor and the elephant, and he was hailed as a hero by everyone. The people of the town asked him to stay and live with them, but Valiant Victor declined the kind invitation, saying that he was seeking fame and fortune and must carry on his journey.

So Valiant Victor left the town and continued to wander, not knowing where he was heading, until he came to a place that was being terrorized by a savage tiger. He would come in the night and make off with a calf or a goat, and the people were so afraid that they would lock themselves in their houses until daylight. When Valiant Victor heard this, he said, 'Have no fear, Valiant Victor is here, and I will catch the tiger!'

That night Valiant Victor waited in the darkness for the tiger to arrive and, sure enough, after a short wait he saw the great cat quietly padding towards him.

When the tiger saw Victor just standing there waiting,

he decided that he would make a fine meal. The tiger leapt into the air with a roar. It was then that Valiant Victor's courage deserted him and he turned and ran away as fast as he could. But the tiger simply took another great leap and almost grabbed the running Victor with his sharp claws. Unfortunately, the tiger didn't see the overhanging branch of a tree and he launched himself through the air with all his strength. He came to a sudden halt as his head smacked against the branch and he fell unconscious at Victor's feet. Victor could hardly believe his luck, for without a doubt the tiger would have killed him if it had not been for the branch.

Valiant Victor thought he had better do something before the tiger woke up, so he called out to the villagers who were hiding inside their houses: 'Come on out! I have knocked the tiger out with one blow; help me to tie it up!'

The people slowly opened their doors and came out one by one, and when they saw the tiger lying at Valiant Victor's feet they could hardly believe their eyes. They quickly brought a rope and tied the tiger's feet, and then took the animal to a cage ready to be taken to a zoo.

Of course, Victor was a hero and news of his daring deeds spread far and wide. As he continued on his way people would come out to see this great hero as he passed through their villages.

One day Valiant Victor came to the palace of a great rajah and he went up to the gates and said, 'Open the gates! Valiant Victor is here, and I wish to see the rajah!'

The gates were opened at once and the rajah came out to greet the famous Valiant Victor. 'Come in,' he said. 'I am honoured by your visit. Please stay here for as long as you wish.'

Valiant Victor liked the look of the palace so he decided

to rest there for a few weeks before going on with his travels. 'Thank you, Your Majesty,' he said, 'I don't mind if I do.'

He was made very comfortable in the palace and was waited on hand and foot by the rajah's servants, and as the days passed he became more and more settled. This is the life, he said to himself, I think I will settle down here and marry the rajah's pretty daughter.

The rajah was more than pleased to let Valiant Victor marry his daughter. After all, Victor was a great hero whose fame had spread across the land. So he was married to the beautiful princess and they lived in the palace in luxury for several months. Valiant Victor grew fat from all the lovely food he ate and became so lazy that he hardly ever left the palace. But one day the peace and quiet was broken by a messenger who rode into the palace courtyard with the news of an approaching army of brigands. The palace was in uproar as they had no means of defending themselves against such a threat.

The rajah sent for Victor and said, 'Thank goodness you are here, Valiant Victor. You will defend us, won't you?'

'Three cheers for Valiant Victor!' the people all cheered.

But Victor was not very happy about this; he had been lucky with the elephant and the tiger, but taking on a whole army of brigands was an entirely different matter. That night he decided it was time to leave the palace before the brigands surrounded it, so he went to his rooms and collected together all the valuable gold cups and plates he could find and put them into a sack. Then he crept quietly out of the gates and hurried away as fast as he could into the darkness.

What he didn't know was that the brigands were at that moment creeping quietly up the road towards the palace, hoping to take it by surprise. As Victor ran at full speed

round a bend in the road he went crashing headlong into the leading brigands. The gold plates and cups went clattering and crashing in every direction, making such a noise that the brigands thought they were under a full-scale attack from a terrible army. Victor screamed with terror but this only made the brigands think their leading group was being killed. There was so much confusion that the brigands set upon each other in the darkness and killed each other. The few who were left turned tail and ran away into the night.

When all the noise had died down, Victor crawled from under a bush where he had been hiding and looked around him. He bent down and picked up a sword that had been dropped by one of the brigands, and just then the rajah and his servants, who had come to see what all the noise was about, came round the corner. Well, you can imagine what they thought when they saw Victor standing there with a sword in his hand surrounded by the dead bodies of fifty or so brigands.

Victor was carried back to the palace shoulder high, and everyone came out to see the great hero who had fought an army of brigands single-handed. The rajah was so grateful that he gave Victor half of his wealth and made him heir to his throne.

So Valiant Victor, the luckiest hero in the world, lived happily ever after, and no one ever suspected that it was all because of luck that he was a hero at all.

The Metal Man

Once upon a time, in Africa, there lived a chief who was very powerful, but also very foolish. When he did foolish things, none of his advisers had the courage to tell him he was being foolish in case he had them thrown into prison.

One day the chief called all his advisers into his hut, where they all waited nervously for him to arrive. It wasn't long before the chief swept in and sat down on his chair.

'Last night', began the chief, 'I had a dream in which my enemies came and surrounded my kingdom. They came in such large numbers that our warriors were outnumbered by ten to one and it looked as if we would be defeated.' The chief paused for effect and the advisers shuffled about uncomfortably in the silence. Then he went on, 'Just as all seemed lost, a mighty warrior marched forth carrying my battle flag above his head, and the enemy turned and fled like cowards!'

At this, the advisers thought they had better do something, so they jumped up and down and cheered. This pleased the chief and he smiled cheerfully. Then one of the advisers stepped forward and cleared his throat before speaking: 'Ahem! Who was this mighty warrior, Sir?'

The chief was glad someone had asked that question for it was exactly what he had wanted. He rose to his feet. 'He was a METAL MAN!' he shouted triumphantly. 'The

spears and arrows of the enemy just bounced off him. He was invincible!'

The advisers clapped and cheered at this wonderful story, then they turned to each other, shook hands and slapped each other on the back. By the time the noise had eventually died down the chief was sitting on his chair again and when he had their full attention, he said, 'Go and fetch the blacksmith who made the fine jewellery for my wife. He must make me a metal man so that our kingdom will be safe from attack.'

Well, you could have heard a pin drop. The advisers just stood there with their mouths hanging open.

'Go on,' yelled the chief. 'Get on with it!'

At this, they all snapped out of their state of shock and ran in every direction, falling over each other in the process. 'Send for the blacksmith at once,' they all said, and a messenger was sent to the village where the man lived.

A short time later the blacksmith was escorted into the chief's hut. 'Good morning,' said the chief pleasantly. 'I have a very important task for you, blacksmith. I hope you will not let me down.'

Now the blacksmith thought the chief wanted him to make some more jewellery, so he replied, 'Have no fear, Sir, my work is of the highest standard. I will not let you down.'

'Good! Good!' said the chief. 'Here is what I want you to do. You must make me a man out of metal who can defend us against attack from our enemies, and you must do it quickly in case my dream was a warning that we are about to be attacked. Your reward will be a rich one, blacksmith, for this metal man will keep your countrymen safe for ever.'

Well, the poor blacksmith was so amazed that he didn't know what to say. He just nodded and left the hut as fast as he could. When he got outside he began to wonder just what he was going to do. It was impossible to do as the chief had asked, but if he admitted as much he would more than likely be thrown into prison.

All the way home the blacksmith tried to think of a way out of the terrible situation he was in, but to no avail. When he reached home he told his wife all about it.

'Why can't his advisers tell him what a foolish chief he is?' she cried. 'They should have the courage to stand up to him.'

The next morning the blacksmith went to his forge and sat down beside it feeling very lonely and miserable. Just then along came an old woman who had come to the village to sell herbs and potions to cure illnesses. 'What is wrong, blacksmith?' asked the woman. 'Perhaps I can help you.'

'I don't think so,' sighed the blacksmith, and he told her the whole sad story.

'Oh, I think I can help you there, you know,' chuckled the old woman. 'This is what you must do. You must go back to the chief and tell him that before you can make the metal man you will need some special ingredients that only he can supply. Ask him to order all his people to shave off all their hair and put it into baskets which are to be delivered to the village by noon tomorrow. Tell him that you need the hair to make a special fire to forge the metal for the metal man. Then tell him he must command all his people to cry into their buckets until they are full of tears and to bring those to the village by the following noon. Explain that you need the tears to quench the metal you are to use for the metal man.'

The blacksmith did as the old woman had said, although he could not see how it would help him. He went to the chief, who listened intently to what the blacksmith asked.

After a few moments the chief turned to the blacksmith

and said, 'I am sorry, but you cannot have the ingredients you ask for. I cannot order my subjects to shave all their hair off; and as for filling a bucket with tears, why, that is impossible! No, no, your request is foolish.'

'And so is yours, Sir,' said the blacksmith.

For a moment the chief looked as if he was going to explode with rage, but then a smile came over his face. 'You are right, blacksmith, I have been foolish. I asked for something impossible. It is quite clear that no one can make a living man from metal. You may go, and thank you for having the courage to tell me I was being foolish. As for my advisers, not one of them had the same courage and as a result they will all be dismissed immediately.'

The blacksmith went back to his village and thanked the old woman for helping him; he made her a special bracelet as a token of his gratitude.

FALL ABOUT WITH FLO

Floella Benjamin

Between the pages of this book, Floella Benjamin, regular presenter of TV's 'Playschool' invites you to have a good laugh with her over some of the funniest jokes you've ever heard. Come along and join the fun!

What's green and hard?
A frog with a machine gun.

Doctor, doctor, I think I'm a billiard ball!
Get to the end of the queue.

FLOELLA'S FUNNIEST JOKES

Jokes from TV Star Floella Benjamin

Presenter of TV's 'Playschool' and star of
'Fast Forward', Floella Benjamin here tells some
of her very favourite jokes.

What's JR's favourite sweet?

Ewing gum.

Where do spiders live?

Crawley.

Floella says:

*'It was great fun compiling my favourite joke book.
It was a real family effort and we were all in stitches thinking
up new jokes. I hope you have a giggle reading them.'*

WILL THE VILLAINOUS MAN OF LIGHT HALT SAM'S QUEST FOR POWER?

Sam rebounded.

The Man of Light blazed before him, glowing bulk filling the tunnel. There was no way around the Man. Sam darted away into a side passage and almost immediately pulled up short to avoid running into the Man of Light again as the gleaming figure suddenly flared into existence in Sam's path. Sam spun to retrace his path, but, again, the Man confronted him. He twisted his head to look over his shoulder.

It was dark. By the time he had turned around, the Man was there, in front of him. Sam raised a hand to shield his eyes from the brilliance.

The Man of Light laughed at him.

SHADOWRUN: CHOOSE YOUR ENEMIES CAREFULLY

**Exploring New Realms
in Science Fiction/Fantasy Adventure**

Titles already published or in preparation:

The Day It Rained Forever by Ray Bradbury

Myth-maker extraordinaire Ray Bradbury has created in his writing a world of uncanny beauty and fear. In this collection of twenty-three classic stories there are the gentle Martians of *Dark They Were and Golden-Eyed*, the killers of *The Town Where No One Got Off*, the sweet sounds of *The Day it Rained Forever* and much, much more.

Of Time and Stars by Arthur C. Clarke

Strange new worlds stretch the imagination and the emotions as Arthur C. Clarke writes of Earth's destruction, trouble with computers, creatures from other planets, spaceflight and the future.

The Neverending Story by Michael Ende

Bastian Balthazar Bux is nobody's idea of a hero, least of all his own. One day he steals a mysterious book and hides away to read it – only to find himself stepping through its pages into the world of Fantastica. Enchanted, perilous, dying, Fantastica is waiting for a Messiah, its faery people doomed, until Bastian appears as their Saviour ...

Walker of Worlds Book 1: Chronicles of the King's Tramp by Tom Dehaven

Jack, a Walker, is in danger. He has learned a secret; he has earned an enemy. Jack must flee the world of Lostwithal. He must flee to Kemolo. The secret he carries could mean the end of all the worlds, not just his own. But Jack cannot violate the Order of Things, not even to preserve it. Jack, a Walker, must walk the worlds.

SECRETS OF POWER
VOLUME 2

SHADOWRUN:

CHOOSE YOUR ENEMIES CAREFULLY

ROBERT N. CHARRETTE

A ROC BOOK

ROC

Published by the Penguin Group
Penguin Books Ltd, 27 Wrights Lane, London W8 5TZ, England
Penguin Books USA Inc., 375 Hudson Street, New York, New York 10014, USA
Penguin Books Australia Ltd, Ringwood, Victoria, Australia
Penguin Books Canada Ltd, 10 Alcorn Avenue, Toronto, Ontario, Canada M4V 3B2
Penguin Books (NZ) Ltd, 182–190 Wairau Road, Auckland 10, New Zealand

Penguin Books Ltd, Registered Offices: Harmondsworth, Middlesex, England

First published 1991
10 9 8 7 6 5 4 3 2 1

Roc is a trademark of New American Library, a division of
Penguin Books USA Inc. SHADOWRUN, and the distinctive
SHADOWRUN logo, are trademarks of the FASA Corporation,
    1026 W. Van Buren, Chicago, IL 60507
Printed in England by Clays Ltd, St Ives plc

To Crick, who didn't believe me about Battletech either.

PART 1

We All Wear Masks

1

Three days ago, the pain had seemed unbearable. But as time passed, the constant discomfort lessened the burden by dulling her senses. As late as this morning, she thought that she had grown used to it. Then the cramps had started. The crippling agony had wracked her with increasingly frequent spasms all day. Now, it was almost dark.

She didn't dare cry out.

A new spasm tore at her intestines and clawed its way up her torso, firing her insides with blazing agony. Despite her best intentions, she screamed as her muscles knotted in the brutal grip of the convulsion.

As the wave of pain ebbed, she lay panting, certain that she had betrayed herself. Slowly, painfully, she dragged herself deeper into the gloom of her chosen shelter. The inhabitants of this rundown building, if there were any, remained hidden. Her only company was her misery. Moaning at the pain accompanying her every movement, she forced her legs to carry her up the stairs. If she could get far enough away, they might not find her tonight. The ravening fire in her belly threatened to overwhelm her, but she hugged one arm across her stomach and continued, bracing herself against the stairwell wall with the other.

She only made it up two flights before she collapsed, whimpering. Silently she cursed her waning strength. Orks were supposed to be tough. The physical power she had known for the last year had been the only compensation for her change, and now that strength had abandoned her. Just like Hugh. And Ken before him. Even her brother had left her to be disposed of with the rest of the unsightly trash.

They could all rot in hell.

The blaze inside her had died to coals, a hot pain but bearable. In the recession of the pain, she became aware of a bone-numbing ache in her limbs. Her muscles, exhausted from her climb, trembled. Her skin was clammy with sweat and itched unbearably. She wanted to puke.

Her position on the landing offered her a view into one of the derelict apartments. The darkening sky was framed in the room's window. Outside, the lights of Hong Kong sparkled awake, forming constellations of sublime and taunting beauty. The thin, seesaw wail of a police siren drifted in through the open aperture. It offered no hope of rescue. None of the corporate police ever came to the Walled City. Not even the Enclave Police Agency, money-grubbing hirelings that they were, could be easily bribed to appear in the Walled City after dark. Gangs ruled the Walled City, and many of them hunted the changed for fun.

A scuffing sound came from the bottom of the stairwell and she froze. Her physical torment vanished in a rush of fear. Praying all the while, she strained to hear anything further. The noise began again, and she recognized the sound of footsteps on the stairs.

She pushed off with her arms, forcing herself upright. The world spun around, but she managed to stay on her feet and stagger up another flight. This landing was as littered with trash as the last, but several of the rooms on this floor still had doors. That meant someone still lived here. Hoping the hunters wouldn't press the search into occupied areas, she chose an open doorway and headed for it. As she attempted to pass through the doorway, her head slammed against the lintel. The shock forced an involuntary grunt of pain.

In the distant lower darkness, there was a sudden silence.

She listened, but there was no sound. The hunters would be listening, too.

Minutes crawled by.

Her eyes were good in the dark. If she stood by the railing and looked down, she might be able to see who was on the stairs. She didn't dare try. Even if she managed to suppress the vertigo, she would be exposing herself. There were others who could see in the dark even better than she.

Her legs began to tremble again, and she felt her fear-induced strength fading. She wouldn't be able to remain standing for long. Ducking her head, she slipped through the doorway. She stretched out an arm and gripped the door, swinging it slowly closed. It made no sound that she could detect. That was good. If she couldn't hear it, they probably couldn't either.

The locks on the door were gone—only splintered wood marked their former presence. Not that it mattered; if the hunters tracked her here, a locked door wouldn't stop them. Her only hope was that they would pass by.

The room was a sty, a haven for drifters and the homeless. From the discarded chip casings scattered about she knew that it had seen its share of Better-Than-Life parties. It would take a simsense world to make this dump vaguely resemble a place to spend any time at all. Any time at all? She might be spending the rest of her life here.

She could see nothing that might conceivably be used as a weapon. That really didn't matter—she barely had the strength to stand; she would be useless in a fight. She staggered across the debris-strewn floor, barely reaching the far wall before her limbs failed her. She found herself on the floor, not knowing whether she had made any noise in falling. There was no sound of eager ork-bashers rushing up the stairs. Maybe her collapse had been silent. Maybe they would not think to look in this room. Maybe she could go back to her old life.

This squat was an awful place to die. Huddled and heartsick, she waited. If she had had the strength, she would have cried.

From the other side of the door she heard the soft scuff of a cloth sole. Someone had found her hiding place. Faintly, she heard the sound of the lurker sniffing the air. It was an animal sound, like that of a hound on a scent. After a moment the noise stopped, then she heard a brief scrape of clawlike fingernails scratching the wood near the top of the door. There was a brief return of the sniffing sound, then all was quiet again.

There was no reason to believe that the lurker had left. Perhaps he was patiently listening at the door, waiting for her to make the movement that would betray her. If she'd had the strength, she would have crawled out the window and taken her chances on the crumbling facade. A week ago she would have been strong enough to scale the wall to safety. Now, her muscles were too weak. Only her fear was strong.

She knew she had not fooled them when she saw the doorknob begin to move. It turned slowly, as if the lurker himself was afraid. Afraid of sudden movement that might frighten his prey. Predators moved that way; slowly and with deliberate care.

She began to think that she had guessed wrong about the nature of her hunters. Gangs made a show of their kills. This sneaking caution wasn't their style. They wouldn't be worried about disturbing any squatters in the building. They would just barge in and, if they had picked the wrong apartment, barge right out again. This stealthy approach argued a hunter who did not wish to disturb any residents. Deciding that she was not being stalked by ork-bashers gave her no relief; there were worse, far worse, hunters that stalked the night in the Awakened World.

The catch disengaged, the door swung open. Moving languidly, it yawned wider, until she could see the landing. There was nothing there.

Helpless before whatever was stalking her, she stared at the opening. There was a movement low on the left side of the frame, and a face appeared there. The angle of the head suggested that the face's owner had crouched before peering around the frame—a simple precaution to avoid offering an immediate target.

Her stalker's face was long and drawn. Sallow skin stretched tightly over prominent bones, and dark, dark eyes were pools of night under slanted lids. Nostrils distended, and she heard the sniffing sound again. The lurker straightened, head twisting as he took in the room and its contents. As he focused on her, he grinned. His mouth was overfull of sharp, pointed teeth.

Lord almighty, you have delivered me to ghouls!

A second face appeared on the other side of the doorway. It too was almost skeletal in its thinness. Unlike the first, his dark eyes were not slanted, but his skin was as pallid. The flesh of both ghouls was tinted a sickly yellow.

The second one mimicked the actions of the first, turning his head with sharp motions as it surveyed the room. Apparently satisfied that she was alone, he entered. He was big and filled the frame as he passed through. His entry stirred the stagnant air of the room, swirling dust aloft and carrying a putrid scent to her

nostrils. The owner of the first face scurried in behind him. She could see others gathered on the landing.

The two ghouls moved toward her cautiously, as if they expected her to attack. She had intimidated a lot of people in the last year. She shifted and raised a hand. It was all she could do and she almost blacked out from the effort. Unaware of how helpless she was, they flinched back. It was a small victory, but all she was likely to get. She had no strength to resist them. The ache in her limbs had kindled to fire and she wilted in the rising blaze.

When they saw that she made no further motion, they resumed their approach. Just short of her out-stretched leg, the big one halted. The smaller one si-dled carefully up to the other, sheltering behind his broad back. The big one crouched. With a start, the other followed suit to avoid being exposed. A soft hissing came from the others gathered in the hall.

The big one reached out a tentative finger to poke her. When she didn't respond, he ran his hand down her calf in a caress as he spoke to his companion. Most of his words sounded like gutter Chinese, but some were Japanese and English. His accent and the speed with which he spoke left her uncomprehending. The small one straightened and took a step back. Watching her with wary eyes, he backed away.

They remained like that for a time. She lay still, her only action an occasional convulsion or shiver. The big ghoul stood silently by the door, watching her and waiting. Maybe they had to gather the rest of the pack before they feasted. Now that they had cornered her, she found it hard to care. If they killed her, the pain would stop. Once she was dead, what they did to her body wouldn't matter to her. Having surrendered to her despair, she found it easy to contemplate surren-dering to the insistent call of oblivion.

A commotion roused her from her drifting semiconscious state. Though still racked with pain, she found herself able to shift her head slightly. It was night—or night again. She had no way of knowing. The big ghoul was still in the room, but he had changed his position. The small one was returning, leading a figure much bigger than himself. She wasn't really sure who or what the newcomer was. She couldn't seem to focus clearly on him. One moment he seemed huge and menacing, a lumbering furry hulk; the next, he was a slim, strongly-built man attired in street leathers.

He entered the room, moving confidently and showing none of the fearful reticence of the ghouls. Kneeling beside her, he placed a hand on her wrist. To her surprise, he showed no reluctance to touch her. Hugh hadn't been reluctant, either. The stranger felt her pulse while he visually examined her. She noted that his eyes stopped at the band on her left wrist. Completing his survey, he looked her in the eyes and smiled.

"Don't be afraid," he said in Japanese. "They won't hurt you."

"Why'd you pick Japanese?" she asked. She wasn't ready to trust him yet. Anyone who ran with ghouls was an outlaw. But then, she was an outlaw herself now.

He briefly shifted his glance to the band before speaking. "I've been to Yomi, too."

Nothing else was said for a minute. What needed to be said? Anyone who knew Yomi understood pain and fear. She felt suddenly reassured. Not all outlaws were criminals by choice. Maybe he was a shadowrunner, one of those renegades from the corporate world who fought injustice. Or he might be a murderer. How could she know?

"What is your name?" he asked.

"Janice."

"No family name?"

"No family."

"I see. I am called Shiroi, Janice. I am most pleased to make your acquaintance."

His politeness seemed all out of place in the crumbling ruin, but still she felt embarrassed by her churlishly terse responses. Nevertheless, doubts and suspicion ruled her tongue. "Why is that?"

"There is no need for you to be so defensive. I would be the last one to take you back to Yomi."

"I didn't think that you were *jigoku-shi.*"

"I am no master of hell. I assure you that I have no connection with those abhorrent racists."

No, he wasn't. He was too handsome to be *jigoku-shi.* But no man walks the face of the earth alone. "Who do you work for?"

"Myself."

So ka. If he wasn't lying, he'd want to be recompensed for his trouble. In the last year she had learned about paying her own way. "I haven't got any credit to pay you."

"I am not asking for payment, Janice. In my own small way, I am a philanthropist. I take joy in helping people adjust to their new lives. I look forward to helping you find your way."

Could she believe him? "All I want to find is a way to escape this pain and a way to get out of this dump."

"That I can arrange."

He began to sing softly. Succumbing to his song, she passed away from her pain and suspicions, falling into a healing sleep.

2

The passengers were nervous—with good reason. Sam Verner was nervous himself, and he didn't have any guns pointed at him. To the terrified corporates huddling in their seats, the shadowrunners would seem much like rabid beasts, ready to savage them for no reason. Such an evaluation might in fact not be too far from the truth. It was certainly Sam's own assessment of the unstable muscleboy in front of him.

Jason Stone was short, but he didn't need the heavy-barreled Sandler TMP submachine gun in his hands to give him a dangerous presence. The Indian's rebuilt muscles and quick, nervous motions told their own tale. He was what was known in the alleys as a street samurai, muscle for hire, chromed with cyberware to set him beyond the frailty of the flesh. Like many of his kind, the trade of meat for machine meant that some of his spirit had been tossed out with the undesired body parts. The cold chrome eye shields shuttered the windows to what was left of his soul, but his leering smile exposed what was left of his emotions, leaving no doubt that he would be happy to use his weapon.

At the other end of the cabin, Fishface George and Grey Otter were menacing the crew in similar fashion. They were samurai too, though less extreme examples of the breed, and neither walked as close to the edge of sanity as their leader. That was just as well. Sam needed the muscle for cover, but he didn't think he could deal with more than one samurai of Jason's hellbent aggressiveness.

Sam slid past Jason. He knew that he was blocking some of the samurai's field of fire, but he was confident that the others would cover the gap. They always had before. They might not like Sam, but they knew he was their meal ticket. They'd keep him safe until they were paid off.

"Two minutes, Sir Twist," buzzed the receiver in Sam's ear. Sam nodded unconsciously to the speaker, but Dodger couldn't see the acknowledgment. He was on a remote broadcast, the only way to link the elf's position in the Matrix with Sam's ground team aboard the shuttle craft. Dodger could have left the mundane time count to a subroutine, but his personal attention indicated his concern. They were all expecting the run to be easy, but Dodger was playing cautious. If anything blew up, a subroutine would be outclassed and purged by intrusion countermeasures before Sam could know about it. An on-line decker was Matrix security that every shadowrunner wanted.

In two minutes, the craft's preplanned ground time would be up and, by then, the Aztechnology shuttle was supposed to be airborne, on its way to the Sea-Tac international airport. If the runners delayed it, the metroplex air traffic control would be alerted. The plan called for the shuttle to lift on schedule, giving the runners time to get away with their prize before pursuit could be called in. They had managed to board just as the craft was leaving the gate, successfully slipping past the ground crew. So far, only the passengers in the main cabin knew of their presence. Dodger's black box had frozen communications with the pilot's compartment as soon as Sam had affixed it to the wall. They should have been gone already, slipping away into the night, but their man hadn't responded to the code phrase when they had announced their presence to the passengers. Time was trickling away.

Where was Raoul Sanchez?

Sam moved down the aisle, checking faces. The craft swayed as it continued its taxi. Fringes on his jacket's arms brushed across the tops of the outer seats as he passed, occasionally flicking into the face of one of the seated passengers. No one complained.

Was Sanchez really on-board? The passenger manifest Dodger had boosted had said that he was. The man should have reacted to the code words, but he hadn't. Maybe he was scared, getting cold feet now that his escort away from cozy corporate security had arrived. Sam was annoyed. What did Sanchez have to be afraid of? His corporate exile would only be temporary. Mr. Johnson had a comfy hideyhole all ready, and in a week or two Sanchez would be back at work, safe and sound in his new corporate home.

Three rows from the forward bulkhead, Sam found Sanchez. He was staring fixedly ahead, sweating. The corporate's hands were rigidly gripping the arms of his seat. Sam spoke the man's name, but was ignored. Reaching out a hand to shake Sanchez, Sam was surprised when the man shrank away.

"Come on, Sanchez. We don't have time to fool around."

Sanchez finally turned his head to look at Sam. The man's dark eyes stared, wide and full of terror. He swallowed convulsively before saying, "Please. I have done nothing."

Sam didn't know what to say.

"Frag it, Twist. If that's the suit, get him moving." Jason moved up the aisle as he spoke. Reaching the perplexed Sam, he stretched an arm past and pulled Sanchez to his feet. "Last thing we need is getting hosed cause the suit's gone limp."

Jason shoved his gun muzzle under Sanchez's chin, forcing his head up. "You don't jerk us. *Comprendé*, chummer?"

"Please, *señor*. Do not shoot," Sanchez pleaded.

"I do not know what you are talking about. I am only a technician. I am not a *ahman*. I have no access to secrets. I am nobody."

"You'll be nothing but a corpse if you don't get your ass out of here."

Sam reached out to touch Jason's arm but the samurai shifted, placing Sanchez between them. "Jason, I think *Señor* Sanchez knows less about this run than we do."

"I don't care what he knows. We're taking him out."

Sam frowned. There was more going on here than they knew, and he didn't like what he was thinking. "Otter, check outside. Dodger, anything moving on the air traffic grid?"

"Negative, Sir Twist," the elf replied instantly. He must have been monitoring the conversation through Sam's microphone. When she ducked back in, Otter gave the same report.

So much for his first thought. "Well, whatever the screwup is, it doesn't seem to be a trap. Still, we'd better buzz."

Otter nodded and started to undog the cabin door. Fishface looked as blank as usual, but remained standing where he was, his eyes fixed on Jason. The Indian still gripped Sanchez.

"It stinks. It's got to be a trap and this pedro's a part of it." Jason leaned into his gun, forcing Sanchez's head even further back. "Ain't that right, pedro? Sure it is. You're too nervous. Don't like being the bait when the fish have teeth, do you? I don't like being fooled, pedro."

"Chill it, Jason," Sam snapped. "You've got a gun in his throat. Of course he's nervous. Let's just get him out of here. The sooner we're gone, the better."

Jason slowly turned his mirror eyes on Sam. "I say we smoke him. It'll be a lesson."

The Indian was pushing, testing Sam as he had ever since the split with Ghost. Jason liked to claim he was as good as Ghost, but Sam had never seen even a remote resemblance. Ghost Who Walks Inside was a real warrior, cast in the mold of his people's ancient heroes. Ghost was worthy of being called a samurai, unlike this cybered punk. Ghost only killed when necessary, but that was just one of the differences between the two Indians. Jason had never really understood Ghost's principles; he had only been blinded by the glittering street reputation of a man who stood up for his people. Sam couldn't deny that Ghost had embraced violence, but only as a means, never as the end that Jason seemed to believe it was.

It meant nothing to Jason that he was using a man's life in his dominance games. But it did mean something to Sam. There was more at stake than Sanchez's life. If Sam backed down now, he would have no more control over Jason. Too aware of the Indian's enhanced reflexes and deadly aim, Sam straightened. Height was one advantage he had over Jason. He tried to put utter assurance into his voice.

"I said no killing. We take him with us."

Jason simply stared. Sam knew that the Indian relied on the unnerving effect of his chromed eyeshields. Determined to be unimpressed, Sam stared back, but a motion in the back of the craft caught his attention. Someone was rising from his seat. The passenger's right hand was cocked back and a shiny barrel protruded from the base of his palm.

Whether Jason used his own peripheral vision or saw the reflection in Sam's eyes, he was moving before Sam could say anything. The man in the back was moving at chipped speed, but Jason was faster. The Indian shifted sideways, vacating the space in which he had stood. Sam felt the heat of the bullet's passage and heard the slug bury itself in the cabin wall.

The gunman started to drop lower, trying to use a seat and the passenger in it for cover. Jason swung Sanchez around with one arm and shoved his other arm in the direction of the gunman. His movement looked deceptively awkward, almost haphazard. Sam knew that it was anything but. The Sandler TMP had a smartgun adapter, feeding targeting information through the induction pad in Jason's palm to establish a feedback circuit. When the crosshairs appeared on Jason's cybereyes, he could be sure that his weapon was effectively aimed at his target.

Jason fired as he dropped into the seat that had been Sanchez's. The Indian's Sandler shrilled as it spat slugs to rip into the gunman's cover. Blood and polyfoam stuffing erupted into the air. Jason's line of fire skipped up past the head rest and clipped the gunman in the shoulder as he ducked.

Fishface's gun chattered behind Sam. Women's wails and screams of pain joined the noise of the guns. The sea of corporate faces that had been staring at the runners vanished beneath the waves of the head rests. The passengers were huddled, praying, hoping, and pleading that no fire be directed at them.

Slow to react, Sam found himself the only one still standing. He reached for his holster. As his hand closed on the butt of his Narcoject Lethe, he knew he wouldn't be fast enough. The gunman was rising for another shot.

Again, Jason proved faster. The Sandler screamed as it pounded slugs into the man. Sam watched as the slugs chewed away cloth and flesh to reveal the implanted armor that had saved the gunman from Jason's first shot. The impact drove the man back, spinning him out into the aisle. More bullets gnawed at him, pounding their way through his protective plates. He started to collapse, his palm gun firing convulsively, the bullets spanging wildly around the cabin.

The gunfire stopped as soon as the man hit the deck. With Fishface screaming orders that no one move, Jason rushed down the aisle to his victim. He ran a quick hand over the dead gunman. He found a wallet and, after only a brief glance, tossed it on the man's chest. He spat on the corpse and stood. "Azzie corpcop."

Sam relaxed a bit. The attack wasn't the closing of a trap. The gunman might have been an air marshal, or he might have been an off-duty officer on his way somewhere. The man had just been trying to do his job and keep some shadowrunners from killing a corporate. Likely, he had seen the confrontation between Sam and Jason as his chance. He had bet on his own skills and lost.

"Heat's on now, Twist," Jason said. "Pedro's dead weight we can't afford."

Before Sam could respond to the samurai's latest challenge to his authority, he felt a hand grip the fringes of his jacket.

"*Señors*, you cannot leave me now." Sanchez's fear seemed to have redoubled.

"The hell we can't," Jason snarled as he shoved past.

Sanchez winced. His glance darted nervously to the door Otter had opened, then flickered around the cabin. Finally, his panicked stare alighted on Sam. "You have condemned me."

"They saw that you were not involved," Sam assured him. "Your corporate masters understand this sort of thing. They will know that it was all a mistake."

Sanchez shook his head vehemently. "The *ahman*. They will not believe."

"Everyone here saw that he started the firefight. They'll tell your *ahman* what happened."

"No, *señor*. The *ahman* will not believe."

"Why not? You've got fifty witnesses."

"No, *señor*. Look at them."

Sam looked around the cabin at the faces that had reappeared. They were all strangers but he knew them. He knew the grim determination and fear that lived in every one of them. These people were already denying that Sanchez was one of them. Sam understood such draconian group dynamics from his years in Japan. There, an entire family or organization took the heat for the actions of a member. The only way to avoid destruction of the group was to deny the membership of the offender. Sanchez's fear told him that the Azzies believed in group responsibility, too.

The cabin stank of death now. The cowering salaryman was right—it wouldn't stop here if he left Sanchez. An Aztechnology security man and at least two other corporates were dead. Several more were injured. This was no longer a minor matter, and Sanchez's fellow corporate employees would not defend him. The *ahman* might decide that Sanchez was responsible despite the evidence. If the *ahman* condemned Sanchez, those who spoke in his defense would be under suspicion—if they didn't share his fate. Aztechnology was not known for its understanding and forgiveness. These people would not take the chance.

Sam looked down into Sanchez's face. The man was full of fear. He was terrified of staying, terrified by the thought of leaving the corporation, terrified by the shadowrunners, and terrified of his own presumption and desperation. His fears fought their war openly on his face.

Sam understood those fears. He reached down and took Sanchez by the shoulders, drawing him up.

"All right," he said. "Let's go."

The gratitude in the man's face almost masked the fear.

3

The room was quiet, but Dodger knew he wasn't alone in the darkened library. His knowledge wasn't anything mystic; spells, conjurings, and astral voyages were not his kind of magic. It wasn't that he heard them, or smelled them, or, as yet, saw any evidence of them, either. His awareness might have been due to some combination of his physical senses, operating below his consciousness. He didn't need to know how it worked; the fact that it had worked was enough. Still, there was no sense of danger. He had been on enough shadowruns to know *that* feeling. At least for the moment, whoever watched wasn't planning to attack.

"I told you he would be decking."

The voice was deep and throbbed with vindication. Dodger knew that voice too well. Estios had never liked him and never would. The black-haired elf had squared off against Dodger from the first time they had met. Like their hair colors, their personalities were opposites. There was no attraction between them save a mutual call to hostility.

With slow deliberation, Dodger prolonged his disconnection from the Matrix, tapping in a few more commands before logging off. He took the connector from the datajack on his left temple and held it with just enough pressure that the reel wound it smoothly and the plug nestled safely into its niche. Sliding the compartment cover closed, he turned his chair around.

Estios was glowering at him, as he expected. Professor Sean Laverty stood by Estios's side. That was also expected; the officious Estios's words only made sense if he had the professor's attention. Chatterjee stood on the other side of the professor. The Asian elf's presence was not expected but not surprising either; he was a frequent resident of the mansion. Hanging back near the door was the real surprise, Teresa O'Connor. Dear, sweet Teresa. If he had known she was at the mansion, he would never have come.

The professor waited until Dodger wrenched his eyes away from Teresa before speaking. "Dodger, you know the rules."

Indeed he did, but when had that stopped him from doing what needed to be done? Sliding the corners and skipping over the bounds were what made life worth living. True as that was, there were some matters best dealt with carefully. "The cyberdeck's running a sidecar copy now, Professor. I didn't break any of your rules."

"You ran the Matrix without authorization," Estios accused.

"A decker always runs without authorization. 'Tis what decking is all about."

Estios's eyes narrowed. "Cut the snow. You've spent enough time here to know that no one connects to the Matrix from the mansion without clearing it first."

"And if anyone, even you, Estios, can find anything compromising in the copy of the run, I shall submit to any discipline that the professor deems proper."

"We don't need to see your concocted evidence, alley runner. You're not welcome here any longer. Leave now."

Estios stepped forward, apparently ready to enforce his demand, but Laverty restrained him with a touch on his arm. "Dodger may stay as long as he wishes."

Estios turned his head sharply and looked down into Laverty's eyes. "That's unwise."

"Technically, Dodger *is* abusing your hospitality,

Professor," Chatterjee said. "It sets a terrible precedent."

"He should be expelled and banned," Estios said.

"Dodger is free to come and go as he pleases, Mr. Estios," Laverty said.

Chatterjee inclined his head in acceptance of the professor's decision, but Estios just scowled and stepped back to his place at Laverty's side. Laverty gave the taller elf a rueful shake of his head.

"Come, come, Mr. Estios. I feel confident that Dodger would never betray this house. He is difficult on occasion and less than mannerly at most times, but his heart is great. I am sure that there is a good and sufficient reason for his actions."

"Verily," Dodger agreed. " 'Tis most assured that I meant no disrespect for you and your hospitality, Professor. Circumstances conspired to force me to this end."

"Don't they always?" Laverty said, then chuckled. "Circumstances seem to conspire against you regularly."

Dodger shrugged. "Time is an unreal concept in the forest. I stayed too long and found myself in need of a safe place to conduct my business. Lacking access to any other place where my flesh would be safe while I roamed the Matrix, I came here."

"You could have decked from your precious forest," Estios said. "You've done that often enough."

"Alas, I had no transmitter. I had not expected to be gone so long, and so neglected to make such preparations. When I found that time had passed more swiftly than expected, I found myself in an awkward situation. Were it not for my obligations to my fellow runners, I would never have imposed so."

"What do you know of obligations, alley runner?"

"I know that a person is obligated to follow his conscience rather than the letter of orders imposed from above. Surely, even a grand soldier such as your-self can grasp such a basic concept?''

"Enough. There have been enough disturbances of the peace in this house. I do not need you two tearing at each other,'' Laverty said. ''Dodger, this run wouldn't be one of Samuel Verner's, would it?''

Seeing no harm in admitting it, Dodger said, ''In truth, it is.''

Laverty was thoughtful for a moment. The other elves waited silently; they knew better than to inter-rupt the professor's thoughts. At last, he said, ''You have shown a remarkable loyalty toward that man.''

"Any loyalty is remarkable for an alley runner.''

"I said enough, Mr. Estios.'' There was no harsh-ness in Laverty's voice, but Estios looked stung just the same. Laverty's attention remained on Dodger. ''Another data run? Verner is still searching for his sister?''

"Always that,'' Dodger replied. The professor's re-newed interest in Sam made Dodger a little uncom-fortable. ''This run was simply business. Even a knight errant needs operating capital.''

"Another theft,'' Estios scoffed.

" 'Twas was no theft.''

"Call it what you want,'' Estios continued, ignor-ing Laverty's sharp look. ''You can't alter its nature.''

Dodger's initial annoyance at Estios's suggestion of larceny eased as he saw the professor's reaction. Estios lost points by being the first to break the imposed truce. Unable to resist, Dodger said, ''Some people never change.''

A slight motion near the door caught his attention and he immediately regretted his words. In the ex-change with Estios, he had forgotten that Teresa was there. She had been so quiet. Thinking that he had no way to fool the professor, but that he might cover his chagrin from the others, he launched into an explanation of what had happened.

"Our run was supposed to be a simple extraction. A friendly one, at that. The subject had supposedly concluded a contract with new employers, but had failed to secure release from his current corporation. Mr. Johnson assured us that the subject was not in a sensitive position, so it should have been a clean in-and-out. Someone hosed. The pickup apparently had no idea what was going on. He did not even seem aware that Sam and the others were there for him."

"A deliberate ruse to trap Verner," Chatterjee suggested.

Dodger wondered just how much Chatterjee knew. The dark-skinned elf had not been present when Sam had been at the mansion last summer, and normally, he would not have been briefed on old business. Perhaps he only drew the obvious conclusion. "If 'twere a trap, 'twere a poor one. There seemed no reasonable chance of closure."

"A Renraku reprisal, then?"

Chatterjee's mention of the corporation from which Sam had fled banished any remaining thoughts of innocence. Chatterjee's knowledge was a sign that the professor retained an interest in Sam. "An unlikely circumstance."

Laverty nodded. "A conclusion based on your research into Mr. Johnson's real identity."

Dodger tried his best offended look. "A client expects to maintain his confidentiality. 'Tis most unhealthy to inquire into such matters."

"Dodger?" Laverty smiled, and Dodger knew his ruse had never had a chance.

"Andrew Glover of Amalgamated Technologies and Telecommunications. Mister Glover is a vice-president, on the fast track with a bullet. His firm has a pedigree that's about as pure European as they come.

'Tis not the slightest hint of Renraku influence. Of course,'' Dodger added with a sly grin, ''there does seem to be a connection to Saeder-Krupp.''

Laverty raised an eyebrow, but said nothing. Estios did the reacting.

''Saeder-Krupp! They're Lofwyr's puppets. If the beast is making moves in Seattle . . .''

Laverty's voice was stiff as he clipped Estios into silence. ''Mr. Estios, you are being most disruptive today. The dragon's plans are not of importance in this matter. Simple stock ownership is insufficient evidence of the dragon's involvement. Although ATT is owned by Saeder-Krupp, the corporation remains essentially independent, and I think it unlikely that Lofwyr even knows of this operation. Dodger, you did say that your Mr. Johnson was Glover?''

''Andrew.''

Laverty nodded to himself. ''Though I doubt your friend is enmeshed in some dragon's schemes again, I think that he will have need of his budding magical talents.''

Dodger understood the implied question. He even had some idea of the offer that was being made. ''He still won't come to see you.''

''I understand. His rigorous logical training and scientific orientation made a very convincing argument that his mind would be oriented to the hermetic tradition. Your report of his vision of the Dog totem was most startling. I had not conceived of that possibility. It was a most embarrassing oversight. He probably holds me in little respect, since I misdiagnosed his calling.''

Ah, thought Dodger, *if you only knew.* '' 'Tis not the reason. Despite surviving dragonfire, Sam barely believes in his magical powers. 'Tis unlikely that he would fault you for thinking him a mage when he himself will not accept that he has a shamanic calling. He clings desperately to his scientific view of the world."

"Then he has abandoned investigations into his magic?"

"Quite the contrary. He struggles to learn. It's driving Lady Tsung crazy."

Laverty actually looked surprised. "Ms. Tsung is attempting to teach him?"

"*Attempting* is the right word. Were Sam not so stubborn, he'd see that he and Lady Tsung have incompatible magical orientations."

"Given what you have said, his lack of vision now seems unsurprising. Try to bring him back."

"He won't come. He wants to find his sister first."

"Such loyalty is admirable. And very valuable. But do what you can to bring him here."

With that, Laverty turned and left the library. Estios and Chatterjee followed. Teresa remained standing at the door, making no move to leave. Estios aborted his own exit, and they exchanged a few words, speaking too softly for Dodger to hear. After a few moments, Estios straightened and threw a hostile look in Dodger's direction. Dodger returned a smile, which only infuriated the elf even more. He said one last thing to Teresa before striding angrily through the doorway. Dodger was left alone in the room with Teresa. He waited and she made the first move, walking softly across the carpet to the desk where his cyberdeck lay. Dodger stood as she approached.

She reached a hand past him and took the chip that the machine had extruded. She weighed it in her hand and said, "You seem very fond of this Samuel Verner."

"I have told him that I will help him find his sister."

"You've set yourself another task?"

"A noble quest. We have learned that she was sent to Yomi Island. 'Tis a foul place where the Japanese send those unfortunate enough to be inflicted with metahuman genes. We would liberate her from such vile durance.''

"Once you would have gone charging in.''

"Yomi is not the sort of place where one could do that easily. There must be preparations. We will go when we are ready. First, we must gain information and credit because transportation, equipment, and muscle are not cheap. While we gather what we need, we hone our skills with shadowruns. Were Sam less fastidious about the runs, we would be further along.''

She made a tentative motion, almost reaching out to touch him. "You would have made a wonderful paladin.''

The old pain seared. Dodger turned his shoulder to her; he did not want her to see the emotions her words had wakened. "I am no paladin. I never will be. I refuse to be twisted to serve any person's will.''

"Yet you serve this norm,'' she said softly.

"I do not *serve* him. I *help* him.'' Dodger turned to look at her, but her face was shadowed under her hair. His hands hung uselessly at his side. "There is all the difference in the world between those two words.''

"You always did worry about words.'' Teresa toyed with the chip. She would not look him in the face. "Why are you helping him?''

"We are friends.''

She tilted her head slightly. He could see her pensive expression now, achingly beautiful in its somber composure. Her serious mien shifted into a wistful smile. "We were friends once.''

Dodger swallowed hard. "*I* thought so.''

At last she met his gaze. Her eyes were pure emerald and as bottomless as he remembered. He had lost himself in those eyes long ago. He found himself ready to do so again.

"But you left,'' she said.

"I had to."

"Have you come back?"

"I'm not sure."

"I see." She pocketed the chip and stepped around him. Pausing at the door, she said, "Come talk to me when you *are* sure."

She was gone.

The darkness and ancient books his only witnesses, he softly vowed, "I will."

4

Sam looked down at Sally Tsung. She was a beautiful woman. From her artfully tinted ash blonde hair streaming across the pillow, to her slim and shapely feet poking from beneath the rumpled blankets, she was the stuff of a lonely man's dreams. Only she was no dream, and he hadn't been lonely for months. He just didn't understand what she saw in him.

Sally was tall and trim, fleshed where a woman should be fleshed. But hard muscle underlay those shape defining curves. A Chinese dragon, vivid in its tattoo colors, slithered along her right arm. The beast's bewhiskered chin rested on the back of her hand, whose slender fingers were half closed into a fist, almost hiding the missing last joint of her little finger.

She had never told Sam how she had come to lose that joint. Despite what he knew had been an adventurous life, she carried no other scars. Her lack of scars she laughed off, attributing her smooth skin to the power of magical healing. Whenever Sam tried to ask about the finger, she found something more interesting to talk about. If he pressed her, she always had an appointment for which she was late. He had given up trying.

The real issue wasn't the history of her finger. As free she was with her body, she had never let him touch her past. He hoped that in time she might open up and trust him, but as yet his hopes were unfulfilled. Sally Tsung remained mysterious.

A cold nose pressed against his naked back told him that he was not the only one awake in the apartment. Rolling carefully to avoid disturbing Sally, Sam slid from the bed; its ancient springs squeaked only a mild protest. Inu lapped eagerly at his face, and Sam rumpled the dog's fur in an equally happy greeting.

Sam showered and dressed while Inu waited patiently by the door. Sam grabbed his fringed jacket on his way to the door. He really didn't think he'd need its ballistic cloth lining for his run with Inu. Dark hadn't fallen yet, so most of the predators were still abed. Still, the armor lining functioned as insulation, making the fringed synthleather the warmest coat he had.

His runs with Inu gave him time to think. Or more precisely, time to worry. Tonight was supposed to be another magic lesson, and he wasn't looking forward to it. The lessons were not going well. No matter how patiently Sally explained the theory, Sam seemed incapable of grasping any but the simplest of spells. Even those only came after he'd had time to work out his own symbologies. The texts he'd gotten from Professor Laverty seemed only to confuse matters more. Sally insisted that he'd have more luck with ritual magics, but so far she had respected his refusal to even try them. Conjuring spirits seemed wrong, almost unholy.

Why couldn't it have been target practice night, even if that meant dealing with Ghost? With a magic lesson on the docket, facing Ghost's coldness seemed preferable to Sally's vituperous condemnations of his intelligence. Sam knew that intelligence had little to do with getting a spell right. Even Ziggy, that street kid who dogged Sally's steps, could get the spells going. *He* had an IQ several points below Inu's. Still, if it had been gun night, he was sure he would have preferred it to be magic night.

His last several months among the shadowrunners had gone through more ups and downs than a Mitsubishi Flutterer skirting a storm front. Despite it all, he had found himself coming to like life in the shadows. It wasn't always pleasant and certainly lacked the everyday comforts of his former corporate life, but he felt he had been given a chance to make a difference. Here on the streets he wasn't just a faceless minion among other faceless minions, plodding to the company's tune. The street folk were individuals, some extravagantly so. Once they came to trust a person, which wasn't quickly or easily, they were true friends. He found such company exhilarating. He was pleased that, under Sally and Dodger's sponsorship, he had been accepted into their circle.

One of the biggest downs was the estrangement of Ghost Who Walks Inside. The big Indian had seemed pleased to see Sam leave the corporate world. He had even been eager to help Sam redress the wrongs caused by Haesslich's plot. Sam felt good about that; he was impressed by the Indian's quiet strength and focus of purpose. But then something had happened to change Ghost's attitude toward Sam. Since the night they had settled with Haesslich, Ghost had refused to take part in any runs with Sam. Ghost still helped train Sam in the ways of the shadows, but he held aloof, appearing for the lessons and vanishing when the instruction was over. Sally shrugged and Dodger told him it would pass, but no one else would talk to him about it.

Inu finished his business and they headed back to Sam's squat. Turning for home set him to thinking about Sally again. Their relationship seemed increasingly fragile. One might almost say it was deteriorating on every front, except perhaps in bed. There the passion seemed as strong as ever. From her first invitation, he had fallen quickly for her. But now, months later, he realized that he really didn't know her at all well.

When she wasn't with him, he had no idea where she went. She admitted having her own place but had refused to take him there, saying that it wasn't his kind of place. He had never tried to follow her; that would have been a betrayal of trust. But he had wondered a lot about where she went.

No one could spend as much time together as they had and not get to know something about the other person. Between the shadowruns, the training, and their time in the sack, he had come to know something about her personality. He wasn't very sure he liked what he had learned. As far as he could tell, money was her principal motivation. She was mercenary almost beyond ethics; her principles were for sale to the highest bidder. All she knew of honor was what affected her reputation. Loyalty she understood; at least, within the bounds of a run where reliance on the team was, by necessity, absolute. But she only gave that kind of loyalty when she was sure that it had already been given to her. If she had the slightest doubt, she would arrange failsafes, backups to ensure that no one betrayed her. At least she hadn't shown such suspicion toward him. She didn't seem to understand that a shadow team had to be a family. In fact, she didn't seem to understand family at all. Of all her sins, he couldn't forgive the way she always tried to talk him into forgetting about his sister. Even for her, he would not forget Janice.

Inu won the race up the stairs as usual, but Sam was not winded as he would have been last summer. His time in the shadows had toughened him, honing away the fat and softness of his corporate life. He opened the door to the apartment, allowing Inu to scamper in through his legs, and found that Inu's excited yapping had done its work. Sally was awake.

"Get enough exercise?" she asked slyly as she tossed back the covers.

He smiled, knowing what kind of exercise she had in mind. "I thought we were supposed to have a lesson this evening."

"Too much work makes Sam too dull." She stretched, testing his resolve. Seeing that he withstood the temptation, she shrugged and pulled on her shorts. "I thought we'd try a conjuring tonight."

Sam frowned. "Why? You know I don't want to do that kind of stuff."

"Every magician needs to know how," Sally said, lacing the strings on her halter. "If you don't know the basics of conjuring, you can't banish an enemy's sending. That's too useful a skill."

"Banishing is sort of like an exorcism, isn't it?"

"Give the boy a gold star. Yeah, it's like that but it doesn't have any of the religious nonsense attached."

Knowing it was a sore point, Sam said, "Religion is not nonsense."

"Don't start with me." Sally's eyes flashed with adamant heat, then softened. "Anyway, what I wanted to do tonight was to get you an ally spirit."

Sam knew what she meant; he'd done some reading. Perversely, he played dumb. "You mean like a familiar."

"Another star."

"*You* don't have one," he pointed out. He was surprised by the petulant tone in his voice. From the look on her face, Sally noted it too.

"I'm not hung up on learning magic, either. An ally may be what you need to break this block you've got."

She was not going to give up. Well, neither was he. "I won't deal with the devil."

"Idiot! There aren't any devils but the ones running the megacorps. Spirits may quibble and bargain, but they're not demons. They're just energy forms cast into a particular construct by the intelligence whose energy forces them to coalesce. They don't have any connections with fallen angels or cosmic malignancies or anything like that. All that drek is stories made up by pasty-faced old men to scare impressionable kids into following orders that are too stupid to defend logically. I thought you had a better mind than that."

"You're entitled to your opinion," Sam said huffily. He knew that most of what was said about spirits being demons was garbage—he wasn't a total idiot. "This dealing with spirits just doesn't seem right. Even *you* say that they talk. That implies sentience, but whether they are free intelligences or not, talking to spirits is just too crazy for me. I had enough of that in those nightmares last summer when I talked to the dog spirit. I haven't had one of those episodes in months, and I don't want to do anything to start them again. I'm just getting back on track. I've put all the troubles that followed Hanae's death into the past where they belong. I don't want to wake that kind of craziness again."

Sally shook her head, her expression hardening into contempt. "You'll never learn with that kind of attitude."

"I'll survive," Sam said defensively. "I've done all right so far."

"Babe, you're in the woods. You're alive 'cause I keep you alive."

Sally might believe it, but Sam knew better. He had learned his lessons. "You weren't there last night."

"And you nearly got smoked."

"We did fine."

She gave him a look that left no doubt that she didn't agree, but she didn't say anything. Her stony silence indicated that she had taken the subject as far as she thought necessary. Sam didn't want to take it any further, either. They would be snapping at each other again soon enough.

"Are we going to do some exercises?"

"What for? You wouldn't learn anything. You're too pig-headed." Sally gestured, casting an illusion spell, and Sam knew that to a viewer he would appear to be literally pig-headed. It was juvenile of her to resort to such a poor joke.

"I haven't given up trying to learn," he said. "Have you given up teaching?"

She snorted. "You don't pay me enough for this lost cause."

Wondering how serious she was being, he said, "I didn't realize I was supposed to be paying you."

Scowling, she breathed a long sigh. She shook out her hair and turned to stare through the grimy window. Her voice was distant. "Drekhead. You want to learn something tonight, you do it on your own."

Conversation ended; sentence pronounced. There would be no point in trying to change her mind. Sam found that he didn't mind. He almost felt relief. As much as he knew he needed to learn, their sessions had become increasingly difficult. Another teacher might be better. Professor Laverty had offered; so had the dragon Lofwyr. The dragon's offer had surely been false, since his agent had betrayed Sam and the runners instead of helping. And Laverty surely had his own reasons. Sam was sure he did not want to get involved with some as high up in the Tir Tairngire power structure as Laverty appeared to be. Sally had seemed the only mage he could trust, and now he was having his doubts about her. He would have to sort the mess out soon. He'd need whatever magical ability he could muster to go after Janice.

He watched Sally pretend interest in the outside world. She was flighty in her anger sometimes. Maybe she would relent.

"Just as well that we're not going to practice. I've got a meet with Mr. Johnson tonight. I'd like you to run backup."

"Got better things to do than baby-sit," she said without looking around.

Sighing, Sam let the insult slide. It was just her heat. He hoped that she would feel differently later. "All right. I'll catch you later."

"Later," she replied almost inaudibly.

He left her sitting in the apartment. As he walked down the stairs, Inu skipped at his side. Sam wondered if Sally would be there when he got back.

5

As Sam approached the corner of South Main Street and Fourth Avenue South, the dark bulk of the Renraku arcology loomed ever larger before him. The megastructure towered above its neighboring buildings, blocking most of the sunset's red tones. Already lights were sparkling on the east face. Low down on the north face, the glare and blare of the club quarter was awakening. Less than a year ago, the arcology had been his home—and his prison.

He turned right on Fourth. He was less than two blocks from Club Penumbra, but the walk seemed lengthy. The first time Sally had taken him here, he had almost run away when he had realized how near to the arcology the club was. It had only been a month after the firefight on Pad 23, that regrettable battle which Renraku security forces believed that he started. He hadn't really been there, but a deception on the part of Lofwyr's agent had made it appear that he had led the attacking raiders. Sam had been afraid of 'Raku retaliation. The thought of walking exposed anywhere near the megastructure had frightened him. But he had learned that he was just a face in the crowd; no more remarkable than anyone else to the guards on the west face of the arcology.

He still wasn't completely sure the corporation had decided that revenge was uneconomical. He had to force himself to keep pace with the pedestrian traffic around him. He didn't want to attract attention. As a member of the crowd, he could pass, but if he gave the guards cause to single him out, who knew what might result?

He reached the alley that led to the club. He was surprised but pleased to see that one of the three bikes parked against the wall was Dodger's Rapier. Penumbra was no place for animals, so he looked around for Inu to tell him to wait. The dog was scampering across Yesler Way, off to find his own entertainment. He'd be back eventually, as always. Sam had met Inu on the streets and had no worries that the dog would be all right.

Though twilight was still gathering among the rain-laden clouds outside, night had already fallen in Club Penumbra. The gloom was deeper than usual, since the wall-sized tridscreen was dark. Sam picked his way through the entryway mostly by following the sound of Big Tom, the Club's resident sound engineer and backup musician, practicing his drumbeats. As Sam cleared the arch and entered the main floor, Big Tom deflated his throat pouch and hooted the dual tone he used for greetings. Sam did his best to return the sasquatch's sound. Big Tom grinned his lopsided grin which only showed the fangs on the left side of his face. Sam was never sure if the furry metahuman was smiling with pleasure or amusement at Sam's attempts to greet him in kind.

Big Tom took up his practice again as Sam crossed the floor. His was the only music in the place, but it was a weeknight and still early. The Penumbra wouldn't start rocking for another couple of hours. There were a few patrons scattered about at the free-standing tables and in the alcoves along the back wall. That was fine. There were enough people to keep things friendly but not enough to crowd sensitive discussions. The club's regulars minded their own biz.

Jim at the bar inclined his head, and Sam altered his path in the direction indicated. The sole occupied booth in that corner had a black booted foot thrust from its recesses. The stud pattern on the footwear's straps and the faint gleam of a white shag of hair advertised Dodger's presence.

Sam kicked the sole of the boot, saying, "Hoi, Dodger. You're early. Are you feeling all right?"

"In truth I was. Until you wounded me with your remark, Sir Twist." Dodger cocked his head to look up at Sam, causing sparkles of light to flash from the three jacks on his depilated left temple. To anyone who didn't know the elf, the computer interface ports would seem incongruous next to his pointed ears, but Sam knew they were as integral to who Dodger was as his slim elven bones.

"You'll heal. Get anything on Mr. Johnson? Like maybe why things got screwed up last night?"

"Some data has fallen into my hands but, as to yesterday's difficulties, I can do no more than speculate."

"Well if you've got any data, you're ahead of me." Sam slid onto the bench next to Dodger. The elf pushed a minicomp across, allowing Sam to scroll through while he gave a summation.

"As you can see, Mr. Johnson is Andrew Glover of ATT. For someone with his background and standing in the corporation, this shadow work is a bit out of line. The bodyguard is Harry Burke, pro muscle from the European circuit. Very expensive."

"Hmm. Think our Mr. Johnson is moonlighting?"

"Possibly. He might have legitimate ATT business in Seattle, since he arrived direct from headquarters in London on his corporate passport. I'll need more time to check that out."

"So he might be legit or he might not."

"Time is data, and I had very little time."

Sam spotted something and froze the scroll.

"Saeder-Krupp," he said softly. He shuddered, remembering his dealings with the dragon who owned that megacorporation.

"Interesting, is it not?"

"I'd hate to think that this has some connection to Lofwyr. I've dealt with more than enough dragons."

Dodger nodded agreement. Sam returned to scrolling through the data that the elf had collected, but his mind wasn't really focused. The reflections on the screen seemed to echo the glints of a dragon's eye, and he kept drifting back to thoughts of Lofwyr. Sally had robbed the dragon of his prize, and Sam had no idea how Lofwyr had taken that. When Sam had tried to use the telecom numbers he had been given to contact the dragon or his agents, he had found them all disconnected. He had assumed that meant that the dragon was calling it quits, finding revenge as expensive a luxury as Renraku appeared to believe it was. Now there was this connection, tenuous but real. Was he already enmeshed in the coils of another of the dragon's plots? Had Lofwyr only been biding his time? Waiting for the opportunity to strike?

Sam felt an elbow in his ribs as Dodger said, " 'Twould seem that everyone is running ahead of schedule tonight.''

Following Dodger's eye line, Sam saw Andrew Glover crossing the dance floor to the bar. The ATT man was of middling height, narrow-shouldered, and slim. His long, slightly horsey face was relaxed, suffused with the calm of a man assured of his proper place in the world. From his clothes, that place was a comfortable one. His shiny black shoes and grey gloves were spotless, showing no signs of wear. The rest was hidden under a long, caped coat of natural tweed. Despite its expensive material, it would be lined with ballistic cloth. The wealthy took as few chances as possible. Dark spots marred the perfect tones of the coat's shoulders. He slid a hand through his sandy hair, flicking away the water in a casual gesture. His walk was casual, too, as if he was striding through some ancestral manor.

Surveying the club with what appeared to be simple curiosity, Burke followed Glover in. The bodyguard moved with a predator's gait, smooth and calm but ready to explode into instant action. Penumbra's protection would not allow Sam to make a successful astral check, but you didn't need to be a magician to know that Burke had some kind of edge over ordinary people. Dodger had said the man's services were expensive. Since there was no reason to expect Dodger to have gotten bad information, Burke was likely very good at his job. That meant cyberware or magic; simple skills and knowledge weren't enough anymore.

The barkeep directed Glover to their booth. As soon as he saw that it was occupied, Glover put on his corporate smile. He removed his long coat and handed it to Burke who slung it over his arm. The guard seemed to find its weight far less than Glover had. Burke stayed back, letting his charge approach the booth alone.

Glover seated himself on the empty bench, but before he could speak, he was jostled by a new arrival.

Sam hadn't seen where Jason had been hiding. He hadn't even known Jason was in the club until he materialized at the edge of the booth. Maybe the kid had learned something from Ghost. In any case, there had been no time to warn Glover that he was about to have company.

Jason pushed his shoulder against Glover. The roughness of Jason's dermal armor implant snagged the corporate's silk jacket, tugging strands free. Jason placed an Ares predator on the table, the gun's huge barrel pointing in Glover's direction. Jason removed his hand from the butt and rested his palm on the table.

The ATT man reacted well. He expressed only surprise at the Indian's sudden appearance. A quirk at the corner of his mouth hinted at annoyance. Other than that, there was no sign that he was bothered by Jason's typically over-stated threat. Sam was impressed, and warned, by Glover's cool. Some corporates would have started yelling murder at such an unexpected appearance. Glover merely slid over to make room for the broad-shouldered Indian and brushed at the shoulder of his jacket. A negligent wiggling of his fingers sent silk fibers drifting to the table top.

Sam would have expected Burke to intercept Jason. Curious, he looked over and saw the bodyguard standing side-by-side with Fishface. It was unlikely that the professional guard had been intimidated by Fishface's ragged presence. Burke's failure to interfere was more likely directly related to Glover's lack of alarm.

Glover cleared his throat. "This *is* a bit irregular."

"So was the run, chummer," Jason said. "You ain't got problems so long as you play clean, Johnson. We got your warm body for you and want our nuyen."

Glover stared at Jason for a moment, then turned his

head to look at Sam. "Am I dealing with a new principal?"

"No, you're not," Sam replied firmly. "But he is right. The situation was not as you led us to believe. I would like an explanation."

"I just want the creds," Jason said.

The look Glover gave him spoke volumes about the trials of dealing with the lower classes. With slow deliberation to show that he was not reaching for a weapon, Glover slid his hand into his jacket and removed a credstick. It was unmarked by bank seals or the banding of a certified stick. "There is no intent to defraud you. I believe that this will cover the remainder of the agreed-upon sum."

For all his obvious greed, Jason didn't snatch it up when Glover placed it in the center of the table. Instead, Jason poked it with his gun, rolling it toward Dodger. Peremptorily, he ordered, "Check it out, elf."

Dodger plucked the stick from the table without a word. He recovered the minicomp and slotted the credstick. His fingers danced on the key membrane. After several flurries, he looked up at Glover. "Pray tell, Goodman Johnson. Why are the funds locked?"

"What!" Jason's eyes narrowed.

Sam tried to forestall any further reaction by asking, "Is there an explanation you'd care to offer, Mr. Johnson?"

Glover ignored the agitated man at his side, focusing his attention only on Sam. "I believe that I have a question of my own which must be answered before we proceed. Where is Mr. Sanchez?"

The man was so damn sure of himself.

"Being delivered as we agreed."

Glover's face remained deadpan. "I am quite sure that you understand. I must have that confirmed before I authorize the transfer of funds."

Hoping that he had called it right, Sam tried to keep his own voice calm and assured. He hoped he hid his growing trepidation. Corporates away from their safe turf didn't stay so unruffled unless they had hidden assets.

"Then we wait." Jason looked like he was ready to do something else, so Sam said, "Got that, Jason? We give the man a chance."

Jason's sullen glower was his answer.

They sat in stony silence for some minutes until Glover's wrist beeped. He slid back his pristine cuff to reveal a multi-function watch. Tapping in two code sequences, he waited for a response. He seemed satisfied when it came. He tapped in another longer sequence.

"Right. That's it, then, gentlemen. You will find the complete fee available to you now, as well as a substantial bonus in recognition of the alacrity of your performance. I would like to say it has been a complete pleasure doing business with you." Glover started to rise. He made no gesture but it was clear that he expected Jason to get out of his way. "I am a very busy man and I must be getting along."

"Just make yourself comfortable, Mr. Johnson," Sam told him. He was pleased that his voice remained steady. There had been no sign from Jim at the bar that anything was out of place, but that was no guarantee that nothing was wrong. Especially if Glover was an agent of Lofwyr. "You're here until Otter calls in."

Glover drew in a long breath and pursed his lips. He reseated himself stiffly. "I see."

"No need to be put out, Goodman Johnson. 'Tis a simple bit of business assurance. I'm sure you understand."

Glover returned Dodger's smile with a stiff mask, but his detachment was evaporating. The corporate's annoyance was starting to grow. In the middle of the room, Burke was tensed. Sam wanted to defuse the situation before someone did something that they'd all regret. But how?

Forcing a smile that he really didn't feel, Sam called for a round of drinks.

"There's no reason to be concerned, Mr. Johnson. This is simply a business formality. We can still complete this deal without impediments."

"Let us hope so, Mr. Twist."

"I have confidence. However, my friends might feel more confident of our good will if you were to answer my earlier question. They would be relieved if you were to offer some reasonable explanation for the screwup."

Glover shrugged away the importance of the matter with the merest shift of his shoulders.

"It was a simple communications slipup. Mr. Sanchez never received the word that his extraction was to take place. That same glitch deprived him of your descriptions. He would have had no idea that you and your friends were my agents."

"That's it?"

"That is, as you say, it. I accept full responsibility for the confusion."

It would be impolitic to dispute Glover's answer. It was possible that he told the truth. Just barely. Sam tried another approach.

"I realize that you need not tell us, but what will happen to Sanchez from this point?"

Glover looked thoughtful for a moment, then almost smiled. "Mr. Sanchez will receive the most attentive care during his transfer. We want him in the best of health. His role in our organization will be a prominent one. Of course, we will benefit from his participation, but it will not be all one-sided. Mr. Sanchez has special assets. His participation in our ongoing project will ensure that many people lead better and more productive lives. If all goes as planned, he may even be famous one day. So I can assure you that you need have no concerns about Mr. Sanchez's welfare. We intend to see that he has every opportunity to achieve his destiny."

"Too fragging noble," Jason commented.

"Believe as you will," Glover returned. "Some people have concerns beyond their own personal comforts and needs. Some of those people are in positions to act and would find it unconscionable not to act. Can you grasp the concept of altruism, or is that beyond your greedy brain?"

Jason clenched his jaw, his hand slowly sliding up and over the butt of his Predator. Thankful that the insult had only lit the fuse rather than touching off an instant explosion, Sam slapped his own hand down on Jason's. He had no hope of pinning it there, but he might slow Jason's reactions. That delay could give Burke time to kill the Indian. Hoping he had made the right move, Sam glared at Glover.

"That was uncalled for. I think you should apologize to Jason."

Glover glanced at the table before speaking. His voice was neutral. "Where apologies are necessary and appropriate, I offer them."

The reduction in tension under his hand told Sam that Jason had accepted Glover's statement as repentence. The Indian really was dumb. Sam waited until Jason relaxed his shoulders, then dragged the Indian's hand away from the gun before releasing it.

They waited. At last, the bar phone rang and Jim picked it up. He spoke into the handset, nodded, then shoved it into his gut to muffle the pick-up.

"Call for Halifax. Anybody seen her?" Jim shouted. After waiting a moment for a response that never came, he said into the receiver, "Ain't here. It's early, try Damien's."

Dodger sat back and smiled. Sam felt the same relief, but thought it impolitic to let it show. Jim was giving the code phrase that meant Grey Otter had made the transfer and gotten safely away. Jason used the opportunity to snatch the minicomp, letting out a surprised oath when he saw the figures on the screen. He turned the minicomp around again and shoved it at Sam.

"Make the cuts, Twist."

Sam transferred Jason's cut back to the credstick in the machine. He popped it and slid in a blank to take the transfer of Fishface's slice. Transaction completed, he put both on the table and rolled them to Jason.

The Indian grabbed his own first and slipped it into his pouch. Rising, he caught the other as it reached the edge of the table top. He flicked the stick to Fishface.

"Done deal?" Fishface asked tonelessly.

"Done deal. We're outta here."

Glover joined Sam and Dodger in watching the two leave. "Your muscle is flighty. Such an abrupt exit might tempt an ungrateful employer into minimizing his expenses. How can they be sure I will not cause problems now?"

Sam wondered that himself. Not that he thought that they'd care if Glover decided to smoke Sam and Dodger. They had their nuyen and were satisfied to let the future take care of itself. Sam had never been so cavalier about the future, so he hadn't been counting on the lame-brained muscleboys to kept the meeting friendly.

"It was never their problem," he said. "This is a public place where we're well-known. You'll find it difficult to make trouble here. Besides, we all got what we came here for, didn't we?"

Glover pursed his lips and raised his eyebrows slightly. "It would appear so. Yet I wonder, would your associates have performed any differently had this meeting taken place somewhere else?"

"We have friends in lots of places."

"You are commendably cautious, although some of your associations may not be wisely chosen."

"There are always constraints."

Glover nodded knowingly. "Quite. I apologize for my earlier abruptness, gentlemen. Your style is unfamiliar to me and I was slightly discomfited. Having become acquainted with some of the constraints under which you work, I realize now that your conduct was competent and professional."

Sam inclined his head. He wasn't sure what Glover was leading up to, so he thought it best to say nothing.

"I have certain endeavors still uncompleted and find myself somewhat short of competent help. Which is to say, I have another job suitable for professionals of your caliber. It is a similar to this recent operation, which has been concluded with such admirable results."

No thanks, Sam thought. "I think things will be a little warm in Seattle for a while."

"Which is a good reason for you to consider my offer. The job I have in mind is out-of-town work."

"I'm afraid that's not the sort of thing we do," Sam said.

"I assure you nothing like the little mix-up that occurred here will happen there. Having taken your measure, I can also assure you that I can convince my principals that you are worth greater compensation."

Sam started to repeat his rejection of the offer, but Dodger elbowed him in the ribs and said, "We'll give your offer some thought, Goodman Johnson. Mayhap you can provide us with a way to contact you?"

"Certainly, my good elf. But I will need an answer

soon. I have schedules to keep and must leave the metroplex by tomorrow evening.''

Dodger took the card Glover offered. "We shall take
counsel with our associates anon and you shall have
our decision by tomorrow afternoon.''

As soon as the ATT man and his bodyguard had left
the club, Sam rounded on Dodger. "What did you
think you were doing?''

"Looking out for our future, Sir Twist.''

"I don't want that guy in our future. Communications slipups like we had are trouble, deadly trouble,
waiting to happen. Especially if there is any chance
he's connected to Lofwyr.''

"I hesitate to suggest that you speak in haste, but I
fear that I must. There was something I thought you
should see before Friend Glover arrived, but he was
so prompt that opportunity fled.''

"And what is that?''

"A mere tidbit that fell into my hands during my
research. It may mean nothing, but it may have some
significance. I had thought that you would be the best
judge. 'Tis a file I found among the datastores Goodman Glover had transferred to Seattle ATT.''

Dodger tapped at the minicomp, bringing up a list
of seven names. He highlighted item number three:
"Raoul Sanchez, Seattle." The line was marked "In
progress." Two of the other names were marked "acquired.''

"So, Glover is collecting people. Nobody we know
is on the list.''

"So sure, Sir Twist?'' Dodger highlighted item
seven: "Janice Walters, Yomi." "Is it not a custom
of the Japanese to change the names of the changed?''

Sam nodded, his mouth dry. Most Japanese considered having metahumans in their family a disgrace.
The unfortunates were shipped to Yomi and their
names changed, thereby removing the shame from

their family. Could Janice Walters be Janice Verner, his sister?

Sam didn't know if the Yomi officials would have allowed Janice to select her own new name. If so, she might have chosen Walters; it was their maternal grandmother's name. Janice hadn't been born when she had died, but their mother had regaled them constantly with tales of Grandma Walters' world travels. She had been the star of many a bedtime story. Janice had grown up idolizing the woman. When faced with the bureaucratic demand that she cease using Verner as her surname, she might have chosen Walters.

It seemed a slim chance that the woman Glover sought was his sister. But could he afford to take the chance that Janice Walters wasn't Janice Verner?

What did Glover want with all these people, anyway? If one of them was his sister, Sam needed to know. What better way to find out than by becoming part of Glover's organization? It was always easier to snoop around from the inside. But what if he was working for Lofwyr? All the more reason to keep his sister out of the dragon's grasp.

He didn't like it, but it looked as though he would be working for Glover a while longer.

6

Janice thought she understood comfort and easy living. Before her exile to Yomi, she had lived the life of a corporate dependent. It was a comfortable, cozy life complete with all the easy conveniences of civilized society. Renraku took care of its dependents. She had felt safe and secure. Yomi had taught her just how fortunate they had been.

Her corporate comfort had been due to her brother. She had often wondered what would have happened to them after their parents were killed if Sam hadn't caught the eye of old Inazo Aneki, the master of Renraku Corporation. Sam was five years older than she was, and he was only eighteen at the time. There had been no money and few prospects, but Aneki had taken an interest in Sam and seen to it that her brother finished his education. Under the distant but benevolent patronage of Aneki, Sam had gotten started on the fast track at Renraku. Aneki's charity had been like a gift from God, an offering of a long, comfortable life. They certainly wouldn't have been able to make it on their own. Her brother's position was exalted, for a *gaijin*, and she had been proud of him. His salary and position should have ensured congenial accommodations for both of them for life.

Now, her thoughts of Sam's success were less kind. He had abandoned her to keep his sinecure, unwilling to be tainted by her goblinization. *Kawaru* the Japanese called it, a pretty euphemism for an ugly thing. The English word, with its harsh syllables and awkwardness, was so much more fitting.

Sam would call it *kawaru*. He had always been so enamored of things Japanese, aping their attitudes and manners. The Japanese corporate society liked to pretend that metahumans didn't exist, casting them away to rot on the edges of society and to dwell in the polluted shadows of those gleaming corporate towers. The pure stayed home, safe from taint. Secure in their bastions, they ate their regular, balanced meals, slept in their soft, warm beds in their precisely controlled climates, watched their approved entertainments, and ignored what they wished did not exist. Those hypocritical overlords spoke of financial aid, readjustment programs, and subsidized communities, while shipping what they considered refuse to the hell they called Yomi. They had seduced Sam from her. Yes, he would refer to her as a *kawaruhito,* if he referred to her at all.

In just one month Yomi had taught her more about the world and how it worked than her eighteen years in corporate society. The lessons were harsh, but she had learned. She'd had to. Failure meant death. Despite the pain, the rejection, and the horrible realization that she was no longer normal, she had not been ready to die.

She'd learned just how luxurious her former corporate life had been. Renraku menials had a better life than even the self-styled overlords of Yomi. The depths to which the weak and ordinary inmates sank was beyond rational thought. It was just as well that most of those confined to the island didn't remain rational long.

She had learned how to survive.

Over a year ago her body had changed, and twisted her life into a new pattern. Now, for whatever reason, her body had changed again. Was she condemned to keep changing? God forbid that she was infected with some nasty new type of goblinization that never stopped. She had survived one change and was stronger for it. Thus far, she had coped with the new change, but she didn't know how much she could take. What if she changed yet again?

The face she now saw in the mirror was alien. After her first time, she avoided looking in mirrors, having found the asymmetry of her ork physiognomy repulsive. But her new visage was more regular, though hardly more human. She was finding her new body shape more congenial as well. She had expected to find the fur unbearably warm, but it hadn't been so. Her long limbs were still uncoordinated, making her every movement awkward. She felt ungainly and frustrated at her lack of control. If Shiroi hadn't found her in the Walled City, she would have been prey for the jackals who scoured that garbage heap.

But he had found her and offered help. She had been scared when she had accepted his offer. Scared of her surroundings. Scared of what had happened to her. Scared of trusting him. So she had taken a chance. After all, what did she have to lose?

Now, her life was taking another crazy twist. This time it was a dream instead of a nightmare. Her memories of her "luxurious" corporate life were being tattered to shabbiness. With Renraku, one had to be at least a vice-president of a regional branch to rate a private aircraft such as the one in which she travelled.

The flight was over now. The craft had taxied to a halt and the vibration from the engines had stopped. The pilot emerged from the cockpit, nodding and motioning her forward. His smiled was forced. The rest of the crew was nowhere in sight. She'd be seeing Shiroi soon. Who was he, to command such extravagance?

She rose from her seat. With three long, wobbly strides, she reached the pilot's side. Undogging the toggles, he lifted the latch and swung the cabin door wide. Brilliant sunshine flooded through the opening, forcing her to squint painfully. The cabin's climate control coughed and shuddered into high gear to fight the invasion of hot, humid air. For a moment, she was back on Yomi and she shuddered. Remembering to breathe, she sucked in air. It was thin, and she felt light-headed. Even her new, larger lungs didn't seem to have enough capacity.

The pilot stepped through the hatchway and pressed himself against the railing of the stairway. He seemed to want to give her as much room as possible. Up close, she could smell his fear. What did he think she was going to do? Eat him? Ignoring him, she looked out. A short, dark man in a white suit waited at the foot of the stairway. As her eyes settled on him, he smiled.

"Welcome to Atzlan," he said in accented English. "I am Jaime Garcia. I offer Mr. Shiroi's apologies. He was unavoidably detained by business and has asked me to entertain you until he is available. I hope you had a good flight. You have no complaints of your treatment?"

Shivering in the sunshine, the pilot tensed. He relaxed only a little when she said, "Everything was fine."

"Most excellent," Garcia said. His dazzling smile vanished as he turned away to speak rapidly in what she assumed was Spanish. The people to whom he spoke were short and dark like him. Their eyes never left her.

Most of the crowd wore loose-fitting blouses and pants, but a few wore tailored coveralls or suits like Garcia's. He finished with an obvious command, scattering the blouses and coveralls. Minions, jumping at his word. She had seen such feverish obedience once when some important Aztechnology officials had visited the Renraku compound. Was it a universal trait of the underlings in Atzlan-based corporations? She didn't like it.

After a few softer exchanges with the suits, he turned his attention to her again. The brilliant smile returned as if it had never been gone. "Please, *señorita*. Come down and join us."

She wasn't sure it was a good idea, but she stepped through the hatchway. There was something about this Garcia that she didn't like. She ran her tongue across her lower lip, wishing she knew what he hid behind his smile. Her eyes were still hurting as she walked carefully down the stairs. She squinted down at Garcia and realized that he looked different. He was no longer a small man in a suit but a long-limbed, furred meta-human like herself.

In her surprise, she nearly stumbled. He was up the stairs to meet her before she could recover her balance on her own. His grip was strong, steadying her. He was a suit again, armored behind his smile. Solicitously, he helped her down the remaining steps.

She didn't like his cologne.

He seemed unaware of her dislike. "You appear to be taxed by your journey. Perhaps some refreshment would restore your spirit?"

"No, thanks. I'll be fine. Besides, they served a meal on the plane only a couple of hours ago."

"And you found it to your taste?"

He really did seem to be concerned that she be pleased. Maybe he wasn't so bad. She gave him a friendly smile, but she remembered her fangs and closed it down. "The meal was quite tasty. My compliments to your corporate chef. I don't believe that I've ever had meat with quite so delicate a flavor."

Garcia's smile grew wider. "Yes, it is a specialty. I will be sure to communicate your compliments."

Garcia escorted her across the landing field to a waiting helicopter. They climbed aboard and made a short flight over Mexico City. Their destination was a compound on the north side of the plex. The GWN monogram that she had seen on the uniforms of Garcia's minions at the airport gleamed on the side of the eighty-story skyscraper at the center of the enclosed blocks.

Oozing charm, Garcia took her on a whirlwind tour of the facilities. GWN was an obviously successful corporation. Most of the plants were devoted to food processing and nutrient farming; labels on containerized cargo lots told her that GWN shipped worldwide. She wondered briefly what brands belonged to the firm. Comestibles weren't the corporation's only product. Several impressive structures were dedicated to information technologies and small, high-tech manufacturing plants. The combination wasn't surprising; no megacorporation could survive without at least dabbling in the Matrix and data technology. If all of this belonged to Mr. Shiroi, as Garcia implied, her benefactor was a powerful man.

They had just left a building where cheap simsense players were being assembled, and were walking through a section of employee tenements, when a telecom box on a street corner called Garcia's name. He excused himself, leaving her to stand in the heat. Off-shift employees, who had been gathered on the front stoops to take in the afternoon sun, suddenly found business elsewhere, but not before she had seen their fearful glances in her direction. Garcia returned.

"Ah, Mr. Shiroi will see you now, if you wish. But there is no hurry. Plenty of time for you to freshen up or partake of some refreshment, if you wish."

She shook her head. Freshening up was something for norms. Make-up on her face would be a travesty, and she didn't have a curry comb for the fur. Let Mr. Shiroi see her as she was, because that's what he got.

"You are not hungry yet?"

"No. I'm not hungry at all."

"That is understandable. After the change one's appetites are often erratic. It is best to trust your feelings. Your body will know when you need sustenance. One should not overdo."

Garcia took her to an elevator, holding the door open as he tapped a code into the keypad. He wished her well and stepped back, letting the doors slide shut. The car rose silently, with very little sensation of motion. After a few moments, the doors opened on a lavish office. Chill air swept into the car, cooling her comfortably.

The walls were a pale, pale blue. She might have

taken them for white if not for the pure alabaster of the deep pile carpet. The room was huge, but its furnishings were few, and they were dominated by the presence in one corner of a carved column. The stack of stylized faces on it stretched at least three meters; it didn't reach the ceiling yet seemed to fill the room. Two-thirds of the way across the chamber, a dark wood desk stood between her and the tinted window-wall. Behind the desk, in an oddly shaped chair, sat Mr. Shiroi.

"Ah, Janice," he said as he noticed her. "It is good to see you again."

He was smiling, with pleasure she thought. Why he should do that, she didn't know. She wasn't pleasant to see. She felt awkward and out of place.

"Wish I thought so, Mr. Shiroi."

His smile faded a bit and his eyes filled with concern. "You must learn to accept what you are, since there is no way to change it. Denial only prolongs the pain. I do not wish to see you in pain. And please, call me Dan."

She slowly walked across the room, since that was expected. When he indicated the chair in front of the desk, she sat. She started as the soft grey upholstery shifted beneath her.

"Just relax. It will settle down," he said. There was a hint of amusement on his face.

She didn't like being laughed at. Forcing herself to ignore the squirming chair, she waited. The cushions slowed their wriggling and finally stopped. She was surprised at how comfortable it was. She was almost as surprised that the chair seemed to fit her oversize body. Shiroi must have read her reaction on her face.

"You have just had your first experience with a Tendai-Barca Glove Lounger. They are always a little unnerving the first time, but, if you will excuse the pun, one adjusts quickly. I doubt you will find better seating anywhere in the world.''

She calmed her breathing, relaxing. The chair shifted again to accommodate her. Perhaps her anger at his amusement was out of place. Anyone feeling a chair writhe under their butt would look comical. She still wasn't comfortable mentally, though. He had had her brought halfway around the world. Surely, it wasn't all for the sake of this small joke?

''What do you want, Mr. Shiroi?''

''There is no more reason to be abrupt than there is to distrust my motives, Janice.'' He took her bad manners in stride. She even thought she detected a hint of sadness behind his soft voice. ''I want to help you find yourself. I want you to accept a place in my organization. If you choose to follow your own path, I will understand, but it is my hope that you will find us congenial. It is very lonely being on your own. It could also be dangerous.''

''Trying to scare me, Mr. Shiroi?''

He laughed. ''No. The outside world holds enough terrors for our kind. We need not prey upon ourselves. And I do wish that you would call me Dan.''

''Dan. You say 'our kind.' *I* know you and Garcia are like me, but your employees don't know it because you hide behind illusions, or whatever it is you do so that they see you as norms. Why? Why do you hide what you are?''

''Why?'' he asked. All trace of his humor sank beneath an expression of seriousness. ''You should not have to ask that. You have seen yourself in the mirror, Janice. You have seen how the norms react to you. That is the answer. Do you wish to deal with the unreasoning fear all day, every day?''

Of course she didn't. Who would? She had felt the fear and hate too often when she was just an ork. Orks were common. She didn't like to think what was in store for her as a rare, more monstrous metahuman. Against that dread, her objection seemed petty.

"I don't like pretending to be something other than what I am!"

He swiveled his chair ninety degrees, presenting her with a profile. She watched his chest rise and listened as he let the air out in a long sigh.

"We all wear masks and pretend to be something other than ourselves, do we not? The norms do it. Even you did it before your change." He swiveled back to face her, cutting her off before she could object. "Were you not a different person with your peers than when you were with your family? How about when you dealt with your corporate superiors? Every set of people with whom we interact sees a different person, a different facet of ourselves. This magical disguise is like that, a mask of necessity. In our case, it hides the physical reality. Beneath the masks we are still ourselves. The illusion is simply necessary grease for the machine of social interaction. Nothing more. Having spent so much time in the Imperial Japanese Empire, surely you are familiar with the need to smooth relations between people."

At the mention of Japan, she shivered. The chair shifted in response.

"I am sorry. I should not have mentioned Japan."

He watched her for a while, saying nothing. She was glad; she didn't know what to say. He was right, of course. It still seemed . . . odd that someone could make the metaphorical masks a reality. If a magical spell could be called reality. She taxed the Tendai-Barca, seeking to get into a physically comfortable position, while it was her mental state that unsettled her. He, of course, noticed.

"If you will be more comfortable, I will drop the spell. You are among friends here."

"I don't know. I don't know what I want. It's been so confusing. I just want to get things under control."

"I want to help you do just that. Here. Look."

He had dropped his spell. He was huge, bigger than she was. His Tendai-Barca flowed to support his increased size; panels expanded, slumped, and thickened as the chair reshaped itself to accommodate him. His fur was stark white, as pure as polar snow. The skin of his broad face and powerful hands was dark and glossy with health. Once she might have shrunk from his visage, but now she was as monstrous as he. But then, he didn't consider himself monstrous. Or did he? He hid beneath a spell. Or was that true, either? What did he see when he looked in a mirror? The smooth Oriental features of Mr. Dan Shiroi or the wide nose, deep-set eyes, and fangs of his metatype?

"Now that the mask is down, anyone can see that I am of the same metatype as you. Believe me when I say that I understand what you are going through. Between us there need be no false fronts. Illusions are for the norms."

A sudden stir of bitterness swirled across her mind, rippling through what she realized had been a growing sense of fellowship. He might be her metatype, but he was still something she was not. "Even if I accepted your philosophy, Dan, I couldn't do what you do. I'm mundane."

"And how do you know that with such certainty? You cannot be totally without talent if you pierced our illusions."

Once again his expression held a hint that he knew something that she did not. She felt uneasy under that knowing gaze. She felt more disquieted by the growing belief that he meant her well, that he really was interested in *her*.

She heaved herself up out of the chair, staggering a little when it released her more easily than she had expected. Pacing around the desk, she made her unsteady way to the window-wall. Beneath her spread the panorama of the towers of Mexico City. The spires of man's arrogance, lofting above one of the largest cities on earth while the bases of those towers lay hidden in smog. Hidden too were the people who thronged the Atzlan capital. People . . . she wasn't one of them anymore. This city couldn't be her home. Cities were places for people and people had cast her out. Would she ever have a home now?

She had been beginning to think that she might find one with Shiroi . . . no, Dan. But now she saw that slipping away as well. He thought she was just like him, but she knew better. She was incapable of doing what he could, and she knew it all too well.

She owed him for his kindness. His manner was so accepting, his interest in her welfare so clear. The least she could do was to tell him how she knew that she had none of the magic. She turned around to find that he had risen from his chair. He stood a step away, concern and anxiety plain on his face. She smiled sheepishly.

"I've never told anyone, Dan. None of my friends. Not even my brother. I was embarrassed to tell anyone." He reached out a long arm and rested a hand on her arm. She drew strength from the comforting touch. "I was tested for magical ability once."

"By whom?"

"The Hoboken Institute. They are a very reputable firm."

"Perhaps they made a mistake."

"That's what I told myself at first. When I was growing up, I always wanted to be a magician. I never told anyone, of course, because my dad was dead set against magic. He called it all nonsense and tricks. But I was a kid, and I knew better. I knew that I had the magic in me. So I saved every nuyen I could, took an after-school job clerking in a Soy Shack for the extra creds. I didn't have enough before . . . before the accident, and I wasn't able to save much for the next year, till my brother got his stipend from the Renraku grant. Once he was in the university, things got easier and I wangled a corporate temp job. It was boring and deadly dull, but I knew I could last it out because it would give me the credit to get tested and once I was certified as trainable there would be no question. I was going to be a high circle mage. I was so sure.

"Finally I saved enough creds, and I went to the Institute. I was hell to live with for two weeks until the test results came in. My brother never knew why I was such a bitch, and I lost a couple of my few friends. I even risked corporate censure, skipping my work assignment that afternoon in order to run off and find a private place to read the report. It was only one word, but it smashed my dreams. 'Negative.'

"I was crushed. If living with me had been hell while I was waiting, the next two months should have qualified anyone for sainthood. But I didn't have any friends who wanted to stick around for the final exam. I was queen bitch of the Wash-Balt Metroplex Education Center. I really didn't shake off the depression until I met Ken at Tokyo University. He made me feel special. He always said I had enough magic for him."

The memories were too much. She couldn't help it, she started to cry. Her body shook with her sobs. Dan gathered her in, enfolding her with his arms. She buried her face in his fur, feeling it go damp with her tears. He stroked her back, saying nothing until she quieted. When she regained control of herself, he released her and took a step back as if fearing to impose on her. She felt chill without his warm fur meshing with hers.

"Ken is your boyfriend?"

"Was." The pain was old but she still felt the ache. It was duller now, but it still hurt. "He doesn't deal well with *kawaru*."

He nodded with understanding. "Ken refused to see you after your change?"

She sniffed and shook her head. "He wouldn't even talk to me or answer any letters."

"He sounds like so many people I have known. The prejudice and fear attached to the metamorphosis is very strong. I think perhaps even stronger now that it is not so common. Do not think too badly of him. As a product of his environment, he was hostage to his society. Given time, he might have come to accept your change . . . if he truly loved you.

"You need not worry about acceptance here. We all know what you have gone through. We have seen the fear. Some of us have felt it turn to hate and violence. We have banded together for mutual aid and support. I speak for all when I say that we want you to join us.

"I will not be shy in saying that your joining will make us stronger, something we all devoutly want. But do not think that we only think of ourselves. Well, some of us do. But, Janice, I did not invite you here just to strengthen the organization. I felt something when I found you in that hovel in Hong Kong. I don't really understand it myself, but I know it's there. I want you to prosper. I want you to gain the strength to stand on your own feet and take a well-deserved place among us, and I am willing to do whatever is necessary to see that happen."

She turned and stared out at the skyscrapers and megastructures. They reminded her of the guard towers and bunkers that ringed Yomi.

His words were tempting, freely offering what she had longed for in the long months of exile on Yomi. There was a hint of more than fellowship, a hint of something that had been torn from her life by the change. Did she dare believe that he was honest? Did she dare reach out for it? She had been spurned so often. What if she changed again? Would his concern change along with her body? The questions made her head spin.

He placed his hand on her arm. Her muscles locked for a moment, leaving her frozen like a small animal in a spotlight. He waited until she relaxed to make his tentative contact more firm. She felt the warmth of his palm and the prickly touch of his nails through her fur. When she didn't shrink away, he encircled her again in his broad, strong arms. She turned within that enclosure and stared into his face. She found only concern.

"Can I trust you?" she asked.

"As much as you can trust anyone."

"That's not a comforting answer, Dan."

"It is not a comfortable world, Janice. I am fallible like anyone else. Sometimes the best of intents yield terrible consequences and the finest of feelings sour. I will not start our relationship with lies and high-sounding promises, but, by all the lights of heaven, I will vow to help you become all you were meant to be. If you let me, I will be your strength now. When you are strong, we can speak of the future."

"You'll wait?"

"I am patient. I will wait for you at each door until you are ready to step through."

"No pressure?"

"No more than the press of life demands."

His eyes were sincere. She wanted to believe. Wanted desperately to believe. But she was afraid. "Just hold me."

And he did. His arms were strong, and she felt safe.

7

Harry Burke was a former member of the Special Air Services, an organization known for its efficient and multi-talented personnel. To Andrew Glover, he was an unparalleled asset.

Without orders, Burke moved quickly along the macadam and took up a position flanking the alley mouth. If he made any noise, it was lost in the jumble of sound from the busy street. It was barely after midnight, and the Hong Kong Free Enterprise Enclave was still very much awake. The dark alley held no interest for the throngs who surged along the carnival-lit street. No simple passerby would notice the dark-clad man crouched against the building. But ordinary pedestrians did not concern Glover.

Glover reached out and tapped the elf on his shoulder. "Have you broken their codes yet?"

The elf was slow in answering. When he shook his head, the datacord clacked softly against the cyber-deck he cradled in his lap. "Not yet. Invisible work takes a modicum of effort."

"Then get on with it." As dark as the alley was, Glover felt exposed. He wanted to get through that door and into the Mihn-Pao facility. Waiting inside was the boat that would take them across to the mainland. He would be glad to leave Hong Kong behind; he didn't like the city or what it stood for.

There was still no sign of trouble, but his stomach kept getting tighter. He wanted to urge the elf to hurry, but knew that he would get the results he wanted sooner if he left the pointy-eared Matrix runner alone.

Elves were rarely reliable, especially for serious work, but this one had proven himself competent. Glover would have preferred a human decker, but one had to use what was available.

His eyes drifted again to the mouth of the alley. Even knowing where to look, he had a hard time spotting Burke's crouched figure. The former SAS man waited patiently for whatever would happen. Patience was a lesson that Glover had never learned very well. It had been his own impatience that had nearly gotten them caught. That squat little sector guard had been so insufferable. Understandably exasperated by the guard's glacial survey of their papers, he had insisted that they be passed through the checkpoint without delay. Apparently that had set off alarms in the half-pint's miniscule brain, causing him to demand that they exit the vehicle. Corbeau's nerves wouldn't have taken the inspection, although Glover had no doubts that their documents would withstand whatever scrutiny the guards could bring to bear. Burke's rapid departure had left the moronic guard capering and screaming imprecations while he ate the dust their car kicked up. The moron hadn't fired on them. Instead, he set the EPA Patrol Force on their heels, forcing them to abandon their original plan to leave the Enclave.

At least they had slipped the pursuit. Or had they? Burke's action told him that the veteran feared that someone would come to disturb their illicit work. Perhaps his sensitive cyberears had detected a hint of danger to their group. If Burke had been sure, he would have said something. Abruptly, Burke made a chopping motion with his right hand.

"Down, everyone," Glover ordered as he crouched himself.

Two caricature silhouettes stopped at the alley mouth. Padded jackets bulked the shoulders wide, and round helmets made their heads bulbous. Tinned insignia gleamed, confirming that they were Enclave Police Agency officers. The two bought-badges were chattering to each other in the distorted mishmash of English, Cantonese, and Japanese that was the common language of the streets here. Glover couldn't make out a word, but Burke was fluent. He would know what they said and act if they were a threat.

They stood at the entrance, apparently indecisive. The flow of traffic adjusted for their presence. Pedestrians swerved around without seeming to notice them, but no one passed between the bought-badges and the alley.

Trading comments back and forth, they readied themselves. Both drew weapons, and one unhooked the heavy cylinder of a flashlight from his belt. They stepped forward, the flashlight's harsh xenon beam blasting away the cloaking shadows. Within that illuminating cone of light, everything was rendered in a curiously flat starkness.

Glover heard the soft click of a weapon safety at his side. A glance confirmed that Twist had his pistol readied. Commendable initiative, but not the best response, since the weapon did not appear to be equipped with a sound suppressor. Their situation would not be improved by attracting attention. Besides, Burke was on the job.

"Wait," he whispered.

The second bought-badge trailed his companion by a meter or two as they entered the alley. They advanced cautiously, probing the darkness with the light. It had yet to sweep deep enough to discover their hiding place. And it would not. Burke's black-clad shape rose from the shadows and slipped behind the second man.

One arm encircled the bought-badge's throat, elbow cinching his throat tight. The second pistoned a fist into the man's kidneys. Burke lowered the limp form to the pavement. A slight clatter from the equipment on the man's belt alerted his partner.

The remaining cop started to turn. Without time to straighten, Burke dropped lower and swept a leg out into the back of the man's knees. The cop's legs buckled. Burke uncoiled and directed a kick to the man's gun hand. The snap of the cop's trigger finger breaking was audible as the weapon spun away. The bought-badge started to howl. Burke's stiff-fingered thrust caught him in the throat, cutting off the scream.

The patrolman was tough. Gasping, he raised the flashlight behind his head, wobbling into a stick-fighter's en garde. His form was ragged, hardly dangerous. Burke settled into guard as well, his left hand protecting the high line. Unseen by his opponent, Burke's right hand curled in toward his wrist. Seven centimeters of razor keen steel slid from its forearm sheath.

They stood, each assessing his strategy. Burke shifted slightly and the bought-badge must have seen a chance. The flashlight whipped around, its beam cutting a wild arc. Burke's maneuver had been a feint. He stepped away from the incoming blow, spinning inside the cop's reach. His right arm flashed up, the extended blade bisecting his opponent's arm. Flashlight and hand separated as they continued to arc past Burke. He twisted and passed his blade through the cop's neck. The bought-badge's head tilted back, but the flashlight shattered and plunged the alley back into night before the blood fountained.

Twist grabbed Glover's shoulder and spun him around.

"He didn't have to do that, Glover. I could have tranqed them. Those were cops he murdered!"

Glover slapped at the offending hand. "And we're robbers, old chap. Are you aware of the penalty for aiding a contract jumper here in Hong Kong?"

"Enforced restitution labor for a period of not less than one year per salary grade of the apprehended party. Compliance shall be enforced with osteo-bonded monitor and time-release mycotoxin implant. Toxin counteragents only available upon completion of certified production quotas," Sam quoted in a cold voice. "The penalty for being an accessory to murder is worse."

Twist was clearly outraged by what he had seen. Another man in that state might be murderous, but someone who was so offended by violence was hardly likely to offer any serious violence of his own. Since there was no danger, Glover found the runner's hate to be of little importance; it was a hasty, ill-informed emotion.

"I see that you are somewhat versed in local law, but what you saw will not be considered murder, since Mr. Burke is a certified corporate agent. He has been engaged in what the Hong Kong Enclave calls unavoidable destruction of another company's assets. The Enclave Police Agency will be properly compensated. You shall never be involved, so I fail to see why you are complaining."

"Their deaths were unnecessary."

"I shall decide what is necessary. You shall simply do as you are told. I remind you that further argument is likely to draw additional attention to us. A second incident might not be so easily overlooked."

Glover could see that Twist was not satisfied. Why should he be? Killing was a rotter scam, distasteful at best. Had time not been of the essence, a better solution might have been found. But Burke was the expert, and he had determined that these deaths were necessary. Glover trusted his professional judgment; Burke understood that their mission must succeed. If that meant a few innocents died in the process, then the cost would have to be borne. Glover and his colleagues were working toward a great good, seeking to save more than a few paltry lives. They could not afford to let a couple of nameless bought-badges disrupt their carefully laid scheme. But he couldn't tell that to these runners. It was not yet time for anyone outside the circle to know what was afoot.

Throughout the discussion, René Corbeau had listened with wide eyes. No doubt he was regretting his decision to take Glover's offer. Well he might. As stiff as the penalties that Glover and his hirelings would face, Corbeau would see worse: he was the defector. It wouldn't matter to Corbeau's masters that the company transfer offer was false. Their trusted employee had believed it and acted on it. The data he had brought along as an offering would only seal his fate with Automattech HK. Subsidiaries of Mitsuhama Computer Technologies were often more ruthless than their parent. Sibling rivalry for their parent's attention, he supposed; just another dirty part of corporate society. Corbeau should have considered all of that before he jumped. Now he cowered against the wall, as if realizing the implications of what he had done for the first time. Such lack of courage was unseemly. Glover hoped it would not compromise Corbeau's usefulness.

Burke joined them.

"The *gingchat* had already spotted the car and called it in. Neighborhood will be crawling soon."

Satisfied, Glover smiled at Twist.

"There, you see? There was no time for anything other than precipitous action. Standard procedure requires the EPA to inform sovereign corporate security if they are performing a search on adjacent property." Glover turned back to Burke. "Did they?"

"Don't know," Burke answered.

"We shall find out soon," Dodger said, "for the lock is breached."

"No alarms?" Glover asked.

"Never a sound."

Dodger's expression implied that he thought such a question insulting. Arrogant elf.

The elven decker opened the door, but Burke was the first in. Twist entered right behind him, gun drawn. Perhaps he thought if he was in the forefront, he might prevent Burke from more "unnecessary" killing. Twist would have to be very fast indeed if he expected to prevent Burke from doing anything the former SAS man set his hand to.

This was no immediate reaction, so Glover got Corbeau on his feet and guided him through the doorway. Dodger slung his deck and followed. As he walked, the elf finished assembling the compact sub-machine gun he had broken down for their walk from the abandoned car.

The inside of the warehouse was cavernous. Corbeau's footsteps echoed softly in the darkness. He was the only one of the group not wearing soft-soled footgear. Pools of light fought back the dark at random intervals, revealing stacks of crates, pyramids of cylinders, and huge cargo containers. During the day the area would have been a hive of activity. Night made it a sepulcher. With the door to the alley closed, the street sounds had vanished, leaving only Corbeau's soft footfalls and the lap of water against the concrete of the enclosed dock area to break the silence.

They were halfway across the floor, strung out in the dark, when Glover felt a clammy touch at the base of his skull. He shuddered. That was the warning signal he had been told he would receive when magical danger to his person was imminent. He stopped, readying his defenses. Extending his senses to locate his associates, Glover spread the protection to include them. He was barely quick enough. As he closed the shield over Burke, he felt a spell slam against his defensive perimeter, clawing to get in and ravage them.

The magician who cast it hadn't been expecting a
counter; he hadn't used enough strength.

Lights flooded the area. Mihn-Pao security had been
alerted and had lain in ambush on the possibility that
the EPA officers had tumbled onto runners targeting the
facility. Half a dozen uniformed guards were on the
catwalks in the rafters, readying to fire on the intruders. Glover could hear more clattering to join their
fellows. The hard slap of boots on concrete told him
that additional forces were charging to intercept them
on the warehouse floor.

Burke reacted with all of his chipped speed. His
Steyr AUG coughed in rapid bursts as he spun. Three
of the guards dropped in his initial attack, killed or
incapacitated before they could fire. One of the bodies
slipped from the catwalk to impact heavily on the concrete behind Glover.

As the Mihn-Pao squad returned fire, Glover dove
forward to drag the cow-eyed Corbeau out of harm's
way. His back itched. There was a hostile magician
out there. If Glover had to protect Corbeau, he would
be unable to counter the enemy's magic effectively.

Single sharp cracks marked Twist's contribution.
Each shot shattered one of the globes protecting the
lights that robbed the runners of the concealment of
the shadows. They no longer fought in a building filled
with artificial day. The earlier gloom had not returned,
but at least they had patches of dark to hide in.

The elf joined the fray, spraying a lethal welcome
into the midst of the first reinforcing squad on the catwalks. The survivors fell back. No doubt they were
suddenly glad of Twist's destructive efforts as they re-
treated into the cloaking shadows.

Darkness would do little to hide them from the enemy magician. Glover forced Corbeau to crawl faster.
He needed to get the man to a safe place so he could
concentrate on finding his counterpart. Finding a stack

of crates that provided a nook out of the surviving guards' line of fire, Glover directed Corbeau into the recess and told him to keep his head down. That done, he crawled back to the edge of the stack.

Using only his mundane senses, Glover started to search for the enemy magician. The hostile was already active and would likely spot him first if he tried active magic. His saw no sign of the enemy.

Twist was huddled in the shelter of a massive shipping crate. At first, Glover thought that the American runner had been wounded, but he realized that Twist was concentrating. His breathing was deep, almost trancelike. When he had first seen the odd knots in the fringes of Twist's jacket, Glover had thought them merely superstitious claptrap, the sort of charms to ward off evil that so many mundanes thought were effective. Perhaps they signified something more. Twist's shooting had been quite accurate. Was he some sort of warrior adept? Glover hadn't thought that such adepts could focus their energies to improve their ability with projectile weapons, but he didn't know everything about magic. Who could?

Twist released his concentration, spun to his left, and knelt. Cradling his gun in a two-handed grip, he eased forward until he had a line of fire around the crate that had shielded him. Head cocked upward, he seemed to be searching the darkness for a target. Glover followed Twist's apparent eyeline.

There was nothing and no one on the catwalk—at least nothing mundane. Glover shifted his perception and saw the enemy mage. She had been standing there, invisible to the mundane eye, awaiting targets. Before Glover could ready a spell, Twist fired. The Mihn-Pao mage jerked and clutched at her shoulder. As she staggered against the railing, her astral aura flickered and Glover knew she had dropped her cloaking spell. Witchfire flickered around the mage's hand as she tried to summon the energy for a spell. The light faded when she slumped to her knees. It vanished entirely when she toppled backward onto the walk's flooring.

The loss of the mage took the heart out of the Mihn-Pao guards, and the firefight rapidly degenerated into a stalemate. The runners were pinned down, too far away from the boats at the docks to make a break. The security team didn't advance; they were unwilling to face Burke's deadly accurate fire. At least there were no alarms. Likely the Mihn-Pao team leader had no wish to lose face in the corporate community; to call for help against such a small invasion would not be good for Mihn-Pao's public image. The corporation's concern for its image was one of the reasons he had chosen to acquire his transportation from them; they were less likely to report the theft than any of the alternative sources. Mihn-Pao's obsession with image was serving the runners now, but it was a fleeting advantage. Even without an alarm, there would be more troops. Time was on Mihn-Pao's side.

A sudden burst of lambent energy cut the darkness, sizzling past the elf's hiding place and boring a hole in one of the pillars. It was too focused and rigid for magical energy; a new, lethal technology had entered the fray. Glover drifted his astral form free to locate the danger. From the far end of the structure, another Mihn-Pao squad was advancing. They were led by a burly ork enwrapped in the bristly cocoon of heavy armor and a gyro-stabilized gun mount. His silhouette was misshapen beyond the offensive distortion normal for his kind, made hunchbacked by the massive backpack he wore. His burden was the power pack that fed his high-energy laser weapon. The laser, though heavy due to the coolant jacket sheathing its barrel, swiveled quickly under the ork's direction. Glover returned to his body as another bolt tore through the boxes behind which the elf sheltered. Dodger scrambled backwards, seeking new cover. Glover smelled burned hair mixed with the scent of wood smoke and something even more acrid. Small flames played in the charcoaled edges of the hole the laser had drilled through the crates.

Mihn-Pao had played a trump that Glover and the runners could not easily counter. Armor would protect the ork from the runners' guns, but Glover could take out the gunner with his magic if he had a clear line of sight. Unfortunately, that meant the gunner would have a line of fire as well. Glover was quite sure the ork would be faster.

Burke signalled for his attention. Glover softly spoke the words for the spell that would let him hear Burke's words. He didn't like what the former SAS man had to say, but he saw no reasonable alternative. He nodded, and Burke was on his way. Glover started to tug Corbeau out of his hiding place.

Seconds later, Burke opened fire from the flank of the advancing reinforcements. Glover gave the Mihn-Pao troops a second to engage, and shouted for the others to join him in running for the boats. Just as they reached the boats, the survivors of the first Mihn-Pao squad spotted them and opened fire. Corbeau was hit as he stepped into the boat. Blood splattered the coaming as he collapsed over it. Glover jumped in after him, terrified that the man had been killed. Twist and the elf returned fire as they converged on the boat. They must have gotten the shooters, since no more fire raked the boat.

Glover was relieved to find Corbeau only wounded. As he searched for the craft's first aid kit, the laser crackled again. A scream of pain rose from somewhere near where he had last heard Burke's Steyr. There was more gunfire, but only from one side. Burke's weapon was silent.

The Mihn-Pao guards would be continuing their ad-

vance. They would be cautious; they couldn't know
where the runners waited. Several stacks of brilliant
orange cylinders screened the two groups, but only for
a minute at best. Not enough time to get the doors
open and the boat clear. Even if Twist was a warrior
adept, they would not get out alive without Burke.
They were trapped.

New gunfire raked the dock and boat, forcing the
runners to duck. The first of the reserve squad had
arrived. The laser gunner, slowed by his heavy load,
would soon be upon them. The elf returned fire while
Twist struggled to unmoor the boat.

What a rotter! For a chance impatience, the run had
soured. Corbeau would die here and it was Glover's
fault. He could not have harmed the cause more if he
had tried. It was unbearable. There had to be something that could be done. He started to pant as his
panic and anger fought for dominance within him. As
his chest rose and fell within the confines of his armored jacket, he felt a hardness rubbing against his
skin. Bright Lord! He was an idiot whose poor memory disgraced his calling.

Burke had bought them some time at the cost of his
life. Such a sacrifice could not, would not, be wasted.
Glover stripped open the velcro fastening of his jacket
and reached under the neck of his shirt, groping for
the cord. His frantic fingers found the talisman and
pulled it free. His desperate animal self cried for him
to unleash its power, but his rational mind knew that
the object held no power of its own; the amulet was
just a focus, a way for him to amplify his call and
enhance his control. Hyde-White had been right—with
a firefight raging, he needed the concrete object as a
core for his concentration. He intoned the word of release over and over. He willed the guardian spirit to
act, focusing on the Mihn-Pao team and naming them
his enemies.

The laser gunner rounded the corner. He advanced boldly, confident in his firepower and the protective virtues of his armor. His support team fired past him from protected positions.

The shriek of tortured metal from the cylinders at his side brought the ork to a wary halt. One of the cannisters midway up the pile had bulged out as if hammered by some immense force. Metal squealed again as the cylinder distended anew. With an ear-splitting screech, the abused container split. A translucent green column of chemical gel arced from the fissure, curving unnaturally to reach for a Mihn-Pao guard who had used the end of the stack as cover. Tentacle-like, it wrapped around the man. He screamed at its touch. Cloth and flesh blackened, hissing and bubbling under the touch of the toxic slime.

The gunner reacted quickly. He swiveled his laser and triggered the weapon. The dazzling beam speared the chemical tentacle halfway along its length, piercing it and puncturing more cannisters. Chemicals sprayed from the newly ruptured tanks. As if with malign intent, the streams arched and flowed into the tentacle. As its volume increased, the malefic limb swelled and sagged towards the floor, the dark swirling stains from the laser's strike dispersing throughout its bulk. It released the guard it had attacked. He dropped to the concrete and lay twisted, skin blistered and seared.

The gelid mass did not flow to spread out on the floor of the warehouse. It wobbled, an uncanny mound growing ever larger. Pseudopods extended from near the top of the column and stretched forward in parody of arms. Nearer the base, another tentacle grew and flowed out to touch the floor. The shape lurched, its mass shifting forward toward that new contact. It was no longer amorphous. A stretching, rounded mockery of a man, it stepped clear of the cylinders.

The gunner pumped two more shots into it, starting new swirls of discoloration. Chemicals boiled where the beams pierced the shape. All the terrible energy he unleashed seemed to have no other effect. Behind the thing, newly ruptured cylinders contributed more to its mass.

The ork scrambled out of its path, backing away until he was forced to stop by one of the roof's supporting columns. Eyes darting between the advancing horror and his weapon, the gunner fumbled with the laser's settings. A high-pitched capacitor whine overwhelmed the shrill beeping of the overload warning. The ork ignored the sounds, training the laser once again on the monstrous thing that stalked him. With a sizzling crack, the weapon discharged. No longer a brief pulse, the beam was an eye-searing line of energy. The gunner's backpack smoked as the power cells emptied their energy into the shape. Acrid green smoke rose from the surface as the chemicals bubbled and blackened. The pale color darkened, going opaque, and the thing seemed to shrink back. The ork's face contorted as his relief shifted to a savage glee. He took a step forward.

His elation vanished as the shape surged, elongating toward him like a cresting wave. His scream was cut off as he was engulfed. Like sand washing from a hand, his flesh flowed away from his bones. The shape flowed past him, curving and reforming in the center of the aisle. It lurched in the direction of the next nearest Mihn-Pao guard. Behind it a pitted, scorched skeleton tumbled into a heap with the corroded plastic and metal parts that had been the ork's gear.

Glover grabbed Twist by the arm. The American was staring at the spectacle, a horrified expression on his face. The last mooring line hung forgotten in his hands. Twist didn't react, and Glover cast free the last line by himself.

"Let's go," he shouted to the elf.

The boat's engine roared to life. Gathering speed, the boat headed for the opening door.

Once they were through, it would be a short run across the strait to the coast, where they would be harder to spot. Then, a quick run along the New Territories. Once they crossed the Enclave border into the maritime jurisdiction of Kungshu, they would be safe. At least from corporate pursuit. The warlords of the Chinese mainland were united on very little, but resisting further intrusions by the extranational corporations was one cause that bound them. Whatever their history and present ambitions, those warlords all remembered the glittering prize of Hong Kong that was supposed to belong to China and how their pride had been torn and shredded when the region had ripped free from China's control during the troubled times of the early part of the century.

Glover could understand how they felt. Britain had been duped and taken advantage of in that disgraceful episode as well. Believing that the British government would have a guiding role in reestablishing the thriving community that had been the Crown Colony and desperately desiring the bounty such a restored enclave would bring, the government had ignored the warnings of the druidic community. But the corps' encouragement of Britain's participation had been a sham, a way to rally certain elements and pull them into the struggle and thus minimize corporate involvement. They so disliked expending assets when unnecessary.

Had the political leaders listened to those wiser and less avaricious heads, Britain's honor would not have been sullied by participation in the multinational megacorporations' schemes that ultimately resulted in their control of Hong Kong. Britain had been used. The multinational corporations funding the rebellion had also funded dissident warlords, using the breakup of the repressive Shui regime to grab and hold Hong Kong and the New Territories for themselves. Those corporations renamed their corporate state the Hong Kong Free Enterprise Enclave. When Britain stepped forward to claim control, there had been laughter in the boardrooms. The corps had already obtained grants to the disputed territories from a dozen warlords in trade for arms and supplies. It wasn't strictly legal, but they had possesion. The few British ambassadors to Chinese leaders who hadn't had "accidents" were sent away in shame. Liaisons to the corporate consortium waited for appointments that never materialized.

The whole dishonorable episode was over and done before Glover had been born, but he felt the pain as if he had been one of those embarrassed ambassadors. Growing up, he had heard the stories from veterans of the expeditionary force, and had wondered why they didn't match the official histories he was taught in school. It wasn't until he was at university and under the tutelege of druids that he learned the true story. The duplicity and betrayals were so much like what he himself saw in Britain today. He had become certain that the megacorporations would very much like to see Britain dead, and that certainty had crystallized his belief that Britain could only be restored to glory by a return to the old ways.

They crossed the strait without incident and turned northward along the coast. Within an hour they would reach the inlet where the aircraft was hidden. Then, he would be on his way home with the prize that would make possible the first steps in restoring the glory that was Britain.

He looked back across the dark water. The glittering spires of Hong Kong were alight with the dazzle of false promises. They were ugly. This place made him feel soiled; he set his thoughts to the future.

8

Sam stared at Dodger. The elf sat slumped in the padded armchair he had appropriated, lost in the world of the Matrix, his fingers occasionally tapping a staccato rhythm on his Fuchi cyberdeck. Dodger looked relaxed, which was annoying. Sam poked him.

"Find anything yet?"

"By all that's good on the earth! Do you want to do it yourself?"

The elf's annoyance triggered Sam's own pent-up frustration. "Maybe I should!"

"Maybe you should just ask our host to shoot you. Glover's system is tough; it's a lot better protected than it should be. You may have been a hotshot researcher but you never were much of a decker. Besides, you're months behind the SOTA."

The elf's harsh appraisal of his abilities stung. "I don't need to be state-of-the-art to bust his hincky system."

Dodger laughed scornfully. "You're so hot! So sure! This 'hincky system' has got protection that has fried deckers better than you could ever dream of being."

"Well, if you're not getting anywhere, somebody has to."

"I've been working the deck for three days now. There are layers of this system that are glacial with IC. Positively cryogenic. You want to fry your brain? Do it with somebody else's hardware. I won't have you getting my chips iced just because you can't wait for a professional to do his job."

Dodger was right, of course. The elf was a pro at

unauthorized computer access. Even with the elf's guidance, Sam had been a barely adequate decker when they had run against the Renraku architecture last year. With all of his magical study and firearms practice, Sam had found no time to pursue Dodger's peculiar technomancy. Besides, the computer interface still gave Sam headaches, and the awakening of his magical powers had made the Matrix an even more uncomfortable place. His brash assertions and challenge of Dodger's competence were just manifestations of his frustrations.

"I'm sorry, Dodger. You're right. Do what you can."

" 'Twould seem my own patience is frayed as well, Sir Twist. I like this enforced guesting no more than you. 'Twould be best not to disturb me whilst I work, for I spoke truly of the devilish complexity of the system. Were you to distract me at the wrong moment, you would learn nothing more than how to care for an elven vegetable."

"That's not something I want to do, Dodger. Just let me know when you get something."

"I shall. But wander not too far lest you not be available should their ice lock me in."

"I'll be here," said Sam.

Dodger smiled with confidence. "I shall count on it."

The elf returned his attention to the Matrix, leaving Sam to contemplate their position. Glover had brought them to England, alleging that he needed them to protect Corbeau now that Burke was gone. Some need! The flight had been uneventful, Corbeau being delivered to a minor ATT installation without incident. Glover had told them to wait at his mansion, offering a handsome retainer. That had been four days ago. Four days in which they had not seen or heard from Glover.

Sam had already been suspicious of Glover's motives. He didn't like the man's attitude. Why had he let Dodger talk him into continuing to work with the man? Why? Because of the chance to find Janice. That slim hope had dwindled to nothing. Janice was on Yomi; she couldn't be further away from England.

But leaving wouldn't be simple. The mansion's population seemed to consist only of a handful of servants, who knew nothing. They were polite and efficient, but totally unhelpful. There were uniformed guards with guns as well, but he and Dodger only saw them when they tried to go beyond the immediate grounds. So far everyone had remained polite, but he was sure that the guards had orders to prevent Sam and Dodger from leaving the estate. Sam had tried an astral survey of the place and found many of the rooms blocked to him. He hadn't tried to get through those blocks, for there were half-world presences drifting around the mansion, hostile spirits that threatened him when he attempted to probe in certain directions.

As much as he disliked his surroundings and the treatment they were receiving, he knew that he couldn't just leave. He had seen the thing Glover had summoned in the Mihn-Pao warehouse. All of his senses screamed that it was *wrong*. His hair had stood on end when he had seen it form, his head throbbing with a warning howl. Glover had called it, and the list Dodger retrieved from Glover's computer said that he wanted a woman who might be his sister Janice. Now, whether or not the woman Glover sought was Janice, Sam wanted to know just who he had been working for. He had to know more about Glover and his organization.

It was hours before Dodger jacked out. His eyes were sunken and rimmed with the bruising of exhaustion.

" 'Twould seem that René Corbeau is not now nor ever has been connected to ATT.''

"You're sure?"

The elf quirked his mouth up in annoyance.

"Sorry." Sam ran his fingers up through his beard until his palms cradled his jaw. "Then Glover is a rogue."

" 'Tis a strong possibility."

"What about Burke?"

"The man is a shadow. There are tracks here and there, the occasional oblique reference, but all vanish if followed. Naetheless, the pattern is similar to one I have seen before. *That* shadow was a covert operative for the British government. By all the signs, I would venture that the late Burke was a special agent of some kind."

"A government agent?"

Dodger sighed. "You have been unbearable for days. Have you gone deaf now, too?"

"Sorry, Dodger." The apologies were becoming a habit. Sam's nerves were frayed, but Dodger's must be worse. The elf had been doing all the hard work.

"Apology accepted, Sir Twist." Dodger massaged his forehead, then stared down at his hands. Without looking up, he said, "I fear that I have not helped matters, either. I wish I had never gotten you involved in this."

"I got myself involved. You may have found the list with a name that might be my sister's, but I was the one who decided to chase that phantom. Going to the Orient was supposed to get us closer to her trail. We were supposed to find out what Glover was doing and who the woman was. Now look at us. We're in England and practically under house arrest. We still don't know anything."

"Not entirely true. We know that Glover, ATT rogue or not, is part of an efficient organization. While we were helping him acquire Sanchez and Corbeau, someone else has been completing the rest of the list.

At the rate they are moving, whatever plans they have are coming to a head soon.''

"You've gotten an update on the list? Let me see it.''

Dodger furrowed his brow as if the request was an annoyance.

"Wait a minute," he said, tapping keys. He snapped open the back of his cyberdeck and rolled out the monitor screen. After locking it, he turned it so Sam could see. "Here it is.''

Sam read it quickly. Five out of the seven names were listed as acquired. Janice Walters, still last on the list, was unacquired. Reason enough to stay. Her acquisition might be why Glover had retained them.

"So what do we do now?''

"Wait. With time and additional endeavor, I shall uncover more details.''

Sam shook his head. "You've done more than enough for today. If you decked now, you'd trip over the first node you encountered. You need a rest.''

" 'Tis true.'' Dodger stretched. Sam could hear his joints crack. " 'Tis also true that I need to get some exercise. Mayhap a walk in the garden would get the blood flowing again.''

The late afternoon sun slanted across the garden, throwing chill pools of shade from the carefully trimmed evergreen trees and shrubs. Winter had stripped the massive oaks of their leaves, leaving their shadows a net of enmeshing branches. Oppressed by the image, Sam guided their walk into the topiary maze. Within its walls, the grasping oaks were only visible near the outer edge.

The curving paths went from shadow into sunlight and back again, alternately chilling and warming them. They took turns at random, not caring whether they reached the maze's heart, simply satisfied to be moving. After a while, they found themselves at the edge of a clearing. The grass was brown, withered into dormancy by the season. In summer, the circle would have been lush, a quiet, pleasant place to laze in the sun. A quartet of stone blocks, apparently seats, were set at the cardinal points.

Dodger headed for the one bench still touched by the sun and stretched out on it. The block was long enough that only the elf's feet hung over the edge. Sam sauntered over to join him. When he reached the stone, he crouched.

"What do you make of this?"

"A popular place to look at the scenery?"

"No, these symbols. There's something carved along the side of the stone."

Dodger rolled over onto his side and ran his fingers along the carving. "Hmmm. Writing. Most of the letter forms seem to be roman, but the frequencies and juxtapositions are not English. 'Tis not a language I know."

Sam stared at the words, if they were words. Most of the letters were familiar, but they were not ordered into words he knew. Silently, he tried sounding out the syllables he knew. There seemed to be a rhythm to the sounds, an interlocking cadence. Like the locking spell Sally had taught him.

"Didn't you once tell me that all mansions had secret passages?"

Dodger chuckled. "You don't think that this is some kind of hidden entrance to an underground tunnel complex where Glover and his fellows plot the overthrow of all who stand in the way of their re-establishment of the British Empire? Speak the incantation and the stone shall rise?"

"Since you put it that way, why not?"

"Because this is not some cheap piece of fiction."

"But there does seem to be a crack. Like the top of the stone is a lid."

Dodger slid from the stone and examined the shadow Sam pointed out. "Mayhap."

"Give me a hand to lift it."

Lifting didn't work. Nor did sliding, pushing, pulling, or twisting. Sam knelt in front of the stone, frowning at it. Dodger sat on the grass, leaning back on his hands.

"A trick of the light. A crack in the rock."

"I'm going to try something," Sam said.

He stared at the symbols, clearing his mind of his frustration. He focused his magical energy, using the rhythmic mnemonic by which he recalled the counter to Sally's locking spell. Into its steady but broadening cadence, he wove the rhythm he had discerned in the carved symbols. Nothing happened. He tried again, working at smoothing the flow of his thoughts, forcing them deeper into the pattern of the spell. This time he felt something in the stone relax.

Tentatively, he reached out his hand and pressed on the top of the stone. The upper surface slid back slightly, revealing a dark hollow wide enough for fingers. Sam stood and slipped his fingers into the gap. He braced himself, ready for the weight, and found the stone swinging up far more easily than he expected.

Visions of concealed stairways and torch-lit underground passages flashed through his head. With a final heave, he swung the slab back. It rocked up, but instead of sliding free, stayed upright as if hinged to the back of the bench. He looked; it was.

The bench contained no entrance to secret places. It seemed filled with carefully folded white cloth. Sam tugged on one pile. It unfolded to reveal that it was a robe. Complex swirls were embroidered on its chest.

"Tacky rags," Dodger said. He was standing too, looking over Sam's shoulder.

"Wizard stuff."

" 'Tis hardly a surprise. We saw what he did to that Mihn-Pao gunner.''

"I've seen these symbols somewhere.''

"Mayhaps Friend Glover is Merlin Ambrosius re-awakened to save the world.''

"Merlin?'' Sam asked thoughtfully.

"Sir Twist, I jested.''

"But you jogged my memory. When I was studying about magic, I read some about the different kinds. A lot of sources suggest that Merlin, if he existed, was a druid. These are druidic symbols.''

Dodger poked at the bundles of cloth still in the bench. He disturbed the piles enough to reveal a golden glitter. Careful not to snag the cloth, he removed a small sickle. Its blade glittered a ruddy gold in the sunlight.

"A sacrificial knife?''

"A ritual implement for the cutting of the holy mistletoe. Druids are nature magicians, shamans of a peculiar breed. They were very prominent in the restoration of the wild lands in Ireland before the Shidhe took control.''

"Driven out like the snakes before Padraigh's wrath.'' Dodger tossed the sickle back into the bench. "There are enough robes here to clothe a dozen or so people. 'Twould seem Friend Glover is part of a circle of druids. Mayhap he acts in their interests and, if so, he might even be a government agent.''

"How so?''

"Know you not that the Lord Protector is a druid?''

"I didn't.''

" 'Tis true. His Green Party is a coalition of members of both Houses of Parliament.''

"I didn't realize the Greens were druids. I remember hearing how they ousted the last Conservative government after the restoration of the monarchy.''

"They were instrumental in the restoration and have

yet to face a serious challenge to their control of the government. England has not seen such a powerful interest group since Cromwell's Puritans.''

''Well, I hope that the druids are more open-minded than the Puritans. With the power they have in this country, they'd better be,'' Sam said. ''Everything I read about druids makes them out to be benevolent sorts. Of old, they were lore keepers and law speakers, prominent and worthy members of the community. In modern Britain, they are active in the recognition and training of magically active persons as well as taking a prominent role in higher education.''

Dodger prodded at the robes. '' 'Twould not be wise to expect more tolerance than the Puritans offered. Was not druidism a sort of a religion and druids its priests?''

''Before the Awakening, maybe so. The cults subscribing to druidism built their belief systems on idiosyncratic reconstructions of old Celtic paganism. They had more than their share of egotistical false prophets. Nobody really knows exactly how the old druids operated, since they kept no written records.

''The druids of the Sixth World are the inheritors of that tradition, but I'm not sure that any of them are direct descendents. When the magic came back, some magicians built their focus parameters around what they believed to be druidic tenets and rituals. Their totems were things like Sun, Oak, Zephyr, Stream, and Stag. Forest and growing land stuff. Naturally, they called themselves druids. Maybe it's their mindset or maybe it's the way the magic works, but mostly they have confined their activities to Europe. Although they were quite active in the restoration of the land in the isles and on the continent, they weren't aggressive like the tribal magicians in North America. I hadn't known they were so involved in British politics.

"England has been prospering under the Greens. If Glover is a druid, we're probably being paranoid about his motives; the delay may be nothing sinister at all. He may just be waiting for the right phase of the moon or something to undertake the next part of his operation. Druids worry a lot about astrological cycles."

Dodger rubbed his fingers together, switching his gaze from them to the contents of the bench. He said thoughtfully, "Let us hope that he is not a fanatic about this stuff."

9

Glover was uncomfortable in the closeness of the room, finding the scent of the many bouquets oppressive. Some of the flowers were wilted, some fresh cut. The mixture of floral perfume and organic decay was an olfactory confusion. How did Hyde-White stand it? Or was the old man no longer able to smell the blossoms with which he surrounded himself?

Hyde-White sat enthroned behind an ancient oak desk whose top was eccentric, the shape of a crosscut bole. His massive gut was wedged into a concavity that allowed him easy reach of the telecom on one hand and the bank of internal intercoms on the other. The grey light of the telecom monitor, the brightest source of illumination in the room, lit his face from below, reversing the normal pattern of highlights. The lighting roughened the softness of the broad face and made his eyes a glitter in pools of darkness.

Glover felt sweat snake out from his armpits to trickle down his sides despite the room's lack of heat. He didn't have Hyde-White's insulation of bulk, but his fear of the old man's disapproval warmed him uncomfortably. He felt the temperature rise as the dark eyes across the desk left the telecom screen and focused on him. It was as bad as it had been at university when the old man had been his teacher.

"So you called upon the guardian I set over you."

"I did."

A bushy, white eyebrow rose. "And?"

"It was a powerful spirit, sir." That was no more than the truth. He wished that he knew how to control such spirits. "You are an accomplished conjurer."

"And you are jealous." Hyde-White interlaced his fingers and rested his hands on the rotund vastness of his belly. "Jealousy is a power that can fuel a man, goading him to reach for his dreams. You could have such spirits at your call, you know. I sense that you have the potential. You need only harness it. A man who possesses such power can rise far."

"I am content with my place, sir," Glover lied.

"If I believed that, I would not bother talking to you." Hyde-White chuckled. The sound was an almost subsonic rumble. "Ambition is not a sin, Andrew. A man without ambition is a husk. A useless scarecrow upon whom the crows shall sit and laugh.

"I am old, Andrew, and not what I once was. In these latter days, it is necessary for me to work with others to accomplish all that I desire. Were I younger, things might be otherwise. But time has taught me that one can get lost pondering might-have-beens. The world's enduring lesson is that opportunities must be seized. Fail to act with resolution and you are lost. All your dreams turn to dust."

The old man was being annoyingly roundabout; making suggestions and prodding him. Was this a test? Or was it something more complicated? A bid for power within the Circle, perhaps? Glover knew his personal power was greater than Hyde-White's; he had read the old man's aura during working sessions. But raw power wasn't everything. Hyde-White was steeped in knowledge, experience, and subtlety beyond even *his* venerable years. Glover had no intention of being Hyde-White's stalking horse.

"What do you mean by all this, sir? Are you suggesting that I disrupt the Circle in some sort of bid for power? I am loyal to the cause, sir. I will not throw our Circle into chaos on the eve of our triumph."

"The Circle is weak."

"We shall be strong when the ritual is completed. The blood will restore the land and the Circle shall become its guardians. We need no longer chafe under the short-sighted leadership of the Lord Protector."

"Perhaps the Circle will be stronger. But a circle is chain of individuals dedicated to the same ideals. Like any chain, it is no stronger than its weakest link, and no chain can remain intact when that weak link is subject to stresses beyond its strength. The ritual we contemplate is a powerful force. It must be, to restore the balance so woefully tilted when the Lord Protector snubbed unforgiving stars and neglected proper observances. This work shall demand much of any who attempt it, and the forces which will rise to our call shall demand even more from the leader of the ritual team. Our leader must be strong, else things will go awry. We may do more harm than good."

The old man's words were disturbing, but not just for their content. "Why are you telling me this?"

"Because I have studied you. I think that you believe as I do. That the land should always have been our first concern, and that we have failed as its custodians. We were blinded by our arrogance and thought ourselves rulers instead of stewards. Our species has failed the earth."

Hyde-White was perceptive and had touched the truth of Glover's convictions. Or at least the surface of them; even stewards had ambitions. But a good steward knew enough to set those ambitions aside until his charge was healthy. For what was a steward, after all, but a parasite? No parasite survived by killing its host.

"I see by your face, Andrew, that I am right about you. The land's pain echoes in your ears as loudly as it does in mine. I am speaking to you because I do not believe you are one of Neville's sheep. You do not seek the land's restoration out of some misguided longing for the restored glory of an aristocratic heritage. You know that it is a task that must be done for our very survival. What ambitions you have, you have harnessed to await that time."

"At first, I thought that you were proposing that we break the Circle. I will not do that. The land must be restored and the ritual is our only chance," Glover said. "You yourself brought the text from which we devised the ritual to the attention of the Circle. Why are you so troubled about it now? Are you having second thoughts about its efficacy?"

"Second thoughts came and went three years ago. I have progressed far beyond them. While Neville and his misguided followers have been chasing down the bloodlines, I have been studying the lore. I fear that all may not be as simple as Neville would have it." Hyde-White paused, allowing the brief moment of silence to add weight to his next words. "The ritual is not entirely safe."

"We all know that there will be some personal danger. All rituals involve risk."

Hyde-White nodded gravely. "Risks to the participants are unavoidable; but that is not what I mean. If the ritual is not performed absolutely correctly, the consequences may be grave, indeed. The gathered power may be warped and, in its corruption, grow to threaten the land itself. Are you ready to unleash more horror on our burdened land?''

"Neville would never allow that. For all his arrogant assumptions of superiority, he feels the land's pain as much as we do. He would not harm it.''

"He may not be able to prevent the harm from happening.''

"And you can?''

Hyde-White pressed his thick lips together, the area around his mouth going pale. ''I do not know. When we realized that the Lord Protector was blind to the need, we formed our circle and elected Neville as archdruid of our ritual circle. I fear that we may not have chosen wisely and that his leadership will have dire consequences. But my fear will not lead me to abandon you all, and my conscience will not allow such a breach of trust. I will be present and do all I can to see that the ritual proceeds as it should. But if it begins to go awry, I would like to know that there is someone else who appreciates that we may have to change our plans. Someone strong enough to take charge and lead us away from disaster. The land needs our help, Andrew. We must do whatever is necessary to heal it.''

"So we all swore.''

"Indeed, we did. But an oath is not strength in itself. I fear that Neville will not have the strength to see us through.''

"He is a greater shaman than I.''

"You are young and strong. Though your skill and knowledge may be less than his, your power is greater. Skill and knowledge may be increased with relative ease, but raw power is the gift of the young. Once squandered, it may only be bought at a dear price.

"I am old. With age, my mundane power has grown, while the tribulations of life and magic have leached my occult powers slowly away. I believe I can see clearly what must be done, but I am no longer sure I have the power to do it. You have that power, Andrew. I feel it pulsing in you. I can show you the way, and you can do what must be done.''

Hyde-White lapsed into silence, apparently content to let Glover consider his arguments. If the old man's fears were real, there was no recourse. The land came first. If this was all a smoke screen for a power play, Glover wasn't sure that he wanted to be involved. Neville was an influential man; his friends were primarily members of the nobility, who could use their influence to make or break Glover's mundane career. But Hyde-White was a power as well. His GWN Corporation held a significant portion of ATT stock, as well as controlling interests in several other minor multinationals. The sum of his interests gave him considerable direct influence in the corporate community and made him more powerful than any one of Neville's cronies. Glover would need time to sort out his options.

''I will think about what you say, sir.''

Hyde-White smiled broadly. ''I have faith that you will make the right decision, Andrew.''

10

''So his lordship wants them drugged, does he?''

Sam's hunger vanished and he stopped instantly, his hand mere centimeters from the kitchen door. Finding the servants' attentions uncomfortable, he had approached quietly, not wishing to disturb them. If they had known he was hungry, they would have insisted on fixing something for him rather than letting him get his own. Their solicitousness, while pleasant at first, had begun to chafe as much as the confinement. Now he was glad that he had tried to keep his kitchen raid quiet. He listened to the voices on the other side of the door.

"That's what Norman said," a deep voice replied. "I don't know why, though."

"You never know, Cholly."

"Cholly's got a point, Bert. They may be Yanks, but I don't like the idea of slipping them something. I mean, what's it gonna be next? Slitting their throats while they sleep?"

"Criminy! You're such a whiner, Georgie. You're almost as bad as Cholly. It's not like we were poisoning them or nothing. The stuff is only going to put them to sleep a little early. They won't feel a thing."

"But how do you know, Bert? The stuff in that bottle Norman brought could be poison. We'd never know it until the Yanks died in their chairs. Then we'd be murderers."

"You ain't got nothing to worry about, Georgie. I used this stuff before. Got me my last three wives."

"Bert, you hound."

Laughter erupted. The loudest seemed to belong to Bert.

"They'll never even taste it in the wine. A couple of sips and fifteen minutes later, they'll get real sleepy and want to head straight to bed. We just let them. If they was birds, we could have a grand old time. They'd never know. Course they might feel a bit sore in the morning."

Cholly's deep voice trammeled on the last gasps of a fresh burst of guffaws. "Burt, why do his lordship want them to sleep?"

"Blimey, but you are slow, Cholly. His lordship's got company coming in tomorrow night. He obviously don't want his house guests to know about it."

"Why don't he just ask the Yanks to stay in their rooms?"

"Because they are Yanks, ya twit. Yanks never do what they're told to do."

The scattered laughter was punctuated by the scape of a chair. Sam backed away from the door. The talk continued, but he couldn't hear it distinctly. He had just settled in a dark corner where he thought he would be safe from a casual glance, when the door swung wide spilling light into the hall. Bert the groundskeeper stepped through.

"Keep the fire burning, boys. I'll be back after I make my rounds."

Assurances and mock insults drifted from the kitchen. Bert waved them off and shuffled down the hall, oblivious to his surroundings. Sam didn't move until he was sure that Bert had enough time to leave the building. Then he headed back upstairs. There'd be no raid on the larder tonight.

Pretending to be affected by the wine had been easy—far easier than waiting for the servants to make the check on the supposedly drugged guests so that they could assure their master that the ploy had been successful. But they came at last, and Sam's lack of response to their calling of his name and the tentative prods that followed satisfied them that the Yanks were safely under the influence.

The house grew quiet.

Sam crept to Dodger's room, avoiding the boards he had learned creaked the loudest. Together they waited while they heard Glover go to the door to greet his guests. When things again quieted, Sam and Dodger crept forth. From the landing, light spilling into the main hall told them that Glover had chosen to entertain in a room that Sam had been unable to penetrate astrally. A quick check assured him that the barrier still held. Any penetration of Glover's secrets would have to be physical.

Sam and Dodger skulked through the upper hall, settling where they could get a view of the meeting chamber. The room's only illumination was the fire in the massive stone hearth at one end, but that made it far brighter than the hall and upper stories. The sliding doors to the room were open, allowing a rectangle of flickering light to fall across the ancient flooring and scale the paneled wall opposite the door. At first Sam thought that Glover and his cronies were foolish to leave the panels open, but then he remembered his own eavesdropping of the previous night. No servant would creep to the door and listen from concealment, for they would be seen. Any who crept close would be disclosed to those within the room as well; the hall's flooring would announce their passage and alert the conspirators. Likewise, a servant returning from the upper stories in defiance of his earlier dismissal would be betrayed by the creaking of the old staircase.

Sam's position provided him with a partial view of the room. Near its center, Glover sat in a comfortable armchair. In a matching chair at his side, a position of honor, sat an older man with grey hair and a trim grey mustache. From the deference shown to him, Sam pegged him as Sir Winston Neville, the only name he had heard Glover use in greeting the others. Neville's welcome had been the most effusive, so it was likely that he would be given the most honored seat. A younger man, by the cast of his aristocratic face a son or cousin to Neville, stood behind the chair. Occasionally Sam caught glimpses of three others moving about the room.

The great outer door opened, swinging wide on silent hinges. There had been no knock or bell chime. A man entered, striding ponderously forward. He was huge and walked with a huffing that emphasized the difficulty he had in moving his enormous bulk. The moonlight sent glints from the sweat that beaded among the sparse white hairs of his head. A casual swat sent the door arcing shut as he started down the hall.

"Hyde-White is here," announced one of the men in the room. They were all staring at the doorway when the obese man reached the arch.

Newcomer and gathered conspirators faced each other. They exchanged words in a language that Sam didn't recognize, although it seemed to have echoes of English. Having finished what seemed a ritual greeting, Glover inclined his head and waved a hand in invitation.

Hyde-White rolled forward. As the jutting prow of his obesity passed over the threshold, the air in the doorway shimmered. A line of sparks ran around the fat man's shape, making a glittering outline as he passed the magical barrier that sealed the room. He spoke as soon as the last sparkle died, his voice a resonant rumble like the distant growling of summer thunder.

"Please excuse my tardiness. There were some affairs in the Atzlan office to sort out, and my personal attention was required. I trust you have not reached any important conclusions without me."

"We were having Barnett fill us in on his last acquisition," the grey-haired man said.

"My apologies for the interruption, Sir Winston. Please continue, Mr. Barnett," Hyde-White said as he marched deeper into the room. "I'm sure I will be fascinated."

The fat man ponderously passed from view. Sam could tell when Hyde-White sat, for the bannister in front of his face trembled slightly. The pinch-faced man, who was obviously Barnett, cleared his throat before continuing.

"I really don't have much more to say. My mission went smoothly and there were no problems. It's a shame that we cannot all say the same. Eh, Glover?"

Glover, who had been staring at the fire, swiveled his head around to face Barnett. "Are you suggesting that I have failed the Circle, Mr. Barnett?"

"Anyone could lose valuable employees in such a venture. Although Mr. Burke was one of our more exceptional agents, I would hardly fault you for his passing. The fortunes of war, I am sure." Barnett sniffed. "I am merely referring to certain loose ends."

Stepping around from behind the chair, the younger Neville said, "Yes, Glover. What has become of the shadowrunners who acompanied you from Hong Kong? We have heard that they are still in the country."

Glover addressed his answer to the older Neville, as if he had spoken, instead. "They are upstairs, asleep."

"Why haven't you dismissed them? Were they to stumble downstairs into our meeting it would be most inconvenient. You should have left them in Hong Kong." The younger Neville's pointing finger of accusation didn't distract Glover.

"I did not think that a wise idea at the time, Sir Winston. With Mister Burke eliminated, I deemed the additional protection they could offer to be necessary. Had I encountered additional difficulties, the safety of Monsieur Corbeau might have been threatened. I saw his safe return as my primary responsibility. The day draws near."

"You should have dismissed them as soon as you arrived here safely," young Neville insisted.

Glover shook his head slowly. "By then, they had seen enough to connect me to ATT. I thought it inadvisable to let them loose with that knowledge."

"Then you should have had them killed," Barnett

said. "You swore the secrecy oath along with the rest of us."

"Indeed," Glover said, folding his arms across his chest. "That is precisely why they are still alive. If they were not disposed of cleanly and completely, there would be an investigation. We do not need inquiries from the Lord Protector's Oversight Board at this time. But once we have completed our ritual, we will no longer need to remain hidden, and without a need for absolute secrecy we may dispose of them easily. For now, they remain here, believing themselves on retainer for an upcoming shadowrun. The deception is sufficient; they remain ignorant of the Circle and our goal."

"You have badgered Mr. Glover enough," rumbled Hyde-White. "The crucial question is the suitability of Mr. Gordon."

"Suitability has been addressed and confirmed beyond any question. While Mr. Gordon remains uncrowned, there is no question of the sanctity of his bloodline. Had not the father-in-law of the current holder of the throne been so prominent in the work of gathering the scattered survivors of the royal family, Mr. Gordon would be our crowned sovereign. That unfortunate turn of events is but one of the hurdles we strive to overcome. The false king only contributes to the land's woes. But crowned or not, Edward Arthur Charles Gordon-Windsor is the chalice of mystic power necessary to restore the land." Sir Winston Neville threw back his shoulders and tugged at his waistcoat to seat it properly. "I spoke with him before coming here tonight. I can assure you all he is ready to accept his part in the ritual. He seems eager to take his place as the seventh, for he believes as we do. The land must live."

"The land must live," the others echoed.

The seventh? If Gordon was the seventh, what was

the name of Janice Walters doing on Glover's list? Sam looked at Dodger. The elf was staring fixedly ahead. He seemed intent on listening to the conspirators. There would be questions to ask later.

11

Illusion was the heart's blood of the Shidhe Courts.

When Hart glanced around her, taking in the wild array of sights, sounds, and smells of the Seelie Court, she could never be sure if what she saw was real or an image that was the result of a magical spell. Checking astrally didn't always help. The great amounts of magical energy and the almost continual activity of the magicians of the court made assensing difficult. Much of the magic was defensive, for members of the court were often at odds with each other. Open warfare was forbidden, but pranks, taunts, and even clandestine, oblique struggles were common. Some of the magic was defensive on a less immediate level. The court had attracted elves and dwarves from around the world; some were concerned that their appearance was not up to the court standards. They used illusion to glamorize themselves, for the ugly were perforce members of the Unseelie Court, the co-ruling rivals with whom the Fair Folk shared the control of the Shidhe Dominion of Ireland.

The Seelie Court proclaimed Ireland to be a magical state, claiming that the Shidhe lords were the ancient proprietors who had returned to claim their rightful lands. But although they reveled in magic and officially held technology in scorn, the magician lords took every advantage of science. The computer facil-

ities and combat simulators she had been using for the past week were ample proof of that. Of course, the Shidhe would not speak of such things in public forums. They denied having or even needing such things. They had them, all right, and their technology was cutting-edge. They simply hid their technological workings or cloaked them in illusion. Image was very important to the metahuman rulers of Ireland.

The great double orichalcum doors to the inner court opened, swinging wide until they came to rest against the walls of vines in which they were set. Two elves, outsiders by their dress, walked through the arch. As they passed Hart, the woman nodded in friendly recognition. It was nothing personal. Hart's upswept fall of hair was the latest style outside. Even though she wore local garb, the hairdo marked Hart as a visitor to this fey land, and most visitors, though strangers to each other, found other visitors more congenial company than the locals. The man, glowering beneath his dark brows, didn't seem to notice Hart existed.

A voice from beyond the arch called Hart's name; it was time for her audience. She felt no trepidation. She had been expecting the summons to come soon.

She almost tripped as a gaggle of leshy scurried by in front of her just as she stepped forward. The short humanoids were a common sight among the verdant forest-city of the Seelie Court, but Hart didn't like them. They were flighty, dirty, and unkempt; their bark and leaf garments were rudimentary and showed no sense of fashion at all. She often doubted if they were truly intelligent at all. Even when she could make out the words their high-pitched voices mangled, the leshy were always either asking an impertinent, silly, pointless question or expressing some obscure and contradictory concern about the harmonious nature of what was going on around them. She cursed the group that had impeded her, and they scattered, laughing.

The doors closed behind her as she crossed the threshold. For a while she walked in darkness, which defeated her elven eyes. The floor beneath her feet felt like earth, firm yet with a resilience unequalled by synthetic carpets. The light level increased until it was comparable to that in a deep forest at night. She could smell the leaf mold and the fragrance of night-blooming flowers. Ahead of her she saw an open space. The light was brighter there, as if stars and moon shed their full light. No city-born plexer had ever seen such a night sky. No one would expect to at this time of day; it was mid-afternoon.

She entered the clearing, finding it little more than a wide lane between the great boles of ancient rowan and hawthorn trees. Amid the trees she could see the strolling or standing shapes of members of the inner court. None spoke to her, or even showed interest. She continued walking ahead.

At the end of the lane, the packed earth mounded in several steps to a raised area, behind which stood a singularly massive oak tree entwined about with mistletoe. Three thrones stood on the flat surface. The seat on the left was placed near the front edge. Though it was small, bold carvings painted in bright colors embellished every surface, making it seem larger than it was. Symbols of life and energy dominated the decorative motif in a vibrant statement of youth. The center throne stood well back, almost hidden in the shadows. Though the light which struck it revealed an intricacy of carving, Hart could discern no details. To the right of that great chair and set nearer and fully in the light was the third throne. Like the others, it was a masterpiece of the carver's art. The bold relief was accentuated by subtle painting that enhanced the relief to the point that many of the designs seemed to stand free from the panels. Of the three thrones, it was the only one occupied.

The woman who sat in the chair was exquisite, of a delicacy that even made Hart's own elven slimness seem fleshy. The lady had the ageless look of a mature elf, a youthfulness that would fade only as she approached the end of her allotted span. Her hair was of such fineness that it drifted in the slightest breeze that snaked across the dais, becoming a mist floating about her shoulders that owed more to light than to substance. Slender fingers toyed with a few errant strands, absently plaiting knots that vanished in a flick of those same tapering digits. Her eyes were the transparent blue of deep ice. Though she wore no symbols of rank, Hart had no doubt that she was the ruler here; the woman's bearing was that of a sovereign.

A male elf stood on the first step down from the dais. His name was Bambatu and his dark skin was an ebon contrast to the porcelain fairness of the hall's mistress. He no longer wore the elegant business suit in which he had recruited Hart. His bare chest shone as if it had been oiled, which perhaps it had. Around his loins he wore a cloth of many bright colors woven in mystical designs. Bangles, bands, and chains of gold and brazen orichalcum hung around his neck, waist, wrists, and ankles. He made a magnificent barbarian. She found his long, smooth muscles much more appealing than the over-developed travesties that norms seemed to insist their trid heroes possess. He watched her, too, his large dark eyes pools of sparkling interest.

When Hart reached the dais, she knelt at the beginning of the steps, holding her head bowed. The text she had read on formal courtesy suggested that such behavior was appropriate.

"The Lady Brane Deigh bids you stand, Katherine Hart," said Bambatu.

Hart did as she was bidden. Bambatu had recruited her, but Lady Deigh was her employer. The Lady's eyes met hers in a coolly appraising stare. Suspecting the importance of the moment, Hart held her gaze steady. A ghost of a smile touched the lady's lips.

"You have sheltered under my roof and accepted my coin, Hart. By the laws of the land that makes you *milessaratish*. You understand this obligation?"

Hart inclined her head. "I do, Lady." *But understanding doesn't mean agreement. You've hired your talent, but I haven't become your liegewoman. That sort of thing is your concept, not mine.*

"Very well. You were told of our opposition to the Hidden Circle, that you might prepare yourself to face them. Lord Bambatu informs me that you have availed yourself of our resources, seeking to hone your skills and study your adversaries. This is laudable. But the time for preparations is past, for tomorrow is the Solstice. Do you stand ready to confront them?"

"Yes, Lady."

"Then you have my blessings, Hart." She stood and walked across the dais towards Bambatu. He bowed to her as she approached. The Lady paused at the edge of the stairs and turned her face to Hart. *"Ozidano teheron, milessaratish. Imo medaron co versakhan."*

Hart replied to the formal dismissal with the ritual recasting of Lady Deigh's commands. "I leave my existence behind, Lady. At your word, I am the death of your enemies."

12

The sky was beginning to grey with the coming of dawn. As it grew, the light let them make out the sentry. Their patience had paid off; he was drowsing.

So far their departure from the mansion had gone unnoticed. The last barrier, the gate, lay before them. Once through, they would be out of Glover's hands. They knew from Dodger's tap of a NavSat that Glover's estate lay in the southwest of England. There was a town only a few miles away. From there, transportation to the Bristol metroplex would be a simple matter.

Sam drew his Narcoject Lethe.

The guard jerked at the impact of the dart and slid to the ground in a subdued clatter. While Sam injected an antidote, Dodger tapped into the gate control system. Three minutes later they were on the road to Taunton, the gate closed and locked behind them. In a few more minutes, the sentry would awaken, propped against the guard house. With little evidence to the contrary, he should think that he had dozed off naturally. If their luck held, it might be an hour or two until their absence was noticed.

The Black Down Hills were strange territory, but for those first minutes of freedom, Sam felt more at home than he had on Glover's estate. The growing dawn dampened his spirits as it unveiled a desolate landscape. Like much of England, the hills had been ravaged; first by overpopulation and industrialization, then by the ecological terrorism to which the country had been subjected in the early part of the century. It was a scarred and battered land, tortured further by the natural and man-made disasters that had plagued it in the last few years. The awfulness began to weigh him down.

Dodger trudged at his side. He and the elf had talked little beyond the necessary planning for their escape. Dodger's contributions had been terse, completely lacking in his usual banter and archaic style. Sam hadn't minded; he wasn't sure that he wanted to talk to Dodger just yet. The druids' talk last night had raised uncomfortable questions.

They reached the outskirts of Taunton without observing any signs of pursuit. The relief must have heartened Dodger; the elf tried a conversational gambit. Perhaps he was motivated by the need to discuss some matters before they were surrounded by curious ears.

"Sir Twist, don't you find it intriguing that so august a personage as Sir Winston Neville would be involved in these druidical shenanigans?"

"No," Sam replied brusquely. Druids weren't the only ones who were pulling shenanigans.

"What about this 'uncrowned sovereign' business? Does not that compel your curiosity, Sir Twist?"

"No."

"Sir Twist, the paucity of your response suggests that you harbor some unspoken concern. Is this so?"

Of course it was so. Dodger's nagging at the druids' plans only gave credence to Sam's suspicions. They were not safe yet and they were beginning to encounter people, so all he said was, "Yes."

The elf lapsed into silence again.

Taunton's grimy buildings soon surrounded them. The town offered them a chance to get some supplies. Beyond the obvious necessities of food, water, and ammunition, they had need of protective gear; there was a stage four smog alert in Bristol and a sane person wouldn't be outside a breath mask. If they wanted to reach their destination quickly, they also needed a means of transportation.

Finding connections wasn't easy, and Sam didn't make it easier. He stubbornly remained silent, forcing Dodger to do all their talking. Watching the elf struggle to conduct his dealings with the locals, Sam felt a perverse satisfaction when he saw the sidelong glances that the passing Brits gave Dodger. Though most concealed their feelings behind a veneer of politeness whenever addressed directly, Sam was sure that the locals didn't like elves much.

They got what they needed, but the locals drove harder bargains than seemed reasonable, even allowing for the fact that they were dealing with strangers. Dodger was forced to pay a premium price for the beat-up old bike, which was the only vehicle anyone would part with. The decrepit thing was alcohol-powered, and its hard rubber tires were gouged and greying. They'd be lucky if it didn't disintegrate at the first bump, but they didn't have time to wait for a better deal.

Though pursuit remained unseen, they had no assurance that the druids were not busy trying to track them down. Dodger and Sam would be safer in a metroplex where outsiders were more common and they could lose themselves among the masses. The sooner they hit the plex, the safer they'd be.

The ride to Bristol was every bit as bone-shattering as the bike's condition promised. Unlike Seattle, Bristol didn't have a wall; it wasn't an enclave of alien territory in the midst of a green and fertile land. The drab grey and brown countryside gradually seemed to blue into drab grey and brown cottages that merged almost imperceptibly into drab grey and brown multistory buildings. They passed the boundaries of the sprawl without noticing.

Dodger abandoned the decrepit bike as soon as he spotted a rail station, announcing that they would be able to use the public transportation from there. Bristol, though a separate entity, had good transport links with the great English Sprawl that slashed across the island from Brighton to Liverpool. The elf seemed to assume that the bigger metroplex was their destination, and made vague references to connections he had there.

Now that they were in an urban environment, Dodger appeared to be in less of a hurry. He dragged Sam through a series of seedy pubs and squalid shops. Several rounds of haggling later, the elf was in possession of the access code to an over-priced, under-heated flat on the twentieth story of a pillar high-rise.

The building was supposed to have been part of the support system for an enclosing dome, fashioned after the one over the London district of the English Sprawl. Bristol's dome, like those of every other sprawl district except downtown London, had never been completed. Fragments of the biofibre mesh that had stretched between the pillar high-rises still clung to one edge of the building. The splotchy fabric fluttered in the clammy breeze from the Bristol Channel. Sam wondered how much the ambiance contributed to the price.

The apathetic owner did not bother to accompany his new tenants to their flat. While Dodger prowled around, Sam stared through the filthy transparex. Across the channel, Sam could see the smog bank that hid the Cardiff plex. Beneath him, grey Bristol bustled about its business; but the smog covered any sign of the activity and hid the tawdry Christmas decorations and neon and trideo exhortations for gift-giving that had festooned the streets. It could be any day, any sprawl.

He and Dodger were safely ensconced for the mo-

ment, anonymous among the masses of humanity. Time for a confrontation.

Without turning from the window, Sam said, ''You knew that Janice was never on their list, didn't you?''

The sudden cessation of sound behind him told him he had achieved the effect he wanted. He turned to find Dodger staring at him. The elf's expression was uncertain.

''Sir Twi . . . Sam, I will not lie to you. I knew, but . . .''

''You already have lied to me,'' Sam said bitterly.

''I never said that the name on the list belonged to your sister. I merely suggested that . . .''

''You meant for me to believe it. You deliberately deceived me. Go ahead. I want to hear you deny it.''

Dodger swallowed, then spent a moment considering what to say. ''I cannot deny that I deceived you.''

''Why not? What's another lie? You're very good at words; surely you can find some. Don't you want me to trust you anymore? Or doesn't it matter anymore?'' Sam asked. ''Why not lie again? Tell me that you were deceived, too. Tell me that somebody forced you to fake the list. I'll believe it. I'm just a stupid norm, ripe for a few elven tricks.''

''Sam, I . . .'' Dodger ran a hand through his shock of hair. ''What does it matter? Whatever I say, you won't believe me. How you got involved isn't really important. You're involved now, and you have to believe what is happening.''

''Do I?''

''Yes, you do. These druids are serious trouble. They've got to be dealt with. You may not want to believe me about the importance of what is going down, but the facts should convince you.'' Dodger tapped his cyberdeck. ''Before we left Glover's mansion, I swiped a few copies of a few files and stashed them in a little-used corner of an ATT mainframe.

Once I knew we were dealing with druids and that the Solstice was almost upon us, I used the date as a cue to run a similarity search. I could see that I was getting somewhere, but that it would take time, so I set a few special programs to work. If no one has disturbed my creative time-sharing arrangement, I should have a few revealing files to be read. Will you look at them?''

Sam shrugged. "I'm not going anywhere for a while; looking won't hurt.''

Despite his predisposition to disbelief, Sam found himself engrossed by the files Dodger had cracked. If they were real and not another concoction, Glover and his cronies were involved in evil doings.

The files told a tale worse than Haesslich's murders. The dragon had sacrificed lives in his search for personal aggrandizement; murders, yes, but incidental to his desires. These druids were methodically planning death.

Most of the data was in a language that the computer tentatively identified as Old English. Without the proper translation programs, most of the files remained unreadable, but enough of the contents were clear to make the druids' intent unmistakable. It all seemed to revolve around a special ritual of immense power. There were several unambiguous references to the "king who must die" as the key to the "cycle of restoration." Other passages referred to "scions of untainted bloodlines" as important components of the ritual. Sam had little doubt that these "scions" would turn out to be the people on Glover's infamous list. They, too, were to be sacrificed as the druids sought to end human lives for the magical energy that would be released. Deliberate, cold-blooded human sacrifice. Black magic of the worst kind.

It was all too horrible to believed. *If* it could be believed.

"I don't like what you are showing me, Dodger. I don't like it at all."

"Neither do I, Sir Twist. 'Tis what I feared, though. Suspicion of this evil drove me to deceive you. Had I simply told you about it without evidence, you would have rightly scoffed."

The elf so casually admitted his toying with Sam's belief in his honesty. Hadn't they been friends, shadow brothers? Where was the elf's trust? Didn't he think he could be open with Sam? Sam had considered Dodger a friend ever since the elf had helped him after his escape from Renraku. How had he deceived himself into believing that this elf was his friend? Friends didn't lie to friends. Friends didn't deceive friends.

He let his bitterness fill his voice as he said, "You deceived me right into helping them with their foul magic."

"I had thought that we could stop it from the inside," Dodger said forlornly.

Sam couldn't help but wonder if the hint of regret he detected in the elf's tone was real. If it was real, did the elf regret what he had done or did he regret the lost opportunity to work against the druids? Did it matter?

"Well, we're not inside anymore, and I don't see how we can stop them. If the druids mean to try their ritual on the Solstice, there's no time left. We're thousands of miles from our home turf. We've got no resources but what we're carrying, and some of these druids are the heads of major corporations. They could put out a contract on us and the bill would show up in petty cash. What could just the two of us do?"

"I have friends in London."

"Why am I not surprised? Why didn't you just take on these druids with them? Or was it too much fun to dupe the norm?"

Dodger sighed. "I thought you would understand. I

thought that you would see the need to stop these people.''

"Oh, I can see the need to stop them, all right,'' Sam snapped. "Anyone planning their kind of evil magic must be stopped. I would think so even if you hadn't dragged me into the middle of this. You could have just asked me, but instead you had to play the puppet master. You made sure that I was involved, didn't you? You made me a party to their crime.''

Dodger straightened away from Sam's accusing finger. "We both became involved inadvertently, Sir Twist. I will not take your guilt on my shoulders alone. You agreed to and completed the snatch on Sanchez before anyone knew what these druids planned.''

Dodger was right about that. They had gotten involved before Dodger had shown him the false list. Sam had been the one who had arranged the run with Mr. Johnson-Glover. Dodger had had nothing to do with it beyond his decking responsibilities.

If Dodger hadn't led him into sticking with Glover, Sam might never have learned of the druids' plan until after they had performed their sacrifice. Then, he would have been an accessory without any chance to avert the crime. As things stood, he had a chance to rescue Sanchez and Corbeau and the others. Were Sam's hurt feelings worth people's lives?

"Your London friends have resources?''

Dodger nodded.

"Then we'd better figure out where and how to apply them.''

Dodger offered a tentative smile. Sam returned it, offering a truce. Once the druids were foiled, there would be time to sort things out. Until then, there was work to do. Constant argument would not get it done.

"I will contact my friends immediately,'' Dodger said.

"Hold on. I want to make sure we are in agreement

as to exactly what is going on. We can't know what we need to have until we know what we need to do. I want to have as little involvement with your 'friends' as possible.''

"Very well, Sir Twist. I trust you will evaluate the problem clearly. I trust you.''

Dodger paused, offering Sam the opportunity to make a statement of reconciliation. Unready to do so, Sam let the silence grow. Dodger cleared his throat and said, "So, Sir Twist, where shall we start?''

"If this ritual involves the shedding of royal blood, it is designed to channel a lot of power. That kind of magical energy needs to be confined and focused. They would need a special ritual site, someplace that would allow them to concentrate and then direct the energies they unleash.''

"'Tis a reasonable conclusion. From the look in your eye, Sir Twist, you have a thought.''

"Yeah. Remember what I told you about the druids being something of a religion?''

"Yes.''

"Well. Religions have holy places and an important shrine would seem a likely place for their ritual. For the druids, holy places were groves of trees and circles of stones. Once Britain was dotted with them. By now though, most of them are gone.''

"Mayhap archaeological survey records?''

"It would take a lot of time to sort through. England's got a lot of history. Besides, we don't really know what might be druidic and what's not. We could play guessing games for days.''

"'Twould seem that there is no other choice.''

"I recall a theory that stated all magical places are connected magically. According to the model, there are connections between such places through which mana can flow, sort of like datalines in the Matrix. Once the magic came back, some magicians

found that these connections actually worked sometimes, allowing spells to be cast beyond normal parameters. Nobody really understands what these
manalines are or how they work, but most of the
research was done in Britain since there seems to be
a high concentration of them crisscrossing the island. A lot of the pathways coincided with a network
of religious and archaeological sites charted about a
hundred and fifty years ago by a guy named Watkins.
His charts don't match the modern ones exactly, I
don't know how; my memory's kind of fuzzy on the
subject. I do remember that these pathways use the
name he coined, ley lines. If we can find where
bunches of these ley lines meet, we might find a
likely place for the ritual.''

''Render unto me the references for the magical
texts, Sir Twist. If they are on-line, I shall strip them
of the pertinent material and mate the data with current orbital cartography. Within half an hour, we shall
have a map of places of power and the highway of your
ley lines.''

In manipulating the Matrix, Dodger was as good
as his word. Using a hookup to the squat's trid unit,
the elf displayed the map he had constructed with his
cyberdeck. Sam stared at the screen, scrolling the
image and tracing the lines. Line after line converged
on a nearby nexus, but the node was small compared
to a greater one to the southeast. He checked the map
reference and sighed. He should have known from the
start, but how could he have been sure that it was
still there? So much had changed in the world, so
many antiquities destroyed, and England had seen its
share of turmoil. But the site remained. And it was
only two steps from a minor nexus at Glover's mansion.

Sam tapped out commands on the cyberdeck's keyboard, expanding the image until a ghostly picture of

sarsen stones filled the image area. Dodger's eyes widened in recognition.

"Stonehenge," they said together.

13

Hart knelt by the heel stone. She had felt the power of the place as soon as she entered the avenue. Even at a distance, astral perception had been difficult; this close to the henge the residual energies produced a kind of glare, effectively cutting off that avenue of scouting. Cautiously, she rose and moved ahead. At the slaughter stone, she cut across the path and slipped down into the ditch. She worked her way past the north barrow before cutting in toward the megaliths of the inner rings.

She halted almost at once.

An elf woman was briefly visible in the open space of the outer ring. She was gone almost before Hart registered her presence, but the sighting was enough to check Hart's approach. There were others present at the henge. Hart waited, but no one else appeared for a quarter hour.

She studied the shadows into which the woman had disappeared. Scrutiny of the megalith's shadow found the woman and revealed another elf, a dark-haired man. Both of the skulkers wore black suits similar to Hart's. She flicked the control on her goggles, switching from unaided to IR reception, and found that their garments masked their body heat. The thermal dispersion factor seemed to be even more efficient than her suit. Their equipment was top notch and their lack of nervous movement marked them as pros. As yet, they seemed unaware of her presence. Were they scouts?

Movement in the darkness caught her eye. A third elf approached. The one wore black synthleathers, and his pale hair was cut in a sprawl shag that rippled as he moved. He had a flat case strapped to his back, which she recognized from its silhouette as a cyberdeck carrying case. There was no use for decking equipment here; the leather elf was out of his element tonight.

A fourth person followed him, not an elf but a human. He moved with a slightly awkward run that nevertheless covered the open ground quickly. The fringes of his jacket swayed with his movement, blurring his outline.

Alert and quiet, the four waited at the side of the sarsen stone for several minutes. Apparently satisfied that they had tripped no alarms, they held a hushed conference before spreading out to take up ambush positions among the stones of the henge.

Interesting. Were they also after the Hidden Circle?

She worked her way in. With others already present, she was denied the perch she had thought to take; climbing to the capstone would attract their attention. Without knowing who they were and what they wanted here, she could not afford their attention. After all, she had no proof that they weren't an advance party for the Circle, come to secure the site.

It took nearly an hour to get into her alternate position, almost due east from the altar stone. The view of the interior of the circle was nearly as good, but more than half of the approaches, including the avenue, were screened by the megaliths.

Her researches had not told her what time might be appropriate for the ceremony, only that it must take place before dawn. She settled in to wait.

She was not sure when she became aware of it, but she realized that the energy of the henge was shifting.

Somewhere, someone was creating a powerful magic that touched the henge. She slipped into astral consciousness and tried to assess the nature of the energy. It didn't feel like a normal ritual, and she could assense no spotter making a ritual link to the henge. The astral glare of the henge was shifting, breaking up. She could discern spirit presences amidst the energy that swept among the stones, like fish on a reef. Those spirit forms were agitated. Moving ever faster, they began to stream out of the henge. Others drifted in, only to follow the path taken by earlier spirits. She shifted her perspective, floating high above the stone circle, and saw that the spirits moved along distinct paths. The ley lines were active.

"Damn!"

The oath focused her attention back to the mundane plane.

The human had come out of hiding and was standing in the center of the circle. His hands were on the altar stone and his face turned to the sky. "They're not here," he shouted. "Those druid bastards are doing their black magic somewhere else."

She recognized the voice, though it had been months since she had heard it. Samuel Verner. She had heard that he'd taken the street name Twist since their last encounter. She had not recognized him when she had seen him, but that was easily explained by the darkness and distance. From his curse, it was clear that he was not part of the druids' plan. Verner was a runner, not a mover; his presence meant an unknown faction was involved.

The other skulkers left their places to join their partner in the center of the ring. The decker elf would be Sam's buddy, Dodger. The other two she didn't know, but as soon as she saw them plainly, she realized that she recognized them. They were the pair who had been leaving the Seelie Court as she had been entering. Was Lady Deigh running parallel teams, or were they the agents of some other power? Had the Lord Protector learned of his renegades? Whoever these runners were, they hunted the Hidden Circle as she did.

Already she had been misled by the quarry. If would take fast work to make up the ground. If the energy she had sensed building was as great as she thought, she would need help. And luck. Verner had been lucky before. Since Sam's group was already after the Circle, they might be willing to share the hunt. She wouldn't have to pay them, and might even be able to arrange for them to take any heat the operation generated.

She left her hiding place, arms held clear of her sides, and walked forward. She was acutely conscious of the Beretta Model 70 hanging on its TEAM sling and slapping against her butt. It wouldn't do to be shot by friendlies.

"I'd wish you a good evening, but it doesn't seem to be one. It appears that we have all been disappointed."

The dark-clad elves drew weapons and trained them on her. Dodger, still fumbling to clear his gun from an entanglement with his cyberdeck, stepped into the woman's line of fire. She looked annoyed, but shifted competently to get a new line. Sam tensed and Hart felt a flicker of power. *Something in the air,* she thought. Sam had not been magically active when they had last met. She waited while they searched the surrounding darkness, seeking to assure themselves that she was alone.

"Perhaps we can join forces," she said. "With some fast transport, we might be able to raid them before they finish their ritual. The circle's not too far away."

"What do you have to do with this?" the dark-haired elf asked.

Sam ignored his companion, took a step forward, and asked his own question. "To the southwest?"

She nodded.

"Glover's estate," Dodger said.

Sam slammed his fist onto the altar stone. "We were right on top of their site and never knew it. If we'd stayed, we might have done something, but we'll never fight our way in now." Turning to Hart, he said, "Unless you've got another dracoform for a partner."

"No more dragons," she said. He gave her an odd look, and she knew that she had not masked all of her emotions. What signal she had sent him, she didn't know. Months later, she still didn't fully understand her own feelings on the matter and Sam's place in them.

"Well, I guess I'm not surprised. A strike team, maybe?"

She shook her head.

"We'll have to try, anyway," he said. "They can't be allowed to complete their ritual."

As Sam started to leave the henge, the dark-haired male elf stepped in his way. "Can she be trusted?"

Sam looked up in the elf's face. He waited until the cool blue eyes met his, then said, "I was once told never to trust an elf, Estios. It's always seemed like good advice around you."

Sam looked around at his companions, making Hart very conscious of her metatype. The points of her ears felt hot with blood.

"But it seems that I have little choice. I'm a minority of one in this crowd. At the moment, I have to trust anyone who looks like they can do something about the druids. Hart's a professional shadowrunner, ready for action, and willing to help. You want to pass up another soldier? The druids will be prepared for trouble and Glover will have tightened his security. We'll need all the help we can get."

Estios remained stiff for a second, as if to assert his command of the situation. "Very well. I will call the aircraft."

14

The wicker man stood to the south, facing across the chalked lines toward the bare, shield-shaped patch of earth across which they had all entered the ritual area. The silver bowl of blessed water rested in the western point, and the scent of burning herbs rising from the eastern point's brazier filled the clearing. Only the upper portions of the wicker man would be visible from beyond the surrounding topiary maze.

Save for the wicker man, Glover found it all very familiar. Normally, the golden-tipped spear stood at the southern point, but this was no normal ritual. This was a ceremony of high sacrifice, the holiest of druidic rituals. Bound within the wicker were the six chosen sacrifices, the scions of untainted blood. Each limb held one, another lay wrapped within the body and the last was curled in the head. Gordon stood before the mannikin holding an unlit torch, half concealed by the flowing sleeves of his plain white robe. He seemed pensive and subdued. Was he contemplating his forthcoming role?

The symbols were all in place; it was time to begin. Gordon abandoned his vigil in front of the wicker man and walked to his place near the center of the ring, careful to avoid stepping on any of the chalked lines. As he reached the unfinished pentacle in which he was to stand, he was met by David Neville. Gordon took his place, and young Neville completed the diagram. Across the clearing, the druids moved to their stations, ghostly white shapes drifting in the dark. Each wore a ritual robe topped off with the golden brow band and head cloth of an initiate. Sir Winston, leader of the ceremony, was distinguished from his peers by a heavy gold pectoral bearing the sun-in-splendor insignia of his totem.

Everything was in order. Glover could find nothing amiss, nothing to hint that Hyde-White might be right. The ceremonial ring was laid out exactly according to the specifications in the ritual they had all worked out. The geometries were accurate, the symbols appropriate. What could go wrong?

Neville stood in the center of the ring, naming each participant and building the protective magics. Glover studied the archdruid. Neville appeared steady and in control; only a touch of anticipation marred his calm. A faint glow was beginning to manifest around him as the energies awoke.

Glover joined the circle, adding his energies to the spell. Neville continued around the ring until he reached Hyde-White. With the inclusion of the fat man, the ritual circle was complete. Glover noticed that Hyde-White's aura was subdued, as if he had not committed himself wholly to the ritual. A less competent shaman might have fatally flawed the ritual by such reservation, but Hyde-White's power was well above the commitment needed.

Neville led the opening chant, his reedy voice ringing out to be answered by the combined voices of the other druids. He called upon the earth to heed their call, offering praise to all that was natural and stating the Circle's commitment to restoring the land's balance. He paused before making the offer of sacrifice.

Neville nodded to Gordon, who held his unlit brand on high. Gathering strands from each of the druids' power, Neville wove them into a lance of light and speared it toward Gordon. The amber beam struck the torch, igniting it in a burst of flame and spark.

To the accompaniment of the rhythmic spell chant,

Gordon walked to the edge of the ring and faced the wicker man. He held the torch to the end of the mannikin's left arm until the flames caught. Then, he thrust it deep into the leg and released his grip, leaving it to kindle another nest of hungry fire. He bowed to the wicker man before returning to his place in the center of the pentacle and facing Neville.

"We give holocaust. Let the sky accept our offering," he said.

The druids continued their spell song, raising their volume as the fire spread through the wicker man. Sanchez, the first of the sacrifices to be consumed, died without a sound. The druids sang louder.

The howl of tearing metal and the crack of splintering wood ripped across their voices, driving the chant to an abrupt halt. The cacophony issued from somewhere near the house. Glover searched for the source.

Behind the outbuildings, an unkempt shape was rising. The irregular mass of shifting material humped up into a huge, dark mass of refuse and debris until its top was several meters higher than the roof of the nearest structure. The thing taking shape beyond the hedges lurched, its bulk shifting toward the circle. It might have been tottering, about to fall, but a second lurch dispelled that illusion. Whatever the thing was, it had begun to move toward them.

"David," Sir Winston called calmly above the excited questions of the other druids. "We must not be interrupted."

"I will hold it, father."

David Neville eased his energies from the complex that the druids had created. Glover pushed harder, taking his share of the slack. His concentration was lacking, for his eyes were continually drawn to the approaching entity.

The growing light of the burning wicker lit the shape. With each step it became more defined. From an amorphous thing, it was resolving itself into a gnarled and hulking man shaped of refuse from the midden heap and fragments of the abandoned carriage house. It was a golem made of trash, and its outline was the same as that of the wicker man.

One of the sacrifices screamed, the flames burning through his drugged haze, and the thing jerked. Piece by piece, Barnett's car, an ancient petrol-burning antique, tore itself apart, chunks whirling free to soar through the air and join with the mound. It grew and shambled forward.

David Neville faced it from within the ring of hedge. He was careful not to step past the safety of the magical barrier provided by the chalked circle. He stood straight, arms outstretched and palms raised to beseech aid.

"By the powers of sky, I command thee. By the powers of the earth, I bid thee be gone. I stand firm on the land, caressed by the wind, and cast thee forth."

Attuned to the astral, Glover could see the energy gather around David before bursing forth to strike the thing. The glittering darkness of the monster's aura absorbed the power, swallowing the bright beam as if it had never been. Glover's mouth went dry. Young Neville was a prig and a snob, but he had power and had specialized in dealing with astral entities. Glover had seen him dismiss unruly spirits often enough. Whatever this was, it already had power enough to resist him.

A gap opened in the chest of the trash thing, a dark maw fanged with leaf springs, bumpers, and metal fragments, and a stream of semi-liquified garbage spewed forth to drench Neville. He stagged back, retching. The pool of refuse at his feet solidified and trapped him where he stood. Dripping tendrils of slime hardened, freezing his motion. His legs disappeared, encased in the ever deeper flow of filth that poured from the horrid monstrosity. Neville tried again to shout the formula of dismissal, but the commands gurgled to a strangled stop as the growing mound overtopped his head and entombed him.

The thing convulsed, apparently collapsing in on itself as if Neville's dismissal had finally taken effect. It was a false hope. The narrow bridge of offal and rubbish expanded where it met the golem. A bulge, like a pig in a python, moved along the connection of garbage. The greater part of the monster's bulk formed that bulge as the great mass outside the maze transferred itself along that slender bridge. The mound that concealed young Neville thickened, ballooning out as the mass concentrated. The debris pile stretched and contorted until the trash thing reformed its shape and stood on the spot where he had opposed it.

Barnett cast a spell at the monster, flames arcing from his outthrust hand to splash against the hulk. Steam and smoke billowed up, but though small fires flickered on the affected area, the garbage golem did not react to the attack.

Hyde-White stood riveted in trance, sweat rolling in sheets across his vast expanses of flesh. Like Glover, he gathered in the strands of power as druids left the ritual to devote their energies to fighting off the intruder. Glover had little time to appreciate the old man's struggle; assimilating his part of the added burden was taxing his own control.

The other druids cast spells and attempted their own banishments. Their efforts had some effect; the monstrosity seemed confined between the outer and inner protective rings of the great chalk circle. Fitzgilbert ventured too close to the thing and was struck down by a flailing limb of rusted metal and decaying wood. Debris showered them as he collapsed to the ground, his neck broken by the blow.

Glover's arm was seized in a bone-racking grip. Hyde-White had crossed the ring. Leaving his place had been a necessity for the fat man; the trash thing occupied that space.

"Andrew, now you see what Neville's obsession has led us to. He has no control over this corrupted spirit. As I feared, there is a flaw in the ritual and so this thing has been spawned. If the sacrifice is completed, there is no telling what strength it will have."

Glover stared at the monstrosity. It was fascinating, at once compelling and disgusting. Its power was enormous, but its very unnaturalness was the final proof of Hyde-White's argument. "We must stop it."

Hyde-White's chin disappeared in the folds of flesh that hid his neck as he nodded. "If the spell is broken suddenly, there may be a backlash. I will guard the link with Neville while you do what must be done."

What must be done.

Glover looked at the wicker man. The flames had already consumed its left half and were spreading. Where it had burned fiercely, the sacrifices were no longer moving. Corbeau lay bound within the mannikin's right arm. The fire ravened closer, and he was beginning to stir as the heat and excitement penetrating through his drugged haze. So much effort to get him here, and now it was spoiled by Neville's arrogance.

In the center of the circle, the older Neville stood tall and straight, the golden sickle raised above his head. His eyes were closed and his lips moved as he feverishly spoke the words of the ritual.

"We offer blood to the earth. Let the land drink from this divinely ordained vessel and be refreshed."

Gordon walked toward him intoning the prayer of offering, naming himself as the gift and offering his own blood to revitalize the land. He knelt before Neville, stretching his head back to offer his throat.

Glover couldn't allow that royal blood to feed the monstrosity. Hoping that he was not also destroying the land's hope, he gathered his power and sent it in a blast that ripped the right arm from the wicker man in an explosion of green witchfire. Corbeau screeched as the arcane energies shredded his flesh and boiled his body fluids. It was a faster death than the creeping sacrificial flame, but no less harsh.

"You fool! What have you done?" shouted Neville as he stumbled across the ring to seize Glover.

"Stopped your abortion." A sweep of his arm broke the old man's grip.

"You have destroyed all we have worked for!"

"I have saved it. Look!"

The garbage golem swayed wildly. Tilting at nearly forty-five degrees from the vertical, it suddenly lost cohesiveness and shattered into its component elements. The stench of decay and putrefaction burst over the clearing as rusted metal and rotted organic matter pelted the ground. The half-decomposed corpse of the young Neville lay amid the debris, its white bones gleaming in the firelight.

"See what you have done, old man, and what your warped ambitions have cost you. Your son lies dead. That's a price you'll have on your conscience to the grave. Pray that your conscience won't be burdened by worse. We can only hope that your folly hasn't cost us the land."

"What are you talking about?" one of the others asked. They had gathered around the quarrelers.

Glover stabbed a finger at the heap of debris that had stalked their ceremony. "That. We all saw how that thing grew as the sacrifices were consumed." Glover turned his wrathful face on Neville. "Had you completed the ritual, that thing would have been empowered in a way beyond our dreams. You would have spawned a scourge for the land."

"No!" Neville's face was twisted with denial. "It would have been destroyed. The corruption would have been swept away."

Glover sneered at the desperation in Neville's voice. The man couldn't even convince himself. "Then why did it disperse when I interrupted the ritual?"

Neville's eyes darted across the assembled survivors. There was no comfort for him in those faces.

"I don't know," he mumbled.

"Well, I have seen enough to know. You have misled us, old man. Your way has been shown to be flawed and unwholesome. We must find another way to restore the land. We must hope that it can yet be done, and that your perverse meddling has not closed the door."

Barnett made a show of turning his shoulder away from Neville. "Glover, you are the one who saw what needed to be done. What should we do now?"

"Whatever is necessary," Gordon said. When all eyes were turned to him, he added, "I was ready to give my life that the land be restored. Who could ask for more commitment? I need only be shown the way. If you see that way, Master Glover, I will follow your lead."

"It is an awesome responsibility," Glover said.

"Which you have shown yourself strong enough to take on."

Glover's spirit soared. Acclamation from His Highness! Hyde-White had been right. Opportunity was rising before him; he would be a fool and a weakling if he did not seize it. He tried to mask his elation, to present a properly stern face as Ashton, who had been Neville's student, removed the archdruid's pectoral from the old man and held it out to Glover. His hands trembled as he accepted it.

"I serve the land as you do, Highness. As you have come to understand, we must all do whatever is necessary to see it healthy again. As leader of this Circle, my goal will be to see the land restored to its glory. Nothing shall deter me.''

He felt the strength of his conviction as he spoke. He *would* do anything to see the land saved. Behind him, he felt Hyde-White's presence, massive and supporting.

PART 2

There Are Always Choices

15

London stank.

It wasn't just the fumes and garbage stenches that permeated everything, although the city had those, just like every other major metroplex. London's peculiar effluvium was a legacy of the terrorist attack of 2039, when the radical group called Pan Europa had released a bioagent in retaliation for England's supposed part in the break-up of the EEC. The bug had been supposed to break down the sheathing element of the metroplex's newly completed dome. The terrorists must have been pleased to see the biofabric skin had evaporated under the ravenous organism. But had they known what effect their organism would have on other biological fibers?

Intentional or not, once the bug was released, there had been no way to recall it. Much of London's historical legacy had been destroyed when the uncontrolled organism had devoured the city's paper and wood. The panic riots that had followed had devastated the city, vandalizing its present and almost completely devouring its past. The spirit of London's people had failed as well, the dreams of leading a new Europe dying in the mouldering aftermath.

Now, the bones of the abandoned dome arched over

the city like the broken ribcage of a rotting antediluvian beast, as the fungi of skyscapers, towers, and communications arrays clawed toward the sky through the bleached struts.

Sam saw those gleaming spires of the new plex as monuments to the megacorporations' contempt for the common folk. Instead of nurturing the people's hopes, the corps had defied the growing power of the Green Party and taken advantage of the chaos and built to their own whims. With bought votes in Parliament and sweetheart deals for the still-landed aristocracy, the megacorps had twisted English law, shattering the people's dreams of safety and protection. Despite the restored constitutional monarchy, George VIII, the Lord Protector, and Parliament didn't govern the country alone. The megacorps ruled much of England as surely as they ruled their own boardrooms.

But London was a modern metroplex, and in the shadows of the corporate towers there was another world; one the megacorps and the Lord Protector's Greens didn't rule. London had its shadow world, not unlike Seattle's. In the corners and the darkness, men and women, shadowrunners, fought the aggressive, uncaring domination of the corporate powers. And when the corps struck back, the runners hid . . . in the abandoned stretches that reminded Sam of Seattle's Barrens, in the teeming hives of the Public Zones beneath the corporate towers, and in the dank tunnels of the service ways and sewers that made up the undercity. Especially in the sewers.

The cold, slimy water trickled through his close-cropped hair. If his hair were longer, the chill splash would have been softened; he wouldn't have felt dampness until the noisome liquid threaded its way unto the bare skin on the back of his neck.

Why was Hart late? Fifteen minutes already. In their three weeks of haunting the London shadow world, she had always been on time, if not early. Even in those rare moments when they had met to relax, she had been prompt. Unlike Sally.

Sally wouldn't like it here. She hated the dark, closed-in places. He remembered her curses when they broke into the Renraku arcology so long ago. So long ago? Little more than two years had passed. He had been living in another world then, living a different life. Since then, he had entered the shadows and found a new life. Was he on the verge of starting down yet another new path?

When he thought about Sally, he remembered the good times they had had in bed, the intensity of it all. But he also remembered the fights and the sniping. He had always had the feeling that he somehow didn't measure up to Sally's standards. Well, drek! He didn't measure up to his own most of the time, but that didn't make him worthless. Times changed; people changed. He had.

Had something happened to her?

Sam's worry was real, but the face he attached to it was Hart's. That surprised him. How easily she had slipped into his thoughts to displace Sally. Almost as easily as they had slipped into bed together. At the time, it had just seemed right somehow. And now? Well, now it still seemed right.

What about Sally?

"What about Hart?" Estios whispered belligerently.

"She said she'd be here."

Sam wished he felt as assured as he sounded. Or did he sound confident at all? Estios seemed as nervous as he ever got. The tall elf was always so cocky; the absence of his partners didn't usually affect him. Was he worried about Hart, too? It seemed unlikely. Ever since they had met in the circle of Stonehenge, Estios had distrusted Hart. Even though she had saved them all from blundering into the ambush at Glover's estate that night, Estios had remained distrustful. His every comment was laced with his suspicions. She just laughed off the hostility, but Sam worried. How could they all work together without trust?

Who was he to talk? These days he had to weigh every word Dodger said, wondering if there was a new lie hidden among the flowery phrases. Then there was Estios and his crew. Chatterjee seemed innocuous enough, quiet and competent. O'Connor was the friendliest of the bunch, but she seemed to know Dodger from a long time ago. Who knew what that meant? Certainly Dodger did, but he wasn't talking. Estios himself was a very cold fish. As much as he resented Hart, he seemed to resent Sam even more. Beneath the surface of politeness, Sam sensed that the tall elf was chafing under some kind of restraint, almost as if someone had ordered him to remain on relatively good terms with Sam. Perhaps someone had. As far as Sam knew, Estios was exclusively employed by Professor Laverty. That made Sam wonder what interest the professor had in the current situation. Just who could Sam trust?

Himself, he supposed. Inu, too. But Inu was only a dog, and besides, he wasn't here. In London, the elves with whom he hunted the druids were his only close contacts. The elves had shadow connections in the plex, almost all normal humans. Sam trusted most of those connections less than he trusted the elves, but he would be lost in the plex without them. Then again, without them, he would be on his way back to Seattle.

A short series of taps reverberated faintly down the tunnel. Estios drew his weapon and faced toward the source before Sam had sorted out the echoes. There were familiar scents beneath the sewer stink. Feeling secure that Estios would handle any physical threat, Sam activated his astral senses and scanned the tunnel.

The approaching aura was familiar, and comforting. It showed no sign of injury or emotional distress. A further probe revealed that she was not being followed.

"Is this the whole party?" Hart asked as she arrived.

"Where were you?" Estios snapped, scowling.

She ignored his question. "Let's go see Herzog."

"I don't like it," Estios said.

"Do you like anything? You didn't have to come."

She brushed at a drip spot on the arm of her Scaterelli jacket. Her annoyed frown would seem to be directed at the spoiled fabric, but Sam knew better. Estios pressed.

"We need not involve him in our affairs, Hart. You have compromised our security enough by sending Twist to him."

"She hasn't compromised anything, Estios. Herzog is just a teacher. You should be grateful for that; it'll make me more valuable."

"Learning from the gutter is worse than no learning."

Hart laughed. "Learning is learning. I suggest that you keep your attitude to yourself. I don't think our host will take kindly to your carping. If Herzog were here . . . "

"But Herzog *is* here."

The new voice belonged to a bulky figure that emerged from the deeper shadows of the tunnel. Sam had smelled Herzog's distinctive odor and had known that he was somewhere nearby, but the others, for all their darkness-piercing elven eyes, hadn't seemed aware. Estios swung his weapon to bear and Hart tensed. The newcomer rumbled with amusement.

"No fight today," he said.

Herzog was big for a human, weighing more than many orks. Most of his mass was muscle and bone, hidden under a layer of smooth fat and a mound of patchwork clothes. He was unnaturally strong, a gift of nature boosted by his totem rather than by artificial enhancement. Despite his bulk and the array of fetishes festooning his garb, he moved almost silently as he stepped up to them.

"Good evening, Herzog," Hart said. "I'm pleased to see you."

"You have work for me."

"Direct," Estios commented.

"The night still grows, elf. I must be about my own work. If you find my manners abrupt, you need not deal with me."

"Ignore tall, dark, and ornery, Herzog," Hart said. "We need your help."

"To do?"

"To get us going. Our probes are getting nowhere; our adversaries seem well prepared for our hermetic intrusions. I thought that your talents might offer a more productive approach."

"Your adversaries are not mine."

"They are everyone's," Sam said.

Herzog turned to Sam. "So. Why have *you* not done what the elf asks?"

Sam didn't want to answer. Had he been alone with Herzog he might have, but in front of Hart he felt inhibited. He didn't want her to know how much he hated talking to Dog, how much he feared the irrationality of the spirit form's essence. And he didn't want her to know about that other presence that so terrified him.

"I can't," he said.

Herzog half turned in a sudden rattle and clash of fetishes and power objects. "You have the power. You know how to free your spirit. Why have you stopped this time? The Dog or the Man of Light?"

Sam hesitated, and Hart shot him a look.

"What is the Man of Light?" she asked.

"Nothing," Sam said quickly to keep Herzog from answering. "It's nothing. Just some kind of subconscious symbol. I'm still having trouble breaking through to the spirit realm that I'd need to reach to do what you want."

Hart stared at him but said nothing. Sam gave a brief prayer of thanks when she returned her attention to Herzog.

"So, shaman. Will you do some *recce* for us?"

"I will. It will take time."

"Then we will leave you to it," Estios said. The deal made, the tall elf vanished into the darkness. Hart delayed to thank Herzog, then reached for Sam's arm. The shaman stopped her.

"He stays."

Sam saw the surprise in Hart's face flash to annoyance. He himself felt afraid. "Why?"

"You need to learn."

Sam started to object, but Hart spoke. "He's right. You need to learn as much as you can. Besides, if you're here, you can make a first call on whether what Herzog finds out is important. It might save a lot of time."

"But you—"

"But nothing. You know he won't work with anyone other than a shaman present."

"I'm not a—"

Herzog exploded with the huff of air that was his laugh.

"You are what you are. You must come with me now; the badges are coming."

Sam looked around. He could see little in the darkness, but he could hear distant splashes. Someone coming all right, several someones. There was too much noise for them to be runners, so the approaching persons were most likely one of the local constabulary's periodic sewer patrols, and magic wouldn't hide them from the patrol magician. When he turned back, Hart was already gone. She had slipped away silently into the dimness, where her elven eyes could see what he could not. He would never catch up to her. Left with no other choice, he followed the retreating Herzog. Even the grumpy Gator shaman was preferable to a brush with the metroplex police.

They stopped when Herzog was sure they were safely away from the sweep patrol. Herzog leaned against the tunnel wall, immobile. Sam could barely hear him breathe. The Gator shaman had never shown much altruism before, yet he had accepted Hart's charge without dickering on the price.

"Why are you doing this?"

"Need."

"But we haven't offered you anything. Don't think Estios will pay whatever you ask. You didn't name a price, so he won't pay one."

Herzog's huff was soft, too soft to carry back down the tunnel, but Sam heard it clearly enough.

"I do not do this for the ice-eyed elf. Nor for your paramour Hart. I do this for you. You must see that the way is safe, that you can walk the path if only you accept what you are."

"I have accepted it. I've learned spells. I can project astrally at will."

"You delude yourself. If you had accepted your shamanic nature, the path to the spirit planes would not be blocked. Until you accept the other reality, you will not achieve what you seek. Until then, you are your own worst enemy."

16

What Dan Shiroi said made sense to Janice. His attitudes and reactions were all reasonable, given the context in which he had to live his life. But that context was hers, now. Like Jaime Garcia and Han and all the others who were part of Dan's hidden organization. Wherever in the world they lived, they were all the same breed of metahumanity.

Dan was a good teacher. With his guidance, she was doing things she would not have believed possible. The spells and the focusing of astral senses came so easily. Already she could mask her appearance with a spell and walk among norms without their knowing what she was. Her childhood dreams of magic were being fulfilled.

The magic had come with her second change. It was a blessing. And a curse. Masked by magic, she heard the norms talk when they thought that they were among their own kind. She heard the slurs, the jokes, and the put-downs. She heard the hate. It curdled her soul.

Dan was right; their kind had to band together. Norms hated anything that was not just like themselves. They hated metahumans worst of all. The larger and stranger the metahuman, the stronger the norms hated. Once, she had believed that the hate was driven by fear, the terror of the strange and unknown. She had begun to suspect that the hate came from somewhere else, some dark part of the human soul. Wherever it came from, the hate was real.

And there were so many more norms than metahumans. Even great strength and superior senses couldn't keep her safe from a mob. That early excursion when she had let her concentration slip had shown her a vulnerability that she had thought she had left behind. Her thoughts fled back to that awful snowy day when her illusion had faltered and she had stood revealed on the street. The norms had turned on her, calling her a monster and an eater of children. She had fled from their shouts and they had chased her, cornering her in an abandoned building too much like the one in which Dan had found her. But this time, it hadn't been ghouls who pursued her but normal people, people who had only moments before been conversing politely with her. And this time she had been healthy, for what little good it had done her. The mob's hatred and invective had flayed her worse that their fists. If Dan had not found her again, she would have been ripped to pieces by the norms. Though they had hurt her badly, Dan's healing touch had soothed her.

She had learned who her friends were. She had been taught her place in the world.

She looked down at Dan's sleeping form. The setting sun's rays insinuated themselves through the shuttered windows to tint his fur with rosy color. He would awaken soon and be about his business. He always said it was her business as well, but as of yet she had little to do, save study the magic he taught.

With the magic, she could touch an essence that was pure, and strong, and free. Dan had led her through a cave at the center of the world and shown her the marvellous land that lay beyond. There, she had met her totem. She had seen His flashing eye and felt the full softness of His fur. In the stillness of the night, she had heard His soulful call and looked up to see His silhouette racing across the sky to dance with the moon. Wolf had chosen her as His own. She felt proud that the old woods runner had found her satisfactory.

She was slowly coming to understand Wolf, coming

to feel the predator in herself. Her heart was full of the clannish pull to stay with and defend her own kind. Her limbs held the strength of the wild. She was ready to stand against those who would sunder her from the pack. Wolf offered her the power to make her own way and rend the weak-willed souls who would keep her from her destiny. Yes, she was beginning to understand Wolf. And she was a bit frightened of herself.

Dan's hand on her shoulder awakened her from her reverie. She realized she was standing at the window, staring at the darkness gathering over London's old East End. The rebuilt district was little different from its predecessors. Killers stalked the dark streets and purveyors of every vice made their lairs there. The East End was still a teeming hive, full of nasty, ugly people and suffused with their sufferings and depredations—an urban wilderness. Dan said that made the area suitable for her current stage of magical development. And so they stayed in a fortified apartment building. He promised that soon she would be ready to move on.

"Is something bothering you?" he asked.

"No," she lied. Her fears and concerns were too vague for words. Her inability to articulate them would lessen her in his eyes. He prized strength, and she would be strong for him.

"Good." He kissed her. "I thought that tonight we might try another journey to the other realm. Your last was encouraging."

"All right." She felt a thrill at the thought of seeing Wolf again.

He took her hand and led her down to the basement where they held their practice sessions. Han was already there, spreading herbs to scent the air. As usual, he said nothing, but nodded in acknowledgment of Janice's greeting before settling his furry body behind the drum. Janice lowered herself to the floor, stretch-

ing out while Dan intoned the spells that would ensure
their privacy.

"Ready?" he asked.

"Eager," she replied.

He sat cross-legged by her head and rested his palms
on either side of her face. He began to sing the travel
chant, and Han picked up the beat with the drum.
Janice listened to the music until the words were lost
to her as voice and instrument blended.

The sound throbbed through her, its pulse filling
every cell of her body. She let herself drift into the
cadence, riding the flow deeper into a shamanic state
of consciousness. The dark hole opened before her, but
she had become familiar with it and was not afraid.
She slipped through the opening and flew downward.
The passage was short, free of hindering shadows,
and she emerged in the other world.

The moon shown, just clear of the horizon. It was
full and lovely. She greeted it and heard the answering
response of Wolf. Her joy swelled. This was how she
was meant to live, unfettered and free to do as she
would, feeling the cool air on her fur and smelling
the myriad glorious scents of the other side of day. The
night had become her favorite time.

She ran.

There was no urgency in her pace, just exuberance.
She ran because she wanted to run, to feel her muscles
moving in vital rhythm. A white wolf ran at her side.
He was larger than she, stronger too, but he was no
threat. This was her mate and they ruled the pack.
They were strong and healthy. None could challenge
them.

They ran.

The moon hung in the sky, but she didn't need its
light. Her eyes were keen, her nose keener. Little escaped her notice, least of all the scent of prey. A flash
of white—a startled rabbit burst from hiding. They

gave chase, bounding over obstacles and racing past obstructions to herd the prey. Sometimes she would close on it, only to have it make a rapid turn and elude her. Sometimes he would crowd it, forcing it toward her.

A hedge of tangled brush loomed ahead. The rabbit, sensing safety, redoubled its speed. He surged ahead, cutting across its path. The prey hauled up short, quivering. It turned, ready to continue its flight. Seeing her so near, it froze. He pounced, slapping the rabbit to the earth with a paw. It struggled against his indomitable strength, to no avail. He looked at her, offering her the honor of the kill.

The rabbit sensed their exchange and turned fearful eyes on her. It pleaded for its life. Didn't it know that its place in the natural order was to serve as her prey? Why did it struggle harder as she approached? This was the way of things. The wolf was the hunter, the rabbit the prey.

Frightened, terrified eyes.

She hesitated. *It's just prey,* he said. *Meat.*

Yes. Just meat. Why couldn't she bring herself to close her jaws on its throat? She hung her head and turned away. She didn't want to see the scorn in his eyes.

The rabbit gave a soft cry as he dispatched it. She listened to the sounds of him tearing up the carcass. When he finished, he offered her meat.

She took the meat. Its juices rushed the taste through her mouth, blasting the sensation to her brain. This was the food she was meant to eat, no other. Wolves ate rabbits. It was the way of the world. She bolted another strip of meat.

In time, he said. There was no accusation, no scorn. She felt his patience and basked in his love. He understood. He would wait for her to take the steps at her own pace. He had promised that there would be no pressure, and he was living up to his word.

She loved him.

After they had eaten their fill, they ran again, racing the moon to the horizon. She was exhilarated by the physical effort, made more alive than she had ever been before. Their running pace eventually slowed, speed waning as their fleet paws matched rhythm to the measured beat of the drum. The journey was ending.

She awakened from the trance, feeling rested and well fed. Dan had her recount the experience and said he was pleased. She knew he meant it.

He had some things to take care of before bed, so he went away. She wandered back upstairs and stood at the window, wrapped in the lassitude of satiation. Down in the streets of the East End, the morning crews were cleaning up the debris of the night. Scavengers. No doubt they helped themselves to whatever the true predators had left behind. She watched a scruffy pair haul a maimed body from a building. Another derelict being taken away, another victim of the plex. Another day in London.

17

An ebon boy in a glittering cloak of silver danced along the electron pathways, but the pattern faltered. A whirling measure would abruptly end in a few stumbling steps. The dancer was eager, but his steps were constrained as though the dance floor was slippery. In every direction there were datapaths in all of their myriad multitudes, but none offered what he sought. Following any one only led to frustration, the dance halting as the pathway expanded into a diffuse and indistinct mass of branches. Each branch was a trail of connections that vanished, becoming an array of untraceable links. The only ones that stayed solid led to unbreakable ice or mundane and unimportant data.

He was frustrated. And angry. The ebon boy folded his cloak around himself. Dodger jacked out, and the boy vanished from the Matrix.

Dodger stared down at the datajack. He couldn't figure it out. There should be more connections than he could follow in a day. The circle of druids they chased were prominent people in England. At least the ones whose names they knew were prominent—highly placed businessmen and -women or members of the aristocracy, whose everyday lives were matters of public record.

The Hidden Circle was living up to its name.

Why couldn't he make connections? Secret societies rarely managed to avoid leaving a trail, especially in these modern times when no organization functioned without some computerization. Magical organizations were usually even easier to track down; their members rarely comprehended the intricacies of the consensual hallucination that was the Matrix, that hypothetical pseudoreality that was a second home to Dodger. In the Matrix, a good decker should be able to trace the connections between people and organizations. And Dodger knew that he was better than good.

These druids, despite all their magic, were a techno-savvy bunch. There was not a hint in the Matrix that any of them were more than they appeared to be in the mundane world. He had not even been able to learn the names of the unknown members of the Hidden Circle. Without records of the Circle's organization, he couldn't tell who among the contacts of the known Circle members were also members. Looking for registered druids was no real help. Many practicing magicians didn't bother to comply with the Registration Act, and the members of the Hidden Circle seemed likely candidates for such an act of civil disobedience.

From the absence of data, he might have given up, believing that there were no other members. But Sam insisted that there had to be more, and Hart had backed him up. They said that a druidic circle was three times three. The runners had names for six of the Hidden Circle and two of those were dead.

The Hidden Circle was too well hidden. Three weeks and Dodger had gleaned next to nothing. There had to be another way to track them down.

A soft hand slid along his shoulder. He knew that touch, and it triggered a rush of memories he struggled to suppress. The past was the past.

"No luck?" Teresa's tone made the question a statement.

Dodger didn't bother to answer. She knew him well enough. Having seen his expression when she entered the room, she would have had her answer. He looked over his shoulder; she had come alone.

"Pray, tell. Where is our chaperone?"

"Chatterjee is downstairs."

With a slim-fingered hand, she slid away the Fairlight cyberdeck and perched on the edge of the desk. Her slim hips spread slightly under the pressure, edging the hem of her skirt higher on her thigh. In his memory, he felt the exquisite smoothness of that graceful arch. His eyes traced the familiar curves up until he reached the equally familiar lop-sided smile of amusement. Her eyes sparkled.

"Have something in mind?" she asked.

He stood and reached out his hand to caress her cheek. Memory blurred with current perception as if there had been no gap. She slid from the desk and into his arms.

"I thought that meat was a drag on the electron spirit."

" 'Tis true."

"I've missed you."

"And I you."

"Estios would not approve."

"Estios can . . ."

She hushed him with a kiss. The moment seemed an eternity.

"Dodger, why didn't you stay?"

"Why didn't you come with me?"

There were no words to say, for they had all been said before. He had no new answers that would mean anything. They held each other closely, entwining the rhythms of their hearts. Her voice was muffled by his shoulder.

"Some things never change. They only fall apart when things around them change."

"It need not be so."

"Are you so sure?"

"No." He wished that he were.

"Neither am I. What's to become of us, Dodger? I thought that I'd be able to work with you without remembering. I'm not as strong as I thought."

"You have more strength than I."

"Liar."

"Is our fate to be the doomed lovers, then?"

She hugged him harder instead of answering.

"I would not compromise you with Estios," he said.

"I would not let you."

That wasn't the answer he wanted to hear.

An unwelcome sound intruded on them; Chatterjee was coming down the hall. For an elf, he was making a lot of noise. Did he know?

Teresa heard the other elf as well. She moved almost as quickly as Dodger. By the time Chatterjee walked through the archway, Dodger was back in his chair and Teresa was sitting demurely on the desk.

"The keyboard was quiet, so I came to see what progress you had achieved. You have information?" Chatterjee asked.

The frustration of the flesh was bad enough. Dodger didn't need to be reminded of how little he had achieved in the Matrix as well. "Nothing new."

"Estios will not be pleased."

"Tough," Dodger snapped. "That slick is never pleased unless he's got his butt . . ."

"Dodger!" Teresa's voice was suitably chastising, but Dodger caught a hint of her quirky smile.

So, the lady has not been totally wooed by the party line.

Chatterjee remained unperturbed. "Your personal evaluation of any member of the team is irrelevant. However, your lack of results is pertinent and distressing. It limits our course of action too much. I had been informed that you were a decker of exceptional competence."

" 'Tis a fact. For the moment, however, 'tis also a fact that there is no joy in the Matrix."

"You have exhausted all avenues?"

"All? A decker of my 'exceptional competence'? Hardly. 'Tis true that I have run all of our current leads to ground. Beyond confirming that the younger Neville is dead, we are no nearer to them than we were on the Solstice."

"Without their full circle, they are weak," Teresa said.

"Yet not weak enough," Chatterjee said. "The optimal result would be their complete dissolution, but reduction beyond the ring of three should be sufficient for present purposes."

"One cannot 'reduce' the unknown effectively. We are no closer to naming all of the Circle than we were three weeks ago. And without knowing all of their identities, we dare not move against those we have identified."

"Precisely," Chatterjee agreed. "You must intensify your endeavors."

Dodger folded his arms and stared at the ceiling. "Let Estios intensify his."

"He already has," Chatterjee said.

He would have. Always going one up. Fragging slick. "Then when he returns with usable data, I shall use it."

Chatterjee frowned. "Time passes."

"What matters time to an elf?"

"Flippancy is inappropriate. Estios prepares for action and we must all be ready to move if the arcane reconnaissance results in useful data. Even if the shaman learns something of worth, it will be unlikely to have much pertinence with regard to your Matrix efforts. I suggest that you immediately pursue whatever avenues remain open."

"Verily? Then I suggest that you . . ."

"Dodger," Teresa warned.

Dodger sighed. Baiting Chatterjee wasn't worth upsetting Teresa. "Perchance I shall try a blind shunt; some of the data we do have should serve as hooks."

"Explain," Chatterjee ordered.

So ho, Squire Chatterjee. Must you now acknowledge that the Dodger may indeed be of exceptional competence? "A blind shunt utilizes a sophisticated series of mask and camouflage programs that render transparent a decker's presence in the Matrix. Unfortunately, the technique leaves the decker vulnerable as well, but what isn't seen by intrusion countermeasures is not attacked by such defenses. While cloaked, the decker waits; for to take active measures is to destroy the illusion of transparency. The hooks are data bits to which the decker attaches his invisible persona, waiting for the data to move. The assumption is that the hook will be taken legitimately into a place where the decker cannot gain entry through conventional hacking. The procedure takes time, but I don't see anything else to do. Mayhap we shall be lucky.''

Teresa reached out and laid her hand on Dodger's arm. He could feel the electricity through his leathers. She didn't seem to care that Chatterjee was watching.

"Dodger," she said. "Don't do that. It's too dangerous. A blind shunt could drag you into heavy ice."

"Fear not, fair maid. The Dodger has not yet met the ice that can trap him."

He was lying, of course. He had been trapped by ice—once and only once. It was an experience that haunted his nightmares. But he didn't need to fear a repeat of that experience. The artificial intelligence—if that's what it really was—that controlled the deadly ice lived locked away in the Renraku Matrix, and he was never going to enter that terrible black pyramid again. No matter how slick these druids were, their deckers couldn't be playing in the same league as the megacorp that controlled most of the world's public data structures. He would be safe from anything he would encounter.

Teresa's eyes bored into his, her expression flickering with an emotion he couldn't read. Her hand left his arm as she stood. Had she read the lie?

"Yet," she said softly.

Dodger was sure she hadn't intended him to hear.

18

The man entering the room was not a man at all. He went by the name Hanson, and looked like a man to the unaided eye, but Andrew Glover knew better. Glover had assensed Hanson when he had first shown up bearing Hyde-White's letter of introduction, and Glover's exercise of his mage sight had shown him that Hanson was not human. What Hanson was remained an open question; Glover had never before seen such an aura or astral image. There were no astral image files, no aura records to consult that would reveal what kind of metahuman Hanson was.

The fat, old man could not have failed to penetrate the illusions cloaking the metahuman from the ordinary eye. So why was he recommending a nonhuman like Hanson?

Hyde-White had sworn the same oaths as the rest of the Circle, dedicating himself to restoring the rightful monarch and purifying the land. Such purification applied not just to the pollution but to the corrupting influence of metahuman genes as well. Glover's ancestors had fought to preserve British purity against the influx of the less advanced races. Their struggle seemed petty compared to the battle he fought against the scourge of mutated humanity that threatened to overwhelm even the debased blood of the lower classes.

Metahumans were little better than beasts, and Hanson, with the bestial aspect he presented astrally, was clearly one of the worst kind.

Hyde-White was devious, but he was also a practical

man. Like all well-brought-up men of his class, he understood the nature of the underclasses. Just as Glover himself did. Which was, of course, the answer. Hanson would only be a tool, a resource to be used up and disposed of when he was no longer useful. That made sense. It was only an unpleasant necessity that required Glover to deal with Hanson personally.

Hanson seemed unaware of Glover's distaste for him. Or, if he was aware, he was indifferent. Either way suited Glover. Hanson's repugnant presence was a temporary annoyance, one more burden to bear in the furtherance of the cause.

"They are ready," Hanson said.

"Then we should not delay."

Glover swept past Hanson and entered the room. In its center five people lay bound. They were dregs chosen from the flotsam of the metroplex, three of them orks. They were a far cry from the pure bloodlines of the sacrifices in Neville's ritual. Glover personally found such submen repugnant. There would be no room for them in his resurrected Britain. The mongrel half-breed foreigners who made up the rest of the sacrifice were little better, but what they were was unimportant. It was what they represented that mattered.

Power.

Such sacrificial offerings had given their energy to aid the Circle, restoring the power lost by the deaths of Young Neville and Fitzgilbert. Even without the full nine, Glover could feel that their ritual workings were stronger, and Hyde-White had suggested that they would grow stronger still. Each completion of the cycle would double their power. It was an added benefit that they could purge the land of such misfits while they gathered strength to restore it.

Too bad there were no elves among tonight's participants. Their legendary physical beauty belied their deceptive and corrupt natures. They had cost Britain dearly. When the restoration came, they would pay for the land they had stolen and for the souls they had corrupted, but first the Hidden Circle needed strength. He turned his mind to the matter at hand.

Glover shrugged back the shoulders of his topcoat, revealing the golden pectoral he wore in his office as archdruid. Hanson's solicitous hands removed the outer garment. Gordon straightened from where he had been bent over to talk to one of the orks, and took his place among the acolytes. Glover nodded to each of the druids present. Of their diminished circle, only Hyde-White and Neville were absent. Neville would attend the next ritual and Hyde-White the following one as they brought the current cycle to its conclusion.

As each druid walked solemnly to his appointed place, Glover stretched wide his arms and intoned the blessing. His words called the earth's spirit to witness the ritual they enacted here tonight for its benefit. The other druids sang counterpoint.

Across the circle, Gordon echoed his words. His eyes were closed and he spoke with prayerful intensity. Glover suspected that Gordon believed in this new path more fervently than did any of the druids themselves. Glover was pleased. Hyde-White's tutoring was having a most salutory effect; the royal heir was wholly committed, embracing their course with all his heart.

Glover was momentarily startled as Gordon's eyes suddenly opened and met his. The belief he had supposed lay there, mantled in the strength and authority of the true king. Glover bowed, an acknowledgment of Gordon as the heir to the land, its heart and the barometer of its health. The bow was not subservient, though. As the keeper of the land, its magical arm of retribution, and its physician, the archdruid was a sovereign of sorts as well. Both king and archdruid had their spheres of power. Together they would lead the way to a new era.

Gordon returned a nod to Glover's bow. The archdruid bowed again, this time to the sacrifices stretched on the floor between them. The derelicts stared with wide eyes, frightened beasts. The first didn't start to scream until he saw the golden sickle in Glover's hand.

19

Willie's signal indicated that she had found something of interest in the derelict building. Sam thought that the structure looked unsafe, teetering on the edge of disintegration. That made it just like all of its neighbors. The whole neighborhood seemed to be decaying.

It had been several hours since they had lost Glover's trail at the edge of the sleazy East End. Sam had held little hope of picking up the druid's trail, but Estios had insisted that they sweep as much territory as possible. Expecting little, Sam had agreed. They all felt the pressure of time.

Willie signaled again, just after Sam had conducted his own astral reconnaissance of the building. The whole place had felt uncomfortable, and he hadn't been able to get a good look at several areas; the psychic static was too strong. It was as if something terrible had happened within, something . . . he really wanted to say evil, but it sounded silly and he had no desire to be laughed at by Estios. He tried to shrug off the sense of foreboding. At least he hadn't seen any live opponents. Willie's signal confirmed that there was no one there.

Estios went in first. The tall elf was arrogant and unlikable, but he had courage. In this benighted part of the plex, there was always the possibility of a trap. Some thrill seeker might set one for kicks, or some paranoid squatter might be defending his stash. Astral senses couldn't detect mechanical or electronic mechanisms with any reliability and Willie's sensors weren't infallable.

O'Connor remained with Sam and Hart. The division of forces was uneven but had become standard procedure. The suspicious Estios always wanted one of his party with Hart at all times. Sam suspected that O'Connor had orders to kill Hart if anything went wrong.

Estios waved from the doorway. Trying to appear casual, Sam and the others crossed the street one by one and disappeared into the building. Estios led them to the basement, toward the place where the psychic static had been the worst. Before they reached it, Sam could smell the stink of blood and feces.

The room was an abattoir. In characteristically opportunistic fashion, the sprawl's scavengers had gone to work. Already the remains of the butchers' handiwork were being spread around. Sam counted five skulls, three orks and two norms. Chittering and squalling at the interruption, the scavengers fled.

Willie's drone sat in one corner. A red telltale winked several times in greeting as its camera eye swiveled to track the motion of their entrance. The upper ring of blades just under the comm dome began to whirl, buzzing as they did. The lower ring began its counter-rotation. As soon as both sets achieved speed, the drone lifted from the floor and folded its five-part landing gear together into a cone. The half-meter-long cylinder, with its twin whirring necklaces of distortion, flitted through a window. Willie would be standing sentry while they investigated.

There were little more to the remains than skeletons. Organs were strewn and dragged around, but there was a noticeable absence of meat. A close look showed that the bones had been cut and there were scrape marks where flesh had been razored away.

"This is a Bone Boy kill," Estios said.

"What's this got to do with the druids?" Sam asked.

No one answered. Sam stood in the midst of the carnage. He could do no more than stare. He had heard of the Bone Boy killing spree on the media, but it had seemed no more than the everyday violence associated with the overcrowded sprawls. Even the most sensational reports didn't match the reality of standing in the place where helpless victims had died. He understood the psychic static now; his astral senses had been defeated by the pain and suffering of the dead. His stomach roiled.

"No, Hart," O'Connor said.

Sam turned to see what she was forbidding Hart to do and found O'Connor staring at the skeleton. Hart and Estios were in conference by a doorway that led deeper into the building. O'Connor had been talking to herself.

She had said *no heart*.

O'Connor looked up to find him staring perplexedly.

"There's no sign of the hearts of any of the victims."

Among all the organic debris, Sam wondered how she could be sure. "It could have been eaten."

"The other organs have been gnawed. Some have been almost completely devoured, but there's enough left to identify them. I don't see any heart tissue at all. The killers must have taken their victims' hearts along with the flesh."

"Then, it's not ghouls," Sam said.

"Not their pattern," O'Connor confirmed. "They might have taken the meat, but if they were organ eaters, they would have taken the rest as well."

"The kills were physical, but there is residual spell energy," Estios said.

"It isn't random violence," Hart said.

"Did you seriously think for a minute that it was?" Estios asked sneeringly.

Sam didn't like it when Estios talked to Hart that way. His anger leaked heat into his voice. "Why couldn't it be? There are senseless killings every day. The sprawls are full of crazies and people who would kill for any one of a thousand reasons, including the thrill. Some of them even use magic."

"Why, then?" Hart asked Estios as if Sam had never spoken.

"Isn't it obvious?" Estios replied. "It's a ritual killing."

"The Hidden Circle?" Sam didn't really want an affirmative answer.

"Insufficient data." Hart's brow furrowed as she thought. "The timing of the Bone Boy spree is suggestive. Our having lost Glover even more so. If he had help, there would have been more than enough time for this atrocity."

"There was help. Marks in the blood show at least a half dozen individuals," O'Connor said.

Sam was distracted from the continuing evaluation of the evidence by the receiver he wore tucked in his ear. Its insistent tone told him that Willie had spotted somebody. The coding of the tone said police.

"Badges coming," he told the others nervously. "We'd better get out of here."

Estios cast a spell to clean their shoes and garments as they left the massacre room. They would leave no tracks of blood. It was only a short walk to a tube station, where they buried their trail in the crush of humanity.

20

Eyes of molten gold stripped away her soul. Janice was as she had been, a human woman. She was weak, powerless. She could not lie to those eyes. They knew when she lied.

The man with the golden eyes had been asking her questions. It seemed as if her whole existence had been a cycle of questions and answers. He asked and she answered, but somehow her answers didn't satisfy him. The truth, her father had said, would set her free. She had told the truth and remained shackled.

"What is your importance to them?" the man asked.

"I don't know what you're talking about," she replied.

"Denial will not save you," he said sternly.

Pain.

Her muscles spasmed as the fiery agony shot through her. What had she done to deserve this? She had told the truth. Why wasn't she free?

"Tell me."

"I don't know!"

Tears streamed down her face. He touched her shoulder and she flinched. His touch was a spider crawling along her neck and onto her face. She tried to flinch away, but her limbs would not obey her. Something held her in place. She looked down to see dark bands encircling her wrists and ankles. Had the restraints been mere iron, she would had struggled to break them, but her bonds were hard chitinous bands, alien things from which there was no escape.

"Do not resist."

Fear seized her. No longer able to endure the horror at his touch, she screamed. Despite the hopelessness, she threw her head from side to side and wrenched at the restraints. She wanted to be free. She had to be satisfied with dislodging the hand which caressed her face.

"Remarkable."

The next words were distant, lacking in the obscene clarity of the previous ones. It was as if someone else spoke in a language that she did not understand.

"It is as you say."

More bodiless voices murmured to the man and he spoke back. His comments and questions melded with the susurrus of the distant voices until at last he said, "She shall at least be useful."

A new face rose before her eyes. It was masked and hooded, swathed in cloth of pale green. Dark eyes regarded her without emotion. She might have been a bench. An impossible mouth opened in the masked face, its teeth a glittering array of hypodermic needles. The mouth drew nearer and she screamed again. And again. Unable to move, unable to even turn her head, she stared in deadly fascination as the obscene visage drew closer. Closer. The violator's lips touched hers and her mouth went numb.

Her vision fogged and star-shot darkness swirled around her. She felt detached as the violator's face lifted from hers. The needles were gone. There were only dark, lustrous, slightly slanted eyes behind the green mask. Then the mask melted away and she beheld the face of Hugh Glass. His fine elven features were as beautiful as ever.

How had he come to be here? He had rescued her from Yomi, promising to take her to safety. Had he come to take her away again? But she had been an ork when she had met Hugh. Now she was human. She reached out, longing to convince herself that he was real. She so desperately wanted the nightmare with the golden-eyed man to be over that she was happy to see even Hugh. She looked at the hand she was lifting to touch his face. It was furred and taloned. She wasn't human anymore. She would never be human again.

Hugh smiled at her. His lips parted as his grin grew, and the perfect white teeth that she remembered were not there. In their place was a writhing mass of corruption. He laughed as she screamed.

She clawed at him, feeling grim satisfaction as she felt flesh tear under her talons. Then her arm was restrained again with a harsh, hot pressure around her wrist. But she smelled blood. It was good. It was real.

She awoke.

Her wrist was held by Dan's strong hand. Bright blood welled from scratches in the dark skin of his face, but his expression was not one of anger. His eyes were full of concern; for her, she realized. As soon as he understood that she was fully awake, he released his grip. She started to shake and he embraced her, murmuring soft reassurances.

In her dream, she had seen him as Hugh and struck out. But he was not Hugh. He would never be Hugh. Hugh would have struck her back. Dan was always gentle with her, a kind spirit in a bestial body, the exact opposite of the handsome Hugh.

Teary-eyed, she examined the wound she had caused. It was already healing. She sniffed and gave him a weak smile.

"It's all right," he said.

And it was. She felt safe, secure. Shiroi's love was real, unlike the false promises of Hugh. If she had harbored any remaining doubts, his patient, caring reaction to her violence banished them. Shiroi's love was no sham, no ploy to use her for his purposes. She knew Shiroi loved her for herself. How could she not love him back?

21

The man of Light confronted Sam again, blazing with the intensity of the sun. Sam could not look at him, could not stand before him. The heat scorched Sam's skin, driving him to retreat. Sam's earliest manifestation of shamanic power had been a spontaneous protection from fire, but this was a fire from which he was not safe. He howled in frustration, a frighteningly animal sound.

The Man of Light laughed.

Sam fled the laughter all the way to wakefulness. The room in which he had been sleeping was cold, but the sheets were soaked with sweat. Seeking comfort, he reached out for Hart and found she was gone. He was alone in the twilight gloom.

Through the open door he could hear the tapping of fingers on a keyboard in the next room. The rhythm wasn't Dodger's; there were odd patterns in the tapping, so it must be Willie rigging. There were no voices. Most likely, the technomancer was alone. Sam wondered where Hart had gone.

Sam threw back the clammy sheets and got out of bed. He was shaking, and he knew that it was from more than a chill in the room. Every time he even thought about the Man of Light, he felt the terror rise.

He didn't know where the Man had come from. It seemed to Sam that He hadn't always been there, blocking the way to the shamanic planes. But Sam wasn't sure. Sam had never been comfortable with the idea of being a shaman. Perhaps the Man of Light was only a manifestation of his own fears. The Man might simply be a symbolic representation of his own reluctance to practice the shamanic powers.

The water from the sink didn't flow very quickly. His fingers were numb from its frigid touch before he had gathered enough to splash into his face. The shock was bracing and cleared his head a bit. He ran his damp hands through his hair and beard, smoothing them into place. Trying to put his night fears behind him, he dressed.

"Hoi, Twist," Willie greeted him as he entered the room where the dwarf woman was engaged with her hardware. "Kaf on the plate."

"Thanks," he mumbled. He got some juice out of the refrigerator. "Working?"

"Just testing my eyes and ears."

"Hart say where she was going?"

"Neg."

"How about when she'd be back?"

"Neg."

Great.

"Null the glum, chummer Twist. Let me give you a little something for your other set of brains. Stayed around after you meatfeet left the squat with the bods and watched the badges. They didn't spend a lot of time, but they did mess up the scene and didn't take any evidence. In fact, it looked to me like they were deliberately destroying some. So I got suspicious and followed them. They met with Inspector Burnside. He didn't seem very surprised by their report, and that got me really suspicious." She waited for Sam's reaction and shrugged when he had none. "That didn't add, Twist. Burnside's a copper's cop, straight as they come. The whole shadow world knows that he's a hard-nosed, real believer in justice that don't bend the law. But those jokers reporting to him had done just that. And he just listened. I tell ya, Twist, it don't add."

"Maybe he's changed."

"Burnside's immutable."

"Maybe somebody's blackmailing him."

"Possible, but unlikely. Even if he'd done something wrong that your somebody could hold over his head, Burnside would more than likely bring them up on charges, even if he took a fall himself."

"I wish we knew more. Dodger could deck into his files, but he's not here. I don't suppose you could do it, Willie."

"Why don't you do it yourself? You've got a jack."

"I don't deck anymore."

Willie gave him a look that told him she thought that his mind was short-circuited. In her world, nobody ever gave it up until they died or brain-fried.

"I suppose I could, since your elf buddy is still busy. If you've got access to a good enough deck. No guarantees, though. It's not my line. A rig may look like a deck but it's completely different where it counts."

"I understand. I'll see what I can do."

It took Sam less than an hour to make a deal with a fixer he had met through Hart. The negotiation wasn't easy, and Sam came away owing more than he cared. He also came away with the cyberdeck he needed.

A few hours later, Willie jacked out and said, "Don't that beat it."

"What?"

"Burnside is the officer in charge of the Bone Boy Murders investigation. Has been since the third batch of skeletons turned up. Direct transfer from on high."

"Who?"

"Been taking a course in interrogatives, Twist?" Willie's laugh would have been a giggle if it had been higher pitched. "Well, there are the usual official orders, but they're not quite right. Wrong incept codes. It took a little doing but I found a trail that leads right on up to the Ministry of the Interior."

"The government's involved." Rogue druids, megalomaniac corporates, and fanatical aristocrats weren't enough.

"Part of it, anyway." Willie positioned the soles of her boots against the edge of the table and rocked her chair back. "What now, Twist?"

"Let's start with the police. Check Burnside's duty roster and compare it with that of the two officers you followed last night. See where they coincide. We'll want to know how wide the conspiracy is. And see if there are any shifts from a regular schedule. Back check it, too."

Willie grumbled, but she went back to work.

When she jacked out again, Sam said, "I'll bet you came up with a correlation between sudden duty for Burnside and his friends and the dates and times of Bone Boy hits. Or at least a correspondence with the discovery of the bodies."

"So why did I have to do all this work?"

"I was just guessing. We can't afford to guess."

"Yeah, well. Did you guess that there's a pattern to the Bone Boy killings?"

"What kind of pattern?"

"A nasty one. There's a few breaks in the first set, but it's pretty clear, anyway. The second set confirms it."

"Confirms what, Willie?"

"The pattern. The number of bodies goes one on the first night, two the next time, three after that, and so on until there are seven victims. Then it starts again."

"Seven? Not nine?"

"Affirm."

"There were nine druids in the Circle."

"And two of them croaked on the Solstice."

"They might have restored their number. That would be the smart thing for a magical circle to do. Maybe the Bone Boy killers aren't the Circle."

"Whoever is doing the killing, they're methodical. Seven days between the first and second killings. Six between the second and third, and on down to two between body count six and seven. Just one day, then a single Bone Boy kill. Seven days later, a double. And so on. Three days ago, we got five bodies. Get the picture?"

"Very methodical. Tonight should be a six-victim killing. Whether it's the Hidden Circle or not, this is a ritual spree."

Willie and Sam progressed from arguing the possible connection to the druids to using Willie's spy drone to monitor the progress of the police. If they followed the pattern, the Bone Boys would be active tonight, and if the police were involved, the runners might lead the watchers to the site in time to determine the nature of the perpetrators. At the very least, they might be able to rule out police collusion. Willie's drone headed for the Burnside's stationhouse, and they only had to wait a half-hour before he left. He was joined by the two detectives the runners had previously almost encountered. Willie and Sam watched the trio set up a tail on an individual who emerged from a fancy townhouse in Regent's Park. They were hunched over the receptor screen when Hart returned.

"What's going down?" she asked.

"We're waiting for something to happen," Sam replied abstractedly.

Hart squinted at the display screen. "That's Burnside!"

"Uh-huh."

"What's going on?"

Sam explained what he and Willie had found out and the theories the data had spawned. Hart joined them at the screen.

Willie's drone was focused on Burnside and the two officers who accompanied him. All were dressed for

undercover work and blended in with the street crowd.
The only thing which set them apart was their apparent
nervousness. After some minutes, Burnside sent his
two officers away. Willie sent the drone flitting after
them and discovered that they were taking up independent surveillance positions around the building the man
had entered. The policemen had set up an old-
fashioned stakeout. They could have used a drone
similar to Willie's, but they didn't—a sure indication
the operation was not official, since police use of remote pilot machines needed to be recorded.

Willie sent the drone higher to cover the whole
block. It was another hour before anything happened.
Then Hart spotted someone leaving the building and
directed Willie to send the drone in for a closer look.
Careful to keep her machine out of sight, Willie positioned it for a zoom-in shot of the persons exiting
the building. A woman led a pack of three men, who
struggled with plastic sacks. None were familiar, but
Willie recorded their images.

The drone returned to station in time to catch a second group almost vanishing from its camera range.
The sacks on the backs of that group's laggards
prompted a quick pursuit. This time, the runners were
rewarded.

"Glover," Sam said quietly.

There was no doubt about his identity; Sam knew
the face too well. Willie recorded the images of the
strangers accompanying the druid.

"Back to station, Willie," Hart ordered. "They're
leaving in small groups and we don't want to miss any.
If the pattern holds, my guess is that all but one were
present tonight."

"Roger."

The drone flitted back. It swooped four more times
to record the passage of furtive groups leaving the
scene. When the last group had left, the policemen

began to move in. Taking a risk that the badges would spot the drone, Willie sent it in ahead of them for a fast pass to confirm the contents of the building. Deep in its heart lay six skeletons, already being attacked by scavengers.

"Do we tell Estios?" Willie asked.

"Not just yet. Let's run down the images first," Hart suggested.

"It's your call, Twist," Willie said.

Sam sighed. "We'd better identify them first."

"Roger," Willie responded. She dumped the recordings to the cyberdeck and began the process of image enhancement and correlation.

Sam hoped it wouldn't take long. If the pattern held, and he had no reason to believe it wouldn't, seven more innocents would die in less than forty-eight hours.

22

"Your report was most enlightening, Katherine." Bambatu smiled, his teeth a dazzling white against the darkness of his skin. "But I fear that you must change your plans. The Lady has considered the information and is determined on a new course of action. The foolish druids of the Hidden Circle have embarked on a course that the Lady believes will be their downfall and that of the Lord Protector. She is convinced of it. In fact, she is sure that they will collapse in such a decisive and spectacular manner that they shall need no help from us. Such self-destruction suits the Lady's plans better than the original plan to disrupt them from outside. Therefore, she wishes that you no longer participate in any operations that will curtail the Circle's activities.''

''What about Verner and the Estios's crew?''

''They must not be allowed to disturb the Circle, either.''

That was a troublesome order. Sam was not going to be easy to dissuade. She had encountered his dogged persistence during the doppelganger affair. And since they had become lovers, she had learned how deeply his passion for justice ran. He would not give up on this chase until it was concluded. He would be impossible to live with if she forced him away from his quest to make the Circle pay for their evil. To her surprise, she found herself worried about that possibility. Why? He was just another bedmate. Wasn't he? She hadn't even begun to consider the implications of her concern when Bombatu resumed speaking.

''The Lady has decided that eliminating Verner from the situation would disrupt the runner operations most effectively with the least repercussions. She expects you to handle the details with your usual efficiency.''

''I'll get him out of the country immediately.''

''Oh no, Katherine. That will not do. He must be killed.''

23

''West on Romford Road.''

The audio signal was a surprise. Willie didn't often speak while rigging. She claimed that it disturbed her rapport with the machine.

She was trailing one of the newly identified druids, Thomas Alfred Carstairs, Lord Mayor of the industrial

Birmingham District of the London Sprawl. The Lord Mayor was accompanied by a pair of toughs who registered as enhanced on Willie's scanners. All three were carrying weapons. Beyond his bodyguard-servants, the Lord Mayor had dispensed with the usual entourage. He had business tonight; private business.

The pattern of killings predicted that tonight would see another kill of seven, one for each druid. The runners knew now that the Hidden Circle had not replaced the members lost on the Solstice. They had not recruited replacements to restore their number before engaging in further ritual activities. Did they feel the press of time? Were they facing some deadline? The runners were still in the dark as to the reason for the Circle's nefarious activities.

Sam hoped that Carstairs was going to be easier to trail than Glover had been when they had first discovered the connection between the Bone Boy killings and the Hidden Circle. The runners could not afford the time to search house-to-house if he lost them as he neared his proposed murder site. Sam didn't want to see anyone else die to serve the Circle's ends.

Following Inspector Burnside was also no longer an option. That course had gotten expensive when he had spotted one of Willie's spy drones and had it skragged by a mage from the precinct anti-surveillance squad. The dwarf rigger had flatly refused to send any more with him.

With the night of sacrifice upon them, they had just finished identifying the Circle's members by name, and there had only been enough time to locate one of them, the Honorable Mister Carstairs. Like all of the druids, the Lord Mayor was a magician, and that made it risky to follow him astrally. The ground team worked a mundane trail, supplemented by Willie's drone.

The group of hunters managed to move through the crowds and cold winter fog without incident. Willie signaled that Carstairs had reached a destination, and the runners regrouped. Carstairs had entered an old warehouse, its name and trade long obliterated by time and the corrosive action of the London atmosphere. The broken pavement of the street sloped and Sam knew they were somewhere near the river; the fog was always thicker there.

"Recon, Willie," Sam ordered. "Find out where they've set up and signal when they begin the ritual. We'll want to catch them then. That'll be as low as their guard will get before they start killing people."

One beep signaled Willie's affirmative.

They waited.

Estios and his team checked their guns, returning them to concealment under their long coats whenever a passerby wandered close. Hart fingered one of the decorations on her belt. They were deadly throwing weapons but looked like mere decorative flash. Fidgeting wasn't like her. She had seemed distracted for the past two days, but she had shut down his every attempt to talk with a shake of her head and a sad smile. Her attitude only increased his own nervousness. He jumped when Willie sent twin beeps to the receiver in his ear.

That wasn't the pre-arranged signal. Sam's mouth went dry.

"Willie?" he asked tentaively.

"What's going on?" she replied. "Where are you guys? It's been twenty minutes."

"We're holding for your signal. You didn't signal."

There was a pause. "Couldn't you hear the screams?"

"Drek!" No sound had reached the watchers.

Sam leaped up, drawing his Narcoject Lethe as he did. The tranquilizer gun felt light and insubstantial. People were being tortured to death and all he had was a toy gun. Was that justice?

Estios was already halfway across the street by the time Sam left the sidewalk. Chatterjee and O'Connor were only a couple of meters behind their leader. As usual, the tall elf was going to be the first one in. Hart hung back, pacing Sam. He knew she could move faster than that. Didn't she feel the same urgency as the rest of them? They were only five people and a drone against the seven druids and an unknown number of flunkies. Sam wished Dodger and his Sandler were along, but the elf was still haunting the Matrix.

Estios barreled through the doorway, only to be flung immediately back. Sam skidded to a halt and shifted to his astral senses. A glow lit the doorway, a magical barrier. Estios picked himself up, his own aura flaring as he did. Sam watched the color shift toward the hue of the barrier as Estios attuned himself to its psychic frequency. The tall elf leaned grimly on the luminescent wall until the tones matched and he passed through.

Chatterjee grabbed O'Connor, enveloping her with his own power and dragging her through. Sam shifted back to normal perception and followed. Maybe it was a good thing that Dodger wasn't there; Sam didn't know Chatterjee's trick and Dodger would have been unable to pass the barrier.

Hitting the wall felt like pressing through a plastic bag. It stretched and strained until it suddenly released him and he was inside in the deeper darkness of the building. Now he could hear the screams. Impelled by a new urgency, he barreled forward, only to be caught by O'Connor.

"No so fast, Twist. You're no shock trooper," she whispered urgently. "Dodger would never forgive me if I let you rush to death."

She was right. Getting themselves killed wouldn't help those poor unfortunates, and rushing blindly in would get them killed. There had been one barrier, and there might be more. There might be physical traps as well. Or hidden guards.

Estios, Chatterjee, and O'Connor scanned the dark with their elven eyes. Feeling inadequate, Sam tugged out his light amplification goggles and donned them. The murk lightened a little.

Estios cursed. "This fragging rattletrap distorts sound. Call the halfer and get a precise location. I want numbers of hostiles and weapons."

"What about electronic intercept?" Sam asked.

"They're busy. Remember?"

A long quavering scream punctuated Estios's question.

Sam passed Estios's request on to Willie and switched his receiver to full speaker mode.

"Two flights down in the sub-basement," she reported. "About ten meters northwest of main door. Seven druids and eight assistants present. Don't know where the rest went. All have knives. All assistants and most of the druids are packing—nothing heavy. Access on north and west."

"Frag it! I wish we had a picture," Estios said. "Can't be helped. Chatterjee and I will take the north approach. It'll take us a while to get into position, so the rest of you get to the west entrance and wait. Nobody moves until we go in. Got it?"

"Yes," O'Connor answered.

Sam nodded.

It wasn't until he and O'Connor were crouched just outside the entrance to their destination that Sam realized Hart was not with them. But the shattering impact of the scene before him drove all worry about her from his mind.

The chamber was huge. Great arches and porticoes extended it beyond Sam's line of sight. The floor on the east side dropped away abruptly in an embankment. An arm of the Thames had been diverted into this area. Sam noted distortion on the water surface and searched the shadows until he found Willie's spy drone, hovering near the vaulted ceiling. From the scattered piles of moldering crates, this place had once been a loading dock. In olden times it had held the hustle of honest workmen, or perhaps dishonest ones. Now it hosted workmen of an evil bent. Its stone walls range with the screams of their tortured victims, scattering the echoes into an infinity of agony.

The druids were gathered in a cleared area about five meters south of the west entrance. Magefire lit their work, providing enough light for Sam's goggles. Far too much light. He had no need to see them slicing flesh from the victims who remained alive. They were moving briskly; there already were three skeletons on the dank floor.

"This one is diseased," Carstairs announced as if observing the color of a house.

"Dispose of the affected parts. Such flesh is unsuitable," Hyde-White told him.

Carstairs nodded. The golden sickle in his hand rose and fell. The Lord Mayor's victim shuddered and went limp, her screams abruptly cutting off as she fainted. Or died.

Sam's mouth filled with bile as he watched Carstairs hold out a severed limb to one of the assistants. The man who took it was tall, well-dressed, and almost regal-looking. He seemed pleased to be of service. He carried the arm reverently across the chamber and stopped a foot from the stairs that led down to a river landing. Throwing underarm, he pitched the limb far out into the polluted waters where it splashed softly and disappeared. The man returned to his station, oblivious to the blood on his hands.

A flicker of motion caught Sam's attention. Two men were moving in from the north entrance. Estios and Chatterjee. Sam watched them crouch in the lee of a pillar and begin a mystical centering process. He turned his attention to the druids, drawing a bead on Glover. He was not happy to see the pectoral of the archdruid on the man's chest.

Estios and Chatterjee unleashed a brace of fireballs. Mystic energy exploded on either flank of the druids' gathering, flinging flaming men and women in all directions. Sam saw Carstairs go down.

At the sudden violence, Sam flinched involuntarily, but his target reacted better. Glover's body flared with a defensive spell as he ducked for cover.

"Hanson," he shouted. "Protect me."

Sam lost his clear shot as the big acolyte stepped between him and Glover. *Just delaying the inevitable, Glover.* He shot Hanson, but the man didn't go down. Another dose of the Lethe tranquillizer might overload his system and kill him, but given the man's involvement in the druids' affairs, Sam didn't care. He fired again. Hanson staggered, but still didn't go down. He showed no sign that the drug was having any effect at all. Sam emptied the rest of his clip into Hanson, rapidly reloading as the man stumbled forward.

By Sam's side O'Connor opened fire, raking the crowd with her H&K G12. Sam watched her hose down a group clustered around Hyde-White. His protective flunkies fell like mown wheat. The fat old druid sagged as O'Connor's slugs reached him. He joined his followers on the cold, damp stone.

Taking down half of the Circle's numbers wasn't enough to stop the fight. The enemy had split up, scattering around the chamber in search of protected firing positions. Fortunately, the enemy's actions remained uncoordinated. Better still, they were indecisive. That was good; the druids probably didn't realize that they had the runners outnumbered, outgunned, and outmagicked. The imbalance of magicians was what worried Sam the most. Flashes and bursts of sound and

smell from the far side of the chamber raised his worry to fear as Estios and Chatterjee came under magical attack. Their defenses and luck were holding, though, and the sharp buzzsaw sound of their G12s made it clear that they were still functional.

A throbbing moan announced the arrival of the runners' equalizer, Willie's combat drone. Unlike the smaller spy drone, this machine was armed and armored. It was also far from quiet; only the sound of the combat had allowed it to approach undetected. But it was here now and odds shifted more in the runners' favor. The drone's high-tech nature made it largely immune to magic, and its firepower alone was probably more than the druids could deal with. Panels slid back along the cylinder's side and gun muzzles snouted forth.

Before the drone could open fire, the room was suddenly lit by an enormous flare of white light. Sam screamed as his amplification goggles overloaded, the compensators not quite quick enough to spare him from all of the burst. The shouts and howls from the druids' forces showed that the runners weren't the only ones caught unprepared for the tactic.

Sam dropped to the floor and ripped the goggles free. He rubbed at his eyes as if he could scrub the whirling spots of color away. Blind, he was helpless.

The drone wasn't firing. Had Willie's sensors been affected too? If so, they were hosed.

Several people ran by his position, but he could do nothing. He heard O'Connor's G12 fire and send slugs into the wall. Her sight was affected as well. They would have been dead now if the druids hadn't been more interested in escaping.

Sam's eyesight cleared with maddening slowness. But when he began to focus on his surroundings, he almost wished he couldn't.

Some kind of dark slimy sludge was puddled near

the body of an acolyte who had fallen near the open sewer. Contrary to the slope of the floor, the puddle was moving. Sparkling with an oily iridescence, the polluted surface of the river was flowing up and over the cornice. The leading edge of the slick reached the fallen woman but instead of creeping along and under her outstretched arm, it crawled up and over. Black smoke rose hissing where sludge contacted flesh and cloth. Sam saw bone where spatters of the slime had leaped ahead of the puddle's leading edge.

As the body disappeared under the advancing foulness, the slime began to bubble. A mound humped where the woman had lain, welling up into a hideously humanoid column.

Sam flashed on a warehouse in Hong Kong, remembering the thing Glover had raised there. Then, the toxic spirit had saved Sam's life, even though the result had only been incidental to saving Glover. This time, it was Sam who threatened Glover.

The noxious parody of a man lurched toward him.

As the slime thing rose, the remaining druids and their acolytes burst from hiding. Under cover of magical and mundane firepower, they made a concerted break for the northern entrance. Estios and Chatterjee, unable to reply to the concentration of firepower, couldn't stop them. Leaving their dead and wounded behind, the druids fled.

As soon as he had a chance, Estios fired at their retreating backs. He rose from his hiding place and shouted for the runners to follow him in pursuit. He didn't wait to see if he was obeyed. Chatterjee was hard on his heels, and O'Connor hurried to join her fellow elves. Sam hesitated, unsure of the wisdom of pell-mell pursuit into the dark; he had lost his goggles. In that moment, the thing moved between him and the northern door.

Like an angry wasp, Willie's drone buzzed the slime

shape, 5.56mm machine guns blazing. The drone's high velocity slugs tore through one side of the thing and out the other with no apparent effect. The thing's half-formed head swiveled to track the drone as it circled.

Willie concentrated the fire of both guns on the shape's malformed shoulder. Bullets slammed into the viscous goo, perforating the limb. The guns raked up and down, dumping a volume of fire that eliminated in-pouring slime before it could reseal the breech. The right arm that had been reaching languidly toward the drone dropped to the floor and splashed on the hard stone.

A rapid series of beeps from the drone was Willie's cheer.

Sam didn't join in. He was watching the puddles of the arm coalesce and flow into the base of the shape. Willie wouldn't be seeing it; she would be concentrating on amputating the thing's other arm.

The second limb splashed down only to trickle back to the parent mass. Willie was keeping its attention but doing no significant damage. Sam thought it would be wisest to get out as soon as he could. A bulge was beginning to develop on the monster's right shoulder. It would be restored to itself soon, and Willie's ammo supply was limited.

Sam was looking for a way past the thing when he realized that it wasn't reforming an arm. Its shoulder just continued to bulge until it began to look hunchbacked. Willie's fire gnawed at its neck, but the thicker attachment was proving more resistant to the drone's fire.

With appalling speed, a tentacle burst from the growth on the thing's shoulder, whipping out and wrapping itself around the drone. The shock and mass almost brought the machine down, but Willie revved the rotors. The blades sliced gobs from the pseudopod and the drone rose again, but it was still trapped.

The monster pumped its substance into the tentacle, becoming thinner and thinner as the portion gripping the drone bloated. It was nearly a caricature stick figure by the time the mass overcame the drone's lift capability and the machine crashed to the floor. The drone's landing gear was still retracted and the rounded lower end offered no stability. The cylinder canted sideways immediately. Guns firing wildly, the drone toppled.

With the drone down, the massive cord wrapped around its middle sagged. The walls of the tentacle relaxed, letting its toxic substance flow across the surface of the captive machine. The shining metal pitted and blackened everywhere the slime touched. A shower of sparks erupted as the first drip slithered through the open gun ports. The drone crackled with miniature lightnings, and acrid smoke billowed out through seams and service ports. A strangled machinery sound began to come from somewhere inside the drone, rising to an unbearably high pitch before suddenly cutting off. The lights which had begun flashing as soon as the drone hit the ground winked out.

The hovering spy drone's rotors cut out, and it dropped into the river with a splat.

Sam hoped the electronic feedback had only knocked Willie off line. There was no one there to jack her out if the destruction of her combat drone had caused a lethal interface loop. She might be dying alone.

He, on the other hand, was facing a messier death. He watched the slime flow and reshape itself into its hulking, humanoid shape.

24

Hart knew that she should have done something sooner, but she had been paralyzed by an uncharacteristic indecision. While she had dithered, the runners had set out after the Circle. Her arguments against precipitous action had been overriden by an equally uncharacteristic agreement between Dodger and Estios that they could not wait. Having those two elves backing him was all that Sam had needed.

His obsession with seeing the Circle stopped was every bit as strong as his fixation had been with bringing Haesslich to justice. But this time it was purer, more noble. It was more than just a revenge scheme. He was working against the Circle because he had been tricked into helping them with their plots. Deep down, though, he was out to stop them because they needed to be stopped. And he was right.

Maybe that was why her arguments had lacked force, why she had not found other ways to handle the problem.

When she had not been able to deflect the runners from charging in on the Circle's ritual, she had gone along. Opportunities could not always be predicted. Besides, if they had all been out of her sight, she would have had no way of keeping track of their actions, no hope of guiding them. She had still been looking for a way to short-circuit the raid when the precipitous rush into the old warehouse had begun.

The Lady would not be happy.

Hart had seen most of the druids escape the runners' attack. Given their capabilities, she had no fear that they would not escape Estios and the others, especially now that Willie's surveillance drones were neutralized. The Hidden Circle would re-form to perform their dirty magic. They were still a functional ritual group; even though they had lost members, their leaders and strongest magicians survived. Perhaps that would be enough for them to do whatever it was that the Lady expected them to do. If so, Hart's lack of action would be excusable. Except for one matter.

Sam.

From beneath the cloak of her invisibility spell, she watched him scramble about the warehouse looking for a weapon. He snatched a pistol from the hand of a dead acolyte and began firing at the slime thing stalking him. His calm was commendable; he grouped his shots neatly between the dark pits that would have been eyes if the monstrosity had had a face. His shots inflicted no significant damage.

The stubbornness that made him so persistent had betrayed him. Had he faced his true nature, he would have known how to deal with this summoning. This was a thing of magic; evil and twisted magic to be sure, but magic nonetheless. Short moments ago he had seen how ineffective the combat drone's machine gun fire had been. Had he studied spirits as he should have, he would have known that the minimal firepower of a pistol could not affect it. Magic must needs be fought with magic.

It would be so easy. All she had to do was turn her back and it would be over. She wouldn't even have to do it herself. Sam would be dead and the Lady would be satisfied. Or reasonably so. Distracting or eliminating Estios's crew wouldn't be so hard. By the letter, her contract would be fulfilled.

So why didn't she? Why was her heart racing and her palms sweating? She felt her concentration slip, and the invisibility spell die.

Sam's attention flickered from his opponent to her as she appeared. She saw fear in his eyes, and when he shouted, she knew what he feared.

"Get out! I can't stop it! Save yourself!"

Could she?

She summoned energy, twisting it into the shape of her most powerful spell of banishment. She felt the thing become aware of her. If she failed, it would come for her and she, exhausted from the attempted dismissal, would be easy prey. She unleashed the first tendril of magic to bind the spirit into submission. The spirit howled astrally as the ribbon of azure energy touched it. It struggled.

She sensed a vague familiarity—a feeling of previous acquaintance—as contact was made, and shuddered. She had never summoned such a thing. This was a toxic spirit such as could only be summoned by a demented magician. She would have no truck with such warped evil.

Her revulsion fed her will. The second tendril wrapped the spirit, adhering more tightly than the first. The spirit struggled against the bonds. Its efforts tore the first, but Hart replaced the sundered binding with a third and fourth. The thing's attempts at escape weakened. It began to plead wordlessly, but she had no pity for such a monstrosity. She tightened her spell, squeezing the toxic spirit out of existence.

What should never have been, was no more.

The world spun and her vision greyed as she slumped against the wall. The sludge spirit was banished, its animating presence terminated. Sam ran to her, carefully avoiding the puddles of caustic slime that were all that remained of the thing.

Practical. Even when running on emotion. If she had been so practical . . .

She blacked out.

25

Sam didn't know what kind of magic Hart had worked to destroy the sludge monster. He hadn't thought her capable of such a feat. Maybe she wasn't—she had collapsed almost as soon as she had finished the spell. He hoped she was all right. He knew that it was possible for a magician to cast a spell more powerful than she normally handled, and that the price for such sudden power was almost always death.

He was relieved to find her still breathing when he arrived at her side. He crouched and felt for the pulse in her neck. It was strong; she would be all right. *Thank you*, he prayed. He kissed her, thankful for the grace that had allowed her to perform the rescue and more thankful that she had survived it. He felt her return his kiss and knew she had revived.

''Ain't that a touching sight?''

Sam froze at the voice. Hart's narrowed eyes told him that the newcomer was armed. Moving slowly and carefully so as to not alarm him, Sam straightened from his crouch and turned around.

The man who had spoken wore a trenchcoat and a battered tweed hat. Sam didn't need to see a badge to recognize him as a London Metroplex detective; the outfit was almost a trademark. If they had been any doubt one look at the square, pock-marked face would have dissolved it, for Sam recognized the man as one of the detectives they had been investigating.

The policeman held a gleaming, big-bore pistol, pointing it unwaveringly at Sam. Though not a hardware fanatic, Sam knew enough to tell that this was no tranquilizer weapon. It was a mankiller. Sam had read that British police had once gone about their ordinary business without firearms, issuing weapons only in dire circumstances, but that practice had long since been abandoned. From his stance, it was clear that this man knew how to handle this weapon.

"Let's see your sticks. On the floor and roll them."

Sam cautiously accepted Hart's credstick and rolled it and his own across the floor as ordered. The detective retrieved them without taking his eyes from his captives. With deft motions he slotted Sam's stick into a reader he fished from his coat pocket. The reader gave off a two-tone beep after a minute. In another two minutes, it gave the same response to Hart's stick.

A second detective arrived.

"What have you got there, Dellett?"

"Two of the downsiders that were hanging around outside."

"ID?"

"Nothing real. SINs are d-code."

Dellett didn't sound surprised. Sam was only surprised at how quickly the cop's system had flagged the System Identification Numbers on their credsticks as belonging to deceased persons. The knowbots the detective had accessed were very good.

"Hey, Inspector," Dellett said. His face was lit as if he had gotten a bright idea. "Maybe we just caught ourselves the Bone Boy killers."

The inspector stepped out of the darkness. "Go help Rogers."

Dellett slid his pistol into a concealed holster and walked jauntily over to his fellow cop. Rogers was busy divesting Carstairs's clothing of anything secreted in it. Dellett began to strip the body. Saying nothing, the inspector watched Sam watch the process. When the two detectives had Carstairs's effects bundled together, they lifted the naked body and walked it awkwardly down the stairs to the river. Sam listened to the count that preceded a heave that forced a grunt from each of them. Dellett cursed when the splash threw some sludge onto his trenchcoat.

Given the disposal of Carstairs's body in such a way that his death would look like a simple downsprawl killing, Sam knew that the policemen would not be leaving until they had eliminated all evidence of the highly-placed people who had gathered here. He expected them to perform a similar duty for Hyde-White's body, but the detectives stood talking quietly at the top of the landing. Sam was confused. Why one druid and not the other? He sought out the spot where he had seen the fat old man go down, looking for the corpse. He didn't see it. The only body approaching the druid's bulk was that of a large furry thing. The metahuman's head had been raggedly severed from its body and was nowhere to be seen. Sam had met a similar creature once before, and it had concealed its true form behind an illusion. In that encounter, Sam had learned that his astral senses could pierce the illusion, but Sam had never had a chance to assense Hyde-White. The fat old druid's appearance must have been a lie. His reversion to true form at his death was saving the corrupt cops a bit of work. There was no need to conceal the manner and location of death, since no one would know the furred metahuman had been the fat industrialist.

But cops were supposed to stop crimes, not help commit them. The whole thing had smelled when he first learned of the apparent cover-up. It stank worse now that he had encountered it personally.

"I'd heard you were incorruptable, Burnside. Guess I heard wrong."

The inspector gave him a sharp look, and Sam knew he had made a mistake by using the inspector's name.

"Shut up, cypher," Burnside commanded.

"Don't you understand what's going on here? Do you have no idea what you're helping hide? Have you any idea how widespread the influence of this evil is?"

"I said shut up. I don't need a sermon from a cypher. Just because I'm part of the system doesn't mean I'm stupid. I understand what's going on here better than you do." Burnside let his gaze slip away from Sam and survey the carnage. "You're not just a cypher; you're a Yank cypher. That means that you couldn't have the faintest idea of what's important here and why."

Sam didn't think the English had a monopoly on knowing what was important. "I understand evil when I meet it. I know it has to be stopped."

"Maybe you should understand this, cypher. What happened here tonight is unhealthy. For you. For your friends. You're going to come along with us and be our guests until I'm satisfied that you're not trouble. For your sakes, I hope you don't know too much."

"I think you're trying to cover this up. I think you're as dirty as they come."

"Think what you want."

Sam could see that the inspector was nettled about something. Burnside was no happier about what he and his detectives were doing than Sam was. Sam suddenly thought he knew why the inspector was involved. "It's Gordon's involvement, isn't it?"

"I told you to shut up, cypher."

That touched a nerve. "You can't muzzle us."

"Can't I?" Burnside asked. "Remember, you're cyphers. Nobody'll miss you, or even know you're gone. You should know enough to choose your enemies carefully. If you say the wrong thing to the wrong person, don't expect to see tomorrow. Keep your mouth shut, and maybe you walk away from this."

Sam decided that keeping his mouth shut was a good idea; aggravating the inspector would only make things harder. His silence seemed to mollify Burnside. The detective called Dellett over to watch the runners and went to have a conference with Rogers. Dellett leaned against the west doorway and ignored Sam and Hart. He knew they weren't going anywhere as long as he was in their way.

As soon as he felt sure that Dellett wasn't paying attention, Sam whispered to Hart, "We've got to get out of here."

"Do tell. I'm too bushed to do much."

"Can you run?"

"If I have to. But no magic."

"Leave it to me. I've been wanting to show you something Herzog taught me when you weren't around."

"You sure you can do it?"

"No."

"No second chances, Sam, but you can't fly with your feet on the ground."

Sam concentrated, trying to remember the words Herzog had used for the spell. The memory was slippery, and he struggled to get it straight.

"Forget the words, remember the song."

Sam stiffened. *Drek, not now. Why does stress always trigger this schizoid stuff? Go away, Dog.*

"It ain't the stress, it's the pattern. Sing the song, or sing for the coppers."

I know.

"Then do it."

Get out of my head.

"Do it," Dog's voice said in a faded musical echo.

Sam caught the tune and sang silently to himself. The power gathered, shaping itself to the melody. When he had the rhythm just right, Sam released it.

Angry voices drifted into the chamber from

somewhere beyond the north entrance. They grew louder, as if they were approaching.

Burnside cursed and rushed for the archway. The other two policemen drew their weapons and followed. For the moment, their captives were forgotten. The spell had worked. While the detectives paid attention to the illusory voices, Sam and Hart slipped through the west entrance and away.

As soon as they hit the sidewalk, Hart started a staggering run toward the riverside.

"Where are you going?" Sam asked.

"Had a boat arranged in case we got hosed. The landing is only a couple of blocks."

"What about Willie?"

"We'll come back for her."

"She might need help now. The slime shorted her drone, and the feedback could have hurt her. Drek, it might have killed her."

Hart looked over her shoulder as if she expected Burnside and his goons to come pelting out of the warehouse at any moment. "If she's dead, we can't help her. If she's alive, we can't help her by getting locked up. Let's get out of here."

"If she's alive and we don't help her, she might not stay that way long. The Bone Boy may not be a ghoul, but that doesn't mean there aren't any in the East End. If Willie's out cold and exposed, she's easy meat."

"Sam, we . . ."

"I'm going after her. I can't abandon her."

Hart shook her head. "Okay. Let's go."

They ran up the street away from the river.

Since she disliked operating at extended range in the plex, Sam knew that she would have parked her van somewhere close by. He and Hart started checking likely places. They found the battered panel truck in the third place they tried. It looked barely functional, more like a derelict than a working vehicle. Appearances were deceiving; its motor and running gear were superbly maintained and its cargo area contained a multi-slot rigger board, multifrequency transceivers, trideo monitoring systems, and drone storage cells. In short, it was the rigger's camouflaged, rolling command center. Sam fidgeted while Hart disarmed the truck's protection, relaxing only when they opened the back to find Willie semi-conscious. The rigger let go her hold on awareness as soon as she realized her friends had found her. Hart gave the van a set of coordinates and told him that they were headed for a place she had used before.

They had been at Hart's safehouse for an hour before Willie responded to the drugs from her van's medical kit. When she opened her eyes her pupils were dilated, but Sam wasn't sure if it was because of the drugs or the rigger-loop feedback. Willie's words were slurred.

"What happened? Where's everybody?"

"Hart and I are here, Willie. You're going to be okay."

"Others get out?"

"Haven't heard from Estios and his crew since they took off after the druids. Nice of them to leave us with that slime thing."

Willie started to shake. Sam reached out to steady her.

"It's okay. Hart got it. It's gone, Willie."

"Sure?"

"Sure."

"I hate magic."

Me too, Sam wanted to say. He thought it more useful to stay positive. "Raid's over now. We must have done something right, we survived."

"What was that furry thing?" Willie asked.

"Looked like a sasquatch to me," Sam said.

"More likely was a wendigo," Hart opined.

"Though the two look a lot alike. Can't always tell even from the aura."

"Why do you think it was a—what did you call it?"

"Wendigo," Hart replied. "The flesh angle. A wendigo is a pananormal thing that eats human flesh. The Circle was probably stripping the corpses to keep it fed. Nasty business."

"Well, it's gonna be hungry for a long time now that its mouth don't connect to its stomach. I stitched the head clean off the furball."

Willie's smile stayed plastered on her face as her eyes sank closed and she began to snore.

26

It had been three microseconds since the activity monitor had registered data manipulation. A long time. Dodger considered the merits of opening the bubble that sealed his persona within the masked credit file he had uncovered in Glover's ATT discretionary funds. The number of manipulations the shunt bubble had passed through had been high, much higher than a legitimate or even an ordinary illegal transfer of funds. The bubble had traveled far, perhaps as far as the druids' innermost computer system. He knew he should wait longer. The operator who had called for the data he had piggybacked on might not be out of the system. Tired of waiting, he was ready for action. While it was a risk breaking out now, remaining encapsuled could be a greater one. He cancelled the program, restoring his ordinary Matrix persona and functionality.

The ebon boy stretched as if awakening from sleep,

then froze. There was no swirl of glitter around him. His dazzling cloak was gone, replaced with another kind of shine. His arms were encased in gleaming metal that was articulated in the style of antique armor. More than just his arms, his entire body was armored. The construct imagery was superb, but not his style at all. Dodger hit the reformat key, but the construct remained. He tapped out a routine to alter the imagery, and still got no result. A diagnostic on the cyberdeck registered nominal, which meant that the persona construct imagery was being imposed by the host system. Such an effect required a powerful system.

A look around told him just how powerful. Most systems, even imposed imagery systems, had a hint of the electron reality about them. Even the best virtual recompositers didn't always provide a truly realistic image, and they only supplied the specific translations to their slaved deck; other users still perceived the basic interface illusion. But this place was beyond the ordinary. Had he not known that magic was impossible in the Matrix, he would have thought the landscape touched with enchantment.

All around him lay a green and pleasant land. He stood at the edge of a forest looking out on rolling hills lush with croplands and scattered copses of woods. The forest behind him, a beautiful climax system, stretched away to the horizon in either direction. It was lush and burgeoning with woodland life. The sight, sound, and smell of it filled him with wonder. If it were real . . .

Dodger turned away and stared once more across the open vista. He could not afford to lose himself in amazement. For the moment, the forest was only a distraction. Perhaps when he had done what needed doing and seen what needed seeing, he would come

back to explore this marvelous construct. For now, he had to be about his work.

A careful visual search revealed no signs of habitation beyond the fields. Given the imagery, he thought it likely that any datastores or other useful computer nodes would appear as man-made structures. Given the girdling forest and the lack of buildings, he felt sure that he was on the fringes of the system. He would need to get deeper to find out anything.

Obstructed somehow by the interface, his standard programs failed to move him through the architecture at a reasonable pace. He tapped keys, improvising variations in a search for a compatible set of parameters. Frustrating minutes later, he finally realized that many of his tricks were inappropriate. Passwords and subroutines here would be strongly influenced by the imagery. Symbolically, not literally, for nothing was literal in the Matrix. He suspected that many programs in this system would have strategic orientations that could only be expressed in such a way as to manifest an appropriate construct imagery. A clever, if convoluted protection system. Any decker unwilling to accept the parameters of the imposed imagery would be paralyzed. But, as he had told uncounted admirers, he was not just any decker.

His fingers flew across the keyboard, searching out the avenues of correspondence with self-contained routines. Having grasped one of the master program's constraining strategies, he was able to formulate more appropriate responses and begin to manipulate the system. Successes began to accumulate, culminating in a soft whicker. He turned to pat the destrier that stood by his side. The horse nuzzled his hand and bumped his shoulder with its snout. Like a proper steed, it was eager for adventure. He mounted the milk-white stallion and settled into the high-cantled saddle. Then they were off, the horse's alabaster mane and tail streaming back in the wind.

The destrier's stride was steady and strong. The countryside rolled past. Despite deviations into likely valleys and detours to check out farmed land, Dodger found nothing more elaborate than thatch-roofed sod huts. Such were certainly nodes, but unlikely to hold anything of import. This system's imagery pattern demanded that what was important look important. He rode on until at last he glimpsed golden spires on the distant horizon. Turning the horse's head toward the structure, he spurred the beast forward.

The destrier climbed the last rise between them and their destination as swiftly as it had climbed the first. The road they had followed for the last several apparent miles led down the gentle slope to a bridge that spanned the valley's wide river. Beyond the water, the road climbed a well-grassed knoll and disappeared through the gates of the structure Dodger sought. The magnificent castle spread over the crown of the hill and its nacreous walls shown in the sunlight. Bright pennons fluttered on the conical peaks of dozens of subsidiary towers, but the spire of the great central tower flew a single flag. There a red banner with the three golden leopards of Britain flapped boldly in the breeze.

Was this the computer system of the English crown?

There was one way to find out. Dodger urged the horse forward.

The destrier's hooves thundered on the wood of the bridge, the noise of them jangling Dodger's nerves. Stealth and the roundabout way were his preferred approach. The bridge seemed to go on and on, its span stretching far further than it had appeared to do. Dodger's suspicions were only beginning to rise when the black knight appeared at the far end. The knight's midnight steed reared slightly as it began its charge.

Clattering steel and the ringing of iron-shod hooves filled Dodger's ears.

Ah, a countermeasure at last.

The need for action released his tension. Dodger's fingers flew across the keys of his cyberdeck, priming his attack and defensive programs and tweaking them to suit the imposed imagery. The ebon boy in the mirror-polished armor held out his gauntleted hand and a crystal lance appeared in it. A shield as reflective as his armor came into being on his left arm. He lowered his weapon into the slot on the shield, using the resting point to steady his grip as he spurred forward.

"Have at thee, Sir Ice."

The two charging chevaliers met in a crash. The black knight's weapon was longer and he struck first. Dodger felt the lance point slam into his shield. For a terrifying instant it hung, pressing him back against his saddle's cantle and threatening to unhorse him. But then the point slid free and slithered along the curve of the shield and away.

His own point slipped past the knight's shield, catching him full on the helm. The shock ran straight through the lance into Dodger's arm and threw him back into the cantle again. His point had struck cleanly and he had braced well for the shock. The knight's helm lifted from his shoulders and flew backwards to strike the bridge surface with a clarion ring.

Unmasked, the knight was revealed as an empty suit of armor. He and his destrier faded and vanished even before Dodger came abreast of them. Unimpeded, the milky stallion raced on.

On a whim, Dodger dipped his lance and speared the fallen helm. He lifted it high, allowing the lance point to pass through the eyeslit so that the helm could slide the length of the weapon. Since he had no further need for the shield, it vanished, allowing him to use his freed hand to remove the red and yellow plume from his vanquished foe's headgear. Dodger retired the attack program as well. When the lance misted to nothingness, the knight's helm volatilized into smoke and blew away.

Feeling exhilarated by his victory, Dodger affixed the plume to his own helm. *A suitable token of prowess,* he thought.

He slowed his destrier as he approached the gate to the castle. No sense rushing in before gauging the opposition. He expected another black knight at the very least. The castle was moated; might he face a monster?

To his surprise, nothing moved to bar his path as he started forward. The drawbridge even remained down. The inhabitants of the castle continued about their business. The gate guards even greeted him pleasantly when he drew near. He was puzzled at his acceptance until he noted the predominant color scheme of the castle's denizens. Everyone wore a favor or plume of red and yellow, if not full livery of the two colors. The plume he had snatched from the black knight's helm was red and yellow. No doubt, it was a passcode. Grinning, he guided his horse across the drawbridge and into the courtyard.

He dismounted, his horse vanishing now that it was no longer needed, but he kept a copy of its program in storage. He might need it for a getaway. The courtyard was bustling with activity, servants and craftspeople attending the multitude of tasks necessary for the running of a castle. How much was analog for computer activity and how much was simply local color he didn't know. He wandered about, looking for a way into the keep.

Long minutes of searching proved useless. Either he was missing something, or he hadn't understood the parameters. If this were a real castle, and he a real knight, all he would have to do was stop a servant and ask directions.

That, he realized, was the answer.

Interrupting a working functionary would be too obvious a disruption of routine. Dodger waited until one of the many liveried folk who appeared to be messengers of some sort passed near him. He stepped into the servant's path, blocking him only long enough to learn his destination. He heard his own voice asking directions. The imposed imagery again, converting his realworld decking into apparent actions that suited the milieu.

He got into playing the game. From servant to servant he passed, each one dressed in fancier clothes than the last. He passed through the ranks of the castle's hierarchy until he faced the seneschal. Dodger was pleased. The seneschal was the keeper of the castle, the repository of all having to do with its function. He suspected that he had reached the main databank. Unlike the other constructs, this one, a beefy red-haired man wearing a furred cloak over his rich garments, spoke to him before he had said a word.

"Good day, Sir Knight. I am at your service, save you demand aid at variance with my fealty to my liege. I am Cai."

"Cai the Seneschal?"

"Certes."

"As in foster brother of King Arthur?"

"That is my honor."

"And this castle is?"

"Camelot, of course."

"Of course." *What else would it be?* "And what is Camelot, Good Cai?"

"Camelot is the stronghold of Arthur, my liege and the rightwise true king of all Britain. All the lands you see about you are his realm. From here he sallies forth to fight the forces of encroaching darkness with the aid of his loyal knights. The land is all.''

If this was Arthur's turf, Dodger had just taken down one of his knights. Or had he? ''Do his knights wear black armor?''

''The knights wear whatever they find suitable to their own nature. They are a brave and hearty lot and serve our liege well. 'Tis they who have won him the lands from which his revenues come. Had they not done so, this castle would not be so great. Arthur is well served.''

''And where are these knights? I see none in the court.''

''On quest at the moment. As always, the king's knights strive to enlarge his realm. Soon Arthur's loyal vassals shall win him more followers, the king's retinue shall grow, and he shall establish his rule over all the land. Then, the land shall prosper and Camelot shall come again unto the world. All of its might shall stand in service to our lord's right.''

''And where is the king himself?''

''He sits at table, enjoying the royal entertainment.''

''May I see him?''

''I regret that he sits not in open court, but you may enter the vestibule and gaze upon him, if you so wish.''

''I so wish.''

Cai led Dodger to the great hall. Cai was careful to remain between Dodger and the door, but Dodger could see most of the interior. It was thronged with courtiers, entertainers, and servants whose moved in a kaleidoscope of color and sound.

An elevated dais ran the width of the far end and was backed by an opulent cloth of estate. The king's throne was positioned in the center. The king stood before it, his face turned away. He was leaning on a long table that ran before the throne. Golden plates and goblets adorned the table, which was covered in brilliant white samite cloth on which had been embroidered scenes of the hunt. The king's fidgety stance suggested that he was waiting for something. A flourish of trumpets pulled Dodger's attention to the other end of the hall. Obviously, a feast was in progress, for servants were carrying a great roast beast from the kitchens. They carried their burden the length of the hall to lay it before the royal presence. As it passed by, Dodger thought that there was something odd about the animal; although it looked mostly like a pig, the roasted corpse seemed to be too long in the body. Its oddity did not bother the king. As soon as the servants set it down he took up his knife and sliced himself a portion.

Having served himself, the king sat and Dodger was able to see his face. The decker had been expecting some idealized noble visage but instead saw a very human face. That was startling enough; Matrix imagery was normally not configured that way. This system was really strange. A wisp of fear flitted across his mind. Was his own face on display?

The king's face was one Dodger had seen recently. It took him a moment to remember where: this man's picture had been among those Willie had taken of the druids' acolytes. Why was he here playing the role of King Arthur? What kind of place did he have in the system? If his was some kind of position of control, what about the druids?

The king was not the only one sitting at the table. The faces of the others were veiled in shadow, however. Were this a real court, they would have had to be great lords and high vassals to sit at the king's side. All the seated figures were as still as statues, but none of the courtiers in the hall seemed to notice. A system operations sign? Were the shadowed constructs place-holders for other members of the cabal who were not presently active in the system?

"Good Cai."

"At your service, Sir Knight."

" 'Tis I who may perhaps be of service. To His Majesty, that is. But before I petition to enter his service, I would like to know my place lest I inadvertently offend one of the nobles of the court. Pray, tell me of the great ones. Who are the greatest of His Majesty's servants?"

Cai smiled and gestured toward the hall. Soft light from an unknown overhead source illuminated the seated figure on the king's immediate right. "Without a doubt, his enchanter stands closest to His Majesty's ear. The wizard is the king's tutor and dear to my liege's heart. Merlin is his name. He is a mighty wizard as well as a master of statecraft. 'Tis Merlin who gathered the knights of my liege's Round Table."

Dodger recognized the new face: Hyde-White the fat druid.

The light died over Merlin and the figure to the king's left was bathed in light. Cai continued. "Foremost among the knights of the hall is Lancelot."

The seated knight bore the face of Andrew Glover. Dodger's expression tightened but Cai apparently didn't notice his audience's reaction.

"He and the Orkney Knights are all the remain in the inner circle of knights, Arthur's closest confidants and staunchest defenders."

Lights played across faces. All were those Willie had tagged as druids. "All that remain?"

"Alas, some of Arthur's truest knights have recently fallen in battle. There is evil abroad in the land, foul foreign knights who would frustrate Arthur's dream and throw the land into turmoil. This must not be."

Cai's eyes narrowed in sudden suspicion.

"The land is all," Dodger said quickly.

Cai smiled, and Dodger relaxed. He had chosen the right password to escape the intruder detection routine. For the moment, he was still safe. He didn't know for how long. The Cai program obviously had triggers near sensitive points, or a random check function on interfacing users, or both. Already Dodger had gathered a lot of information, even if it was couched in arcane form. Analysis would surely straighten some of it out.

What else could he do here that would not raise immediate alarms? What might a travelling knight be free to see? Not the defenses certainly, or the treasury.

"Cai, I have travelled a long way and seen many strange things. Have you a sage or a chronicler to whom I relate my tale?"

"Certes. Do you wish to see him?"

"I so wish."

They turned around to find a page standing in their way.

"Sir Dodger, I bear a gift from an admirer," the young boy announced in a reedy voice.

Beware of constructs bearing gifts, a wise decker had once said. What was going on now? Was this some sort of subtle attack by the ice?

"I may not accept a gift," he said, improvising. "I have made a vow."

"You cannot refuse," Cai said. "This page is in the service of the Lady Morgan Le Fay. None may refuse her gifts."

" 'Tis true, Sir Knight," the page concurred. "Accept the Lady's gift, given in all honor and courtesy, for she sends it with all good will. She knows of your recent victory and is impressed by your skill with the lance. She finds you worthy of reward. Please, Sir Knight.''

The page held out the packet. Wishing he could think of something else to do, Dodger took the offering. When it did not discorporate his construct, lock the persona into stasis, or send him into instant brain seizure, he felt relieved. He unfolded the wrappings to reveal a jumble of computer chips, credsticks, and corporate identification cards. A quick survey showed that they all had the same codes; he held in his hands the complete Matrix record of one Samuel Verner.

''What is going on?'' he asked aloud.

The page answered, obliquely. ''My lady wishes as well to apologize for her lack of courtesy when last you met. She thought that this offering would please you and demonstrate her good will.''

''The last time we met?'' Dodger felt faint, but persona constructs don't pass out. He didn't like the way this new twist pushed against the limits of the imposed imagery.

''She comes now.'' The page bowed and indicated an approaching figure before vanishing as if he had never existed.

The woman wore a long, flowing dress that fit snugly to her full and fetching figure. The gown was midnight itself, swallowing all light. The skin of her throat and neck was brilliantly contrasted against the fabric. It seemed to gleam. It did gleam. Her skin was not the pale tone fashionable in the court, but a faint silver. As silver as her perfect face and delicately rounded, hairless skull.

He recognized the woman identified as Morgan and felt his loins heat up.

This is impossible!

When last they had met, she had effortlessly hijacked him through the Renraku Matrix and held him prisoner. He didn't know why; he didn't want to know. The thing calling itself Morgan Le Fay was neither decker nor system construct. Though he was not sure, he suspected it was something that should not exist; an artificially created machine intelligence, an AI, a real ghost in the machine. During his first encounter with it, the AI had presented itself to his perception as a female counterpart of his own persona construct while simultaneously displaying an entirely different image to another decker. This thing had abilities he couldn't understand. It was apparently sentient, but if its actions were any indication, it was slightly crazy. But crazy was defined by the human norm, and who could know what the norm was for an entity dwelling totally within the electron space of the Matrix? He had thought the AI confined to the Renraku Matrix.

He was obviously wrong.

Morgan Le Fay smiled warmly at him. He fled the only way he could be sure to evade her. He jacked out.

27

Sam didn't like Dodger's analysis one bit, but it made sense. It matched too well against the data they had gathered while Dodger was pursuing the blind shunt that had led him to the Camelot system. It fit with the police cover-up. Most of all, it explained the strange alliance of corporate and political figures who made up the Hidden Circle.

The druids were apparently operating in the interests of Gordon. Their patron wasn't the crowned king, but only barely. In the turmoil of political compromise and under the economic pressure of the corporations, Windsor-Gordon's faction had lost the bid for his affirmation as the true heir to the throne. George Edward Richard Windsor-Hanover, the other principal claimant, had been crowned instead.

Since his ascension to the throne, George Hanover had often favored corporate interests. No doubt, the European Corporate Community was pleased at having found the technical loophole that assured the superiority of Hanover's claim to Gordon's. But minor technicalities couldn't change Gordon's bloodline. His connection to the House of Windsor made him successor to the throne should George VIII and his children die without heirs. Given Gordon's strong association with the Green Party, the ECC would find him an uncooperative king. Thus, while the ECC made sure that their boy George and his family were well protected, they would not mind seeing Gordon do something to bar himself forever from the throne.

Their attitude was not universal. Gordon's bloodline was more than enough for royalists like Burnside. Whether they favored the current king or Gordon, the royalist factions had worked too hard in restoring the shattered monarchy. The last thing they wanted was to see their handiwork be swept away in a scandal. They would do whatever they could to cover up Gordon's misdeeds and polish his image as a suitable member of the royal family. The inspector and his cronies would suppress Gordon's part in the killings if they could.

The whole arrangement stank. It was a stench Sam was coming to know well, the corruption of power. Power was what it was all about. Gordon grasping for the throne and the druids of the Hidden Circle reaching to further their own interests. It was just barely conceivable that they sought to install Gordon as king because they believed he was the rightful king. More likely, they wanted a puppet who owed them everything.

Gordon courted the druids for the power they represented. No doubt, he expected to control them once he was king. No ambitious man could ignore the power a circle of druids offered. The Hidden Circle commanded considerable magical power as well as substantial mundane power through their advantageous placement in political and corporate struc tures. So great a concentration of influence would be hard to duplicate in such a small number of British citizens.

Sam didn't know who was using whom in this arrangement, and it didn't really matter to him. They were all participating in the magical sacrifices. They were all guilty.

Justice seemed further and further away, as the runners' forces disintegrated. Two nights ago they had disrupted the druids' ritual and achieved one confirmed kill and a second probable, but it had cost them. Estios, Chatterjee, and O'Connor were still missing. Dodger was fretting and had abandoned his affectation of ornate speech. He had to be pulled away from his cyberdeck to eat, and he barely stuffed down food before jacking back in. Hart maintained that the raid on the warehouse had effectively scuttled the Circle's scheme. She insisted that there was no need to do anything else, and that it was too dangerous anyway, as the disappearance of Estios's crew showed. She refused to do any legwork or magical searches. If their sack time hadn't been full of heated apologies, Sam would have thought she had finally gotten bored with him and was anxious for a more attractive partner. Only Willie seemed to be staying on track. Her payments had vanished along with Estios, but she was still on the job and sending second-rate drones anywhere she thought she might pick up a lead.

The night's arguments had wearied Sam more than the long days without enough sleep. Dawn was beginning to lighten the sky from black to indigo. He rubbed at his eyes and felt their puffiness. Almost a new day and they hadn't heard anything yet. Maybe Hart was right.

"There it is," Willie announced.

Sam's stomach flopped.

"Hey, Hart," Willie called from her seat by the rigger board. "I thought you said that with the wendigo dead the Circle was out of business. Morning screamsheet's got a Bone Boy kill. One victim. Just like we never bothered them."

"Must be a copycat," Hart said sourly.

"Sweet dream, elf, but no joy. It's them, or I'm an unjacked ferrophobe. Wendigo or not, they're still on course."

"We can't let this go on," Sam said.

"What are we supposed to do about it?" Hart asked. "They know about us now. Willie can't get a drone near enough to follow even the acolytes. Dodger's off chasing who knows what. Without surprise, we won't be able to crack their security. If we try to catch them in the act again, they'll be waiting. Even if we still had Estios and his bunch, we'd only get ourselves wasted."

"We've got to do something. We can hire muscle."

"With what? We don't have the resources. Even if we had muscle, what about their magic? Those druids are pulling down some powerful mana."

"We'll get the resources," Sam insisted. "We'll find a way to cancel their magic."

"How?"

"That's a question I've got to ask too, Twist," Willie said. "I'm not gonna quit on you, but you gotta know that we ain't gonna get much help on the street. Burnside's been spreading the word that anybody who works with us, crosses him.''

"He's just one cop.''

"Maybe he's just one cop, but he's got a lot of hooks in the shadow world. Most runners still got to live in this plex with that one cop.''

Sam hung his head and massaged the back of his neck. After a few moments he let his hand drop. "Then we'll do it ourselves. Dodger can slice loose some of the druids' own money. With enough nuyen we can refit your drones, Willie. Cog's a good connection; he can get us combat drones.''

Hart forced a hissing breath through her teeth. "Willie's firepower didn't do much against their summoning in the warehouse. The mundane approach won't work without some serious firepower. Even then, it's not sure. With preparations, and they will be prepared, they can raise stronger spirits. Lots of them.''

"Then we'll need magic to take care of the spirits.'' Sam stared her in the eye. He willed her to put aside her negativism. They all knew it wasn't going to be easy, but they had to do the right thing. Why was she being so difficult?

"Don't look at me that way,'' Hart snapped. "I'm not sure I have the juice. Putting down that last one almost broke me.''

Sam was disappointed. Had the dismissal of the spirit really been so hard for her? Since that night she had been so defeatist, not like herself at all. As much as he hoped that she would be by his side to face the Circle, he knew he would face them without her if he had to. The Circle and their pawn-patron Gordon had to be stopped. If she wasn't going to be there, he'd find another way.

"Herzog will help," Sam said. He tried to sound assured. "He's always said he's a master of spirits."

"He won't leave his sewers."

Hart's statement was made with utter confidence. Sam's hope sank. She had known the Gator shaman longer than he had; she feared she was right.

"Then he'll have to teach me how to handle the spirits, because I won't let those druids sacrifice another person."

28

Dan had not come home for days, but Janice wasn't worried. He was strong; nothing could harm him. With him gone, her lessons had perforce stopped. She had grown bored and begun to prowl the maze that made up the residence floor. It was a fascinating place, full of mementos, books, and art. There seemed to be artifacts from all seven of the continents. Many of the more curious items were magical, and those were the most fascinating. She had never dreamed that there were so many different kinds of aids for magical operations. When Dan returned, she would badger him into explaining them to her.

She had known that his corporate holdings were widespread, but her browsings in his library and databank showed her just how extensive they were. Through networks of holding companies and brokerages, he held controlling interests in more than a dozen corporations of varying sizes. GWN was the largest, but not by much. He could go to any of the world's major cities and find one of his corporate enclaves.

Her readings uncovered a curious fact. None of the heads of his corporate empire had ever met, despite a strong interweaving of business efforts. The presidents and CEOs must be very good to pull off such an arrangement, considering the disparate natures of their businesses and the spheres in which they operated. Dan must have chosen his subordinates well. Intrigued with how he had found so many loyal followers, she delved deeper.

She began to wonder if all of Dan's top corporate officers shared his metatype. Garcia and Han were both of the metatype and so were important officers of his operations on different continents. While the computer records showed all of the principal officers as norms, she knew better in at least one case. Dan himself was head of GWN despite the registered smiling face of a blond man named Doug Randall. Therefore, there was no reason to believe that the other records told the truth. The photographs accompanying annual reports could only be considered circumstantial evidence at best. Some megacorps deliberately published false pictures of their officers as a security measure.

In the beginning, Dan had said that he wanted her to join his organization. At the time she had been scared and disoriented by her change. She had thought him hypocritical for hiding his own nature within an illusion of normal humanity. She had learned otherwise, been educated in the necessity of his approach.

In her second change she had lost her self, but with his aid she was finding that self again—or rather, redefining it. She no longer wanted to consider herself human. Humans were petty beings full of hate and prejudice. She wanted no connection between herself and those awful creatures.

She had come to see Dan's mask as the way of sur-

vival, appreciating its necessity and adopting one of
her own. Thus, she was not surprised when the bits
and pieces began to fall into place, and she realized
that all of the presidents and CEOs were Dan himself.
There was no need for them to communicate with each
other. Each knew all of the others' plans, hopes, and
aspirations. Each agreed whole-heartedly. It was a
wonderful joke.

She scanned the executives' pictures over and over,
imagining Dan's toothy grin lurking behind each face.
The collection was a wide sampling of racial and bod-
ily types. The choices showed a clever imagination.
Would he ever consent to wearing one of his masks as
they made love? Most of his guises were handsome in
human terms, but a few were less than appealing, especially the grossly fat Hyde-White. She wouldn't care
to share her bed with that one. She finally decided that
it wouldn't matter. Her astral senses were becoming
so tuned that she could pierce an illusion spell almost
automatically.

She hoped he would return soon. She missed him.

Hart kept her face carefully neutral. She didn't want
to give anything away. Bambatu's expression was one
of stern disapproval.

"You have not fulfilled your orders, Katherine. You
know that the Lady will be displeased."

"But you haven't told her, have you?"

Bambatu's mouth quirked up in irritation. It spoiled
his good looks.

"Are you guessing, or are you better informed than
I think?"

His question answered hers, but Hart just smiled in
response to his query. Let him worry.

"The actions of the Tir elves continue to be a
problem, but not an insurmountable one. Since their

split from Verner's team, they have done little to harass the Hidden Circle. Burnside's efforts are keeping the elves off balance and ineffective. However, Verner is still alive. He remains a focus for the efforts against the Hidden Circle, and I expect that sooner or later the Tir elves will rejoin their efforts to his. If they do, there is a reasonable certitude that the Circle's plans will be disrupted before they can become the undeniable embarrassment to the Lord Protector that the Lady desires them to be. With minimal planning and firepower, Verner's team and the Tir elves managed to reduce the Circle's numbers. Further reductions might prove sufficient to disrupt their plans completely. The Lady no longer wishes to see the Hidden Circle die a quiet death in the shadows. She wishes to see these druids fail spectacularly, damaging the credibility of their uncorrupted brethren and drawing the House of Britain down with them.''

Hart shifted uneasily. Did he know she had actually saved Sam? "I'll take care of it. I have my reputation to consider."

"You must take positive action, Katherine. Your results to date have been unsatisfactory."

She rose to leave.

"Soon, Katherine. The Lady has a habit of discarding unworthy servants."

"Worried about your own butt?"

"I am an elf who wishes to live a long and full life."

"That makes two of us."

The first-level precautions had proved adequate; there had been no interference in the first ritual of the new cycle. Glover felt charged with energy. He wanted to call Hyde-White, but his secretary reported that the fat man still had not arrived at his office. Glover had not seen him since those wretched American runners had ruined the second cycle's closing ritual. Hyde-White might be dead, but Glover doubted it. He felt sure that the fat man's death would resonate in the Circle's ritual. Glover had felt no diminution of power; therefore, the fat man must still be alive.

He thought it unlikely that the runners had captured the fat man. Hyde-White was too powerful, too resourceful to be held captive by the inexperienced magicians in the runners' team. Perhaps Hyde-White had been injured and was lying low, while he recuperated. Careful treatment was required to restore a magician to health without harming the delicate mana pathways through which he channeled his power. If the fat man was licking his wounds in private, he would not want to be disturbed.

The Hidden Circle had lost one member to the surprise raid by the runners. But then, Carstairs had been something of a weak sister, though not as bad as Neville. Too bad the fireballs hadn't caught him instead. The simpering old fool was weak-willed despite his considerable mana-manipulation ability, and Glover would gladly have accepted the drop in the Circle's power. Such a power loss would only be temporary, for the rituals were raising the pool of mana which he, as archdruid, could direct.

The day of restoration approached nearer with each soul whose blood bathed the land.

Still, it would be some time until they could complete the full cycle of rituals as Hyde-White had prescribed. Until then, mosquitoes such as the American runners could continue to plague them. Perhaps something more direct should be done about them.

Glover poured himself another brandy and reseated himself before the fire to contemplate the situation.

29

Sam's eyes jerked open. He tried to force his muscles to relax, but they only tightened more. His shirt stuck to his sweat-soaked torso, chafing the sensitized skin. As his breathing slowed from panting to a more normal rate, he levered himself up on his elbows.

Herzog was watching him. The Gator shaman's face was shadowed by the snouted headdress he wore, but Sam didn't need to see that visage to know that it bore an expression of disgusted contempt. Herzog reverently placed his drum to one side and stood. Fetishes and power objects clattered against each other and the bone-studded vest that the shaman wore as he heaved his bulk upright.

"You returned far too soon," Herzog said.

"The Man of Light was there."

"You knew he would be. He has been there as long as Herzog has known you. Herzog does not believe you thought tonight would be different."

"I had hoped. You said that if my need was great, I could transcend the barrier."

"Did you really try?"

Sam rolled over to escape Herzog's stare. He was ashamed. His consciousness had fled from the Man of Light as soon as the apparition had turned its blazing eyes toward him.

"No," he whispered as he stood.

"Louder! Admit what you have done! Accept what you are! If you do not, you cannot progress. You learn nothing from Herzog. Herzog is wasting his time.''

The Gator shaman stamped his foot. The slap of his bare foot against the concrete was a sharp crack of thunder in the small chamber. The echoes of the sudden noise were engulfed by the rustling of the shaman's accoutrements. The cacophony subsided, damping down into a heavy silence.

"Go away," Herzog boomed.

Sam wanted to go, but he knew he couldn't. As much as he disliked and distrusted magic, it seemed to be a permanent part of his life now. Certainly magic had its attractions and uses; it had saved his life time and again. But those magics had been spells and the use of enhanced senses, things which were relatively easy for him to accept. Spells were just manipulations of energy. The ability to see into the astral planes was a sensory ability. Natural, or rather paranatural, stuff. But now it seemed that he needed to master another aspect of magic, one that touched the supernatural. He didn't like it at all, but he knew he had to find a way to come to terms with it.

"I need you to teach me how to harness my power so that I can control spirits," he said.

"You tell Herzog that Dog speaks to you. You tell Herzog that you have seen Dog. You do not lie when you say these things, but you do not believe in Dog. You think that you have power in yourself." Herzog huffed his laugh. "Power you have. But Herzog tells you that the universe is not just man's playground. Herzog tells you that you are a chosen one. Dog is your guide. Dog himself. You must listen because Dog is you and you are Dog. Listen to Dog and not yourself, for Dog is the way of your power."

Herzog's logic made Sam's mind reel. Logic? Too rigorous a word for arguments that doubled back on themselves. "I wish you could just explain things more clearly."

"There is nothing for Herzog to explain. Dog is your totem."

"Totems aren't real. I read Isaac; they're just symbols, psychological constructs that allow a shaman to focus his personality and will. They're not true spirits or even angels. They're not real."

"Totems *are*. You must believe."

Sam could see Herzog believed in his totem. Did he worship it? Many shamans seemed to do just that. Sam could not follow that creed. "I believe, all right. I believe in God, not some mystic canine archetype. I'm a Christian, not a pagan. The Lord told us not to put false gods before him. What *is* a totem but a false god?"

"Totems *are*," Herzog said flatly.

Sam waited for Herzog to say more. He wanted to hear how the Gator shaman would defend his beliefs. But Herzog remained silent.

Frustrated, Sam took a deep breath and exhaled it slowly. Herzog professed Gator as his totem, yet he lived and worked powerful magic in the sewers of a great metroplex. The shamanic mindset often put restrictions on its traditional practitioners. Commonly, the magic available to a shaman was limited if he was not operating in an environment believed to be favored by the totem. Despite decades of urban legends, alligators lived in swamps, not cities. Where was the favored environment? Herzog operated in England, where there were no swamps. As far as Sam knew, the burly shaman never left the metroplex, and he rarely stirred from the tunnel complexes. Still, Herzog's magic was effective. Was that a contradiction? Or a clue?

You must believe, Herzog had said. Belief was the key to shamanic mindset. Belief also terrorized generations of urban children who had heard and *believed* that alligators dwelt in the sewers of their cities. Did that make Gator an urban totem? If that were the case, a totem was no more than a symbol, a way to place the mind in a receptive frame. Issac's writings had implied as much, but Sam hadn't grasped the emotional core of the concept. Now, he began to see.

"Look," he said to the implacable shaman who was still frozen in his stance of dismissal. "I understand symbols. I used to do work in the Matrix, where computer programs take on imagery to make it easier for the human mind to grasp. I can see that magic could work like that. Magical theory is full of stuff about symbols. I don't know how it works or why I picked the imagery, but I can see that Dog is a symbol that my mind has conjured to allow me to manipulate magical energies. If I need to learn other symbols to manipulate the magic imagery, teach me. I can do it. I have to do it."

Herzog simply stared at Sam.

"Herzog, I've listened to your lessons and I've learned some spells from you. I'd be happy if that was all the magic I'd need. The spells don't need this Dog construct to work. But I've seen what the druids of the Circle can do, and I know that it'll take more than spells to stop them. We need the energies of spirit constructs to fight the spirits they can call up. It smacks of devil worship but, Lord help me, if it takes spirits to fight spirits, I'll call them up."

Herzog pretended an interest in the ceiling. "Your need lends you strength."

"Show me how to use it."

The Gator shaman lowered his head and gazed at Sam out of the corner of his eye. "You accept Dog as your totem?"

Hadn't Herzog been listening? "I'll have to, won't

I? If the image of Dog as my totem is the key to using the magic, I'll talk to the damn hound. If I don't, people will die. That's something I won't let happen while I can do something about it.''

"You know what Herzog tells you is true, but you do not accept." Herzog shook his head slowly and sighed. "You will fail."

"I will not!"

Sam stared Herzog in the eye. The Gator shaman's pupils were contracted despite the low light level, making more of his uncanny yellowish-green irises visible. The shaman's stare was unnerving, as much for its intensity as for its uncanniness, but Sam held his gaze fixed.

Several long minutes passed before the Gator shaman bowed his head. "Herzog will drum."

The shaman shambled back to his instrument. Sam waited until Herzog had settled down before stretching himself out on the cold floor. Sam began the exercises of relaxation, readying himself for the shamanic voyage. Lying on his back, he could smell the must in the cracks of the concrete. At least the floor wasn't wet.

"Accept Dog," Herzog said as he began to beat the drum.

"I'll use the image for all its worth."

"Accept Dog," Herzog repeated. The shaman's drumming blended with his words, the music repeating the phrase over and over with increasing insistence.

Sam felt himself slipping down into trance. Closing his eyes, he let himself go. The darkness behind his eyelids shifted like a field of dark stars whizzing past a trideo starship. A brief perception of light intruded on the pure sensation of motion and he recognized the tunnel before all went dark again. *The tunnel is the passage to the otherworld,* Herzog had said, *the way to the land of the totems.*

Although he knew he was in the tunnel, Sam really couldn't see anything. There was no indication of which direction he should take. He felt lost and abandoned. Herzog had said that the tunnel would lead him; all he had to do was follow it. How did one follow something that led nowhere?

Dog is your guide, Herzog had said. *Well Dog, where are you? I need guidance.* Feeling remarkably silly, Sam called out. But nothing answered to Dog's name. He called again. Nothing again. He turned in place, trying to perceive some difference in the darkness. Slowly he realized that he was beginning to see the walls of the tunnel. A distant sound reached his ears, like a faraway trickle of water striking stones with a steady beat. The drumming. Herzog was helping.

A faint glow appeared almost straight down from his position. Sam stepped forward, feeling a certainty that the passageway led toward the distant light source. Though the tunnel led directly downwards, Sam had no trouble negotiating a passage. He simply floated along the gallery. Anxious to get on with it, Sam flew down the tunnel. The sooner it was done, the sooner it would be done. He sped down the passageway, the light growing ever stronger.

"All right, Dog," he called. "Here I come."

The light grew brighter as he traveled. The walls became visible, then washed out as the illumination increased. Light filled the passage. In the midst of the harsh brightness stood a massive figure.

Sam rebounded.

The Man of Light blazed before him, glowing bulk filling the tunnel. There was no way around the Man. Sam darted away into a side passage and almost immediately pulled up short to avoid running into the

Man of Light again as the gleaming figure suddenly flared into existence in Sam's path. Sam spun to retrace his path and was confronted again by the Man. The dying of the light behind him and its flaring as he turned had barely been noticeable. He twisted his head to look over his shoulder. It was dark. By the time he had turned his body around and taken his first step in that direction, the Man was there. Sam raised a hand to shield his eyes from the brilliance.

The Man of Light laughed at him.

In the Matrix, one operates by accepting the imagery and responding appropriately. If one's software was good enough, one's action was translated into a computer reality. Here in this magical realm, Sam was faced with a terrifying obstacle. He wanted to run and hide, but he knew the results of that response. There had to be another way.

When one ran into trouble in the real world, one yelled for help. Would that work here?

"Dog!" Sam shouted. "Help me! Where are you?"

Sam was relieved, surprised, and a little frightened when he got a response.

"Here, boy." Dog's voice was faint, as if the words were muffled by an intervening door.

"Where?" Sam asked. He could see nothing through the burning radiance of the Man of Light.

"Here," Dog answered.

"I can't see you."

"But I'm still here."

"If you're here, you can help. Come to me. I need your power."

"Come yourself. What do you think I am? A cocker spaniel looking for a handout? If you want power, you come and get it. You'll have to take matters into your own hands."

"How?"

"That's your problem. I've got more than enough to share, but you haven't been very nice to me lately."

Lord above! Was that how magic worked? Did one have to bargain with one's own psychological constructs? Sam began to think that maybe he was crazy. Holding conversations with yourself was a sure sign that a chip wasn't seated right. *Symbolic imagery,* he told himself. Fighting the constraints of the imagery would only make it harder to manipulate the energy. Lacking any idea of what to offer, he said, "I'll be better."

"Promises, promises. I've heard it all before. You want it, come and get it."

"Frag it! How do I get to you? The Man blocks the way."

"That he does. You're a man, too. But then, not all men are men and sometimes you've got to solve problems *mano à mano,* eh?" Dog was silent for a moment, leaving Sam puzzled and frustrated. When the totem's voice returned, it was fainter. Sam had to strain to make out the next words. "I understood that you felt a certain amount of time pressure. Get a move on. I may have four, but two legs are enough to run on."

"Dog, what are you talking about?"

There was no answer.

"Dog? Dog!"

Sam was alone again, save for the Man of Light.

Holding a hand before his face, Sam tried to see through the glare. The looming shape of the Man was indistinct, his outline blurred by heat haze. He was white as if burning brightly. Sam had no doubt that the Man was the source of the heat he felt.

Well, Sam had dealt with heat and flames before. He shuddered at the memories of Haesslich's toothy head rearing back. Sam had been sure he was going to die that night. He hadn't because Dog's song had saved him. The song had been a protective spell which had saved Sam from the dragon's flaming breath.

Confronted by another blazing threat, Sam began to sing the song. Confident in its power, he stepped forward. Even if the Man didn't evaporate, Sam felt sure the fire would be no threat.

At first, his confidence seemed justified. Sam approached the Man with no increase in discomfort. He sweated a lot, but that could have been nerves as easily as heat. The Man seemed to radiate an aura of fearful menace.

The Man stepped into Sam's path.

"Stop," he said.

Sam was astonished. "You can speak!"

"In your mind."

If Sam's evaluation of the process of magic was correct, the whole experience was in his mind. Subjective or objective, time was passing. Sam straightened his carriage, trying to nullify the creeping sense of peril that clawed its way up his spine. "Let me pass."

"No."

Sam tried to step around the Man. A arm that felt furred in fire smashed into his chest and knocked him backwards. He landed butt first and then sprawled to slam his head painfully against the floor of the passageway. Dazed, he stood again. He had to get around the Man of Light.

"You shall not pass," the Man said.

"I must," Sam insisted. Did one of his teeth feel loose? "Get out of my way."

"I oppose you because you hunt me and mine. Leave us in peace and I shall not trouble you. She is no longer part of your world. Return to Seattle and forget all you have learned here in England. It will be better for all."

"Better for you, you mean."

"Yes. But for you also. I have been lenient. Trouble me further and I shall show no mercy."

"Mercy? What mercy? I've seen your crimes."

The Man laughed. The sound was loud, almost painful. "You have no idea what you have seen. You are a foolish norm who seeks to meddle in affairs that are not his own. You are manipulated by other forces and you can't even see them. How could you perceive what I am or what I have done? Tell me, little norm. Do you remember your woman in Seattle? What would she say about your little arrangement with Katherine Hart? Your affair is an infidelity by her rules as well as yours. And you can't even remember when it started, can you?"

Sam started to protest that his feelings for Hart had grown naturally and that she had responded just as naturally, but he suddenly realized that he couldn't remember when they had first expressed such feelings to each other. His feelings were strong and clear; he loved her. She was beautiful and caring and . . .

The Man's laughter cut into his thoughts. "Does she feel the same for you?"

"Of course!" Sam remembered the first flare of passion on the cold Solstice night they had found the druids' ritual circle empty. He remembered her eagerness and his. He remembered the heat, the rightness. He remembered . . .

Remembered that the druids' circle hadn't been empty. The false memory of the empty topiary circle faded, and he saw the chalk pentacle, smudged and broken. He saw the blackened heap of ashes and the burned corpses within it. He saw the pile of debris and felt the residual wrongness of its presence. But impressed on his memories like an afterimage was the Man of Light, his burning figure encompassing and shielding the ritual circle.

The Man of Light had been there that night.

"And in your dreams since, little norm," the Man said.

Sam felt violated. When he, Hart, and Estios had attempted an astral reconnaissance of the site, they had met the Man. In a searing moment of pain, they had fallen under his sway. Somehow, the Man had altered their memories, played with their minds.

"So much for your mercy." Sam felt his stomach tighten with cold, congealing purpose. A righteous desire for justice had driven him before. More than the repugnance he felt at having been manipulated into physically aiding the druids, this raping of his mind made it very, very personal.

Was this the taste of hate?

He dropped his hand from before his face. He no longer needed to shield his eyes from the glare now that he perceived more of the nature of the Man who was not a man. The thing he had called the Man of Light no longer looked human. Its three-meter-tall body was furred with a pelt of snowy white, a complete contrast to the dark skin of its face, hands, and feet. Fangs filled the grinning mouth and a dark talon glinted sharply at the end of each of its fingers and toes. Its aura shrieked its nature as a predator in a way he didn't understand. He felt the power of the being and knew the Man of Light as a mere echo of the truth. The Man was not a real entity, but a spell entity cast in the image of its maker. Sam had been ensorcelled.

He was furious.

There was no way for Sam to know if the spell entity spoke for itself or was a conduit for its maker. It might even be no more than a set of preprogrammed responses. But what it was seemed unimportant; what he would do about it mattered. He addressed the spell entity as if he were speaking to the caster. "I will stop you."

"You have not the power, nor will you reach the power."

"I will."

"You will die."

"To hear Dog tell it, I already have."

The flames flickered briefly while Sam spoke, but the Man's voice was still strong. "If so, you will die again. The true death; and your soul will howl as it feeds me."

Despite the dire words of his adversary, Sam felt emboldened. Mention of the totem had triggered a change, an ever-so-slight weakening, in the Man's aura. Maybe now that he knew it for what it was, the Man was weakened. Perhaps Dog was the key, the symbol Sam needed to manipulate to cross this barrier. Dog had told Sam to run. Maybe he was supposed to do that literally, or at least as literally as one could in this never-never land of the mind. Sam squinted, trying to gauge the stance of the Man of Light, to read the readiness of his pose. The Man was tall and massive; maybe he was slow. Big things in the real world were often slow.

Sam steeled himself. The Man seemed to notice Sam's tenseness and began to shift. There was no more time for hesitation. Sam bolted forward, legs pumping. The Man shifted to block him, reaching out with a long, furred arm. Sam dove under it, hands stretched out to break his fall. His palms scraped against the floor of the tunnel and Sam scrambled faster, using all four limbs to keep moving. The Man's clawed hand crashed into the wall next to Sam's head. Sparks leapt in a spray of fire where the talons scratched furrows in the tunnel wall. Sam kept moving, pushing himself upright again and running for all he was worth.

The light expanded around him, filling his vision with an emptiness of white despair. Sam ran. There was too much at stake. Too much he had to do. Then the light and the Man were gone. The tunnel was gone as well.

Sam stood on a dirt road. He felt the soil and stones under his bare feet. A soft breeze caressed his skin. All of it. He was naked, but somehow that seemed all right. The Man of Light was nowhere to be seen or felt. Sam had escaped him. He looked around.

The texts on shamanic experiences had spoken of what the voyager experienced on the far side of the tunnel. Those accounts had led Sam to expect a pristine and vibrant wilderness. The scene that lay before him was hardly that.

There was wilderness here. He could see it on the horizon where the dark shadow of a forest lined the far hills. But the countryside nearer to hand had been transformed from its original state by the coming of man. The dirt road upon which he stood led across gentle rolling knolls, most of which were covered by well-tended cropland. Hedges lined the road and broad shade trees cast their shadow to lessen the sun's burden. Here and there, fruit trees stood in ordered rows quite unlike the irregular clumps of woods scattered about. In a dell just the other side of the first hill, the thatch-roofed buildings of a rustic village clustered around the road and a few lanes that led away from it. Smoke rose from stone chimneys and laundry hung from stretched ropes in rail-fenced enclosures, suggesting that the houses were occupied. Sam saw no people. He also looked for a church, but found none. Save for that lack, it was idyllic.

Sam had never seen anything like it outside of a historical trideo or an art gallery.

"Comfy, don't you think?"

Sam mastered his astonishment and turned to look at the canine sitting by his side. Dog grinned his doggish grin.

"I was beginning to think you were a waste of time."

"What is this place?" Sam asked.

"Here."

"I asked what, not where."

"So you did. Does it really matter?"

Sam chuckled. "Since it's all in my head, I suppose not."

Dog stood and began walking down the road away from the village.

"Am I supposed to follow you?"

"There are always choices, Samuel Verner called Twist. Make your own."

Sam did. He started out after Dog. The totem animal began to trot, so Sam did too. Dog only ran faster.

"Hey, wait up," Sam called.

With looking back, Dog replied, "I don't wait for any man, man."

Sam bit back a response, saving his breath for running. In all his years of raising and caring for canines, Sam had learned that no man, not even a boy with boundless energy, could outrun a dog; the animals always seemed to have more than enough speed to race circles around the slower humans. Sam ran as fast as he could, and to his surprise, the gap between him and Dog closed. As he drew abreast of the racing animal, Dog grinned at him. Curiously, Sam felt unwinded.

"You've got a lot to learn," Dog announced.

"I know."

"That's a start."

For hours they ran and walked and talked. Along the way, Dog taught him a new song.

30

"That's why I wanted to talk to you alone," Sam concluded.

Hart seemed edgy, as if something about his tale of his encounter with the Man of Light bothered her. The nervous play of her fingers in her hair had increased as he told her what the Man had said. Her reaction unsettled him, eroding the confidence he had felt since he'd returned from Dog's green land. So he had edited the story and had not told her of what the Man had said about their relationship. What would she say if confronted with the Man of Light's story that their love was concocted by mind-controlling magics? Would she deny their love was forced upon them? He hoped she would, but he couldn't be sure. Even if she did profess a real love for him, would that be real or just an implanted reaction?

For a minute after he finished, she continued twisting ringlets into her errant locks. Then she tossed her head back, shaking her fashionably curled hair back into place, and gazed out over the rooftops as if searching for a response. He waited. No one would disturb them up here for a while, since Willie was sacked and Dodger still roaming the Matrix. Without looking at him, she spoke.

"Whatever your apparition was, he was a liar. Nobody is good enough to affect all three of us at once. You maybe; you're still learning. But while Estios is an ass, he is a strong mage." She crossed her arms over her chest and hugged herself. "If something raped all of our minds that easily, I don't think I'd want to

face it when it wasn't busy.'' Hart walked away from
the edge of the rooftop and sat on the rusting hulk of
a climate control unit. ''But I don't think that'll be a
problem.''

''Why not? Are you sure that our memories of what
we found at Glover's estate are correct?''

''Yours match mine,'' she said, as if that were con-
firmation enough.

She unslung her bag and dumped its contents onto
the flat surface. She unholstered her onyx-handled
Crusader machine pistol, laying the weapon by her
side before fishing among the haphazard pile of matte
black containers she had released from her bag. She
chose the largest, the one which held her Crusader's
accessories in custom-fitted compartments. She
snapped open the lid and removed the cleaning kit.
Checking her gear was one of the ways she calmed her
mind. Sam let her get the gun disassembled before he
crossed the roof to continue the conversation.

''If the Man of Light wasn't what he said he was,
what was he?''

Hart shrugged and continued cleaning her weapon.
''Don't know. I'm not a shaman, but I've heard that
some voyagers encounter a being that blocks the way
to the higher planes, some kind of guardian they call
the dweller. From the descriptions I've heard, it could
look like anything, even your Man of Light. The way
I figure it, this Man was the dweller—and the dweller,
like the tunnel and the totems, is a construct, a way
for a mind to wrap itself around the possibilities of
magic. All those things are just symbols for a mind
structured toward a mystic rather than an hermetic
approach.''

That was what Sam had thought before he experienced the Man's presence and before his last conversation with Dog. How could Hart be so sure? She wasn't

a shaman and had never talked with Dog. More importantly, she hadn't been there and felt what he had felt. The whole thing didn't add up unless the Man was telling the truth.

Sam watched Hart wipe clean the parts of the Crusader and begin reassembling them. Her hands moved with a practiced quickness; those slim fingers, whose touch he knew so well, deftly fitted the pieces together with a precision born of long habit. Any turmoil that might be roiling her mind was submerged in the routine. To watch her was to see a professional machine that matched her reputation in every particular.

Sam knew better. In their time together he had touched a different Hart, one that yearned for tenderness and love as much as he did. She was hiding that need now, avoiding his eyes and his touch. He wished that he knew what to do, to say, but for all their intimacy, there was a lot he still didn't know about her. Then there was the doubt the Man had left in him. Her own supposition that the Man was a barrier Sam had constructed for himself made him doubt his own feelings. He wanted reassurance that what he felt was real, not planted in his mind for someone's perverted pleasure or, worse, a fantasy of his own to hide his guilt over violating Sally's trust.

"But if the Man of Light was a construct of my own mind, why would he claim he had altered my memories?"

"I'm a runner, not a psychologist. Maybe you were projecting your fears and frustrations onto a convenient scapegoat. I know how much you hate that shamanic mumbo-jumbo. Maybe you should just give it up. We could get out of this place; go somewhere else, where you could study hermetic magic."

"You were the one who suggested I work with Herzog in the first place."

"So maybe I was wrong. Wouldn't be the first time."

Her voice held an unfamiliar note of bitterness; it stung his heart. She had always banished his ill tempers with her sarcastic humor. Trying to use her own medicine, he laid a hand on her shoulder and quipped, "A rare confessional moment from the unequalled shadowrunner."

"Don't push it, dogboy," she snapped, slapping away his hand.

Sam was taken aback. She was not acting like herself at all. Something was seriously wrong. The only thing he could see was that she had lost confidence in him. Confidence and more. How did shadowrunning elves brush off their no-longer-interesting paramours?

"Are you telling me now that you don't think I can cut it?"

"No, Sam," she said softly. For the first time since he began the tale of his power ritual, she met his gaze. Her bronze eyes glistened in the twilight. "I know better. You'll do all you can. That's the problem."

Instead of continuing, she dropped her head and concentrated on her weapon.

"You're not making sense," he said.

He watched her bite her lower lip. When she spoke, her voice lacked her usual resolution.

"It's too dangerous, Sam. The payback's just not there."

"I thought you were a hot-shot runner."

"That's not the point and you know it. The Hidden Circle is bad business. We were outclassed *before* Estios and his people went missing."

"I've got magic now and Dodger cutting a deal that'll get Willie all the combat drones she can handle. We can do it."

"We can get ourselves all killed. The druids have resources we can't match, and we no longer have the element of surprise. If they've taken Estios or one of his people, which is highly likely, they know who we are and what we can do. They'll be ready for us. Is that what you want? Are you trying to get us all killed?"

"I'm trying to see justice done. I'm trying to see that no more innocent people die to feed some lunatics' ideas of the path to power. I'm trying to . . ."

"You're trying to get yourself killed," she said bitterly.

"I don't want to die, Katherine. But I can't let those druids go on with what they are doing."

"It's not worth it, Sam."

She finished reassembling the Crusader. He heard the soft click of plastic as she sought the magazine. Sam took her by the shoulders, but she wouldn't look him in the eyes. He felt the movement in her arms as she loaded her weapon. The job was done and offered no more distraction. Only then did she meet his gaze.

"Are you asking me to run away, Katherine?"

"Would you if I did?"

"You know the answer to that."

"Yes, I do."

He felt her tense and looked down to see the Crusader pointed at his belly.

"I'm sorry, Sam," she said.

Sam threw himself violently to his left. He felt the bullet snag his long coat. The smell of propellant harsh and accusatory in his nostrils, he vaulted over the climate control unit onto a lower level of the roof. He ran toward a workshed that offered safety only a few meters away. Her second shot gouged the wall of the shed as he reached it. Sharp fragments of brick spattered into his cheek. He threw himself forward and down, hoping that the sudden maneuver would spoil her aim as he tried to get out of her line of fire. It was a vain hope. His body twisted as he felt a slug slam into his shoulder. Striking the rooftop out of control, he scraped more skin from his already lacerated cheek. He tried to push himself up, but the muscles of his arms failed and he collapsed. His injured arm was numb and cold. He managed to roll over onto his back as she approached him, gun held ready. Her eyes were sad, but her jaw was clenched with determination.

Feeling betrayed, he blacked out.

PART 3

A New Twist
in the Game

31

The chittering voices of the leshy grated on Hart's nerves. Hart knew her nervousness was adding to the irritation caused by the humanoids. Irritated or not, she had never liked them or their leafmold smell. However, they were the best choice for the task of carrying the bier on which Sam's body lay. Though the body was concealed beneath a cloth-covered framework, the bearers would know what they carried. The other servants of the Seelie Court would spread gossip. Of course, the leshy would too, but few courtiers ever bothered to pay attention to leshy babblings.

So far she had managed to avoid undue notice since her arrival in Ireland. Bambatu had arranged for the landing pad to be deserted. No doubt he'd had a hand in ensuring that the passages through which she passed were nearly empty as well. The few courtiers she encountered either were too busy with their own business to pay much attention to the covered bier, or were cowed by her cold stare. No one hindered her passage.

The designated court was one of a myriad of open spaces in the gloomy half-forest, half-palace that was Lady Deigh's stronghold. A soft, sourceless light defined a circle just over three meters in diameter. The rest of the court was shrouded in darkness. Its floor was moss-covered earth, and Hart sensed great boughs arching over her head, although she could see nothing in the darkness above her.

The rectangular doorway through which they entered the clearing seemed to vanish after they passed through. Hart walked to the circle and stopped on the far side. The leshy carrying the bier almost tumbled their burden to the ground in their haste to stop when she did. She ordered them to set it down and dismissed them. Like children released from school, they scattered, laughing, in all directions.

The clearing grew quiet. The leshy hadn't used the doorway to leave, but Hart suspected *she* would find the darkness impenetrable.

Hart drank in the silence, using its power to calm herself. Before long, a new rectangle appeared, framing an elven woman. The backlighting silhouetted her slim figure through the diaphanous gown she wore. Hart felt a twinge of envy at the perfection of line and form in the woman's body. For all the illusion in which her court was cloaked, Lady Brane Deigh used none to improve her own appearance.

The Lady stepped forward and the rectangle vanished, restoring the illumination in the clearing to its original low level. She acknowledged Hart's bow with a slight nod of her head, but her eyes remained fixed on the covered bier as she crossed through the darkness and into the light. As soon as Deigh reached the bier, she drew back the cloth.

"He breathes."

The surprise Hart had hoped to engender was absent from the Lady's voice. Instead there was a slight hint of annoyance. A dangerous hint. Lady Diegh turned her face to Hart, her green eyes almost luminous.

"Is this how you fulfill your orders, *milessaratish?*"

"A *milessaratish* serves her mistress. I sought only to further your desires, Lady."

"By disobeying orders?"

"A good servant fulfills the desire of her mistress rather than the letter of the request. I was told that you wished that the runners stop harassing the Hidden Circle. Was that not correct?"

"It was correct," the Lady said softly without looking at Hart.

Hart could feel the chill. The earth beneath her feet felt like ice. Fragile ice.

"Killing Verner would not have achieved this end. I have worked with them and know them. They would only have redoubled their efforts seeking to avenge Verner's death. But with him missing, they shall be unsure. More likely they will search for him instead of the Circle."

The Lady finally turned her emerald eyes on Hart. "So you have arranged for them to bother me."

"They will find no connection," Hart said hastily. "I used reliable people who have no connection with the Shidhe."

"If your reputation is half true, you could have made him disappear without bringing him here."

"Yes. But dead, he has no further use."

There was the slightest thawing in the Lady's attitude as she said. "And alive, he does?"

"Circumstances have changed before; they may again. Verner is a ready weapon to send against the Hidden Circle should their actions fail to fulfill your expectations. If he were dead, you would need to find and hone another tool."

The Lady was silent. Hart wondered if she had made the wrong play. Deigh did not like surprises, nor did she like subordinates with too much initiative.

"I do not like being disobeyed, Hart. You were told that Verner was to die."

"I was told that the actions of the runners against the druids must be disrupted. I took that as the primary goal to be achieved. Verner's death was suggested as the most expedient method of achieving that end, but I saw another way to achieve the goal and retain options. My evaluation of the situation was that his death would jeopardize the primary objective.

"Verner's death would be an irrevocable step. His disappearance could still be just as effective. If he were to remain here in Ireland, no one need know he is still alive, and I can arrange that the world outside your court believe that he is dead. Captivity in place of death maintains his value as a pawn in your schemes. The renegade druids of the Hidden Circle have proven to be resourceful and unpredictable foes. Should circumstances arise in which Verner's skills and talents would be of use, he will be available. If he dies, he ceases to be a factor, and you will have permanently expended a potential resource."

"You were thinking of my best interests, then?"

"Yes, Lady."

"Hmmm." The Lady studied Sam's face. A sly smile flitted across her lips. "I begin to see possibilities in what you have done. Mortals can be so . . . entertaining."

Hart found herself bothered by the Lady's words, and even more by the possible motivations behind Deigh's fleeting smile. Hart hadn't brought Sam here only to have him become a plaything for a jaded tart who deluded herself about her immortal elven heritage.

She was surprised at herself, not just at the emotion she felt but at the very fact that she was feeling emotion at all. Jealousy was foreign to her; the hot, angry thoughts that flooded her now were disturbing. But she could not express her feelings. It would be too dangerous for Sam. And for her.

"You will let him live?"

The Lady gave a slight shrug. "Your arguments have some small merit, but I must also consider how it will look. My word is law in the court and you disobeyed orders."

"Only to serve you better. Such disobedience is no crime in the eyes of a wise ruler."

Deigh regarded her sidewise. "As long as the servant is wise as well."

"I believe that I have done nothing to compromise you. And I have my own reputation to consider."

"Ah, reputation. Such a strange master and servant," the lady said wistfully. "You have staked more than your reputation here. Do you think you know me so well that you can rely on my forgiveness?"

Hart knew that the wrong answer to the question could be dangerous. Had she read the Lady wrong? Hoping that Deigh was just playing games, Hart steadied her nerves and spoke.

"I spent weeks in the court before you sent me after the Hidden Circle. I listened to your subjects. Even before I took your contract, I researched you as well as I could. I know you for a strict disciplinarian. But I also know you for an intelligent woman and ruler. You would not throw away an advantage, especially so potentially useful an advantage, over such a small matter as the interpretation of orders. Only your loyal Bambatu and I know the wording of your orders. I have nothing to gain by talking and he has even less. You have something to gain and nothing to lose by accepting the situation as stands."

"I do not stand in need of a lecture," the Lady snapped in sudden anger. She turned on her heel and strode toward the space from which she had entered. The rectangle of light appeared before her. On its threshold she spun and faced Hart again. "And if there is a problem?"

"I guarantee my work," Hart said, looking directly into the Lady's eyes.

Lady Deigh smiled coldly. "Work such as yours is only guaranteed with lives, Hart. Yours shall stand for his."

Hart lowered her gaze. "I understand."

"I don't think you do, but I accept your guarantee. He shall live for now. On my terms."

Lady Deigh gestured; the bier on which Sam lay lifted from the ground and floated away from Hart into the darkness that surrounded the clearing. Hart's elven eyes couldn't pierce the gloom beyond the first few meters. Even shifting to astral senses only revealed the hulking spirits carrying the bier. She watched anxiously as the gloom hid Sam from her sight. When Hart looked toward the doorway, the Lady was gone as well.

Had she done the right thing?

32

Sam awoke to the gentle whisper of someone praying.

He tried to sit up, but the sudden flash of pain in his head doomed his effort. His return to the horizontal wasn't fast enough to satisfy his stomach; it lurched and heaved. Sam rolled onto his side just in time to spew the contents mostly onto the floor rather than himself.

He groaned.

"Ah, you are awake."

A man in dark clothing appeared at Sam's side. The man had a ceramic bowl in one hand and some towels in the other. Without asking, he started to help Sam clean himself off.

Sam let the man take over the job. His head still hurt, almost as bad as after a long session in the Matrix. That was an old familiar pain. It would pass. His belly felt acid-scorched and his muscles ached. He felt like drek. Through the wool that seemed impacted around his teeth and tongue, he asked, "What happened?"

"That I cannot tell you. My first sight of you was when the servants brought you here. From your condition, I'd say you had been drugged."

Hart. In his memory, Sam could see her saddened face hovering over the muzzle of her Crusader. He saw the muzzle flash and felt the slug hit. But it couldn't have been a slug. If it had, he would have been dead. She must have loaded her weapon with tranquillizer bullets. Why? What was going on?

Sam looked around. There wasn't much to see. Rough stone walls defined a circular chamber about three meters in diameter. A small alcove held a pool of water. The walls were beaded with moisture and spotted with patches of luminous lichen. Puzzled that he couldn't feel the humidity or smell the mold, Sam shifted briefly to astral senses. The change in sensory input disoriented him; there seemed to be a severe fuzziness to his perceptions, but he learned that the walls' appearance was an illusion. He and the stranger were being held in a modern cell. The illusory lichens hid lighting panels; the real walls were concrete and embedded with some kind of high-tech circuitry which frustrated his attempts to penetrate with his astral vision. He felt too weak to press the issue, and returned to his mundane senses. If the man with the cloths had noticed Sam's absence, he gave no sign.

"Where are we?" Sam asked.

"In general, somewhere south and west of Dublin.

In specific, a holding cell in the stronghold of the See-lie Court.''

"Dublin?" Sam was stunned. His mind didn't want to work. "Dublin, Ireland?"

"Yes." The man tossed the dirty cloths into the bowl. "You seem surprised."

"Confused would be a better word. You'd be, too. I was shot in London."

"Shot?" The man's eyes grew concerned as he began to search Sam for a wound. Sam was too spaced to do anything. "Ah, the drug. You were shot with a tranquilizer gun, then."

Sam thought he nodded in the affirmative.

"It would seem that you have not slept too long, judging from the condition of your last meal. Who shot you and why?"

He didn't want to talk about it. He didn't want to think about it. Hart had shot him down. Why? Without a word of explanation, she had shot him. Then, he had awoken a captive. Had the bitch sold him to his enemies? They had been lovers; he hadn't thought she could be so cold. He had loved her. He really didn't want to think about it. "I don't want to talk about it."

"Then we shall not speak of it. Perhaps though, it would not trouble your memories to recall when you were shot. I no longer have a timepiece, and I have lost track of the days here. The light, you see, doesn't change and the meals are irregular. There is no way to measure the passage of the time here."

Time? Sam realized he had lost track of time himself. The long days of tracking down the Hidden Circle had all blended into one another. He had barely noted the passage of Christmas and the coming of the new year. The last date he recalled clearly was the Solstice; the Man of Light's words had burned the date into his mind.

"It was late January, the twenty-ninth, I think."

"The twenty-ninth." The man sighed. "It's been over a week and the others have not found me. If the elves' magics are so strong that I have not heard from them by now, I fear I never will. These elves do the devil's work."

Sam's head was slowly clearing. He listened to the man's words, but they only made partial sense. "Who are you?"

"I? I am a sinner who answers to the name Pietro Rinaldi. I am also a priest of the Order of St. Sylvester, and, for the sin of inattention, a captive like yourself."

"You're a priest? But this is Ireland. I thought all the priests had been kicked out when the Shidhe took over."

"I am but lately come to these shores."

"Not a very good start for your missionary work."

"Missionary work is not my calling. Although it is the task of all priests to aid souls toward salvation, the Order of St. Sylvester has another mandate. I am part of an investigative team. While my fellows concentrated on England, I came to Ireland seeking information. I had assumed that the diplomatic pass from His Holiness would have been better respected. Alas, the arrogant leaders of this state seem to have no concept of any authority higher than their own."

"So, you showed up at the airport, and they took one look at your Vatican passport and chucked you in this hole."

"Quite the contrary. I was admitted without any trouble at all. It was not until after I had begun my inquiries that I attracted the attention of the Lady Deigh."

"Who?"

"Lady Brane Deigh, a very rich and powerful elven woman who styles herself queen of the Seelie Court."

"Whoa, father. You're not telling me you're here because you got involved with a woman, are you?"

"Involved with?" Rinaldi blinked in brief confusion, then smiled wryly. "Ah. Yes, involved indeed, but not in the way you think. Since the Reunification, celibacy is no longer required of priests, but my Order still takes the vow for ritual reasons. I have not broken that vow. My fall came not from the temptations of the flesh; my involvement with the Lady, as they call her, was one of matters more arcane than carnal."

"Arcane? Are you going to tell me that you're a magician, too?"

Rinaldi chuckled. "Would it matter if I did?"

"It might."

"Then I hope it is not too much of a disappointment, but I am not. I am a sensitive, however, and so know that you are one, yourself." Rinaldi paused, offering Sam a chance to say something. When he did not, the priest tried another tack. "My limited gifts do not tell me your name."

Sam was embarrassed. Here he had been grilling Rinaldi and had never even introduced himself. He started to give his name, but sudden suspicion stopped his tongue. Names were important, both magically and in the world of the shadows. How did Sam know if this priest—if he was a priest—was who he said he was? Rinaldi had admitted to being involved with this elf queen, Deigh. Maybe his involvement hadn't ended. He might be one of Deigh's flunkies and the whole friendly approach some kind of trap. The suspicion gnawed at Sam, and he hated himself for it.

It had been bad enough when Dodger manipulated him, but what Hart had done . . . her perfidy was shattering. It made him want to believe the Man of Light's implication that their affair had been induced by magic. But magic wasn't causing his feelings now. The anger and pain made mock of any attempt to accept that his feelings for Hart had not been real.

First Dodger, then Hart. Too many betrayals. Could he trust anyone?

"They call me Twist, father," he said softly into the silence. He could see that he hadn't hidden his inner struggle from Rinaldi, but the priest politely ignored it.

"Ah. A street name?"

Sam nodded.

"I understand that the current circumstances do not inspire trust. However, we are both in the same cell and I believe that you might have the power to get us out. Perhaps if I tell you more about myself, you will trust me. Read my aura, if you wish. I have nothing to hide."

Getting out was a top priority, but Sam still felt too weak to do more than sit up and breathe deeply. He didn't feel ready to read anyone's aura, but he didn't have to tell Rinaldi that. Until he was stronger and had a better idea of what was going on, he could at least listen to the priest's words. "Sure. Why not?"

Rinaldi's idea of filling Sam in began far too early to be of any real interest. Sam had no desire to hear about the priest's rough childhood in Awakening-torn Italy. What relevance could it have? Sam let his mind drift, occasionally dropping back to the real world to pick up snatches of Rinaldi's early tribulations with his vocation and final selection of the rule under which he had chosen to live. It was only when Rinaldi revealed the nature of the Order of St. Sylvester that the priest recaptured Sam's full attention.

"You're part of an order of magicians?" Sam asked incredulously.

"I said that the Sylvestrines gather the cream of the Church's magical talent, but not all members are magically active and most of the rest are adepts or students. I myself have but a small gift.''

''Which is?''

''I have astral senses.''

Rinaldi looked embarrassed, or perhaps, troubled. Sam felt sympathy for him. Any magical talent set a person apart from ordinary folk. But to see the magic and not be able to use it? What frustration! Sam didn't think *he* would be able to deal with that kind of limitation.

''That's a valuable talent,'' Sam said.

Rinaldi shrugged, giving Sam a weak smile.

''I am primarily a scholar. My specialty is totemic shamanism, but I have studied several hermetic traditions as well. While I have done some investigations of other more esoteric traditions, I would hesitate to claim any particular expertise. There is so much knowledge, and so little time to acquire it.

''I have spoken long enough about myself and fear I shall have to confess my prideful indulgence. You seem more relaxed now. Perhaps you feel secure enough to tell me what tradition you follow.''

''Can't you tell?''

''Without you actively using your magic? Of course not.''

Sam felt stupid. With his limited experience, he already knew that a person's aura only showed strength. While those with strong auras were often magically capable, it didn't show unless they were actively manipulating mana. Even then, the tradition they followed might not be clear unless the nature of the magic was strongly allied in the form of manipulation.

''I appear to be a shaman.''

Rinaldi looked surprised. ''Appear to be? I should think that someone with your level of power would be quite aware of his orientation.''

''It's what people tell me I am,'' Sam said sheepishly. "Honestly, father, I find the idea uncomfortable. I'm a Christian. All the business about totems is very disturbing to me. I mean, didn't primitive people worship totems as gods? I can't do that. It just doesn't seem right that my magic is hedged around with such pagan symbolism."

Sam's breathless admission seemed to shift Rinaldi's mood. His expression became more serious.

"Do you believe in angels?"

"What's that got to do with anything?"

"Do you?" Rinaldi insisted.

"They *are* in the Bible," Sam snapped.

"Some people do not believe the Bible is literal truth," Rinaldi said calmly. "Do you believe that angels are real?"

Sam hesitated. "Yes."

"And what are they?"

"How should I know? I'm not a theologian."

Rinaldi smiled. "If it makes you feel any better, theologians argue over angels, too. Most agree that an angel is a being, a spiritual entity of a different order than man. I believe that true knowledge of these beings is something that is denied to us as long as we wear flesh.

"In our mortal state, we cannot know the mind of God. Though we each have a sliver of him within ourselves, we are hampered by our physical nature from seeing the truth as it is. For all the wonder and glory of God's creation, we perceive only a part. You, as a magician, are able to perceive more than the vast majority of mankind. You used your astral senses earlier. Didn't you see more than your mundane senses revealed? Of course you did. A small proof that what is available to mundane senses is not all there is to the universe. You have assensed spirits that have no physical presence, haven't you? Aren't they real?"

"They're just energy forms," Sam protested. "It's not the same thing."

"$E = mc^2$. Energy is as real as matter."

Rinaldi's answer was smug, and troubling. "Are you telling me that totems are angels?"

The priest shook his head. "No. Yet I know of no shaman who does not believe in their existence."

So, was Sam supposed to believe that totems had independent existence? "Then totems are not just psychological constructs, tricks to let a brain do magic?"

"I didn't say that either."

"You're making me crazy, father," Sam said exasperatedly. "What *are* totems? Are they real or not?"

"I wish I could give you the answer you want, Twist. I'm not a shaman, so I can never experience a totemic contact or visit the realms where shamans learn the secrets of their magic. The ability to experience such has not been given to me, and the shamanic magic is so very experiential. While in this flesh, I shall never personally know the answer, but all those I have spoken to agree that whether totems are real or not, the effects of totems are real. A shaman must conform to the attitudes and strictures of his totem or lose power."

"You're telling me that I must follow my totem's decrees. What about God's commandments? What about false gods, priest?"

"A totem is suited to your nature, or your nature to it. The order is unclear. Like the very ability to do magic, or the type of magic of which a person is capable, totems are not something that is chosen. A person is as God has made him, gifted or burdened as He wills. We must use our gifts and shoulder our burdens as we attempt to find our way nearer to Him. He has given us free will that we may choose, and He has given us His love to guide us in choosing wisely. Accepting your shamanic nature will not drive you from

Him. Your gift comes from Him. How could He make you so that you are unacceptable to Him?''

Sam felt the wisdom in the priest's words. He said thoughtfully, ''I should have spoken to you sooner, father.''

Rinaldi smiled warmly. ''Regrets gain nothing, son. You must look to the future.''

''Easy to say,'' Sam said with a wave of his hand taking in their cell. He shrugged and said, ''So when Dog speaks to me, it's not a betrayal of God.''

''Your totem is a link with . . . '' Rinaldi quick answer died abruptly. ''Did you say your totem speaks to you?''

''Yeah. He doesn't always make sense and sometimes he talks too much.''

Rinaldi put a hand on Sam's shoulder and stared earnestly into his face. ''But he talks directly to you? In words?''

''How else does anybody talk? Other than dragons, that is.''

''I don't know; I've never spoken to a dragon.''

''Try to avoid it. They're accomplished liars,'' Sam said. Bitterly, he added, ''Like elves.''

''Twist, how many times have you spoken with . . . was it 'Dog'?''

Rinaldi, intent with his own thoughts, had paid no attention to Sam's sour tone. Sam forced thoughts of *her* lies away and tried to answer Rinaldi civilly. ''Dog sure enough; he kind of looked like a mutt I once befriended. I guess we've had three or four conversations now. He teaches me songs. Crazy, isn't it?''

''No, not at all,'' Rinaldi said. He thought for a moment then said, ''When was the last time?''

''Just before she . . . just before I got shot.''

''You were facing death?''

''That was later.'' Sam laughed nervously. ''I guess I'm a little confused, and I'm confusing you. Must be the aftereffects of the drug. When I talked to Dog, Herzog had been helping me break through to the spirit planes. He wouldn't help us against the Circle, but he was willing to take me through the ritual so I could get the power I needed to face the Circle's abominations.''

"The Circle? What circle?"

"A bunch of renegade druids who call themselves the Hidden Circle. They're homicidal manics. My . . . , " Sam paused, ". . . friends and I were trying to stop them."

"Twist," Rinaldi said softly. "Tell me about this Hidden Circle."

Why not, Sam thought. If he and Rinaldi were really captives of elves, nothing would get back to the Circle. Sam knew how much the druids hated metahumans; these elves wouldn't be allied with the Circle. If Rinaldi's presence and the "elven captivity" were some kind of subtle ploy, what did it matter? Sam was on his own now, and even Dog's songs wouldn't be enough if he were in the Circle's hands.

Sam recounted his involvement with the Circle's machinations, beginning with the bungled extraction of Raoul Sanchez and ending with the disastrous raid in the East End of London. The priest's questions were sharp and probing. Sam's answers seemed to disturb Rinaldi. Throughout the tale, Sam observed the priest's growing agitation. If he was an actor, he was very, very good.

Rinaldi listened to Sam's recounting of the runners' speculations as to the druids' plans, then said, "Twist, we've got to get you out of here."

Sam could see the intensity in the priest's face. Sam revised his opinion. Rinaldi had spoken freely and offered aid without asking a reward. If Sam rejected that kind of selflessness, he would never be able to trust anyone again. But then, was trust important to a shadowrunner? Sam was surprised that he didn't need to think about it long.

"Call me Sam, father."

33

Sam and Rinaldi talked for hours before the grinding rasp of the opening cell door interrupted them. A pale-skinned elf entered as soon as the door had risen high enough to clear the shock of yellow and pink hair that stood straight up from his scalp. His pointed ears were especially prominent against the shaved sides of his head. Though his manner was nonchalant, Sam noticed that the elf kept a hand near the weapon holstered low on his right hip.

The elf stepped to one side of the doorway and a short, squat shape took his place in the arch. Their second visitor was neither an ape nor a man, but something in between. Thick brown fur sheathed its torso and lower legs, while a fine, sparse fuzz covered the rest of its body. The digits of its hands and feet had sharp, thick nails that were almost talons. The narrow, broad-nosed face shifted expression from fearful skitteriness to a threatening snarl and back again. It wore no clothes, but carried a bundle of cloth from which Sam could see the soles of a pair of boots projecting.

The elf grunted at the hominid and pointed at Sam. The furred being crouched at the sound of the elf's voice and looked at him. It made a few guttural noises. The elf repeated the sound he had made more loudly and jabbed his hand emphatically in Sam's direction. The creature shuffled forward, side-stepping toward Sam, and rapidly shifted its gaze from Sam to the elf.

When it was a meter from Sam, it tossed its burden at him and scampered out of the cell to stand hesitantly just on the other side of the threshold.

Sam caught one of the boots and what seemed to be a shirt of fine white silk. The other boot and the rest of the clothes landed on the floor around him.

"Drek-eating munchkins," the elf muttered. He made a barking noise and stamped his foot in the direction of the hominid. The munchkin bared its teeth at him and hissed, before spinning in place and scampering down the corridor. When it reached a group of its fellows clustered where the corridor forked, it stopped, hopping back and forth as it screeched at the elf. The elf stamped his foot again, and the whole group of munchkins pelted out of sight around the corner.

"Must be tough getting good help around here," Sam said as he bent to gather up the fallen garments.

Rinaldi chuckled, but the elf only frowned.

"Dress," he ordered.

"There are only clothes for one. What about Father Rinaldi?"

"He stays here."

Sam started to protest, but Rinaldi's hand on his arm stopped him.

"It's all right," the priest said. "But you'd better clean yourself up first. You obviously have an interview with the Lady and there's no point in making a bad impression."

"What about you?"

"I expect she's had her fill of me. Go on. I'll still be here when you get back."

Sam had time to think while he showered in the cell's small sanitary alcove. He continued thinking as he put on the clothes that had been brought for him. He had even more time to think on the trip to the audience chamber. He spent most of the thinking puzzling over the why of his capture. He found no answers.

He realized that he knew damn little about Hart. His runner contacts vouched for her competence in the trade and pegged her as a hermetic mage. Both those things he knew were true from his personal experience of her. But the streets had no tale to tell of her origins. She was supposed to be a mercenary, but what if she were not? What if she had been an agent of the Shidhe all along? He knew so little about her past. Although the subject had never come up, he realized that he knew no more about Hart than he did about Sally Tsung. His involvement with Sally had sprung into being almost overnight and become a tempestuous affair quite unlike his earlier involvement with the staid Hanae. Like Hart, Sally was strong-willed and quite sure of what she wanted. Their becoming lovers had been mostly her idea. Mostly. But what of his involvement with Hart? Whose idea had that been?

The Man of Light had preyed on Sam's own loyal impulses when he had suggested that Sam was betraying Sally by his involvement with Hart. But Sam knew Sally had been through lovers before. He doubted she had gone without comfort since he had left Seattle. It just wasn't her style. He was both comforted and disturbed by that thought. She had done a lot in helping him adjust to the shadow life, and he wanted nothing but the best for her, but he had been raised to believe in fidelity.

So what had he been doing fooling around with Hart?

He didn't have an answer. His feelings roiled under the heat of suspicion planted by the Man of Light. Was it real magic or just the old biochemical magic of hormones and psychological need?

He realized that he didn't know Hart well enough to answer for her. Would she tell him honestly if he talked

to her? Could she? That night on the rooftop he had
been afraid to tell her everything the Man of Light had
said, confining himself to the less personal issues.
Still, he remembered how she had shivered when he
spoke of the magical compulsion to forget the encounter at Glover's mansion. What had her reaction meant?
He didn't know. In truth, he didn't know her at all.
He remembered the sadness her eyes had held as she
pulled the trigger. Why had she done it? There was so
much he didn't know about her. For all he knew, Hart
might actually *be* the Lady Brane Deigh.

Did that explain everything? Anything? He thought
about it for a while, too, and finally dismissed it as
paranoid fantasy.

The time for ponderings ended as he was ushered
into the audience chamber. At the far end of a gauntlet
of courtiers was a tiered dais upon which sat three
thrones. The right one was occupied—the Lady Brane
Deigh, he presumed. To the enthroned queen's side
stood a tall, dark-skinned elf. Hart stood among the
courtiers nearest the dais.

Sam was shoved from behind by the elf accompanying him. After an initial misstep, he strode forward,
determined not to show the turmoil he still felt. He
ignored the scattered titters from the crowd as he
stopped before the triple thrones. He stared defiantly
at the queen.

"Why am I here?"

"You are my guest," she replied sweetly.

"Guests aren't kept in cells."

"Let us say, then, that you may *be* my guest. As
such, you shall be given the freedom of the court, but
my guests are well-behaved and display courteous
manners. Though lately you have associated with less
attractive elements of society, you are a child of corporate culture; thus I know you to have been educated
in reasonably civilized behavior. Offend none of my

court, and you shall have a long life among us. Prove yourself entertaining or of value, and it shall be a pleasant life.''

Not a guest at all, but a prisoner. Or worse, a pet. "I want no part of your court.''

"It is not your choice. Are you so ungrateful as to throw away what the Lady Hart has won for you?''

"Oh, I'm grateful,'' he said icily, staring at his so-called benefactress. Hart would not meet his eyes. "And I'm sure there are many innocent souls in London who would gladly cry her praises as well. If they could.''

"You need not concern yourself over matters in London.''

"Then the Circle is destroyed?''

"Broken, certainly. And much of that work was yours. You are resourceful, for a mortal. I like that.''

Sam didn't believe that the Circle was defeated. They had still been active, and he had heard no evidence to the contrary. So why was the Lady complimenting him? Were elves by nature deceitful? He knew the job wasn't done—the renegade druids were still at large.

"You haven't said that they're destroyed; therefore they will still be at their evil work. They must be stopped.''

"They will be,'' the Lady assured him.

"Then you are working to stop the Hidden Circle?''

"They will be exposed and their evil seen by all the world. Their crimes are repulsive to all sentients. Public revelation of their evil will shatter their warped dreams of power.''

Sam didn't want to hear vague promises and flowery rhetoric.

"When?'' he demanded.

"In time.''

Lord Almighty, this woman is playing games with

people's lives. She was far more beautiful in body, but no better in soul than Haesslich.

"No! They must be stopped at once. If you are opposed to them, you must act now. People are dying."

The lady's warm manner frosted over. "Do not presume to tell me what to do. You cannot know of the large concerns at stake here, with your mortally limited view of time. Perhaps you should talk some more with Padre Rinaldi. In many ways he is as intense as yourself, but his organization has learned to take the long view. You could learn patience from him; he has learned his place."

"His place? His place is out in the world, not suffocated here as one of your *guests*. Why is he being held prisoner?"

"He is so very quick of tongue," she said, folding her hands in front of her left breast. Abruptly, a hint of her former warmth returned. "Could it be that he has not told you his tale?"

Suspicious, Sam replied, "He has not."

"Then you see that even he does not consider it any business of yours."

"I do not believe he has broken any laws. Whatever business it is, you have no right to hold him. Keep me here, if you must," Sam said. *If you can,* he added to himself. "But set him free."

"You may make no demands here. Never forget that you are an illegal alien in this land. You live on my sufferance." The lady returned her hands to the arms of her throne. "Still, Padre Rinaldi's wit is quick and keen, and his arguments, though insufficiently informed, did amuse me. However, it is not proper for me to arbitrarily rescind his confinement, and I find that I miss him. It is a dilemma."

The dark-skinned elf spoke into her ear. His words were pitched to carry to the audience as well. "The

Lady Hart is a member of your court. Perhaps she would sponsor the priest as she has the shaman.''

The Lady turned her attention to Hart. ''Are you interested, Lady Hart? A toy for your toy?''

Hart didn't look at her mistress immediately. For a moment she stared straight ahead, then her face turned to Sam. Her left eyebrow rose minutely, a silent question. He thought at first to keep his expression passive, to force her to decide without any input from him. Then, he thought about how much harder it would be to plan an escape without Rinaldi; the priest was his only ally here. Sam had no idea of Hart's motivation in bringing him here, but she had certainly not asked his permission to kidnap him. Would asking her to take the priest's part work for or against him? The moment was stretching out uncomfortably. He nodded to Hart.

''I shall stand for the priest,'' Hart said.

Lady Deigh laughed lightly, then smiled expansively. Sam got the sudden feeling that, in some obscure way, he had served Lady Deigh's ends, whatever they were. If this little tableau had cost Hart something, that was only justice. But he had been set up, too, and he didn't like it. In the past, whenever he had been manipulated to serve other people's ends, bad things had happened. The Lady was playing some sort of game here, and she seemed pleased by Hart's acceptance of responsibility for Rinaldi. Sam didn't know enough of what was going on and that worried him.

The Lady rose from her seat, precipitating a rustle in her crowd of attendants as they moved to anticipate her reaction.

''Let there be music,'' she said. ''I would dance.''

A soft strain of harp music began, filling the room and seeming to come from everywhere at once. The notes were clear, yet held faint echoes of other songs. The trill of a flute joined in, adding its lively tones to the ethereal sweetness of the melody. A drum slipped in and increased the tempo as the Lady stepped up to Sam and held out her hand.

"Dance with me, Samuel Verner."

Not knowing what else to do, Sam took her delicate fingers in his own. He felt coarse and awkward as she turned him toward the open floor, but a sudden flood of insight brought him the steps of the dance. He tasted the magic of the subconscious instruction and knew that the Lady's strong will powered it. She would not be embarrassed by an untutored partner. They were soon whirling across the floor, feet flashing in the rhythms of the jig. Pairs of elves followed behind them; each courtier strove to outdo his or her partner, and each couple attempted to outshine rival couples with the intricacy of their footwork. None danced with such flair or elegance as the Lady herself.

Hart did not join the dance. Each time Sam's gaze swept across her position, he found her cold bronze eyes following him and the Lady across the floor. The music seemed to go on for hours, and Sam danced, but he didn't feel his exhaustion until the music finally ended on a wild, shrill clash. Panting, Sam looked around. He didn't see Hart among the milling courtiers.

34

Days passed. Or at least Sam thought they did. Time seemed to be a mutable commodity in the illusion-ridden palace of the Shidhe. After that first interview with Lady Deigh, Sam had seen nothing of the ruler of the palace. Hart he had seen, but not talked to; every time he approached her, she slipped away.

Father Rinaldi was his near constant companion. The two wandered the halls, groves, and shadowed passages of the Seelie Court, talking. As soon as the priest was released from the cell, Sam had demanded the reason for Rinaldi's imprisonment. The priest had revealed that he was investigating rumors of renegade druids. When his attempts to gather knowledge from the Irish elves had uncovered the existence of the Hidden Circle, his welcome had come to an end. Lady Deigh had called for an interview and Rinaldi had revealed too great an interest in the subject. Apparently, the Lady had her own plans, though the priest had no idea of their content. She had ordered him imprisoned. The priest had not spoken of his involvement in the affairs of the Hidden Circle earlier for fear that Sam would distrust him as an agent of the cabal.

They concluded that the elves had thrown them together in the hopes that they would reveal things about the Circle. Sam didn't know what he knew that the elves didn't. He suspected that they knew more by far and were just being cautious. Once Sam and Rinaldi discovered they were opposing the same adversaries, they postponed their discussions until Sam, with the help of Rinaldi's theoretical knowledge, managed to adapt one of Herzog's spells to cloak them in silence. Protected from prying ears, they pooled their knowledge and reached the conclusion that they needed to escape confinement as soon as possible. The renegade druids had to be stopped.

They wandered the halls of the palace, alert for anything that might offer an opportunity of escape. They knew they were followed, usually by a single elf; the watchers made little secret of their surveillance. Follow they did, but the watchers did not interfere unless Sam and Rinaldi strayed towards one of the zones for-

bidden to them. At such times, the lone watcher was
rapidly reinforced by other elves with munchkin minions who blocked the prisoners' path and ordered them
to turn back. They were never told why they were not
allowed to proceed further. Sam maintained that they
had gotten too near the outer precincts, but Rinaldi
seemed more inclined to think that they had only approached some reserved sector.

Three times the great tables in the main hall were
replenished with the elaborate meals Sam had dubbed
"dinner" before he and Rinaldi stumbled upon a service passageway that led to a space under the open
sky. The Shidhe's cloak of illusion made the open
space appear to be a natural clearing in a forest. The
confusing fog of active magic was weaker in that place,
and Sam's astral senses let him pierce the masking
spell to see open space as it was: a modern helipad
designed to facilitate the loading and unloading of
cargo craft. Four more "dinners" passed before Sam,
using some of Dodger's tricks and paying a terrible
price in headaches, managed to tease a transport
schedule from the palace computer system while the
watcher thought he was reviewing library files.

From that list, they learned of a regular cargo shuttle run. Sam was relieved to see that the aircraft
assigned to the run was an Ares Wyvern, a small
single-rotored cousin of the massive twin-rotored
Dragon that seemed to be the mainstay of the Irish
helicopter transport fleet. He wasn't sure he would be
able to handle the big ship; he was nervous enough
about trying a small helicopter even with the help of
the sophisticated autopilot with which Ares equipped
their aircraft.

Sam and Rinaldi started taking irregular walks,
making sure that their paths frequently took them near
junctions close to the service passage. They honed
their plan to hijack the Wyvern and use it to cross the

Irish Sea to England. Periodically, they checked the palace computer system's bulletin board, watching for the dummy message that was the signal from the knowbot Sam had left monitoring the cargo schedule.

Sooner than they dared hope, the Wyvern arrived. They redirected their path, hoping that they still appeared to be wandering aimlessly while they were in fact taking as direct a route as possible to the landing pad. They wanted to time their arrival to coincide with its final clearances for takeoff, and they didn't have much time.

Two archways from the pad, they ducked into the shadows on the side nearer their goal and waited for the elf who had been following them. Their watcher had grown complacent; he stepped through the archway totally unsuspecting. Sam's punch took him cleanly in the belly. The elf folded, gasping for air. Grabbing handfulls of collar and of pants, Sam directed the elf into the wall. Sam winced at the crunch the elf made but was relieved to see his knees buckle. The elf sprawled on the floor, unmoving.

"Let's go," Rinaldi urged.

Sam tore his eyes from the fallen elf and followed the priest down the corridor. They cut through another arch into a more crowded thoroughfare. It was torture to move at the more sedate pace, but Sam knew they had to do it. He felt that the elves and other beings they passed were aware of what he had done, what he and the priest were trying to do. But despite his fears, no one tried to stop them.

At last they reached the side passage that would take them to the landing space they had discovered. It was a service corridor lined with crates and parcels and bereft of the cloaking illusions so prevalent in the Shidhe palace. This stretch of passage might have been in any airport in any metroplex. Once through the il-

lusion that hid the corridor's mundanity and assured
that the way was clear, they ran.

They couldn't have timed their arrival at the arch to
the landing pad any better. Through the cockpit windows of the cargo helicopter, they could see the pilot
going through his preflight checks. Fortunately for the
escaping prisoners, the pilot had set his craft down so
that the boarding ladder was turned toward them. The
bulk of the Wyvern screened the ladder from the con-
trollers' blockhouse.

Focusing his concentration, Sam cast the spell to
project the words he whispered into the pilot's headset. He held his breath, praying for success. He swallowed hard as the pilot tapped his headset in apparent
frustration over mechanical difficulties. Sam saw the
pilot's lips move as the elf asked for a clarification.
Refocusing his auditory illusion, Sam whispered again
the words he wanted the pilot to hear. To his relief,
the elf listened intently, then took off his headset.

The pilot hauled himself out of his flying couch and
disappeared into the body of the helicopter. He appeared again in the hatchway, kit bag in one hand. The
elf slung the bag over one shoulder before clambering
down the ladder. He walked around the nose of the
aircraft and headed for the illusory clump of trees and
brush that was really the pad's control blockhouse.

Sam allowed himself a sigh of relief before forming
the visual illusion that would cloak himself and Rinaldi, making them appear to onlookers as elven pilots.
Having seen the flight suit and insignia of the departed
pilot made it easier to get the details right. He hoped
no ground crew showed up to intercept them. The illusion was purely visual, since overriding one sense
was all he could handle. Anyone who touched them
would feel the difference immediately. Even sound
could give them away; the imaginary clipboards hanging at their sides would not be making the normal clat-

ter and ground crewmen would not fail to notice that discrepancy.

They stepped onto the tarmac together and tried to look casual. Sam hoped any onlooker would think they were chatting when, in fact, they were watching over each other's shoulder for any sign that they had been unmasked. Sam was sweating by the time they passed the nose of the aircraft and out of sight of the unseen elves in the control booth.

Rinaldi was standing at the foot of the ladder and Sam was halfway up when a cold voice ordered them to freeze. Sam looked down to see the elven pilot emerging from beneath the Wyvern. The elf held an automatic pistol trained on them. For all the awkwardness of clambering out from under the aircraft, the muzzle remained steady, leaving no doubt in Sam's mind that the elf was more than capable of using his weapon. The elf's smile was that of a cat who had just caught a mouse.

"Now just ease yourself down," he said to Sam. "Your work's not too bad for a norm. The aural bit had good resolution, even if you had me wondering why O'Neill had gotten so formal all of a sudden. You really need work on your visuals, though. It was a good likeness, but even if it hadn't been me who saw you, you would have been hosed. Should have varied the spell for the old guy; I'm not twins."

Rinaldi had to move aside to clear space for Sam. The elf didn't react to priest's motion; his attention was mostly focused on Sam. Thus, the pilot was wide open when Rinaldi snapped his foot up into a kick.

The priest's foot connected with the pilot's elbow, wrenching the elf's arm straight. The gun fell from the pilot's suddenly numb hand. Before the weapon hit the ground, Rinaldi stepped toward the elf and grabbed his arm. Jerking the pilot forward, Rinaldi drove his knee upward. Air whooshed out of the elf and he started to collapse, and Rinaldi helped him down by slamming his left elbow into the base of the elf's neck. The pilot's head snapped back and he hit the concrete chin first. Sam heard teeth and bone snap.

Rinaldi snatched up the gun and tossed it to a surprised Sam.

"Don't stand there," Rinaldi said. "Get in the helo."

"But you . . ."

"Did what had to be done."

Rinaldi bent down and slipped his hand into the elf's armpits and started to drag him toward the ladder.

35

Hart knew she was lucky to be the first one to find Donahue. She bent over to check him out. He had been assigned to follow Sam and the priest and had run afoul of them. The signs were obvious. No one in the court would have run him into the wall, or if they had, they wouldn't have left him in one piece. Sam was trying to escape.

Donahue groaned. Hart straightened and stepped away from him, so that when he emptied his stomach, she was well clear. He started to roll over, but she whispered a spell. In his weakened state, he had little resistance and succumbed to the enforced sleep she pressed upon his mind. She tapped the hall's illusions, extending them, to cover the sprawled body. Stretching an existing illusion was something that she couldn't do anywhere, but the mana-rich environment of the palace allowed certain liberties to be taken. The masking was an imperfect job, but it might delay discovery of the sleeping Donahue for a few minutes.

She checked the passageway and found it still deserted. Sam had chosen his ambush site well. Sam and the priest certainly hadn't passed her, so they had to be somewhere ahead. She took a moment to set her ally spirit Aleph on overwatch, warning it to watch specifically for Sam. Then, she hurried down the corridor, trusting her mundane senses to warn her of non-magical problems.

She could do no more than pick archways at random, because there was no way to tell what path the fugitives had chosen. As she crossed a threshold and heard the distant whine of a helicopter engine, she guessed their destination and suspected she was too late.

She ran.

She hit the clearing as the landing gear of the Ares Wyvern lifted from the pad. She could see Sam at the controls in the cockpit. He saw her, too, and smiled savagely.

Hart ducked back through the archway and pressed against the wall of the service passage. No alarms clamored. No one shouted to her. Sam had hijacked the helicopter successfully and she seemed to be the only one who knew. It was important that she not be seen here.

She didn't have much time before the Lady learned what had happened. Hart herself could tell Deigh, but she didn't know if the Lady would have her killed before or after they shot down the helicopter. When aroused, the Seelie Court could be every bit as ruthless as their less seemly cousins of the Unseelie Court. A violated parole and a stolen aircraft would certainly anger the Shidhe.

Hart had taken responsibility for Sam and the priest. Their escape was her failure, her responsibility; by the

Shidhe's law, her life was forfeit. Only Sam's death at Hart's hands might release her from that harsh judgment.

It took Hart three minutes to run through the halls to her quarters. Worry nagged at her the entire way, almost disrupting the concentration she needed to maintain her invisibility spell. She knew some of the palace's guardian creatures had marked her passage. The damned, chittering leshy seemed to see her too, but none of the elves she passed were aware. That was good.

There were no guards at her quarters. The alarm had yet to be given. She wasted no time packing, only grabbed the working bag she had kept ready out of old habit. Before leaving the room, she used the computer to log a ''do not disturb'' order and a delayed order for a meal delivery with the palace household staff. It was a weak ruse, but it might buy a few minutes.

On her way to the outer precincts, she only paused once at a storeroom. The room was supposed to be secure, but she had penetrated better systems. She was in and out at the cost of only a few precious minutes, her bag stuffed with Sam's gear. There were ways to use the items as tracking links.

Just before she hit the outer, public section of the palace, she dropped her invisibility spell. There would be mages on watch at the boundary, and her concealment spell would only mark her as someone to be detained. To her relief, she found at the gate that her privileged status hadn't been revoked. The guards listened dutifully to her story about a trip to the southwest, and even offered her good wishes as she left the building.

She passed through the park surrounding the palace and entered the rail station without incident. Her good fortune held; a train was in the station. She slipped a certified credstick into the turnstile slot and dumped enough nuyen for a month's open pass. The gate opened and she made it to the platform in time to board just as the doors were closing.

By the time the train pulled into the main station in Dublin and she left the car to mingle with the city crowds, she had worked out the bones of her plan. Her first step was to contact her decker Jenny and arrange transport to England. As soon as she secured a little backup, she would intercept Samuel Verner. She was very sure she knew where he was headed.

Dodger had never felt so tired. He stared at the dataplug in his limp hand for a full minute before letting it drop to the idle cyberdeck. He was hungry and his muscles ached from hunching over the cyberdeck. His meat was failing under the strain. Running the Matrix steadily ground a decker down. Trying to do the work of a whole team of deckers changed the grinding wheel of exhaustion from carborundum to diamond grit. He was worn down.

The search for Sam and Hart had been a total bust. The Matrix offered no hints of any operation, and his checks on druid holdings gave no indication that they had anything to do with the sudden disappearance of his fellow runners. Willie had come up with zilch as well. Even Herzog's street contacts had nothing, no matter what price was offered. No avenue Dodger had explored had yielded any information on the platinum-haired lady elf or the brown-bearded American shaman. Neither should have been able to hide for so long in the London sprawl.

Dodger was frustrated. Hart he could take or leave; something about her flashed a warning mode. But Sam . . . Dodger had gotten him into this mess and now his friend had vanished without a trace. His feelings of guilt were uncomfortable as much for their rarity as for their strength. Those feelings were exaggerated every time he thought about how much time he was spending on the other problem.

The hunt on that issue had turned up only negative clues, but the puzzle drew him like a siren. Driven to look, and repelled at the same time, he haunted the Matrix searching for anything that might tell him more about the Artificial Intelligence that had called itself Morgan le Fay.

Dodger had visited with some of the best deckers in the Matrix, but they knew nothing. The rumor mill at Syberspace was empty. Or rather, it had been when he checked into the virtual club. It wouldn't be now. He knew that he would have started a whirlwind of speculation with his guarded questions. The habitués of the decker club were not stupid—nobody stupid could deck through the ice that armored that exclusive little Matrix hideout. His fellow Matrix runners would guess what he had hinted at and begin looking for themselves. Soon someone would know.

Or would they? Was the AI too good for mortal deckers? Could it hide in the Matrix in ways beyond any decker ability to detect?

He wished he knew.

All he knew was that Renraku still had not announced the Artificial Intelligence's existence to the world. That meant that something in their program had fouled up. If they were sole owners of a functioning AI, they should be media-blitzing. The technological coup was worth too much.

Unless they were using it for shadowrunning. Could the rewards of applying it subversively be greater than the killing to be made on the open market? The AI had been present in the Hidden Circle's architecture. Dodger's investigations had revealed no significant connection between Renraku and the Circle. There were the usual minor connections between some of the druids' corporations and the megacorp, but no more than could be expected in the interconnecting world of modern business. Renraku had contracts with the British government, but Dodger had been unable to detect any unusual activity or connections there, either. Normally, he would have assumed that everything was just too well hidden. But with the AI involved, he couldn't be sure. The Hidden Circle's antics just weren't Renraku's style.

So what was the AI doing in the Circle's architecture?

His first thought had been that Renraku might be moving against the Circle, too. Such criminals might attract the attention of a civic-minded megacorp. The publicity for squashing murders and terrorists was always worth a few points on the stock exchange. But the AI hadn't done anything to the Circle's system, and Renraku operations were quiet. The fragging local Red Samurai contingent had just been withdrawn for temporary assignment on the continent. Dodger's every runner sense screamed that Renraku wasn't involved.

So who was running the AI?

It wasn't the renegade druids. If they had that kind of Matrix power, Dodger would be a vegetable by now. The AI was just too much Matrix muscle.

For all its power, the AI was a riddle. It had found him in the Circle's architecture. How? It had even brought him a present. Why? Could it have been following him? Again, how and why? What in all the electron heavens and hells was going on?

Dodger had begun to think the only one with the answers was the AI itself. If he met it, he could ask. That was a concept that burned while it froze. When he was jacked in and experiencing the AI in the Matrix, he had no desire to stay in its presence. No rational desire, anyway. But an irrational attraction was there. He could no longer deny it. There weren't supposed to be emotions in the Matrix. The electron world had no pheromones to clog a man's brain and force animal reactions on a rational mind. When he stood under the electron skies, in the presence of the mirror woman with the ebony clothes, something called to him in a way he had never experienced before. At least not in the Matrix. He felt very afraid when he realized that the pull was too much like what he felt in Teresa's presence.

The meat and the mind, enemies ever.

So what was going on?

He was tired and confused and hungry. Knowing he wouldn't be able to deal with any problems if the meat collapsed on him, he rose shakily from his seat and stumbled across the squat toward the refrigerator. He hoped Willie had stocked the thing before she had relocated her base of operations.

He hadn't thought that was a good idea. Sam or Hart wouldn't know where they had gone, and leaving a message with a map was just as dangerous as staying put if the bad guys tracked them down. More dangerous; in a new base they'd feel safer than they were. She'd argued that splitting their reduced forces was dangerous, and been incensed that he refused to leave. But then, she'd already been smoking over the time he spent chasing his Ghost in the Machine instead of looking for Sam.

The refrigerator door didn't rattle when he opened it. Even as bleary as he was, he knew that wasn't a hopeful sign. The vegetable bin was empty save for a browning, wilted bunch of celery. The shelves held a few soggy pasteboard cartons sagging with the weight of their contents and a trio of bottles of Kanschlager fortified ale. The detrius of their patronage of the local food merchants he understood, but Willie's abandonment of some of her booze was a surprise.

He picked up one of the bottles. He squinted his weary

eyes at the label, but couldn't read the fine print. *How the mighty have fallen from their lofty ideals.* Alcohol was another sin of the flesh that dragged the mind from the clearer realms. Still, it would taste better than what they called water around here.

A sudden clatter from the doorway showed him just how strung out he was. He dropped the bottle. It shattered at his feet, spraying shards of plastic and sticky ale over his bare feet. A glance over his shoulder wiped such petty concerns out of his foggy brain.

Two men had entered the squat. The noise had come from the one clothed in dark garments. He had slipped on the remains of Dodger's last meal and grabbed the table where the cyberdeck and Willie's radio lay. The rattle of equipment had betrayed their entrance.

The second intruder was already halfway across the room. At first, Dodger thought he was a Shidhe because of the cut and material of his clothes, but the wild beard that spilled from the shadows of the hood dispelled that thought. Emanating menace, the intruder closed the distance between them in four quick, long strides. Dodger tried to move out of the way, but his flesh, the poor abused meat, betrayed him. The norm caught Dodger easily as he tried to slip past to reach his gun.

Pain shot through Dodger's spine as he was slammed into the edge of the kitchen counter. The norm forced him into the counter, grinding the edge into Dodger's arched back. The cold muzzle of a gun forced his chin up.

"So confident that you didn't even bother changing your base of operations? Should I shoot you now or let you try to lie your way out of it again?"

Dodger was shocked to recognize the voice. "Sam?"

Sam grinned with surprising savagery. "Surprised, aren't you? She couldn't hold me."

Sam wrenched Dodger upright and shoved him

against the refrigerator. Dodger's right elbow caught the edge of the door painfully. He cried out and grabbed for it with his other hand as he struggled to stay on his feet. Sam took two steps back and leveled his weapon at Dodger's chest. The gun's muzzle seemed far too large for the pistol's size.

"Sam, that's not a tranq gun."

"No, Dodger. It's not. Give me a good reason not to use it on you."

"Use it? What are you talking about? What happened? We've been trying to find out what happened to you and Hart for a week. We were really worried. Who's the other guy? Where's Hart? Is she okay?"

Dodger knew he was babbling, but the words just kept pouring out. Sam's face was stony. His lack of reaction and warmth rattled Dodger almost as badly as the gun his friend was pointing at him.

"Hart's in deep drek with her friends. Excuse me, *your* friends."

"*My* friends? What are you talking about?"

"Dump it, Dodger! I've had enough of your lies," Sam shouted. His hand was shaking with the violence of his emotions. "Look at you! You're pathetic. What's the matter, chummer? Drinking away your sorrows? Or are you trying to get up enough courage to sell Willie into captivity, too? Why don't you just have her killed? It'd be kinder than putting her into some elf zoo. See the halfer rigger and the crazy wildman from Seattle! Amusing! Entertaining! All courtesy of Dodger and Hart Enterprises. You've conned me for the last time."

Dodger let go of his bruised elbow and drew himself to his full height. If this was going to be the end of the flesh, he wouldn't cringe. He didn't know what had set off his friend, but there really wasn't anything he could do about it. Sam was obviously confused, maybe mind-controlled, and he wasn't listening. But talk was the only weapon Dodger had.

"You're wrong, my friend. Whatever happened to you, I had no part in it."

"You're a liar!"

Sam raised his pistol.

The muzzle pointed directly between Dodger's eyes. Death was a finger twitch away. Sam's hand began to shake.

"Drek! I can't do this!"

Sam threw the gun across the room. His companion stretched out an arm to catch the weapon, but its trajectory took it just out of his reach. The pistol hit the wall, gouging the wallboard, and rebounded onto the mattress Dodger had been using for a bed. For the first time, Sam's companion spoke.

"It's just as well, Sam. I don't think the elf is lying. His aura indicates that his confusion is real."

Sam turned away from both of them. His hands clenched and unclenched at his sides. Sam's companion stood silently watching him, an expression of concern on his face. The companion turned to look at Dodger, his eyes full of curiosity.

Dodger didn't know what to do. He was shaking himself. While he dithered, Willie's voice burst from the radio receiver.

"Twist! Is that you, Twist? What's going on?" There was a pause. "Frag it! Somebody answer me!"

Sam walked to the radio, avoiding eye contact with anyone.

"I'm here, Willie," he said shakily.

"Frag, but I'm glad you're back. Where ya been?"

"Took an involuntary vacation."

"Hell of a time to go sightseeing, but you could've come back sooner."

"Would have if I could have, Willie." Sam took a

deep breath and released it. When he spoke again, his voice was steady. "My tour guide had other ideas."

"What counts is you're back. You ready to run again, chummer?"

"All cylinders."

Dodger thought it sounded likle false bravado, but Willie obviously took it at face value.

"Good 'cause the ante's going up and you're the last magicker on-line."

"The last . . . what's happened?"

"Just had a drone in for a meet with Herzog. He's dead. Somebody raided his sanctum, but he put up the good fight. Made 'em pay. Took out four or five, my count on the body parts was a little iffy."

"The Circle?"

"Neg. Not unless they've got a lot broader of mind while you were gone. The hitters were all elves."

Sam turned to stare at Dodger. "Say again."

"I said the guys who took out Herzog were all elves."

"Elves," Sam repeated softly. "Talk to me, Dodger."

36

Jenny's check on the power draw for the squat confirmed that either Dodger or Willie was still operating out of the apartment. There wasn't enough usage to supply both the elf's cyberdeck and the rigger's board. One of them had moved out. The broad-band receiver Hart carried didn't show any unusual broadcast activity, so she assumed it was the elf. As far as she knew, Willie didn't use booster stations to hide her location.

Hart's surveillance hadn't picked up any activity for over an hour. Jenny confirmed power draw, so that meant Dodger was decking and the others asleep. It was time to move.

She left her perch and made her way down through the building, exiting around the corner and out of sight from the runners' lair. Timing her crossing to coincide with traffic, she crossed the street screened from the apartment's window. Once on the same block, it was easy to move unseen through an adjoining tenement and up onto its roof. She leaped across the gap between the tenements and landed with satisfactory silence. Crossing the rooftops, she hesitated only a moment near the brick shack that Sam had tried to use for cover against her shots. She shook off the thoughts that threatened to upset her centering and proceeded to the cornice at a position above the flat's biggest window, where she set her bag down. In a few minutes, her gear was rigged, and she sat down to do an astral scout of the squat three floors below her; she didn't want any surprises.

She got one.

The flat was astrally warded! Unable to penetrate the protection to view the interior, she returned to her body. She would have to go in blind, relying on the mundane reconnaissance she had already performed.

There was no reason to delay. She shed her long coat and clipped the drop line to her harness. Satisfied that it was secure, she went over the side, walking the wall past darkened windows.

The winter air was chill, but she barely felt it. Her doubts kept her warm. Was she doing the right thing?

With a swiftness born of familiarity, she squirted lubricant into each side of the window frame. She let it penetrate for two minutes, then tried to lift the sash. It moved smoothly and silently; as she had remembered, there was no lock.

With the kitchen window open, the blackout curtain was the only impediment to entrance. She folded her legs, then straightened them, pushing off from the wall. The extra force from her right leg angled her return so that she would pass through the aperture. Her feet brushed aside the curtains and as her hips went through the frame, she hit the friction clamp and released its tension. She hit the floor and tucked herself into a forward roll. The soft clack of harness buckles against the floorboards was the only sound she made. She came up into a crouch and froze, listening.

The apartment was silent save for the soft background hum of an active computer system. The soft glow from a terminal screen was the main room's only illumination. No one moved in what she could see of the room.

Hart remained in place for five minutes or more, and heard nothing else. Satisfied that she had alerted no one, she stood up and stepped forward. Her curse broke the peacefulness.

There was no one there. The computer hummed only to itself, but there was a message on the screen:

It read:

"Not what you expected, is it?

"Too bad.

"There's a new twist in the game.

"Press ENTER for more."

She knew better than that. She left the way she had come in.

"A return to old haunts when the other side is on to you can be fraught with danger," Glover said pedantically. "But then, I suppose you have already learned that. The restraints are not too uncomfortable, I hope?"

The captive had only one eye, since the other had

been closed by the purplish black bruise covering most of one side of his face. Still, he glared. Glover found it amusing.

"It would have been better for you had you simply kept running. You could hardly expect to succeed where your associates had failed. You are only one person and nowhere near as skilled as they were. But don't feel too impotent. Your friends did some damage, and they might have done more against us had we not already been alert for those who would sabotage our great work."

"God will see you punished," said the prisoner.

"God? Whose god, my pathetic friend? Yours? In the olden days, they believed that the stronger god would overcome the weaker and set his people above all others. You can see the motif in so many stories that one must think in the days when myths were made, before the old magic lessened, that there was a factual basis for such replacement. Today, you sit defeated, and I stand victorious. Your god has forsaken you, but the Sun shines on me."

"Your pride will be your fall."

"Stubborn." Glover chuckled. "One might almost think you still held hope for a rescue. Do not. The rest of your little band have gone the way of all flesh and, in doing so, have strengthened our cause. You shall join them when the appointed hour comes. Perhaps I myself shall wield the sacrificial knife that drinks your blood."

"You are deluded. Your murders bring you no power. Your path is corrupted."

"How could you know? Our rituals are steeped in a tradition that antedates your pitiful church. We have reached back to touch the old ways, the true ways of power. I have felt it."

"You have felt lies, murderer."

Glover backhanded the prisoner, rocking him back

and almost toppling the chair to which he was bound. Blood spurted from the prisoner's nose to spatter the white cuff of Glover's shirt with incarnadine stars.

"I had thought you an educated and intelligent man, Father Rinaldi. Your fellow Sylvestrines spoke so highly of you in interrogation that I thought you might be able to see beyond your prejudices, once confronted with the truth. I see I was mistaken. Still, your soul will fuel our paean to the Sun."

"Your blasphemy will be stopped."

"Your faith is touching, father. Would it be shaken if you knew one of your fellow priests told us everything we needed to know about your communications with Rome? As far as your superiors know, your team has found nothing as yet. You are, however, pursuing a most diligent investigation. By the time any of the fossils in Rome suspect that they are being fed false information, the cycle of rituals will be complete and our Circle shall no longer need to be Hidden. We shall set the king on his throne, and the restored land shall be as it was."

"You're mad. Corrupted by evil."

"And you're powerless. Consumed with envy." Glover laughed loud and long. "The weak will never understand the strong. Never having tasted power, they are incapable of it. You and your weakling breathren will never know the true power the Circle has touched. Even when we reveal it, you will see only a shadow of the truth. Well, your fellows will see. You, my dear father, will be long gone."

"It shall not be. Even on earth, you are opposed."

"Perhaps you refer to the meddling of shadowrunners. They had been causing us some difficulty, but their masters are too ill-organized to control their minions and insufficiently committed to maintain bothersome pressure. Their bumbling runners ran afoul of their own internal factions, and the team crumbled away, leaving only a handful of pox-ridden elves to annoy us. Stings only. Why, just last night we swatted one of the annoying insects. Their importance diminishes to insignificance as we grow in strength. When we have established the new knigdom, we will deal with the shadowmasters and they will regret opposing us.''

The buzz of the telecom cut off Rinaldi's response. Glover was annoyed; he had ordered that he was not to be disturbed. He returned to his desk, intent on giving his secretary a piece of his mind, but he changed his mind when he saw which line was lit. Tapping the command to transfer the call to headset, he settled the earpiece and opened the line. The call was swift and to the point. Cutting the connection, he faced the priest.

''Someone else has taken an interest in you, Father Rinaldi. You should feel honored.''

37

The garden mezzanine of the Hawthornwaite Residential Tower was deserted save for three animated shadows near the banks of private elevators. Faint music from the bar in the lobby three levels below masked what few sounds the shadows made as they huddled near the control panel. One detached itself from the group and moved to stand by the brazen doors bearing the GWN graphic on the left panel.

Listening at the door, Sam could hear the elevator car approaching. If the car didn't stop, they might as well go home. If they could.

As the car sighed to a stop, Sam cocked the bolt on his

Narcoject Hypnos. The rifle version of the tranquilizer gun felt bulky and obvious. But this was a raid and inconspicuousness wasn't a high priority. If the elevator disgorged security troopers, he'd probably need the extra capacity the rifle's magazine afforded. Briefly, he wondered if he might be better off using the captured LD-120 pistol that rode in the holster at his hip. No, the building's guards would just be doing their jobs. Did that deserve death? The druids and their acolytes deserved no mercy, but what of their unsuspecting minions?

Dodger, seated on the floor next to the doors, concentrated on his cyberdeck. Willie readied the elf's Sandler submachine gun and laid it near his right hand before cocking her own.

"Give me first shot," Sam said.

"You sure?"

Sam nodded.

"Wilco," Willie confirmed as she backed along the wall to give her a line at the part of the car Sam wouldn't be able to cover in the first sweep.

With a pneumatic hiss, the doors slid open to reveal an empty car.

Sam let out a breath he hadn't realized he was holding. With its release, tension drained from his muscles. They'd made it past the first hurdle.

He held the door while Willie trundled inside to catch the door button. Dodger jacked out and began reeling in the datacord he had patched into the elevator controls.

"Hurry up, Dodger," Willie urged.

"Patience, Mistress Machinerider. If aught appears amiss after we depart this floor, the alarums will ring. 'Twould be most unfortunate if haste undid our plans at this stage."

"Just do a good job, Dodger," Sam said.

"Assuredly, Sir Twist."

Dodger finished his fussing and gave the panel a

quick polish with a rag before joining the others in the car. Willie released her button and the panels hissed closed. Sam reached across to tap the bronze strip labeled GWN and start them on their journey to the ninetieth floor.

"Pray tell, Sir Twist. Where is the priest? I thought he had joined our team."

"He had other business."

Willie snickered. "You bust him out, and the first time you need help, he's off doing errands? Some gratitude."

"His other obligations had first claim on his loyalties. If all goes well, he'll be joining us later. With help."

"But not tonight?"

"No, not tonight."

"And why should we need help tonight?" Dodger asked sarcastically. "We are but three intrepid souls invading the residence of a multinational corporation's highest officers. Since we hope to beard their local executive officer in his home, why should we be concerned with numbers? He is only a dreadfully powerful shaman and will, no doubt, have only a battalion or two of mundane guards. What have we to fear from them?"

"Dump it, Dodger." Sam didn't need the elf's sarcasm. They might not know exactly what they were getting into, but they had all studied what information they had. They all knew who the target was. The time for cold feet had been two hours ago. Dodger may not have had anything to do with Herzog's death, but he was not yet back in Sam's good graces. "You know why we're here."

" 'Twas your choice."

"You didn't have to come."

"Pray, tell. What would you have done without me? Scaled the building?"

"We'd have managed," Sam replied. Dodger's whining was beginning to get to him. "Willie's good with electronics."

"Take it easy, Twist. Dodger's just nervous like the rest of us. I gotta admit, I don't like moving on this guy when we don't know if he's dead or alive."

"Alive. Dead," Dodger scoffed. " 'Tis a difference that makes no difference to this run."

"It'll make a difference if the fat man's waiting for us," Willie observed, gripping her weapon tighter.

"The villain is dead. Did not Sir Twist see Hyde-White go down during the raid on the ritual?"

"But there was no body," Sam said.

" 'Twas present if you accept the wendigo corpse as his. Such a hypothesis explains the more grisly aspects of the Circle's operations. 'Twould account for the sluggishness of GWN's business reactions as well."

"Jeez, Dodger. You can't still believe that," Willie said. "The druids are still doing their Bone Boy stuff. That dead wendigo ain't the answer. I think Hyde-White is still alive, but wounded. That would fit with the business problems."

"A clattering fit to the facts, Mistress. The wendigo is dead. Hyde-White is missing. Therefore, Hyde-White is dead."

"That's pretty shaky, Dodger."

Sam interrupted Willie before she could get rolling.

"Whether Hyde-White is alive or dead, GWN is still functioning and serving the Circle. That's more than enough reason to hit it. Since the company's a potential target for more than the opponents of the Circle, we'll be able, with a little luck, to hide our incursion under the guise of an ordinary shadowrun against the corporation. Besides any damage we do to GWN, we should be able to find out the truth about Hyde-White."

"And if he's alive, Twist?" Willie asked.

"We cut him out of the Circle."

Dodger waited a moment before asking, "Sir Twist, are you saying we shall kill him?"

Sam kept his gaze riveted to the doors, but he could feel Dodger's eyes on him. "There are still too many druids to take them on all together. We need to chip away at them."

"You have not answered my question."

The slowing of the elevator was an answer of its own.

"Get ready," Sam ordered.

As they had hoped, the guard at the station was sluggish. He had no time to do more than catch a glimpse of them from the corner of his eye before Sam cast his spell. Sam knew it was a success as a puzzled look crept over the security man's face. He had succumbed to the illusion and was seeing an empty elevator car.

The guard stood up and started around from behind his desk, muttering about technical malfunctions. Sam shot him with the Hypnos as soon as he was out from behind the desk. The guard's puzzlement slipped into bafflement as he sank to the plushly carpeted floor. He was snoring when the runners stepped over him to get to the desk controls.

Willie ran her hands along the controls. Her stubby fingers touched each lightly as if she could divine their function by mere contact. She nodded to herself, tongue sticking out to touch her upper lip, as her roaming hands came to rest on a row of buttons beneath a flat metallic panel. She tapped the first, and the panel clicked, its left side separating from the desk's surface. Willie flipped the panel open, revealing a hidden set of switches and a datacord receptacle.

"Rig option," she announced. "Ain't it nice when the info ya buy is right?"

Her partners didn't bother to answer her question,

but she didn't seem to mind as she settled into the still-warm chair. In thirty seconds she had jacked in and switched the security system management over to rigger control.

Sam had never understood how a rigger made the translation between body sense and the diverse components of a building's systems. Rigger security control was even more alien than the way they piloted vehicles. "Nothing to it," she had said when he proposed the raid. "It's just like a big body; ya get itches where something's happening." The concept was creepy to Sam. It lacked the purity of the Matrix or even the more understandable body-control concept of vehicle rigging. But Sam didn't have to understand or like it. It was Willie's job—all Sam had to do was count on her to do it right.

"What's going on in the residence?" he asked.

"Quiet," she replied. "I don't think anybody's home."

"And no signs of recent occupation," Dodger added confidently.

"Wrongo, elf. Plenty of signs: dirty dishes, rumpled bed, private line call logged out less than two hours ago. But nobody's there . . . wait a min. There's something funny about that level."

"Looped broadcast?" Sam suggested.

"Neg. All eyes are live. But they're not seeing everything."

"Alternate sensors tracking something?"

"Neg on that. There aren't alternate systems anywhere but on this level. I think . . . yeah, it's got to be. There's part of this level that isn't covered by the security system."

"A black room?" Sam speculated.

"Could be." Willie agreed. "Looks like you two will be doing an in-person visit after all."

"Thrilling," Dodger said.

"You can handle the locks, Willie?"

"Null perspiration. You want to go up by lift or stairs?"

"Stairs. More options for retreat."

"Allow me," she said. Across the lobby a doorway opened. Through the arch, Sam could see stairs.

He tapped Dodger on the shoulder and started for the stairs. Sam could hear the elf grumbling under his breath as he followed. The unprofessional bitching stopped as they reached the landing below Hyde-White's residence. Guns ready, they advanced up the last flight. When Sam signaled their readiness to the stairway camera, Willie opened the door. Dodger went through low while Sam covered him.

They got the drop on an empty room.

When nothing reacted to their presence, Sam said softly, "You there, Willie?"

"Affirm." Her voice came from the building intercom speaker. "I see you but they won't. I dumped a copy of an all-camera scan, just in case we need to know the layout of the place for some future op, and I'm using it to run refeed on the room cameras from the five minutes before you got there. If anybody notices, it'll look like a digital overprint. Just let me know if you need more time. But try to be quick, a second blip'll start looking suspicious."

"We'll do that. Now where's this blind spot?"

Hyde-White's residential level was made up of a bewildering arrangement of spaces demarcated by freestanding walls and half-walls and room dividers. There were also several spaces which were completely enclosed. Willie directed them as well as she could, but it still took them five minutes to isolate the area that was in the rigger's blind spot. Dodger found the door hidden behind a tapestry.

"Sir Twist," his muffled voice called. "You must needs see what I have found."

Sam pulled aside the tapestry preparatory to entering the hidden chamber and immediately felt the tingle of magic. Warily, he leaned against the outer wall and probed with his astral senses. The room was surrounded by the rosy glow of an astral barrier. Something coiled about the top of the domed-shaped protection, but it seemed inactive. Sam sensed no threat from it. Concluding that the ward was only a protection from astral intrusion, Sam returned to his mundane senses and probed the open doorway with a tentative hand. Nothing happened, so he followed Dodger into the chamber.

The stench was the first thing he noticed. The place smelled as though something had died there. Rotting meat was Sam's first thought, but the temperature was so low that meat would have been unlikely to spoil. Sam was already chilled despite his winter clothes.

The room was only a few meters across, but it was jammed with an eclectic collection of furniture and artifacts. Dodger was poking about among the jackdaw's nest of furnishings and decorations, but Sam paid him no heed. His eyes were locked on a large oil portrait of a woman that dominated the wall opposite the doorway.

"Quite attractive for a norm," Dodger commented when he noticed Sam's fixed stare.

"Janice," was all Sam could say.

38

"Find anything interesting?"

Dodger reached for his Sandler as soon as he recognized the voice, but she was faster. She snatched the weapon from his fingers before he could get a grip. He kicked the chair back as he stood, but she skipped clear. He spun, hoping to get inside her aim, but again she was too quick for him. He eased back against the table, forcing his muscles to relax. Elven reflexes weren't good enough to dodge bullets at this range.

Hart smiled at him. "Much more reasonable reaction."

"What do you want?"

"To talk."

"That is obvious. Else, I would not be breathing."

She shrugged and lowered the muzzle of the Sandler, but Dodger felt tension in her still. Gauging the distance between them, he briefly entertained the idea of a move, before dismissing it as foolish. He'd seen her in action and knew he wasn't her match. She would be ready for anything he tried.

"Speak, then. You have captured my attention."

She hesitated before saying, "I want to offer my help."

Was she serious? After what she had done to him, how could she expect Sam to let her anywhere near him? "He doesn't trust you anymore. I don't either."

Her smile was sad. "You should understand how compelling previous arrangements can be, Dodger. Have you told him who had you get him involved in this mess, or that you're still passing his plans on to Estios?"

"You didn't tell him, did you?"

"Not yet, but I could."

She gripped the Sandler by its barrel, carefully lowered it to the floor, and leaned it against the wall, and stepped away from the weapon. Her actions were likely intended as a sign of her peaceful intent and meant to reduce the tension between her and Dodger. He found himself considering her motivations, and the possibilities only made him more nervous.

"We can help each other, Dodger."

"If you really want to help, you'll go back where you came from. He's screwed up enough now as it is."

Her brow furrowed. "What's happened? Is he hurt?"

Her concern seemed genuine, but she was a good actress. She had thoroughly fooled Sam. He considered the wisdom of telling her what was wrong with Sam, and decided that her reaction might provide a clue to the motivation behind her recent actions. If not, there was the slim chance that she might have some data that applied to the riddle of the painting.

"There was a picture of a norm woman in Hyde-White's sanctum. He said it was his sister."

She grasped the situation at once. "A *norm* woman? I thought she had goblinized. When was the painting made?"

"The date within the artist's cartouche was this year's."

"And the artist?"

"His identity is a mystery."

"So what have you been doing?"

"He's been brooding when he hasn't been rerunning the tapes we got of Hyde-White's apartment. I've been trying to break into the GWN personnel files."

"With no luck, I expect."

He was annoyed by her casual assumption of lack of progress. "I am the Dodger. It is only a matter of time."

"Isn't it always."

She reached into her satchel, and he tensed again. She offered him a tentative smile along with a raised hand. Her other hand slowly emerged from the bag, holding a slim black chip case. Dodger relaxed as she opened the case and selected an unmarked chip carrier. When she held it out, he recognized the molding as UCAS government issue.

"Try this in your deck," she said. "It's a one-shot can-opener. I've been saving it for a special occasion."

Dodger took the carrier. Unable to contain his curiosity behind the thrust and parry of shadowtalk, he asked, "Why are you doing this?"

"Let's just say I've got an inquiring mind."

The lure of using her toy did not keep him from running diagnostics on it before slotting it into his deck. Slipping into the Matrix soothed him; in the electron world he had no worries. Well, only one; and it hadn't shown its mirror face in weeks. His meat was already at her mercy, but he would be safe enough until she got what she wanted.

He was amazed at the beauty and elegance with which her can-opener cut the GWN ice and slipped him into their files. The hunt was short and successful. He dumped his swag back to the deck and exited the GWN architecture. As he cleared the boundary, the can-opener evaporated. He jacked out.

Janice Verner's name was on a list of special consultants for GWN that he scrolled onto the display screen of his cyberdeck. Most of the other names meant nothing to Dodger; they had never before appeared in all his searching through portions of the Matrix associated with the members of the Hidden Circle. The one name he recognized was that of Karen Montejac. Unfortunately, Hart noticed his reaction to the name.

"You know her?" she asked.

"The, ah, lady works for a . . . a former client."

"So, what's the connection?"

"There isn't one."

Hart wouldn't let it go. "Guessing, or do you have evidence?"

"I have deferred the evaluation of connections to a higher authority who has ruled out the possibility."

The look on Hart's face told him that she didn't like his answer. From her earlier threat, he suspected that she knew he was referring to the professor. She finally nodded in acceptance, apparently willing to concede to the professor's judgment.

"What is in the Verner file?" she asked.

Dodger brought it up on the screen. It took only a little manipulation to crack the lock. The first entry was a transit pass for a corporate flight from Hong Kong to Mexico City.

"Not Yomi?" Hart asked musingly, then she smiled. "There's your answer to your problem. The date on that flight is after Sam's sister's exile. If Hyde-White recruited her, it would have been at the gulag, and she would have been whatever she had turned into by then, no longer a norm woman."

"The painting may have been done from an old picture."

Hart snorted. "Even if it were, what reason would he have for wanting it? *She* wouldn't, if she's like most people who go through the change. No, Sam was meant to see this painting. The fat druid's a manipulative bastard and likes playing mind games."

"How do you know that?"

"Personal experience," she said bitterly. "Trust me. The portrait's got to be a fake, a ploy to throw him off stride."

Something seemed out of place to Dodger. "How would Hyde-White have known Sam was going to see it?"

Shrugging, Hart said, "Maybe he was going to plant it somewhere else."

Her explanation still seemed to be missing a chip. "Why do it at all?"

"I don't know. But I do know that the fat man's a devious bastard and a class-A manipulator. He's the one who really started the Circle, you know. Even led the research that got them the wicker man ritual. He's the real power behind the Circle.''

''As Merlin was behind Arthur,'' Dodger said, remembering the imposed imagery of the Circle's computer architecture.

''What?''

''Nothing. Just a literary allusion. So, what to we do about this?''

''You tell Sam, and then keep me posted. I've got other things to do.''

Dodger's suspicions flared again. ''More trouble to cause?''

''You betcha,'' she replied jauntily. ''When you see him, give him these.''

Hart dug a wrapped packet out of her satchel. The bundled had filled most of the bag's volume and, when the soft sides collapsed, Dodger could see the outline of a gun. He took the offered bundle. From his weight and balance, he suspected a second weapon was wrapped within its softness.

''Why should I?'' he asked as she headed for the door.

She kept walking, saying over her shoulder, ''He'll need them.''

Sam didn't know what he expected to see, but he kept rerunning the tapes Willie had made from the trideo monitors in Hyde-White's residence. Willie watched them with him, getting twitchier with every repetition. The copy spun to an end and Sam reached for the controls to rewind the tape.

''Ain't ya seen enough?''

''One more time, Willie.''

''Jeez. Ya been through through it a billion times. Look, Twist. I'm not a forensic expert, but I am a woman. I'd say there was a woman living in that residence. Ain't that what ya want to know?''

Sam nodded abstractedly as the tape clicked over and started to play again. "But what kind of woman, Willie? A norm, or something else?''

"Do I look like a parabiologist?'' Willie bounced up from the floor, grabbed a half-full bottle of Kanschlager, and downed it. "The blowups show a lot of hair scattered around, but, frag it, that don't tell us anything without chemical analysis. The fat druid and his woman could have a dog; there's enough gnawed bones in the kitchen.''

"It didn't smell like a place where a dog lived.''

"Well, then, a cat! Jeez, Twist, what do you want?''

"I want to know about my sister. They told me she had goblinized.'' Would Sato have lied about that? No, the doctor had said she was in the *kawaru* ward, so it had to be true. But what about later? Maybe she had died, been killed by Hyde-White and his flunkies. Maybe that was why Renraku had never let him communicate with her.

Sam didn't want to believe it. He felt sure he would know if she was dead—he was a fragging shaman with fragging mystical powers! If he couldn't sense the death of his own sister, his only living relative, what good were those powers? Still, he had been a reluctant shaman and had avoided a lot of what he needed to know about his gifts. He couldn't be sure that the magic would let him know if she was dead.

The portrait in Hyde-White's sanctum didn't have to be his sister. It could be a coincidence. So why didn't he believe that?

He tried to picture the painting in his mind. He wanted to remember a detail, any detail that would confirm or deny the subject's identity. All he succeeded in doing was calling up the horrid smell again.

That awful stench seemed somehow . . . familiar.

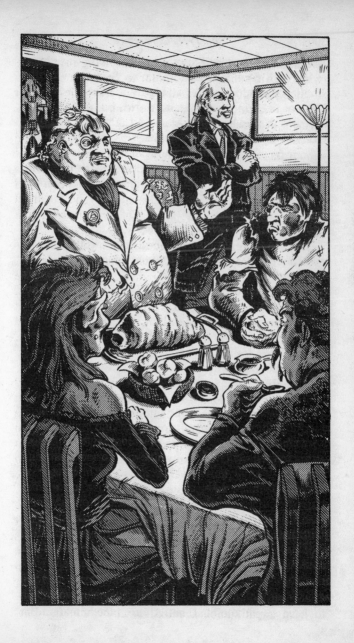

In his memory, it had another quality that was absent in the chill confines of the sanctum. Sam knew he had smelled the odor before; suddenly, he knew where. It had not been in the mundane world, but in the realms of the spirits where the Man of Light had worn fire like fur, and exuded that stench.

Sam remembered what the Man had said about manipulating his emotions and meddling with his memories. Had Dodger seen the same woman in that portrait?

"Hyde-White, old man. Good to see you," Glover exclaimed. "Recovered from your injury?"

"Almost."

Janice knew better. Though Hyde-White still wore bandages and limped, Dan Shiroi had long ago recovered from the injuries dealt him by a ravaging band of shadowrunners. She disliked the fat shape Dan wore. She was not skilled enough to pierce his mask and so, like his coconspirators, she could only see the obese bulk of Hyde-White even though she knew Dan's lean, furred shape hid within it. His obsession with masks no longer bothered her. She understood and embraced the necessity. She looked forward to the day when he would teach her enough to mask her own shape as effectively as he did his own, and she would be able to deceive the slimy Glover and his like.

"Your pet appears as ravishing as ever," Glover said archly.

When he thought he was unwatched, Glover regarded her with the disgust one usually reserved for things that crawled out of one's food. She suspected he knew her true form; he was a druid, after all. She also suspected that his attitude was more than the prevailing English class consciousness. The man seemed to have a pathological hatred for metahumans. But then, did that make him different from the average norm?

Glover struck her as a petty, small-minded man despite his grandiose plans for the country. She didn't like him, and wished Dan didn't find it convenient to associate with him. The other druids were nearly as bad.

Dan had told her how his Hyde-White identity was involved in the plot to replace the monarch. She had thought the plan put him too near the spotlight of publicity, but had dropped her arguments when he explained that his participation would place him in a position to influence policy regarding their metatype. The risk seemed worth it; they needed every protection they could get from the swarming norms. Even if it meant using such unsavory persons as Glover.

With her presence at these increasingly frequent dinner parties, she had come to see just how well Dan had the druids under his influence. They treated Dan like a revered elder. Alone at his home, she and Dan had laughed at them, especially Glover. The archdruid was so devoted to Hyde-White and the cause. Glover, who hated all metahumans, fawned on one regularly without ever knowing the truth. It was a rich joke.

Much better than the hoary jests exchanged by the rest of the druids once she and Dan joined them. There was the usual round of pleasantries from which she was excluded. The snubbing didn't bother her; she only came for Dan's company, and the food.

The seemingly interminable interlude in the lobby ended and Barnett, the hosting druid, opened the doors to the feast hall. The site was one of his company's conference centers, and he seemed unduly proud of it. Janice found the decorations tasteless and boring. The table, on the other hand, was set with superb style.

The selection of condiments and sauces was extensive, offering a wide variety of flavorings for the main course of rare meat which dominated the setting. To either side of the golden platter with its mound of bite-sized morsels, were baskets of sourdough rolls, excellent for sopping juices. Save for the guest's place, each diner's setting included a delicate ewer containing his or her favorite beverage. The guest's plate was flanked with two glass goblets, one brimming with iced water and the other gleaming with a dark wine.

Scattered among the auxiliaries to the main course were small dishes of vegetables and fruits. They added a splash of bright color to the table, but Janice no longer found such foods appetizing. Her changed metabolism was exclusively carnivorous.

The guest was already seated at the table across from the seat of honor, which was always given to Dan at these affairs. The seats for her, the druids, and their companions were ranged along the opposite side from the seated man, flanking Dan's chair on either side.

The guest didn't look up as the feasters entered. In the subdued lighting, Janice at first did not notice the extensive bruising on his face; but as she took her place, his battered visage was obvious. His dark clothes were tattered and stained, and his posture made them hang on his gaunt frame as if he had been shrunken within them. He had the air of a man resigned to an unpleasant fate.

"You could have gotten our guest a change of clothes," Dan said to Glover as he seated himself.

"I did," the archdruid replied. "He refused them."

"Perhaps you should have offered sackcloth and ashes," suggested Ashton.

His remark raised general laughter around the table. Janice didn't get the joke and didn't join the merriment. No one noticed.

"You are impolite, my friends," Dan chided gently.

"Pietro Rinaldi is our guest. If he wishes to attend in casual dress, I will not spurn him from my table."

Rinaldi looked up when Dan said his name and his eyes widened slightly when they rested on the speaker. He looked next at Janice and she smiled at him, hoping to set him at ease. He shivered and his gaze slid away to skim over the lavish meal set upon the table.

Dan handed the great platter of meat to Glover, starting it down the side of the table away from Janice. As he awaited its return, he engaged their guest in conversation.

"I was pleased to learn you had been persuaded to stay with us, Pietro. An opportunity to interact with a person of your quality and distinction is far too rare a pleasure."

Dan waited for Rinaldi to speak, but he rudely remained silent.

"Come now, Pietro. It will not imperil your soul to talk to me."

Rinaldi glared at him before saying, "Will it not? I know what you are."

"Ah. Your gift of sight. Your fellow Sylvestrines told me that it was very strong. It must be difficult, always seeing things and never having the experience to truly understand them. You have my sympathy."

"Spare me," Rinaldi said. Janice thought the tone of his response was rude. "I understand your kind well enough."

"Do you, Pietro. I hardly think we have been represented fairly in the arcane libraries in which you have studied. I expect you have seen nothing but biased accounts, half-truths, and ill-informed speculations. But rather than arguing about what you *think* you know, I'd like to talk with you about something you know very well.

"You see, I know about you, Pietro Rinaldi. I know the facts of your career and numerous small details of your history. But more importantly, I know what kind of man you are. You are a doer, a man of action.

"As I learned of how your gift had been limited, I was saddened. To find yourself only able to watch the magic that makes the world live . . . such a limitation is a criminal shame. You are not a watcher, Pietro. It must gnaw at you to always see and never do."

"I have accepted my lot."

"Fine words, and a noble sentiment. I'm sure your superiors approved and encouraged that attitude. However, acceptance of the inevitable is no virtue. Virtue requires sacrifice, does it not? At the very least it requires voluntary abstention. But your inability to touch the real magic is far from voluntary."

As her own had been, Janice remembered. She had yearned for the magic, and had despaired when she was told she hadn't been blessed with the ability.

Rinaldi said, "I learned long ago not to aspire to what cannot be."

Dan shook his head. "You mean, what you were *told* could not be. Are you really sure that you can never have the magic flow through your hands?"

Janice had been sure until she met Dan. He had shown her the way.

"Pietro, your ignorance made things safer for them. With your access to magic limited, you were no threat to them."

Dan accepted the platter back and forked several juicy chunks onto his plate. "Knowing what I am, you know that I walk ways different from those of the bulk of humanity. Those paths have taken me to places of arcane knowledge. The power I have touched in those places transcends moral strictures, and I have learned how to share that power. I can offer you a way to transcend your own strictures. *Magic*, Pietro! If you accept my ways, the binding can be broken. I can lead you into the realms of power and show you the secret paths. I can give you the magic you long for. All I ask is that you embrace us and our cause." Dan held out the plate of meat. "Eat with us."

Rinaldi kept his hands on the table, but his gaze skimmed along the seated diners. "I know you better than they do. *Retro me, Satanas.*"

Dan lowered the plate and laughed. "I am a persuasive fellow, but I have never claimed to be that particular silver-tongued devil."

"But you are a devil none the less."

"So I have been called, but I am not. I am a creature of the earth, Pietro. No more, no less. The earth is as much a home to me as it is to you, and we each have a place in the grand scheme. I am only attempting to offer you a better place, one in which you can exercise the power that you long for. You are obviously superior to the masses who throng the outside world. The superior are not bound by the conventions of the inferior. It has always been so. Haven't you always known that your destiny was to be a magician?

"Join with us and it can be so."

Rinaldi ignored the newly offered plate and said, "God is my armor. He offers all the power I need."

Foolish man, Janice thought. God set the natural order on the earth and in that order, one relationship was paramount: predator and prey. If you were not one, you were the other, and the superior preyed upon the inferior. Having made the world as it was, God understood. How could Rinaldi not see that?

"Your vision of God offers you nothing but frustration and privation," Dan said. "Knowing no better, you accepted that distortion of reality. But you are no longer an uneducated child, sheltered by a limited view of creation. You have seen magics, great and small. You have seen the spirits moving through the air. How can you just be a bystander? How it must gall you to be unable to partake in the wonders!"

"It is as it must be," Rinaldi said.

Janice thought his voice held less of the obstinate conviction with which he had started. Dan had said Rinaldi was an intelligent man; perhaps he was beginning to see Dan's wisdom. Janice found herself hoping that he would.

"Must be?" Dan questioned. "Very little *must be* to a man who has the strength to seize opportunity. You can see that if you just look around you. My companions have partaken of my table, and they are whole. They are better than whole; they are stronger than they were before they joined me. Your *gift* lets you see that, doesn't it?"

Rinaldi hung his head and said nothing.

"Look at them!"

Rinaldi's head snapped up at the command. He stared at the feasters with eyes as bleak as winter.

Dan sat back, smiled with satisfaction. "Yes, you can see that their auras are stronger for partaking of my feast. You can be stronger, too. Strong enough to burst the bonds that tie you and touch the face of magic. You want to feel the magic, don't you?"

In a very small voice Rinaldi said, "Yes."

"Then join us," Dan said, leaning forward to offer the platter for the third time. "It's not hard. Partake. Take the power of another into yourself. Make yourself strong."

Rinaldi's nostrils distended. He began breathing hard, as if he was exerting himself physically. Sweat beaded on his brow and upper lip. His eyes devoured the meat on the platter.

"Come, Pietro. You can't deny me. I'm only trying to help you fulfill your destiny."

Rinaldi locked his fingers together, elbows resting on the table and lowered his forehead to his hands. He was shaking.

Dan snorted and passed the platter to Janice. She

took a portion for her plate and passed it on. She felt sorry for Rinaldi. Why was it so hard for him to accept a place among them? How could he not want what Dan offered him?

The platter completed its course and the feasters began their meal. From behind the barrier of his folded hands, Rinaldi watched them. His eyes grew wilder.

At last he shouted, "Don't you all realize what you are eating?"

Silence descended on the table. Dan smiled at Janice and she smiled back. "Prey," she mouthed silently to her lover. Dan's smile grew wider. Glover cleared his throat and spoke.

"Oh, yes. We are quite aware. We partake of the ritual portion. It is necessary for the completion of the ritual. We purify the impure and return them to the holy cycle of the earth. Through us they are cleansed and, through them, we are strengthened."

"God save you! You're eating human flesh!" Rinaldi seemed verging on the edge of hysteria. "Give up your sin! Fight off the evil influence of this creature!"

"We partake of a ritual sacrament," Ashton responded calmly.

"And here I thought the Church had become more broad-minded about alternate religions," said another druid.

"We do this for the good of the land," added a third.

Rinaldi tried to get up, but Dan gestured and an invisible hand threw the priest back into his seat.

"It is impolite to leave the table before the meal is finished," Dan admonished him.

"Let me go! I reject you!"

"I am patient, Pietro," Dan said, unruffled by Rinaldi's outburst. "I'll give you another chance."

"I will die first."

"Perhaps. Perhaps not. I am persuasive as well as

patient. I'm sure you will come around to my point of
view. Soon or late, everyone gets hungry.''

39

"I've got a line on the priest," Jenny's synthesized
voice announced from the telecom.

Hart considered telling her decker to put her time
into higher priority searches, but data was data and
Jenny, like any good decker, collected whatever was
lying around. Hart knew she should be thankful to be
relying on Jenny again, instead of the more technically
brilliant, but emotionally unstable, Dodger; but the
stress under which she was operating was disturbing
her usual crisp grasp of the situation.

"What's the word, Jenny?"

"A street runner posted an FYI on the local shad-
ownet after seeing a magically assisted snatch outside
St. Basil's in South London. Dated the op just after
noon yesterday. Victim matches the priest's descrip-
tion.''

"Could still be a thousand people."

"A thousand people don't attract the attention of
other people, two of whom match descriptions with
your druids.''

"You got any more details?"

"Negatively. Spotter didn't want to get involved.
Beat feet soon as he twigged to the op. Said catching
fireballs wasn't his style.''

"Smart.''

There was a pause, then Jenny said in a tentative
voice, "I thought we were, too, boss.''

"You got a problem, Jenny?''

"Negatively, boss," she responded quickly. "You pay the bills and I run the Matrix. What could be better? I just think this one's running a little close to overheat, and you're awful close to the fire."

"Just do your job, girl. I'll be all right."

"Hope so. Just don't want to see the boss getting hurt for no good reason."

Hart didn't like the idea of getting hurt, for *any* reason. Jenny's fears weren't groundless. There were too many factions scrambling around. The sooner things were settled, the better.

"Did you get the mercs lined up?"

"Prepaid bond locked them down, but if they're as good as they claim, we don't have enough in the account to pay the completion fee. Logistics ate a lot of the budget."

"Don't worry, they'll take enough casualties. Feed me the rendezvous data."

The telecom beeped, signaling a datafeed on the second line. Hart split the screen and reviewed the details. They were satisfactory.

"Time to go to work, Jenny."

"I'm gone, boss." Jenny's voice faded out in simulated doppler echoes.

Word of Father Rinaldi's fate finally reached them, and it was not good. In attempting to contact the investigative team his order had sent to the British Isles, the priest had run afoul of agents of the Hidden Circle and been captured. Sam had no doubt that the priest would be one of the victims at the renegade druids' next filthy ritual.

Rinaldi's capture complicated things, and Sam didn't need any more complications. Everything was too confused as it was. He stared at the opened packet that Dodger had brought.

Weighting down the curl of the paper was a pistol holster wrapped up in its belt. The smooth black leather encased his Narcoject Lethe, the same pistol that Dodger had given him and that Hart had taken away after she shot him. The other end of the wrappings was held down by a fossil tooth. "Some kind of Late Cretaceous dinosaur," the paleontologist had said when Sam had taken it to the museum open house. Sam thought he had a better idea of its origin but he had been wounded and delirious that night in the badlands when he had broken it free from its sandstone entombment. Whatever it had been, it had become a power fetish for him when he drilled a hole to take a ritually knotted cord so that he could wear it around his neck. Folded neatly between the gun and the tooth was the fringed kevlar-lined leather jacket that Sally had given him after his first solo shadowrun.

What had motivated Hart to give Dodger this packet of gifts for Sam? It didn't seem to be boobytrapped; Sam had detected no residues of spells, and Willie had confirmed that no technological bugs infested the contents of the package. "He'll need it," she had told Dodger. For what? Against her? If it was meant as some sort of apology, why hadn't she contacted him herself? The unlooked for return of his goods only confused him more, raising additional worries.

Time was running out.

With Rinaldi needing to be rescued, the runners had to split their already pitifully weak forces. It couldn't be helped. If their attack against Hyde-White went off before they rescued the Circle's captives, there was too great a chance that the captives would be killed out of hand. If they made their rescue attempt before the spoiling attack, the Circle would be alerted that Sam's team was back in action. That surprise element was their only advantage, and a pair of simultaneous operations was the only way to use that advantage. It was also a good way for the runners to be defeated in detail.

They were so pitifully undermanned for what they had to do. Herzog was dead, and Willie's street contacts had told her that the shaman's death had effectively cut off any chance of local help. The word on the street was that the run was suicide. Dodger was still trying to contact some out-of-town friends, but Sam didn't have much hope that they would be able to stand up to the druids. He had detailed them, should they show, to helping Dodger go after Rinaldi. With the distraction Sam's attack would provide, Dodger's group shouldn't face organized opposition. At least they had been able to make connections through Cog to outfit Willie for the raid.

The plan was weak and Sam knew it. But they'd make the run. The split weakened the effort, perhaps fatally; but Sam couldn't abandon Rinaldi, and he couldn't see a way to stagger the operations. It was all at once or not at all.

He tossed his head back and closed his eyes, using the exercises Herzog had shown him to reduce the tension. When he felt his neck muscles relax a little, he sighed and brought his head upright again. Beyond Hart's engimatic gift the telecom screen glowed with a frozen image. The screen showed a hardcover book lying on a rug, half covered by a sheet. Due to the forced image enlargement, the image wasn't sharp, but it was clear enough for Sam to recognize it. While Dodger's electronic delvings seemed to contradict Sam's certainty that the woman who was residing in Hyde-White's residence was his sister, the book argued otherwise. And, to Sam, the book won the argument and spurred his haste.

Only the author's name and half of the title were visible, but Sam knew the book, anyway. It was R. Norman Carter's *Queen of Sorceries*. The original spine of the cover was gone, replaced by a strip of plastiboard taped down to protect the binding. Sam remembered his father standing behind his shoulder monitoring him as he carefully lettered the name of the book onto that now-scuffed piece of board. He could hear Janice crying in the other room and the soft, comforting tones of his mother as she tried to soothe her frantic daughter. Sam had still been mad and unrepentant about teasing his sister about her fondness for the story. His father had said it had been cruel to tease Janice, but Sam hadn't understood at the time. He had thought that his father would approve of his attitude. After all, the book glorified magic. Sam had thought he was rescuing Janice from the perils of magic.

What he hadn't known when he was nine.

Even with its shoddy repair, or perhaps because of it, the book had remained one of Janice's childhood treasures. Like their father, she had always been sentimental about books. Sam didn't understand the passion she felt for the physical object, but he knew that she would have used her limited weight allowance to take her favorites with her to Yomi.

Now that book sat in Hyde-White's residence, and Sam could not believe that it belonged to anyone other than his sister. Somehow, Hyde-White had rescued her from Yomi and seduced her. For the first, Sam had to be grateful; the druid had done something Sam had been unable to do. But, for the second, the man had only earned Sam's enmity. Janice had obviously exchanged one form of bondage for another, and she probably was more than grateful for the attention the fat druid gave her. Her goblinized form would not be beautiful.

Sam could not leave his sister living a lie. He was all the family she had left, and he would have sought her freedom even if Hyde-White had been no more than a wealthy and jaded corporate with an exotic taste in bedmates. The druid's evil taint made Janice's rescue and Hyde-White's elimination imperative.

Dodger knew that the electronic contact would have been safer. Not that he was worried about physical safety; he had chosen the meeting site carefully. Though elves were uncommon throughout the plex, their presence in this dive of a pub was less remarkable; London's metahumans showed remarkably more tolerance for each other than the norms did for any of the metatypes.

Even though a Matrix connection would have given him less opportunity to screw up, he wanted an in-person meet. It wasn't because he wanted to deal with Estios face to face—that was a pain on which he would gladly pass. He felt a need to see Teresa again.

He was on this third V-juice when Estios and Teresa entered the pub and took a booth in the back. From his shadowed position at the bar, he waited, watching to see if they had a tail. Satisfied that there were no obvious followers, he flipped a one-band credstick to the ork behind the bar and joined them.

Teresa looked tired and worn down, but she had a smile for him. Beneath the layer of exhaustion, Estios's expression was even more sour than usual. The hand he tapped nervously on the table was wrapped in surgical tape. The exposed flesh at the base of his fingers looked raw.

"Let's get to it, alley runner. I don't like being out in the open like this."

Dodger gave him a smile as wide and honest as that of a megacorp's public relations director. "Indeed, I think 'tis a lovely evening as well, and your inquiries into my health are sincerely appreciated."

"In your pointy ear, smart-ass. We lost Chatterjee the other night."

Dodger swallowed his levity. He hadn't particularly liked or disliked the Indian elf, but he had respected him as a competent runner. "I know. I'm sorry."

"That don't change anything. He's still dead. If we'd had some more muscle on the floor, he might not be."

Dodger's retort was cut off by Teresa.

"There's no need to lay guilt on Dodger. You went ahead with the raid after you knew he couldn't make it."

"Don't start," Estios snapped.

Teresa sat back. Estios's heated reaction seemed to assure her that her point had been made.

"Chatterjee knew the risks, alley runner," Estios said directly to Dodger, as if he needed to explain his own responsibility in the other elf's death. "We're not playing games here. But his death costs the team, and I don't plan on losing anybody just to have a chat with you. Make your point quickly, or we're gone."

"Very well. We've gotten reliable information on the itinerary of one of the Circle. There will be an opportunity for a strike."

"I assume your presence here means that Verner isn't going after him."

"Her. It's Wallace."

"Whatever," Estios said, dismissing the correction with an irritated wave of his injured hand. "You had reported that his strategy was to whittle them down."

Dodger tried to sound properly offended by Estios's implication. "I have reported all with scrupulous accuracy. Sir Twist wants to wait for a shot at bigger fish."

"But, Dodger, why pass this information on to us? If *we* hit Wallace, it'll stir the Circle up," Teresa observed. "That would seem to complicate Verner's plans."

"A successful raid will also weaken the Circle." He turned to Estios. "I think even you can see that an opportunity to weaken them will be to all our benefits."

"There will be just the one?" Estios asked, still suspicious. "They been hanging pretty close since we iced Carstairs."

"For this occasion, the Circle will be separated. One druid and a minimum amount of muscle is all there will be. The Circle continues to expand their shadow contacts, and there is to be a meet with an important runner. Since the site is within Wallace's turf, the politics of the situation demand a show of trust. Security will be light."

"You've got plans for the meet site?"

"Of course." Dodger slid a chip case across the table. "Times and routes as well."

"And you're willing to take Chatterjee's place on this hit?"

Dodger hesitated. "I'll ride Matrix cover."

"Some brave fellow, eh, Teresa? Can't get shot or flamed in the Matrix."

"There are dangers enough in the Matrix," she said.

Dodger wondered if she was worried about him. Estios made his own feelings clear by saying, "Not when we all know the Circle hasn't got a decker in his league."

"Is that a backhanded compliment, Estios?" Dodger said in mock surprise.

Estios glowered at him and stood. He half-dragged Teresa from the booth. "If you do the job, alley runner. We'll take out the druid."

The abrupt end of the meeting spoiled Dodger's hopes of talking with Teresa. His pique roused him to take a jab at the departing Estios. "What's the matter, Mister Competence. Don't you trust me?"

40

Wind whistled past the cockpit. The rush of air almost drowned out the moan and hum of the taut fibercables connecting the Fledermaus to its untenanted twins. The cables slaved the autopilots of the other craft, forcing them to duplicate Sam's maneuvers. The dogbrains were left just enough latitude to compensate for slight differences in the air flow.

In the distance, the triple towers of the Brighton Centrum stood like spires of light against the night. Below and beyond them, the lights of the district dotted the landscape like a mass migration of hopped-up fireflies.

Somewhere down there various radars would be running, watching the skies. The cables ensured there would be no transmissions to unmask them, while the foamed exteriors and composite construction materials masked the metallic contents of the craft. To any vigilant watcher, the vee formation of Fledermaus should look like no more than a small flock of night-flying seabirds.

Sam hoped that was true. Cog had assured him of it, but Cog was safely on the ground. Sam turned the nose of his craft toward the land, riding the predawn seabreeze. Behind him, the other two ultralights turned in his wake like obedient dogs.

Hart tongued the button on the boom mike of her headset, silently acknowledging Jenny's signal. A glance over the edge of the roof showed her the two vehicles carrying the mercs moving into pre-assault positions on the plaza between the towers. It was almost time.

Jenny had managed a reasonable crop, given the constraints of time, and they were every bit as cocky as the decker had said. But then most of their breed were that way; they didn't have enough brains to be otherwise. Still, they were well equipped with untraceable equipment, which she had checked herself at the briefing. More importantly, they were hopped up and ready to go on what they thought was a retaliatory property smash.

Hart had arranged for the bloodballs that they had demanded in their contract. The combat drug would raise their pain thresholds and boost their adrenal functions, making them more effective physically while cutting down on reasoning functions. Just the thing for a shoot-and-scoot where no tactical subtlety was needed. She had sternly admonished them to take only one apiece, but she knew most of them would pop a few more. In fact, she was counting on it, and had made sure the drug was above average purity. A merc who succumbed to its false promise of invincibility probably wouldn't last the fight, but until then he'd be worth two or three straight shooters.

They'd need the edge; she hadn't told them about the magic they would be facing.

Hart laid the Conner grapple gun on the parapet and used the sight to check the opposite roof. It was still clear. She wished she could see inside, but she didn't dare send Aleph or make an astral check herself. Surprise was vital.

She tried to relax as she waited for Jenny's go signal.

*   *   *

"Two doors down on the left."

Dodger watched Estios and Teresa move down the corridor. She'd cover while the black-haired elf moved forward. Then, he'd hold until she joined him. They were careful and quiet. If Dodger hadn't been monitoring the hall camera, he would not have known they were there; the sound pickups didn't register their presence due to Estios's silence spell.

The pair reached the designated door. As Teresa crossed in front to take a position on the side of the frame opposite Estios, Dodger switched cameras and checked the room to satisfy himself that all was well.

"All clear," he sent on the tight band. "Bonding charge is off. Only the panel lock left."

Estios nodded once to Teresa. He barely waited for her to signal her own readiness before stepping away from the wall. He faced the door and kicked. A portion of the frame tore free. Estios used the recoil of his kick to drop back in a crouch. Teresa cut through the door and rolled to the left as Estios aimed into the room, ready to take out any threat.

As Dodger had known all along, there was none.

A dazed Pietro Rinaldi awoke with a start. He blinked sunken eyes into at the gun-wielding elves facing him. Like any intelligent person, he made no extraneous movements.

Estios released he left-hand grip of his Steyr and slammed a fist onto the floor. Furiously, he shouted into his microphone. "What kind of drek you pulling here, alley runner!"

"Please, noble rescuer. Lower your voice. I think you're disturbing the good father. As well as possibly alerting ATT-Multifax's sluggish but still present security forces."

"Father? This guy's a *priest?*"

Dodger was inordinantly pleased with himself. Seeing Estios lose his cool was so gratifying. "Now, now.

Don't let your prejudices show. It's bad for public relations. Times are difficult and 'the enemy of my enemy' and all that. The good father opposes our mutual foe and is their prisoner.''

"That's his problem.''

"You are being short-sighted, Ice Eyes,'' Dodger chided. "This gentleman will have information we can use.''

Estios began to bristle, working himself up for a blistering retort, but Teresa touched him on the arm.

"Dodger's right,'' she said softly. Her words made Estios flinch, but at least he stopped sputtering. "Besides, since he has seen us, we can't leave him for them.''

"And leave you should. I've got activity on the motion detectors in the cross-corridor at junction three.''

"Frag it!'' Estios exclaimed. "I don't like being used, alley runner. I'll get you for this.''

Despite his comment, he helped Teresa get Rinaldi to his feet. An elf on either side, the priest was able to shuffle fairly quickly down the passageway.

Dodger guided them through the building, steering them past guard stations and roving patrols. His best information said that the staff of ATT-Multifax weren't part of the Circle's conspiracy, but their building security was still charged with apprehending intruders. Two elves escorting an emaciated priest would definitely attract their attention.

Once the elves and the priest were in the elevator and on their way to the roof, Dodger decided to switch back to the level where Rinaldi had been held. It wouldn't do to have a hue and cry go up. He switched to the zone in time to see a group of four people moving toward the now-vacant holding area.

"Drek! It really is Wallace.''

"What did you say, alley runner?''

Estios's query made him realize he had broadcast his surprise.

"Nothing," he responded quickly. "Just get in the veetole and go."

Estios made some kind of response, but Dodger was too busy studying the druid's party through the security camera. He couldn't see any transmitters, which was good; he would have a chance to slow them down. He started isolating the floor by activating all the telecommunications circuits for the zone. As the druid's party discovered their prisoner was gone, he was unleashing an expert program that would flit about the system causing mischief. Until someone isolated the bug, it would look as though a bush league hacker had broken through the building's ice and was flexing his muscles by messing with the telecommunications lines. By then, Dodger would be long gone. He hoped.

As he expected, the first move of Wallace and her goons was to use a telecom to alert the rest of the Circle. While they struggled with the phones, Dodger continued his guerrilla tactics. His ground team had exited onto the roof, so he shut down the elevators. He tensely waited for the veetole to lift before initiating the next sequence.

Finally frustrated with the telecoms, Wallace led her goons toward the elevators. He had only seconds before they decided to use the stairs. One by one, he cut off the security cameras in the sub-basement, starting with the one commanding a view of the elevator lobby. He was rewarded when the ATT-Multifax security triggered the building's intruder alarm. The alert status let him tweak the response and initiate the magnetic locking of the stairwell doors, to completely trap Wallace and her flunkies on a level about to be assaulted by security teams. As a parting shot, he programmed the sub-basement's sprinkler system to function in random bursts and set off the fire alarms throughout the basement levels. The noise and discomfort would go a long way toward distracting Wallace from using magic to solve her dilemma.

He wanted to stay and watch the fun, but there wouldn't be much for him to see with the cameras out. Besides, he had places to be. He sent the go signal on ahead and slipped out of the ATT-Multifax system as stealthily as he had crept in.

Glover watched the lights of the departing helicopter disappear into the distance. The craft was carrying Ashton to investigate the trouble at the ATT-Multifax complex. There had been no word from Wallace and something seemed to be amiss on the lower level where Glover had arranged for the storage of Hyde-White's prize captive. The disturbance might have nothing to do with the captive priest; there were enough targets throughout the complex to attract shadowrunners. The Circle had taken care of the rest of the priest's team and were still successfully blocking the Vatican's inquiries. It seemed unlikely that a second team would have been dispatched this soon, and the priest hadn't been in the country long enough to ally himself with other parties. Still, with Wallace out of touch, Glover didn't want to take any chances. If there was a threat to their interests, Ashton's magical muscle and his overly enhanced bodyguards would handle it.

But until Wallace and Ashton returned, the Hawthornwaite Tower's magical defenses were weakened.

With Carstairs' loss to the shadowrunners, the Circle had lost its best situated connection in the local government. The protection afforded their operations hadn't totally disappeared, but it had been reduced, forcing them to regroup. They had been using Carstairs' residence as their chief base of operations, and his death mandated that they seek a new location. Nearby living quarters for all members was desirable for mutual support, and easy access to the lower classes a vital necessity for the continuance of the ritual cycle. Plausible mundane world connections were needed, for the Circle was obliged to remain hidden until the power ritual cycle was completed.

Brighton Centrum had seemed the perfect choice. Sir Winston Neville owned the land on which the Centrum was built, and besides being the leaseholder, he was a major stockholder in the holding corporation which administered the complex. The former archdruid's public connections with Gordon made it easy cover his transfer to the Complex beneath the guise of social affairs. Some of the Circle needed no special arrangements to move their operations to the Centrum. Hyde-White's GWN Corporation already maintained residential floors in the Hawthornwaite Tower, as did Ashton's Miltech Research. ATT had residences in all three towers, and it had been simple for Glover to invoke executive privilege to take a residence in the tower. Bringing Barnett's General Services in to replace the security corporation had only left Wallace without a business reason to be there, and she was rich enough to afford one of the luxury flats. Thus had the Circle gathered under one roof, with no one the wiser.

A buzz from the telecom interrupted Glover's chain of thought. Barnett answered it, as was appropriate: the call tone had indicated the building security line. There was a hushed conversation, most of which Glover didn't hear clearly, but he had caught enough to be unsurprised when Barnett said, "I say, Glover. Security seems to be having a spot of trouble on the plaza level."

"Why should it concern us?"

"Well, really, I am not sure that it does." Barnett stroked his mustache in a nervous gesture that Glover found irritating. "We've been having a rash of alarms throughout the complex tonight. Most of them have been false, but this is most definitely not. Sec desk is reporting ten or more heavily armed intruders wreaking havoc on the lobby and mezzanine levels.''

''Have they attempted to force entry into the Tower proper?''

Barnett shook his head. ''Not as yet. Their violence is without pattern, and individuals are reported to be evidencing berserker fury, which has led Sec Desk to suggest that we are dealing with a flashmob outbreak. Personally, I find the scale of this assault disturbing.''

Glover was annoyed by the whining tone in Barnett's voice. ''Then perhaps you had best attend to it personally.''

''But the Circle's anonymity . . .''

''Will be safe,'' Glover finished for him. ''You are a licensed druid and no one think twice if you defend your residence, especially in aiding a security corporation which you own.''

''Good point.''

Barnett demonstrated his concern by leaving the apartment posthaste. Glover returned his attention to the skyline. Ashton's helicopter had long since vanished. After a moment, Glover felt a presence at his back. Refocussing his gaze, he saw Sir Winston Neville's gaunt face reflected in the transparex.

''*Now* shall we tell Hyde-White, archdruid?'' Neville asked petulantly.

Glover frowned.

Archdruid indeed. The title he had coveted for so long had a hollow ring these days. While Glover wore the title, the members of the Circle always seemed to look to Hyde-White for direction. Without a struggle, the fat old man had leeched the leadership role and prestige from Glover. How had Hyde-White managed it without Glover noticing? He never missed a power shift in ATT and had always moved with the flow to increase his own influence. So, what had happened within the Circle? Without the fat old man actually present, Glover was still master of the others, so Glover was not totally without influence. Hyde-White was foolish in allowing Glover to garner the lion's share of the power their rituals raised; one day that shortsightedness would turn around and bite him. Glover would not stay first in the Circle in name only. He may have missed the opening pitch, but the wickets weren't down yet.

"Archdruid?" Neville prompted.

Glover shook himself free of his brooding and turned to his questioner. Neville stepped back, apparently startled by something he saw in Glover's face.

"I just thought that," Neville began. "I mean—if there is a significant danger, he should know."

"And show weakness by running to him over some petty problem that most likely has nothing to do with the Circle? You don't know him half as well as I do, Sir Winston. You would only earn his scorn."

"And if it does concern the Circle?"

"Then we shall resolve it and present him with the evidence of our efficiency. We captured the priest without his involvement, as you recall. We shall show him that the Circle is no longer weak."

And I will have shown that I no longer need his strength.

Sam could see some kind of commotion at the base of Hawthornwaite Tower. Flashes of light from heavy weapons fire and magical blasts lit the sky with the sudden violence of summer lightning. The arcane bolts were coming from inside the building, which most likely meant that one or more of the druids was involved. The Centrum's security company had no on-staff magical talent, relying on quick response from the municipal police forces. Sam was pleased. The

distraction would only make his job easier, perhaps changing the odds of success from utterly impossible to only mostly impossible.

He banked the Fledermaus, sending it in a wide curve around the western tower. Locking the maneuver into the autopilot, he relaxed and sent himself down into trance to free his astral body. Any warning his reconnaissance might give now would be minimal. He ghosted through the target floor and found nothing alive. The thing coiled on the sanctum's arcane dome hissed at him, but did nothing to impede him. As he passed through an area set aside as an office, a communications device buzzed, demanding attention. An immediate response cut off its strident complaint. There had been a telecom in the sanctuary; Hyde-White must have answered the call from there.

He rejoined his body as the Fledermaus finished its turn. Sam called up an overlay graphic to the heads-up display and confirmed the target floor. Dipping the nose of the craft, he headed in.

One hundred meters from the tower he switched on the auxiliary motors, giving the three craft the extra power they'd need to deal with the updrafts around the building. His screech transmission to Willie was answered at once. Sam blew the armament covers, sending fragments of radar-absorbent panels fluttering toward the ground, then cut the trailing craft free. They'd be under Willie's control for the final approach; there was no longer any need to maintain comm silence.

"Fifty meters, Willie."

"Affirm."

"Launch on three."

"Wilco."

"One. Two. Thr—"

The Fledermaus bucked as it launched the single air-to-surface missile slung under its belly. Flashes of fire lit the cockpit from either side as the remotely piloted craft launched their missiles simultaneously.

The floor-to-ceiling transparex windows of the target floor dissolved into millions of fragments under the hammer blows of the triple explosion. Sam fought the controls as the backblast washed over the Fledermaus. Somehow he managed the keep on the flight path. An updraft caught the craft just as its nose reached where the windows had been. The tail drifted forward and one wing dipped. Dipped and caught against the building. The 'Maus slewed around, flopping hard on its belly. The light craft bounced, then came down again on its nose, balancing precariously. Sam, hanging in the safety harness, saw one of the other craft nose up as it crossed their newly made threshold and kiss the ceiling inside the residence. The collision canceled its momentum. The Fledermaus's tail was still hanging outside. With a grinding roar, the craft slid backwards and out into space again. Sam could picture it tumbling toward the plaza.

Thank you, Lord. That could have been me.

His own craft rocked backwards, its precarious balance disturbed by the rush of air chasing the plummeting Fledermaus. Sam's teeth slammed together as his aircraft crashed to rest in a horizontal attitude. Half-dazed, he flicked the harness's quick release with one hand and with the other triggered the explosive charges that blew the canopy open.

He crawled shakily from the wreckage of his Fledermaus, eyes flying across the area in search of any opposition. Finding no immediate threats, he checked the status of the third craft. The other 'Maus had made a perfect landing and was discharging its cargo. A dozen rigger drones rolled down the extended ramp.

Each drone ran on four fat, deeply treaded tires and

looked remarkably like a child's radio-controlled toy. But no child had ever had such a toy. The drones were armored with ceramic composite plates and armed with fully automatic pistols mounted in extendable turrets. Each was equipped with a dog-brain that allowed it limited tactical responses when the rigger wasn't directly controlling it. The expert system wasn't a great shot or a canny fighter, but the drones would make good pillboxes capable of suppressive fire. Their small size made them difficult targets.

Once off the ramp, each drone turned in a different direction. Most were headed for the entrances to the residence level; their job was to limit reinforcements for Hyde-White. Some stolidly climbed up and across obstructions, proceeding in direct lines to their stations. Others whizzed around debris, taking corners as if they were driven by tiny, demented road rally drivers. Sam thought he knew which ones Willie was running. Within thirty seconds, only three remained in sight, and they had taken up station in a triangle with Sam at the center. Their turrets swiveled to allow gun and camera sight to cover a circular field of fire.

Smoke from the missile explosions filled the air, cutting visibility. Sam crouched, trying to keep his head below the smoke. He had to move cautiously; there were plenty of places to hide in the warren of living spaces that made up the residence level and no guarantee that Hyde-White was still in the sanctum.

Sam drew the Lethe. If by some chance Janice had been present in the sanctum and was now roaming the floor, he didn't want to shoot and kill her. Once he had a better idea where the opposition was, there would be time to shift to the heavy Ares Predator filling the holster on his left hip.

The stalk through the apartment was slow, lengthened by Sam's caution. The metroplex's night sounds were distant. They faded from Sam's awareness. Only what was near at hand mattered. He stepped carefully, trying to move silently. He listened for the slightest sound. The drones escorting him hummed almost inaudibly.

"Bogey. North Quarter," Willie announced suddenly in his ear reciever causing him to jump. "Tally ho!"

A short burst of weapons fire ruptured the silence, followed almost immediately by a howl of pain. More gunfire followed, and the sound of a heavy body crashing into things, but there were no more vocalizations. There was a crack like thunder and a flare of light washed the ceiling in the north quadrant.

"Drek. Oh drek!" Willie wailed in his ear.

Sam's escort drones swiveled their turrets and surged forward. As the last one careened out of sight around a corner, more gunfire erupted.

Sam arrived at a waist-high partition and ducked behind it. Cautiously raising his head, he got a glimpse of the battle. The drones were racing about, dodging beneath and behind blood-spattered furniture while taking pot shots at Hyde-White, who was dodging with surprising agility. He too was using the residence's furnishings as cover while he sought a clear shot at the whizzing drones. The fat druid looked uninjured, and his right hand glowed with some kind of spell held in readiness to cast.

Before Sam could decide on a course of action, Hyde-White spun and faced a drone that had backed itself into a corner. Disdaining to use his prepared spell, the fat druid reached out with a stubby-fingered hand and grabbed. With a casual flip he smashed it into the opposite wall. The drone split open on impact, scattering innards like shrapnel. With a sizzling pop, it tumbled from the drone-shaped dent in the wall and landed sparking on a couch. The fabric began to smoulder.

Sam was startled by the druid's display of strength. Belying their toylike appearance, the drones weighed almost twenty kilograms apiece. They were not easy to toss around, and the druid had thrown one with sufficient strength to crack it open.

Sam's stomach flipflopped. The last time he had seen a man display such strength, the "man" had not been a man at all, but a dragon concealed within a shape-shifting spell. Allowing Willie's drones to carry the fight, he slipped into astral perception.

In his altered perspective, the attacking drones became blurs of murderous intent, their clean-lined mechanical appearance replaced by a fuzzy presence of intent and purpose. As machines the drones were not truly present on the astral planes. But Hyde-White, a living being, remained clear in Sam's eyes. The fat druid glowed with raw power. It was a dazzling aura, but in its tone and strength unlike anything Sam had seen before in a human.

One of the drones must have caught the druid cleanly with a burst for he suddenly staggered backwards. A smaller man might have been dropped by the impact of the bullets, but the massive Hyde-White only reeled. Sam expected to see the man's torso splattered all over his fancy wall hangings, and the live glow of his astral spirit dimmed and dying.

What he did see frightened him badly.

Hyde-White's astral glow remained steady and strong. The image Sam saw looked like a double exposure he had once seen in an old photograph collection. There were two Hyde-Whites occupying the same space, the sharply defined astral image and the increasingly tattered flesh form. Sam saw muscles tear, bones shatter, and blood burst forth from the flesh form to stain the room incarnadine. But the druid did not fall. Torn skin crawled and flayed muscles writhed as though imbued with lives of their own. Splintered bones swayed together to disappear under closing wounds. New flesh spread across gaps where chunks of muscle had been torn away. Once the process began, Hyde-White regenerated the wounds caused by the drone's gunfire as soon as they were made.

Despite the fat druid's appearance, Sam could no longer believe the fat druid was human. Whatever Hyde-White was, he was invulnerable to physical damage. Sam's throat tightened with fear.

41

The explosion on the side of the tower was the cue for which Hart had waited. She settled the butt of the Conner firmly against her shoulder and sighted in. Fifteen pounds of pressure on the trigger ignited the propellant. The grapple gun kicked into her shoulder as it sent its alloy missile two hundred meters across the gap between the towers.

The missile struck cleanly and buried its head in the concrete wall. Moving quickly, she attached the carry line to the tension wire and to the takeup reel. She hit the *go* button and rechecked her gear as the winch reeled in the thin line and dragged the heavier weight-carrying wire through the pulley on the attached grapnel and back to itself. When the load-bearing wire returned, she attached it to the anchored winch. She slipped the wheels of the pulley slide between the now-parallel strands of wire, snapped the cover down tight, and attached the safety wire. Reversing the winch, she tightened the line and tested the grapnel's grip. It stayed firm at four times her weight, so she slacked the tension back.

The gunfire from within the residential level, though nearer, was barely louder than the increasingly sporadic noise from the plaza. There was no time left to waste. She sat on the coping and got a good grip on the handle bar of the pulley slide. She pushed off with her feet and started herself on the slide down to the Hawthornwaite Tower.

Glover felt the tremor in the building. He didn't know what it meant, but he felt sure that it wasn't a result of the ruckus at plaza level. The source of the vibration was somewhere above the level he was on.

"What was that?" Neville asked fearfully.

Glover didn't bother to look at the old fool.

"We must tell Hyde-White."

He may be dead already, Glover thought. He found himself wondering if that would be a bad thing, and after a surprisingly short moment of indecision, decided that it would. The fat old man was still necessary if they were to achieve their goal of restoring the land.

Barnett's office did not offer the full range of surveillance monitors available to the security desk in the main operations center, but the telecom controls allowed an operator to route input through the telecom itself or one of the two wall screens. Glover took advantage of the access afforded to Barnett's station and demanded data on the status of the GWN floors. The computer showed no contact with the security systems on those floors. The condition was flagged with an immediate response request that had gone unanswered, since the building security forces were engaged in the battle on the lower levels.

Clearly, the Circle was under attack. The apparently coincidental actions were obviously planned, designed to separate the members of the Circle. It had been cleverly staged. Glover suspected the enemy's goal was to isolate the members of the Circle and eliminate them individually. It was a clever strategy, but one he would not allow to succeed.

So far, the only direct thrust against a member of the Circle was the assault on Hyde-White's residence. That would be the enemy's major thrust, barring more attacks to come. Whatever the case, the Circle needed to combine their strength as much as possible.

As he reached his decision, the office door slid open to admit a disheveled Gordon. His face was fixed in an angry frown as he swept the room with his gaze. The narrowed eyes lighted on Glover and he strutted up to the archdruid.

"What the devil is going on, Glover? I was enjoying a nice quiet evening preparing myself for the next ritual and then all bloody hell starts breaking loose. First, Barnett stops by my flat and informs me that there is some kind of row going on downstairs. Then, there's a bloody great explosion that shakes the whole building. Is it the shadowrunners again? You must have gotten some of them, since one of their bloody aircraft went tumbling past my window." Gordon stopped suddenly in the midst of his tirade. "Where is he? Is he all right?"

Glover didn't need to ask to know that Gordon wanted to know what, if anything, had happened to Hyde-White. Bel's blistering face! Did no one accord Glover his pride of place as archdruid? Glover stifled the thought. The land came before any questions of dominance, and the needs of the land would not be met if the enemy succeeded. The foremost need was to end the threat to the Circle.

"He is in his residence, Your Highness. Neville and I were just on our way there."

Gordon didn't see the surprised look on Neville's face, and his own words drowned out those of the old druid.

"Then I'm going with you. I must know if he has been hurt. Those shadowrunners almost killed him before. If he's alone, he'll need our help."

Glover shook his head as he stepped past Gordon and grabbed Neville by the shoulder. He hustled the former archdruid toward the door, saying over his shoulder, "There's no need for you to go, Your Highness. Sir Winston and I will deal with any problem that might have arisen."

He might as well have saved his breath. Gordon fell in behind them, and his bodyguards behind him. The parade lasted all the way to the lobby, where Glover stopped in front of the GWN shaft. Gordon's constant babbling about Hyde-White's safety almost made Glover fumble the security code that called a car.

Glover shoved Neville into the car as soon as the doors hissed open. He turned to insist that Gordon remain behind, but before he could speak the man brushed past him and entered the car. Realizing that argument was useless and time was passing, Glover entered the car himself. The two bodyguards crowded in behind him. Glover tapped in the code for Hyde-White's floor. The doors slid shut and the car began to rise.

After only a few seconds, the car lurched to a stop.

"Power's still on," observed one of the guards. "Must be a security check."

"Are you *sure* you entered the right code, archdruid?"

CHOOSE YOUR ENEMIES CAREFULLY 335

Neville's tone was unusually catty for the increasingly timid former archdruid.

"It was correct," Glover replied. He didn't bother to hide his annoyance.

"Well, call security and get this elevator moving again," Gordon ordered. "Hurry! He needs us."

Glover snapped open the panel covering the emergency comm unit with more than the necessary force. The cover rebounded from the wall to rap him sharply. He cursed as the edge jarred his hand with pain.

" 'Tis evocative, but hardly likely," a voice commented from the speaker. The comm screen glowed to life with the image of a white-haired, male elf. "Good evening, archdruid, Your Corrupt Highness. Ah, Sir Winston, I'm very glad you're here as well."

"Who are you?" Gordon asked belligerently.

Sudden suspicion bored in on Glover. "What do you want?"

"Much cooler, archdruid. As to what I want, shall we just say that I hope you're as cool in hell. Going down."

The elevator began to plummet.

The initial lurch of car threw its occupants off balance. As Glover recovered he could see fear etched in the faces of his companions. Even Gordon's bodyguards were afraid—their reinforced bones would not save them from a forty-story plummet.

"No need to bother with the emergency brake," the elf said jauntily. "It's disconnected."

One of the bodyguards slammed the button with his fist anyway. As predicted, there was no response. The guard slammed it again and again, denting the surrounding panel with the force of his blows.

"Do something, Glover! Save us!"

Gordon's voice was shrill with panic. Glover blocked it out and concentrated. Raising his personal protection spell only took the archdruid a moment—a moment in which the elevator car gathered speed in its downward rush. Glover knew that maintaining the protective spell would make other magic difficult, but he was sure he would need the safeguard.

Glover raised his arms above his head and spread them. He focused his energy and blew the roof from the elevator car. Fluorescent panels, structural members, and supporting cable volatilized. The sound of the car's downward passage no longer muffled, a rushing sound filled the car.

Gordon grabbed Glover's shoulder, dragging down one arm. "What in heaven's name are you doing?"

"I'm leaving. The land needs me."

"What about me? The land needs me, too!"

"There are others of royal blood."

Glover struck the grasping hand away and pressed his palms together at chest level, fingers pointing out. He rotated his wrists until his fingers pointed up, and the elevator car dropped away. He remained floating in the shaft.

The decker's frustrated cursing joined the screams of Gordon, the howls of the bodyguards, and the desparing wail of Neville. The din grew fainter as, driven by his will, Glover shot up the now-vacant shaft.

Sam watched as an arcane bolt caught the last of the three drones that had escorted him. Its armor bubbled and darkened. With a burst that sent shards of the device in all directions, the drone exploded, its ammunition cooked off in the magical heat.

A fragment whizzed past his head, scoring his cheek before its tumbling flight buried it several centimeters deep into the wall behind him. He cried out from the sudden pain.

Hyde-White turned to face him. Red-rimmed eyes bored into his own.

"So it is you. You should have heeded the warning, Samuel Verner. You've only brought death upon yourself by coming here."

"Don't be so sure, monster," Sam bluffed.

The druid laughed, a deep booming sound. "Monster? Is that anyway to describe a person who only seeks the well-being of his fellows?"

Hyde-White's reaction puzzled Sam. The savagery of the druid's fight with the drones had been unexpectedly replaced by a calm, and somehow sinister, playfulness. Sam didn't know Hyde-White's game, but every minute the druid talked gave Sam a chance to think of something to do. Unfortunately, every minute also increased the chances that the druid would get reinforcements.

"Your deeds speak loudly enough of your nature. For all that you look like a man, you're not human."

Hyde-White sighed. He looked around for a moment, then sauntered to a chair that remained mostly intact and threw himself down.

"You had me fooled for a moment. I suppose I should have known better. I have been an initiate of my magical tradition for more years than you have walked this wounded earth. It was ridiculous to even entertain the thought that you might have penetrated the mask. I expect I was misled by your potential."

Sam was confused by Hyde-White's ramblings.

"You look so perplexed. It's quite a wonder." The fat man chuckled. "Since your death is inevitable now, the mask doesn't matter anymore. Shall I let you see the truth? You won't like it, and I suppose you might even find it a little frightening, which is all to the good. Fear adds a wonderfully subtle flavor."

Hyde-White stood up again and stretched languidly.

The stretch seemed to go on beyond the bounds of his flesh. He grew taller and slimmer. His arms lengthened, as did his legs, and the clothes covering his body changed to become a white pelt. Wrinkled, liver-spotted hands widened and darkened as fingers elongated into taloned digits. His facial features melted and re-formed into a bestial visage.

The thing that had hidden in the shape of Hyde-White looked down at Sam and smiled a carnivore's smile. Like a stage magician signalling a completed trick, he gave a twisting flick of his hand and said, "You see, I haven't been human for decades."

Sam stumbled back from the divider behind which he had crouched, and bumped into a wall. He straightened up, letting the wall take some of his weight. Otherwise, he feared his knees would buckle.

The stench of decay and corruption emanating from the furred apparition was almost overpowering. Sam had expected the smell after his invasion of the sanctum, but he hadn't expected to see what he was seeing. Like the odor, the being's silhouette was familiar from his troubled dreams and frustrated attempts to enhance his magical power. He had seen a similar creature when they had raided the Circle's murder ritual. Both Willie and Dodger were right and wrong. Hyde-White was a wendigo, but he was very much alive.

"*You* were the Man of Light."

It was the wendigo's turn to look confused. "The what?"

"The one who blocked my path to the totem realms."

"Ah. You use the past tense, implying that you have breached the barriers I set in your mind. This is unfortunate. When I touched your astral form on the Solstice, and learned who you were, I sought to save you from yourself. You have been very persistent, as I should have expected from one with so strong a will. Perhaps I was not so foolish to worry about your ability to pierce the mask.''

Sam shuddered as the wendigo spoke. All lingering thoughts that the Man of Light was something he had dredged from his own subconscious vanished. His mind had been violated, his memories subverted by the wendigo. He felt sick and revulsed. He felt hatred.

''You bastard! I'm not a toy for you to play with. I'm a man, you godless, soulless beast! You fragged with my mind just to frighten me away from the power I needed to stop you.''

''Stop me? A pup like you?'' The wendigo laughed. ''That's rich. But then, she said you had a strange sense of humor.''

The muscles in Sam's face went slack. He felt chill all over as he remembered his not entirely strategic reason for selecting Hyde-White as the first target.

''Janice,'' he whispered.

''Of course, Janice. You knew she was here, didn't you?'' The wendigo paused to study Sam's expression. ''I see you did. So it was she who motivated you to come after me. So much for noble motives. It does always seem to be kinbonds that motivate the hunters. I, of all people, should not have forgotten the power of that draw.''

Indignation fueled Sam's anger. ''How dare you call yourself a person? You're a murderer, an eater of human flesh, and a corrupter of minds. You have forfeited any claim of humanity. God as my witness, you have forfeited your right to life.''

''What right have you to judge me?'' The wendigo pointed an accusing finger at Sam. ''You are of the blood of man, a scion of the long line of corrupters of the earth itself. The human race has fouled its nest since its infancy. Humanity is the true despoiler, and

I am relieved that I am no longer a part of that desecration. Were you able to understand your place in nature as I do mine, you would see the truth.

"By blood, I am born of the earth and I act as my blood directs. By temperament, I have responded to the atrocities your precious humanity has visited upon its collective mother, and have learned to call the corrupted spirits of the earth. I will see the vermin of humanity scoured from the face of the planet they have defiled. I will turn the corruption back upon the real evildoers. All you need to do is look around yourself to see that I speak the truth. If you were truly moral, you would join my crusade."

Sam felt the tug of the wendigo's words. He, too, hated what man had done to the environment. He felt his despair and frustration curdle into rage over the thought of the betrayed trust. Then, he remembered the filthy feel of the wendigo's previous presence in his mind and shouted. "Liar! You twist the truth to suit yourself, and I won't fall for it. *You're* the corruptor, the seducer, the defiler, and the despoiler. You're evil by nature, and I will destroy you."

The wendigo let out a low growl through clenched teeth. Then his lips closed down over his fangs, and he smiled.

"If I am evil, what of your sister?"

"I won't let you hurt her."

"Hurt her?" The wendigo laughed. "I have no reason to hurt one of my own. You are her past and I am her future. She no longer belongs to your world, but to mine. Forget her."

That was something Sam would never do. He felt guilty enough over how little he had accomplished in finding her. "Where is she?"

"She is safe from your misguided attentions. When Glover told me of the disturbance at ATT-Multifax, I thought it best to take precautions."

"What have you done with her?"

"Brought her into the fold."

"No!"

"Oh, yes."

"No!" Sam screamed again. He threw himself away from the wall and summoned his magic. Howling the words of Dog's song, he poured his will into the effort of summoning a spirit. As soon as he felt a presence, he demanded service of it.

A luminous mist rose from the floor. Streamers of mist floated from the walls to join the cloud beginning to swirl in the space between Sam and the wendigo. The mist thickened, becoming almost liquid in density, and poured upwards to form a shape as if filling a mold. The last of the vapor joined the hulking shape, and the whole thing became more solid, taking on the texture of poured concrete.

The floor groaned under the weight of the manifested building spirit. Between its wide, humped shoulders there was a knob that might have been a head. Two pits of darkness opened in the knob, and Sam felt the spirit's attention settle on him.

The spirit's stare unnerved him even more than the realization that he had succeeded in summoning it. The spirit's intensity, underlaid by hostility, scraped stainless steel fingernails on the chalkboard that was the inside of his skull. The spirit was insistent; it wanted his orders, for only by discharging its duties could it leave the physical plane.

"Destroy the wendigo," he told it. "End the blight on the city."

The spirit turned away abruptly. Spreading its arms, it advanced on the wendigo. Each step sent tremors through the floor.

Sam had expected that his enemy might show some fear at this sudden manifestation of power. He was disappointed. The wendigo began to vocalize. The sound started as a deep rumble in the massive chest and occasionally burst forth in a feral growl. The stench of putrefaction increased as the wendigo also spread his arms wide.

The spirit lumbered forward and raised one blocky, fistless arm to smash its victim. The wendigo stood his ground. His only action was to convulse his outstretched fingers closed into fists.

The spirit froze as pain flared in Sam's head. The mystic bonds by which he directed the spirit tattered and tore. He tried to re-form them, but they slipped through his grasp.

Across the room, the spirit turned. The smooth, seamless lines of its form had become more jagged, and its facade was pitted and marred. Like lurid tattoos, graffiti and slogans of violence defaced its surface. It took a step toward Sam. Portions of its outer covering flaked away as it moved. It stalked toward him, leaving footprints of garbage and sludgy residue.

The wendigo gloated. "A poor choice, puppy shaman. Cities are one of the great blights that man spreads across the earth. Know now, if you had not already discerned it for yourself, that Blight is my totem. I have embraced the toxic defilement of the earth to turn it back on the source of the pollution. This cold, concrete tower has no true hearth. By its nature, the spirit you have summoned is more my servant than yours. All you have done is given me the tool for your destruction."

42

Janice was worried as soon as she heard the explosion. Her failure to get through on the telecom only intensified her concern. Suddenly Dan's uncharacteristic request, that she carry a message to a business partner who lived on a lower floor of the tower, made sense. It had just been an excuse to get her out of the residence.

She detached her spirit and sent it upwards through the building. Dan was there and well, but he was being menaced by a hostile spirit. The shaman who had summoned it was there as well, fully capable of more mischief. Since she hadn't yet learned the secrets of casting magic through her astral body, she fled downwards and returned to her physical body.

Hoping to reach the residence in time to help her lover, she ran to the elevator lobby. In her excitement, she fumbled her first try to enter Dan's code. She got it right on the second try, but there was no response, not even a call acknowledgment.

The shaft was the only one with direct access to the residence floor. Frustrated, she slammed her fist into the door. The metal buckled. She hit the door again and a gap appeared between the two panels. She dug her fingers into the space and pulled until she forced the seal. As the pressure lock released, her strength proved too much for the structures. The left panel buckled and jammed, while the right folded and slipped out of its track. She flung the useless thing behind her.

The shaft smelled of magic, making her fur rise.

She stuck her head out over the abyss and looked down. The bottom of the shaft was obscured in a dust cloud. That puzzled her until she realized that there were no cables in the shaft. Someone had sabotaged the elevator, and there would be no car arriving to carry her to the residence.

She leaned into the opening she had forced, keeping her balance with one hand gripping the frame of the opening. With her free hand, she grabbed the rungs of the emergency service ladder and tugged. To her relief, it seemed solid enough to support her weight. Careless of the jagged metal edges protruding in her way, she swung into the shaft. The gashes she sustained began to heal as she started to climb.

The elevator doors on Hyde-White's residence level buckled and blew inward with explosive force. There was no roar of explosives, only the metallic scream of tortured metal and the shattering pop of plastics. Hart knew magic when she encountered its effect.

Toylike, a four-wheeled silver thing rolled out from under one of the lobby's low tables and took up station in front of the opening. As the machine pulled into place, its turret swiveled to point a gun barrel into the shaft.

For a moment, nothing happened. Then, the drone began firing its weapon in shrill hiccups of short-duration autofire bursts. Hart heard bullets spanging off metal and concrete, but there was another sound as well, a high pitched *whang* which a norm would be unable to hear. The source of the sound appeared, as Glover drifted out of the shaft. Flares of light accompanied the strange sounds as bullets struck an invisible shield that protected the archdruid.

The drone briefly ceased fire as Glover drifted over it and touched down on the thick carpet. The drone revved its motor and began to circle him, firing bursts at different portions of his anatomy in a random timing sequence. Glover watched contemptuously as the drone sought a weakness in his defense. On the third circle, Glover lashed out with his foot, deflecting the drone's course. Before its onboard expert system could compensate, the little machine hit a piece of debris from the doors and bounced into the air. It came down on its right front fender and toppled forward. Its momentum was so great that it rolled right through the open doorway of the elevator shaft.

"Pathetic gadfly," Glover sneered as the machine vanished from sight.

Hart dropped her invisibility spell and pointed her pistol at Glover.

"Shouldn't have dropped the levitation spell, archdruid. You don't have an invitation to this party."

Glover started at her words, but recovered quickly. "I have no further need for it and I don't need any invitations, elf. You are no impediment to me. I presume you were watching and saw how ineffectual guns are against a magician of my skills and power."

"I saw."

"You don't seem properly impressed."

"Oh, I was impressed. That bullet shield is a real powerful trick, but I've got a few of my own."

She dropped her aim to the floor by his feet and pulled the trigger three times in rapid succession. The first explosive bullet shredded the carpet and pitted the floor. Its concussive force tossed the archdruid from his feet. The second bullet chewed through the flooring and into the subflooring, and the third punched through the ceiling of the floor below. The destruction was so rapid that the stages were indistinguishable to the eye. When gravity reclaimed Glover, it pulled him through the new hole. As he passed through the opening, Hart saw the shock and surprise on his face, but he looked physically unhurt. She was surprised at the effectiveness of his protection spell.

Hart approached the gap cautiously, carefully testing the footing before trusting her weight to the weakened floor. Looking over the edge, she saw Glover lying on top of a pile of debris. His clothes were dusted over by late-falling chunks and settling dust. She had hoped the fall would kill the archdruid; it hadn't. He was dazed though and had dropped whatever spells he was maintaining. As a mage herself, she knew the strict concentration necessary to maintain powerful spells.

"Are you awake, Archdruid Glover?"

He groaned. Conscious, but not composed enough for magic.

"I actually came loaded for bigger game, but a good hunter never passes up an opportunity."

She fired three more times. Without the protection of his spell, he was just meat. Then, he was no more.

Sam crashed into things as he ran. He needed time to gather his wits. Walls and furniture that were impediments and bludgeoning obstacles to him did nothing to slow the corrupted building spirit; it just walked through them as if the object wasn't there. The only things it detoured around were plants and the thieves' cache of art objects scattered around the residence. Fortunately, the spirit was moving more slowly than he, as its summoner, knew it could. Under control of the wendigo, the spirit seemed inclined to play with its prey.

Gunfire from one of the drones reminded Sam of

Willie. The plan had called for her to concentrate on dealing with physical threats while he handled the magic. Her drone's lack of success against the wendigo in his Hyde-White guise had put the monster in Sam's purview. Sam hoped she was doing better against the security guards who were probably storming up the stairwells by now.

Collision with a musty tapestry told him where he was in the maze of the residence. The wendigo's sanctum was hidden behind the hanging. Its magical barrier would probably stop the spirit, but the small room would be a trap where the wendigo could deal with him at leisure.

But, he realized, what would halt the spirit would blind it as well. In a desperate burst of speed, he cut around to the side of the sanctum, placing its barrier between him and the spirit. A groan like overstressed steel told him that the spirit had lost sight of him. If it hadn't been limited by the manifestation, he would never have been able to pull off this little trick. Sam ran down the first hallway and cut right, trying to keep the sanctum between him and where he thought the spirit was. The longer he could keep it up, the further away he could get. Breathing heavily and lungs burning, he stumbled into one of the few enclosed chambers of the residence floor.

For now, he could run no more. He leaned his back against a wall and let himself slide down to the floor. Opening the seal on his leather jacket, he reached inside and closed his hand on the tooth. *Peace,* he told himself. *Peace to find the center.* His breathing slowed and his fear-fogged thoughts began to focus.

He envisioned the building spirit clumping toward him. He visualized the strings of power that bound it to the building. Tracing their flow from the essence of the structure, he followed the threads to the spirit's manifestation. Because he had summoned the spirit, he knew how those mana threads were twined and knotted as they stretched to twist through the boundary of astral space. Without such a connection, the spirit would not have been able to manifest on the mundane plane. Sam felt along the strands of power, seeking to untangle them.

Sooner than he expected, a groping, handless arm thrust through the partition. A second limb followed, then the rest of the spirit emerged through the wall. It was only a meter away. Sam could smell the mold and rotting garbage odor of it as it cocked one arm back to smash him.

He tugged on the astral strings.

The manifestation jerked. Sam tugged again, harder. The spirit staggered back a step and lost a bit of its substantiality. Digging mental fingers into the strands of power, Sam pried and pulled. As he unraveled the binding of the spirit's form, its physcal shape lost coherence, returning first to the liquid mist and then to nothingness. He had banished his summoning.

It was a short-lived victory.

The wendigo trotted through the door to the chamber. He betrayed no surprise. Having been in control of the spirit, he would have felt its dissolution.

"An excellent banishment, if unexpected. You rebuke my nonchalance, and rightly so. She is coming and it will be better for all of us if you are dead by then." The wendigo bared his fangs and advanced, taloned fingers extended. "It is time for the end."

Sam knew he was no physical match for the three-meter monster, but he scrambled to his feet, anyway. He crouched, presenting a smaller target. He hoped. The wendigo was stronger and faster than he was. Staring death in the face and having no better idea, he dove forward, surprising the wendigo and slipping beneath the outstetched paws. But Sam was not fast enough to escape unscathed. The wendigo whirled and raked Sam across the back, slicing fringe into a scattering of leather scraps and cutting through to shred the jacket and its lining. Four rows of fire burned into Sam's upper torso. The impact knocked him to the floor and beneath of the sweep of the wendigo's second swipe.

Sam rolled away, trying to gain enough room to get to his feet again. Pain seared through him as he flexed his muscles to keep moving. Each time his back hit the floor, the agony spiked.

An immense vise closed on his right ankle and he knew his maneuver had failed. The wendigo lifted him by his ankle and he dangled in the monster's grip. The Ares Predator slipped from its holster, whacking Sam's elbow as it fell. His arm went numb.

"I thought you were Dog, not Rabbit," the wendigo scoffed.

Inexplicably, the wendigo howled in pain and flung Sam away.

Sam was parallel to the floor when he hit the wall. Pain exploded in his chest and he blacked out for a second. He came to on the floor. His ears were ringing and he felt like he was going to vomit. His left leg was twisted underneath him. He felt no pain from it, but by the angle, he knew it had to be broken. It hurt to breathe, causing sharp stabbing pains in his chest. *Ribs broken too,* he thought. No more running now.

The wendigo was clawing at the back of his left shoulder as if madly trying to scratch an itch. He roared in rage and pain. Sam heard a metallic click, and the wendigo straightened up, one arm wrapped across his chest to hold the opposite shoulder.

"Over here, furface."

With the ringing in his ears, Sam thought he did well to recognize the voice as female.

The wendigo turned to face the newcomer's voice. Sam could see blood leaking from beneath the black-skinned hand. Even through the scratches that the wendigo's own talons had made were closing as Sam watched, the monster still bled from the weapon wound.

"You too. I should have known."

"Payback time, furface."

The wendigo dodged to one side and a whirring metal disk rushed through the space he had occupied. The weapon buried itself in the wall over Sam's head. He looked up. It was a spoked wheel with a series of wickedly sharp curved blades along its perimeter. It was a signature design, a shuriken in the shape of a Katherine's wheel.

"Hart," Sam croaked.

He could just catch glimpses of her beyond the bulk of the wendigo. She was a wraith in black leather, night to the day of the wendigo's white fur. Her right hand was cocked back, another of the shurikens ready to throw. In her left she carried a heavy pistol. Having watched the fruitless attacks of Willie's drones, Sam knew the gun would do little harm to the wendigo. The wendigo himself seemed contemptuous of it as well; his attention focused on the hand that held the throwing weapon. It must be the metal. Some awakened beings had allergic reactions to certain metals.

For long moments the two opponents feinted. Each seemed unwilling to commit to a move that might open an attack line for the other. Hart's hand blurred forward suddenly, unleashing a glittering star toward the wendigo. He shifted to his right fast enough that the shuriken whizzed past. He had anticipated her throw, but had not foreseen the diving roll to her right that she made as soon as the throwing weapon left her hand. He checked his charge and started to turn to her new location. Hart fired from the floor and the wendigo's right hand vanished in an explosion of blood and shattered bone fragments.

The wendigo's howl nearly deafened Sam. The sound, which should have been full of pain, carried nothing but outrage. He thought he heard the scream re-echo through the residence as the monster recovered from his surprise and charged Hart.

Trying to stand, Hart missed with her next two shots. The bullets blew craters in the wall. As Sam had done, she tried to duck under the sweep of the wendigo's arms. Also like Sam, she wasn't fast enough. One arm caught her in the hip and sent her spinning into a bookshelf. Covered in blood, she collapsed in a pile of books, artifacts, and simsense cartridges.

In two steps the wendigo reached her, but instead of going for her, he grabbed the top of the bookcase with his remaining hand and tugged. The heavy wooden shelves creaked as they leaned out from the walls, the anchor bolts squealing as they pulled free from their moorings. The shelves crashed down just as Hart scrambled out of their way on her hands and knees.

"Do something, dogboy!" she shouted at Sam. "Throw a spell! Call a spirit! *Do something!*"

What could he do? He had called a spirit already and the wendigo had corrupted it and turned it back against him with contemptuous ease. What could he do against such powerful magic? He was just a Dog shaman.

He was—

He was in a forest glade in the middle of a city, sitting on the grass. A mongrel sat by his side.

"Dog!" Sam exclaimed.

"Man," Dog said, mimicking Sam's intonation. "I was wondering when you'd get to me."

"I thought you were always with me?"

"I am. You're just not always with *me*."

"I don't know what to do, Dog. Tell me," Sam pleaded.

"Tell you? You're the one out in the world, man. You've got to make your own decisions. You wanna be a pup all your life, that's okay. *I* can live with it, but *you* can't, 'cause it ain't gonna be a long life if you don't wake up and smell the world like it is."

"The world smells like death."

"That's the wendigo talking. I thought you were a man."

"I am."

"So show me," Dog yelped. "The men I know don't give up so easily. Fight it, man."

"I don't know how," Sam complained.

"If you don't despair, you do."

Somewhere else, the wendigo advanced on Hart. She drew a dagger from her belt. The orichalcum symbols inlaid in the blade's side glowed slightly, the power of that most magic of metals would enable the blade's kiss to wound the wendigo. But it was only a dagger; he had talons and fangs, and was more than twice her mass.

"He'll kill her," Sam said to Dog.

"Yup," Dog agreed jauntily. "Then you. Then lots more people. You gonna stop him?"

"What can I do?"

"Where's your faith? Us dog types believe in you men types."

Somewhere else, the wendigo smashed the dagger out of Hart's hand. The disarming move cost him a deep gash in his forearm, but he seemed content with the trade. His return strike was an open slap that caught Hart on her right temple. She tried to roll with the blow but the force was too much. She went down.

"She's got no hope, Dog."

"She's got you. Show some spirit, man."

Sam felt utterly stupid. Dog had been telling him what he had to do all along, and he was just being dense. The wendigo had turned the building's spirit because it was primarily the spirit of the place; and places, no matter how pure they had been, could be corrupted. Places were just things made to be used. But people were more than things. Certainly they were physical bodies, but they were more as well, hearts and souls. Hearts could be corrupted too, but the soul's purest essence was not so easily swayed. Confused, tricked, and misled for a while, perhaps; but not forever, as long as there was hope and faith and belief in the ultimate goodness of life.

The wendigo had embraced death and despair, but even his creed was tainted with hope. Though the wendigo called Blight his totem and walked a toxic path, he still saw a hopeful end. He used his corrupt tools in his warped fight to rid the earth of what he considered a plague. His was a terrible path, but ultimately a misguided one. For the shaman, Sam suddenly felt pity. For the wendigo nature of the being he felt no such pity. The being it had been deserved the pity, but that being had long since died inside the great furred body.

Sam opened himself to the spirit world. Brighton Centrum was full of people, full of life. He avoided the dark corners and sought the light. In a rundown squat of a shack cobbled together in the mall space of a section scheduled for reconstruction, he found what he wanted. Nurtured by the love and hope of a family who had taken all the drek that life had thrown at them and stayed a family, a spirit dwelled here. It was a little grungy around the edges, but it had never known despair.

Sam sang the song Dog had taught him, wooing the spirit. At first it seemed deaf to his pleas, but at last it heard the song and stirred. Sam coaxed it from its place with flattery and fed it his strength. The spirit drifted through the distanceless space and joined him. Sam rejoiced. He spoke to it of the urgency of his need. Its aura pulsed, flaring in indignation and rage as he told it of the wendigo. The spirit allowed him to sculpt its raw purity into a concentrated crystal of diamond clarity and adamantine strength.

All the while, Dog sang counterpoint.

As Sam returned his consciousness to the mundane world, the wendigo pinned Hart beneath his foot. He leaned forward, putting his weight onto her chest. Sam heard her ribs crack. He feared for her life, but he was not distracted from the song. If he gave in to the fear, all hope would truly be lost.

The spirit forged of man's nature manifested as a small child. It was dirty and wore ragged castoff clothing. It held a pipe in its right hand which it smacked grimly into the palm of its left.

"Yo, furball!" it called.

The wendigo turned his head at the new interruption. His eyes narrowed and nostrils distended as he drank in the power of the spirit.

"You gotta go, furball," the spirit said.

The wendigo moved faster than Sam had ever seen him do before. The foot that had been crushing the life out of Hart swept around toward the manifestion. The spirit blocked with one hand on either end of the pipe, stopping the blow dead. The spirit then slid its upper hand down to the lower, raised the pipe above its head, and slammed it into the wendigo's still-raised leg. The room shook as the wendigo crashed to the floor. The splintered ends of bones protruded from his leg.

The spirit's assault didn't slow. Its pipe blurred up and down, pummeling the wendigo. The spirit's strength was magical, unconstrained by its physical appearance. The wendigo was no match for its fury. Soon, he lay helpless.

The spirit drove the end of the pipe through the wendigo's left shoulder and into the floor. With two swift hammer blows of its tiny fist, it bent the pipe over, forming a staple that pinned the wendigo to the floor. The fight seemed to go out of the wendigo and he lay limp on the floor. He watched fearfully as the spirit knelt on his chest and placed a hand on either side of his broad head. Their eyes locked, and the wendigo screamed.

The air seemed charged with electricity, but Sam knew it was magic. He slipped into his astral senses and saw the storm of mana that raged between the spirit and the wendigo. Glowing like a sun, the spirit poured golden light from its eyes into the wendigo's dark orbs. At first, all that glorious light fought against streamers of darkness that emanated from the wendigo's eyes and wrapped around the twin columns of light as if to smother them. Seconds later—or was it hours?—the dark wrappings started to fade until they finally turned translucent and drifted away like smoke. The body of the wendigo began to glow from inside as the golden light poured into him from the spirit. The spirit grew dimmer as the wendigo grew brighter and brighter, until Sam could no longer bear the intensity. Just before he dropped back to his mundane senses, he thought he saw a shape within the wendigo's form. But the glare made it too hard to be sure.

On the mundane plane, the wendigo's body looked shrunken, a bag of skin over a frame of bone. The spirit stood by the side of the body and pulled the pipe free.

"The darkness is gone," it said in a voice only Sam could hear.

"You have done all that I could ask, spirit. I can think of no better way to thank you than by giving you your freedom."

"You would do this for me? I still owe you services."

"We fought a common foe. You owe me nothing, and I ask nothing more of you. You are free."

"Honor to you, man," the spirit said as it faded from sight.

Sam could have followed its departure astrally. He wanted to. He desperately wanted to know where the spirit would go. But somehow that didn't seem right.

He crawled past the husk of the wendigo toward Hart. Her breathing was ragged and shallow, and he hurried even though he knew that he was aggravating his own injuries. Pain seemed a small price to pay to be by her side. He touched her face with his hands and found that she was crying. She stirred at his touch and opened her eyes. It took her a few seconds to recognize him. Once she did, she tried to raise her arm.

"Wrist," she gasped.

Trying not to hurt her, Sam unsnapped the cuff and rolled back her sleeve. Sam recognized the name and logo of DocWagon on the circuit board embedded within the clear plastic band she wore. The base color of the board was platinum.

"Don't leave home without it." She tried to smile at him, but the effort to talk had exhausted her waning strength.

He pressed the stud that would summon the medical service.

His own injuries sapped his strength, but he knew that unless he did something foolish, he would probably live. He was not so sure about her. After all she

had done to keep him from stopping the wendigo, she
had risked her life to save him and give him the time
to call the spirit.

"Why?" he asked.

"I wish I knew."

She passed out.

43

By the time Janice reached the residence floor, everything was quiet. That made her nervous. She had
heard his last scream. It had been so full of pain that
she feared for his safety. How could anything have
happened to him? He was stronger than any norm shaman.

She skirted the hole on the entryway floor. Unlike
in the elevator shaft, there was no strong residue of
magic. The destruction here was purely physical.

The doors of the formal entrance were open.
Through them wafted the faint odor of blood. Tense
and alert, she padded through the archway.

There were a lot of scents in the air, but all were
faint; the floor's climate control system was busy
pumping warm air out the shattered northern window
wall and diluting the concentrations below the level
she could track. Still, she identified the scent of
strangers lingering in the air. One, a male, was vaguely
familiar, but the other, a female, was new to her. There
was also the ozone tang of machines like the one that
had almost struck her in the elevator shaft. That odor
was strong enough to indicate that there might be several of the things; they didn't have enough individu-

ality for her to tell if there had been only the one or if more might be lurking about. The machine had been small enough to hide effectively.

The one scent she most wanted to smell was the most elusive.

A high-pitched, sequenced beeping reached her. It was beyond the range of a norm hearing, or even an elf's. It was clearly a signal. She knew of nothing in the residence that would emit such a noise; the device must belong to the intruders. She listened carefully, then shifted position and listened again. The sound seemed to be originating somewhere east of the sanctum. She moved cautiously toward the source.

As she drew nearer, her apprehension grew. With the air flow moving toward her the odors, all of them, grew stronger. Dan's was among them. But her momentary flare of relief was snuffed by the realization that the intruder's signal continued. Dan would not have let it continue if he were able to stop it. Worse, she sensed a lingering tingle of magic.

She stopped before one of the studies where blood spattered the floors and walls. Beyond the hallway in one of the large living areas, she could see a crater in the wall. From somewhere out of sight around a partition, she could hear a male voice whispering assurances. It was not Dan's voice. She crept forward.

She reached the corner, and her wary peering rewarded her with a sight that tore her heart. Dan's body lay sprawled on the floor. His limp form was emaciated, his bones pressing against his once-glossy pelt. The white fur was fouled and matted with blood. A great, gaping wound covered his left shoulder, and his right hand, the hand that had stroked her so tenderly, was missing. It had been jaggedly severed and was nowhere in sight.

Her caution and fear were swept away. She rushed

from concealment and threw herself on him. He was so still. She didn't want to believe he was dead, but her eyes could only see the blood and the wounds. Her ears could not hear him breathe, and her touch found only chill. He was far colder than he should be. Tears streamed from her eyes, blurring her sight. Her ears filled with the sounds of great sobs which she knew were her own. She felt him cold under her hands and wanted to deny what she felt. It was not possible, he couldn't be dead.

"Fragging drek, Twist. It's got a mate."

The words broke through her grief. Those words were meant for the norm shaman and whispered from his earpiece receiver, but she heard them. She raised her tear-blurred eyes and looked at the intruders for the first time.

The woman lay against a wall, unconscious and nearly dead. The man was the shaman she had seen raising the spirit against Dan. He was battered and covered with blood. Though his face was screwed into a rictus of pain, he was struggling to prop up his torso. In one hand he held a dagger of red-gold metal, but he seemed otherwise unarmed. *Save for his magic,* she reminded herself. One of the machines sat near his head; the gun barrel of the tiny turret pointed directly at her.

These were the ones who had taken Dan from her.

She sat back on her heels, noting as she did that the machine's gun tracked her motion. Ignoring them she passed a gentle hand along Dan's face. *They had closed his eyes.* Her fingers lingered on his lips. *They had stolen his smile.* She let her hand trail down to his chest. *They had stilled his heart.*

She focused her intent, wrapping herself in the illusion that she was as she had been, grieving over Dan's body. Beneath the image, she crouched in readiness.

They would die.

She leapt.

Her illusion vanished as she moved. The killers finally reacted, but, they were too late. The gun turret could not swivel fast enough to track her. The shaman was too weak to come close to matching her speed. She was already in the air and soon she would rend them.

She slammed into an invisible wall, and her lethal pounce was converted into an ignominious tumble to the floor. She felt her mind teeter on the brink of madness—the magical barrier tasted of Dan.

As she turned to his body, she found his head turned slightly in her direction. His eyelids seemed to be open, but she could not see the glitter of his eyes.

She returned to him and kissed his lips. Her joy faltered. He was cold, and his chest remained still. And yet, with no air in his lungs to force the sounds out of his throat, he spoke.

"I could not let you do it."

She probed with all her senses and only confused herself. He was there but not there. She wanted him alive. Her tears fell upon his face but not a muscle twitched. She didn't know what to do.

"No kindeath. The blood is too strong. It taints. It's so heavy. It taints. For you, my darling, I fear it would be fatal."

She combed his mane with her talons. "Be quiet, my love. I shall sing the healing songs for you."

"No songs. The meat is finished, and the feaster is no more. From the brink of the dark I heard you weep for me, and your tears, your love, let me save you this once."

"Save me? I would have killed them for you."

"No," his sepulcral voice insisted. "Promise me. Forswear the kindeath."

"What are you saying, my love? What is this kin-death?"

"Promise."

His voice had become fainter and echoed hollowly, but she recognized his force of will in the demand.

"Anything. I promise. No kindeath. Whatever you want. Just come back to me," she pleaded.

"The Dog shaman. He is your brother."

With that dire pronouncement, Janice felt him leave and knew that all Dan Shiroi had been was gone. Forever. She poured her anguish into her scream.

Sam could not believe what he was hearing. The voice from the dead wendigo was something he feared would haunt his nightmares. But as terrifying as that was, the words the voice spoke were worse. Was this great furry thing, this female wendigo, his sister Janice? God could not be so cruel.

He shifted to astral perception and studied the being's aura. He knew now how to recognize a wendigo aura, and he had no doubt that he was seeing one. But he had not been magically active the last time he had seen his sister. Nor had she gone through the change. How would he know if this was she? He could not be sure. Like a half-remembered dream, something in the being's aura nagged with familiarity.

"Janice?"

The red-rimmed eyes that turned to him were bleak. The face in which they were set was totally unfamiliar. He could not find a hint of his sister's fair features. He had already heard this wendigo's voice and found nothing to recognize in it.

"Sam?"

His throat constricted when he heard her pronounce

his name, "Sa-am." His doubts fled. "Lord in Heaven, it is you."

There was so much to say, but Sam couldn't find the words. Ever since he had heard of her goblinization, he had feared for her. His attempts to contact her through Renraku had been inexplicably stifled. But he had never forgotten her, never stopped trying to figure out a way to contact her. She stood before him now and the moment was nothing like any he had imagined. He had been afraid *kawaru* had left her an ork, or worse, a troll—but this! Ever since he had learned what wendigo were, he had hated them.

Janice only stared at him, her dark eyes an enigma.

Finally he stammered, "I want to help."

"Where were you when I needed you before?" she asked accusingly.

"I tried to—"

"If you had really fragging tried, you would have done something. Dan was there when I needed him. You abandon me, then you come back into my life, and you take him away from me. You want to help me? Bring him back."

"But he was a wendigo."

"And what do you think *I* am?" she shouted, slamming a great paw against her chest.

"There has to be a way to help you."

Her laughter was bitter. "And I grew up thinking *I* was the romantic and *you* were the practical one. There's no redemption for me. Don't you see I'm already damned?"

44

"I can't believe that you just let her leave."

Estios stormed back and forth across the short space afforded him. The apartment was one of Hart's safehouses. The back room had been roomy for Willie and her rigger board, but with all the runners gathered, space was at a premium. Most of the fine furniture had been pushed back against the walls to make room for the Mitsuhama Medical Technologies Home Convalesence Bed in which Hart lay. The runners, both the unscathed and the wounded, and their gear looked absurdly out of place among the wainscoting, natural fiber rugs, and timber-beamed ceiling.

As soon as Estios passed him, Dodger stuck a foot into the open space. Estios's attention was focused on Sam; he remained unaware of the obstruction as he retraced his path. Teresa elbowed Dodger in the ribs and he retracted his foot just before Estios would have stumbled over it.

Monitoring the readouts on the MMT bed, Sam was only half-aware of Estios's ravings. Sam was no expert, but he thought the readings indicated that Hart should be conscious. Though her eyes remained closed and she didn't respond when he whispered her name, he felt sure she was awake, refusing to acknowledge anything around her.

He was afraid that he was what she was avoiding. But it might have been that she didn't want to deal with the loud-mouthed Estios, or maybe she just wanted to rest. Either made sense. They had all been through a lot and no one wanted to hear Estios rant.

Sam looked around the room. Dodger and Teresa were holding a private conversation where they sat on the long couch. They were intense and Dodger looked unhappy. Willie sat hunched over her rigger board and was ostentatiously busy with the controls. Father Rinaldi, when they had been exchanging tales in the Shidhe holding cell, had told Sam that he disliked any kind of computer-human interface, but he was helping Willie watch the viewscreen. From what little Sam could see of the pictures relayed from her spotter drones, nothing much was happening. Obviously, Janice was still inside the rundown tenement where she had gone to ground.

Sam suddenly realized Estios had stopped talking and was looking at him. The elf must have asked a question. With no memory of having heard the question, Sam had no hope of answering it.

"Look," he said with a sigh. "It's over. The Circle's broken."

"Weren't you listening? It's not over as long as Ashton and Wallace are still out there."

"If you're so worried about them, go do something about it. I think they were just minor players. With the others all dead, especially the wendigo who built the Circle and fed them the power they thought their sacrifices gained them, they won't be a problem. An anonymous message to the Lord Protector's Oversight Board will get them their come-uppance."

"They might still escape and recruit new members. Even if they do not, the monster's mate is still out there."

Sam buried his face in his hands and tried to massage away the anger he felt toward the obtuse Estios.

"Forget her. She wasn't part of the Circle."

"I can't forget her. She's a wendigo. That's enough reason for her to die."

Sam got to his feet. His ribs ached within the restraint of his torso bandage. He was wobbly, but the walking cast on his leg made a limping shuffle possible. He hobbled across to Estios and looked up into the elf's face.

"You're not going to kill her."

Estios curled his lip; he put his hand on Sam's chest and shoved him backward. Sam landed in a chair with an agonizing shock that sent a wave of blackness and wheeling lights across his vision. He was glad he had fallen in the cushioned chair; hitting the floor or a wall might have caused him to pass out. He didn't think Estios would have cared.

"You're too emotionally involved, Verner. I will assume that the painkillers have fogged your reasoning, and overlook your criminal shortsightedness. She stopped being your sister the day she grew fur." Estios surveyed the room. "We've wasted enough time. Put the drones on standby and transfer control to your van, rigger. Priest, you'll stay here with the wounded. Everybody else, grab your gear. We're going hunting."

Willie looked to Sam. She had never liked Estios and hated taking his orders. She seemed torn between her loyalty to Sam and the weight of the elf's arguments. Her eyes asked for a release from the burden of decision.

Seeing that no one else was going to stand up to Estios, Sam gritted his teeth. There was a table next to the chair, and he grabbed it, hoping to take some of the pressure off his ribs as he attempted to stand. Pain rocked him as he tried, and he collapsed back into the chair.

Dodger was across the room and crouched at Sam's side in an instant. The elf used one hand to steady Sam in the chair while his deft fingers adjusted controls on Sam's torso wrap. There was a brief hiss as more gas pumped into the bandage's tubes to increase its rigidity.

"He's going too far, Teresa," Dodger said. "This is a dangerous plan."

"If you're scared, alley runner, you can stay behind. We'll be playing in the real world where people get really hurt. You wouldn't like it. Why don't you go hide in your electron fantasies?" Estios took a step toward the couch and held out his hand to Teresa.

Dodger stepped forward. "Don't go with him, Teresa."

Teresa stared past Sam, obviously meeting Dodger's gaze. Sam could see wavering emotions on her face. Dodger was out of Sam's line of sight, but he felt Dodger's tension through the elf's grip on his arm. The grip tightened as Teresa dropped her eyes and took Estios's hand.

Estios helped her up, then bent, retrieved her weapon, and tossed it to her. All the while Estios grinned at Dodger like a kid who had won a prize at a carnival.

"Get a move on, rigger," he said, slapping a hand against the back of Willie's chair. "We've got vermin to exterminate."

Estios reached for his own Steyr, which leaned against the table with the rigger board, and froze as a new voice entered the conversation.

"Touch it and your boss will need a new number one, Ice Eyes."

Hart's voice was hoarse. Her eyes, sunken and dark ringed, were open and burned with fever. Their gaze was fixed on Estios. Her left arm lay across her body, which took most of the weight of the gun she held. She pointed the muzzle at Estios. Sam had no idea where she had gotten the weapon, but she wasn't in any shape to use it effectively. He thought he noticed a slight tremor in her hand.

Estios looked at her, his face stony. Then, apparently dismissing the threat, he started to reach for his gun.

Thunder boomed in the room. Estios recoiled as splinters of wood exploding from the table drew blood from his outstretched hand.

"That was your one warning," Hart said. Her complexion was paler, and fresh sweat plastered locks of hair to her forehead. The recoil from the shot had obviously caused her pain. Her hand shook visibly now.

Estios rubbed at his small wounds with the thumb of his uninjured hand.

"Put the gun down, Hart. I could hit you with a power dart before you could fire, and I don't think your spell defense is up to competition levels right now."

"You can try me, drekhead. It's the only way you'll know."

Estios appeared to be weighing the odds.

Rinaldi reached across and grabbed the Steyr by the muzzle. He set it down again against the wall, well out of Estios's reach.

"I think that you might reconsider your position, Estios. One cannot condemn a person for possibilities. If that were so, all people would have to be condemned, for we are all capable of crimes. As far as we know, Janice has killed no one yet."

"But she has eaten human flesh," Willie said. "The other wendigo said she was just like him. We know *he* was a killer."

Rinaldi shifted his stance so that he could speak to Willie without taking his eyes off the stalemate between Hart and Estios.

"We also know he was a liar. If Janice has eaten

flesh, then she has committed a crime and a sin. But the crime is not a capital one, and the sin may be forgiven. I do not find it beyond the bounds of reason to think that she was under the influence of the evil she called Dan Shiroi and did not fully know what she did. If she repents, there is hope for her redemption.''

"Redemption," Estios repeated in a mocking tone. "As long as she is a wendigo, she will crave the meat. Tell me, priest. Can you change her back to the way she was, then?"

Sam's heart raced, ignited by hope.

But Rinaldi turned away from Estios and gripped his left hand in his right. He rocked his hands up and down at waist level and shook his head sadly. "Alas, no. But neither can I condone murder. That is what it shall be if you kill her without evidence that she has succumbed completely to the wendigo nature. Cold-blooded murder."

"Let her kills be on your head, then."

Rinaldi shifted as if Estios's suggestion made him nervous. "Her actions are her own responsibility. As yours are your responsibility. Every individual must make his or her own choices."

Each of Rinaldi's minor changes of position had put him closer to Hart's bed. In a sudden lunge, he snatched Hart's gun. She was too weak to fight him as he easily removed the weapon from her grasp. He slipped on the safety and tossed the pistol into a corner.

"As I said, I will not condone murder," he said to Hart.

She threw back her head and clenched her teeth. Sam could hear her fist pound once against the edge of the bed.

"Nice move," Estios said. "For a priest. Thanks for saving me the trouble."

"I did not disarm Hart for you alone," Rinaldi said. "And I still maintain that you are premature. Janice must live as her own conscience demands. If she is weak and embraces the demands of her parabiology, I will help you hunt her down."

"I don't want any help from you, priest."

"That will not stop me from joining the hunt," Rinaldi said resolutely.

Their casual talk of hunts and death and murder was finally too much for Sam. Janice wasn't an animal.

"Shut up!" he shouted. "Shut up, all of you! There won't be any hunt. She's my sister."

"She's a wendigo," Estios said. "You're a fool to protect her, Verner. That kind of collaboration would get you the death sentence in the Tir. We know how to treat those who help the wendigo. If you think that being her brother will save you from her, you're a double fool. The wendigo is conscienceless evil; it knows no family."

Sam looked at Estios, but his eyes were seeing the events of the previous night. He saw the spirit of humanity wrestle with the spirit of Blight in its wendigo embodiment. He heard the wendigo's voice pleading with Janice. That hollow voice had spoken words that didn't fit Estios's evaluation. Those caring words had come from a husk that had been burned clean of evil, but they had been born of one human spirit, twisted as it was, reaching out to another who responded. He had seen the tears of the wendigo Janice and knew that the human Janice was still alive somewhere inside.

"You just don't understand," Sam insisted. "She's sick."

"You're crazy, Verner," Estios spat back at him. "She's a killer. She has to be stopped."

"She has killed no one," Rinaldi said. "Hunting her down and killing her would be murder."

"She's a wendigo. It's necessary," Estios said.

"It's murder," Sam said.

"It's moot," Willie said. "At least for now. I've called back the drones."

"You stupid halfer," Estios screamed. He grabbed his Steyr and headed out the door. "Come on. If we don't hurry, the beast will get away."

Teresa slung her weapon and started after him.

"Teresa!" Dodger called, stopping her halfway to the door.

"You're not like him, Teresa," Dodger insisted. "Don't go with him."

She stood still for a full five seconds, then ran out the door. She didn't look back. Dodger slammed his fist into the wall, then sought out a corner and collapsed in it, arms folded over his drooping head.

"Willie, what have you done?" Sam asked.

"Got rid of a real loser," she said. "Sorry about your bird, Dodger."

"She made her own choice," Dodger said glumly.

"But they're going after Janice," Sam said. "They'll kill her."

"Neg. She'll be gone. I dropped a drone in to spook her. All they'll find is an empty squat."

"But you have lost her to us as well," Rinaldi pointed out.

"Neg, again. Got a pair of drones still on her tail."

"Clever, Willie," Rinaldi said.

"Affirm," the rigger agreed as she returned her full attention to monitoring her drones' progress.

Sam forced himself to ignore the pain and rose to his feet. Unsteadily, he limped to Rinaldi. Taking the priest by his arm, Sam leaned close. "You're an expert on magic, father. Tell me there's a way to cure her. There must be a way."

Rinaldi bowed his head for a moment, then looked Sam in the eyes. "I just don't know, Sam. Science knows next to nothing of the wendigo metatype, and magical tradition adds precious little. If the tales from the north are true, the wendigo nature is a curse. If that is the case, it may be that she can be restored. But if it is a biological change and nothing more, I fear there is little hope. I will pray that your faith and love be rewarded, but I just don't know."

"You won't really hunt her, will you?"

Rinaldi turned his head away.

"First things first, Sam. You and Hart are hurt and must be taken care of. Janice is fresh and strong, while we are tired and weak. I have no doubt she has been well trained in combat and magic by the evil. If we try to restrain her she will fight, and she might kill most of us."

"She would never kill me. I'm her brother."

"You could be right. I pray that you are. That might be her way to redemption."

Might. Could be. Maybe. Wasn't anything certain?

"I'll never be sure, will I, father?"

"In this life? I think not, Sam. But one can always pray, and trust in the Lord. He is always with us."

Sam said nothing for a few minutes, quiet as he thought about Janice and about what Rinaldi had said. Finally, he said, "I think you're right, father. I think He will be with me in this. You might even say that He's dogging my path."

Frowning, Rinaldi said, "You sound like a shaman I once knew."

Sam just smiled. All those mights, could-bes and maybes were full of possibilities. All kinds of possibilities. It was only despair that made the future seem dark. He didn't have to look at it that way and vowed that he wouldn't. Dog had shown him the enlightening and redeeming power of hope.

Sam knew he'd find a way to do what had to be done.

**Exploring New Realms
in Science Fiction/Fantasy Adventure**

Calling all fantasy fans!

Join the

FANTASY FAN CLUB
for exciting news and fabulous competitions.

For further information write to:

FANTASY FAN CLUB
Penguin Books Ltd.,
Bath Road, Harmondsworth,
Middlesex UB7 0DA

Open only to residents of the UK
and Republic of Ireland